ALONE AGAINST AN
ALIEN INVASION—
AND AGAINST THE LAWS OF
THEIR OWN INTERSTELLAR
COMMONWEALTH

COMMANDER PHEYLAN CAVANAGH: He had watched helplessly as his eight-ship task force was destroyed and the survivors hunted down and vaporized. Now that he was a captive of the alien Conquerors, his only goal was to survive long enough to warn humanity and its allies of the terrible juggernaut headed their way.

LORD STEWART CAVANAGH: A former Parliament member, he would call in every political favor he could to get his youngest son back alive . . . and when that failed, he would go beyond the bounds of law and loyalty to the Commonwealth—to the edge of treason.

ADAM QUINN: Once a member of the Copperhead corps, an elite unit mind-linked to their fighters, he was now the security chief for CavTronics—but he felt his duty extended to the entire Cavanagh family. He alone knew the terrible price he would pay to jack into the Copperhead link once more—but if it meant the life of Pheylan Cavanagh, nothing would stop him from attempting it.

ARIC CAVANAGH: Thoughtful and studious, he had always been the opposite of his physical, adventurous younger brother, opting for a stable career in the family business while Pheylan chose a military life with the Peacekeepers. Now, with Pheylan's life at stake, Aric would stand beside Quinn and become a warrior—and, if their plan went awry, a traitor.

TIMOTHY ZAHN

CONQUERORS' PRIDE

BANTAM BOOKS
NEW YORK • TORONTO • LONDON • SYDNEY • AUCKLAND

CONQUERORS' PRIDE
A Bantam Spectra Book / September 1994

SPECTRA and the portrayal of a boxed "s" are trademarks of
Bantam Books, a division of Random House, Inc.

ISBN 0-553-56892-2

Published simultaneously in the United States and Canada

Bantam Books are published by Bantam Books, a division of Random
House, Inc. Its trademark, consisting of the words "Bantam Books" and
the portrayal of a rooster, is Registered in U.S. Patent and Trademark
Office and in other countries. Marca Registrada. Bantam Books, 1540
Broadway, New York, New York 10036.

PRINTED IN THE UNITED STATES OF AMERICA

OPM   0 9 8

CONQUERORS' PRIDE

1   **T**hey were there, all right, exactly where the tachyon wake-trail pickup on Dorcas had projected they would be: four ships, glittering faintly in the starlight of deep space, blazing with infrared as they dumped the heat that zero-point energy friction had generated during their trip. They were small ships, probably no bigger than Procyon-class; milky white in color, shaped like thick hexagonal slabs of random sizes attached to each other at random edges.

Alien as hell.

"Scan complete, Commodore," the man at the *Jutland*'s sensor station reported briskly. "No other ships registering."

"Acknowledged," Commodore Trev Dyami said, flexing his shoulders beneath his stiffly starched uniform tunic and permitting himself a slight smile as he gazed at the main display. Alien ships. The first contact with a new self-starfaring race in a quarter of a century.

And it was his. All his. Trev Dyami and the *Jutland* would be the names listed in the Commonwealth's news reports and, eventually, in its history books.

Warrior's luck, indeed.

He turned to the tactics station, fully aware that everything he said and did from this point on would be part of that history-book listing. "What's the threat assessment?" he asked.

"I estimate point one to point four, sir," the tactics officer reported. "I don't find any evidence of fighter ejection tubes or missile ports."

"They've got lasers, though, Commodore," the tactics second put in. "There are clusters of optical-discharge lenses on the leading edges of each ship."

"Big enough to be weapons?" the exec asked from Dyami's side.

"Hard to tell, sir," the other said. "The lenses themselves are pretty small, but that by itself doesn't mean much."

"What about power output?" Dyami asked.

"I don't know, sir," the sensor officer said slowly. "I'm not getting any leakage."

"None?"

"None that I can pick up."

Dyami exchanged glances with the exec. "Superconducting cables," the exec hazarded. "Or else just very well shielded."

"One or the other," Dyami agreed, looking back at the silent shapes floating in the middle of the main display. Not only a self-starfaring race, but one with a technology possibly beyond even humanity's. That history-book listing was getting longer and more impressive by the minute.

The exec cleared his throat. "Are we going to open communications, sir?" he prodded.

"It's that or just sit here staring at each other," Dyami said dryly, throwing a quick look at the tactical board. The rest of the *Jutland*'s eight-ship task force was deployed in his designated combat formation, their crews at full battle stations. The two skitter-sized watchships were also in position, hanging well back where they would be out of danger if this meeting stopped being peaceful. The *Jutland*'s own Dragonfly defense fighters were primed in their launch tubes, ready to be catapulted into battle at an instant's notice.

Everything was by-the-book ready . . . and it was time to make history. "Lieutenant Adigun, pull up the first-contact comm package," Dyami ordered the comm officer. "Get it ready to run. And alert all ships to stand by."

"Signal from the *Jutland*, Captain," Ensign Hauver reported from the *Kinshasa*'s bridge comm station. "They're getting ready to transmit the first-contact package across to our bogies."

Commander Pheylan Cavanagh nodded, his eyes on the linked-hexagon ships in the bridge display. "How long will it take?"

"Oh, they can run the first chunk through in anywhere from five to twenty minutes," Hauver said. "The whole package can take up to a week to transmit. Not counting breaks for the other side to try to figure out what we're talking about."

Pheylan nodded. "Let's hope they're not too alien to understand it."

"Mathematics are supposed to be universal," Hauver pointed out.

"It's that 'supposed to be' I always wonder about," Pheylan said. "Meyers, you got anything more on the ships themselves?"

"No, sir." The sensor officer shook his head. "And to be honest, sir, I really don't like this. I've run the infrared spectrum six ways from April, and it just won't resolve. Either those hulls are made of something the computer and I have never heard of before, or else they're deliberately skewing the emissions somehow."

"Maybe they're just shy," Rico said. "What about those optical-discharge lenses?"

"I can't get anything on those, either," Meyers said. "They could be half-kilowatt comm lasers, half-gigawatt missile frosters, or anything in between. Without power-flux readings, there's no way to tell."

"That part bothers me more than the hull," Rico said to Pheylan, his dark face troubled as he stared at the display. "Putting that kind of massive shielding on their power lines tells me that they're trying to hide something."

"Maybe they're just very efficient," Meyers suggested.

"Yeah," Rico growled. "Maybe."

"There it goes," Hauver spoke up. "*Jutland*'s running the pilot search signal. They've got a resonance—fuzzy, but it's there." He peered at his board. "Odd frequency, too. Must be using some really weird equipment."

"We'll get you a tour of their comm room when this is all over," Pheylan said.

"I hope so. Okay; there goes the first part of the package."

"Lead bogie's moving," Meyers added. "Yawing a few degrees to port—"

And without warning a brilliant double flash of light lanced out from the lead alien ship, cutting across the *Jutland*'s bow. There was a burst of more diffuse secondary light as hull metal vaporized under the assault—

And the *Kinshasa*'s Klaxons blared with an all-force combat alert. "All ships!" Commodore Dyami's voice snapped over the radio scrambler. "We're under attack. *Kinshasa, Badger,* pull out to sideline flanking positions. All other ships, hold station. Fire pattern gamma-six."

"Acknowledge, Hauver," Pheylan ordered, staring at

the display in disbelief. The aliens had opened fire. Un-provoked, unthreatened, they'd simply opened fire. "Chen Ki, pull us out to sideline position. Ready star-board missile tubes for firing."

"How do we key them?" Rico asked, his fingers skat-ing across his tactical setup board. "Proximity or ra-dar?"

"Heat-seeking," Pheylan told him, acceleration press-ing him back into his chair as the *Kinshasa* began to move forward to its prescribed flanking position.

"We're too close to the other ships," Rico objected. "We might hit one of them instead of the bogies."

"We can pull far enough out to avoid that," Pheylan told him, throwing a quick look at the tactical board. "Point is, we know the bogies are hot. With those strange hulls of theirs, the other settings might not even work."

"Missile spread from the *Jutland*," Meyers an-nounced, peering at his displays. "They're going with radar keyed—"

And suddenly all four alien ships opened up with a dazzling display of multiple-laser fire. "All bogies firing," Meyers shouted as the warble of the damage alarm filled the bridge. "We're taking hits—hull damage in all starboard sections—"

"What about the *Jutland*'s missiles?" Rico called.

"No impacts," Meyers shouted back. The image on the main display flared and died, reappearing a second later as the backup sensors took over from the vaporized main cluster. "Bogies must have gotten 'em."

"Or else they just didn't trigger," Pheylan said, fight-ing down the surge of panic simmering in his throat. The *Kinshasa* was crackling with heat stress now as those impossible lasers out there systematically bub-bled off layers of the hull . . . and from the barely controlled voices shouting from the audio-net speaker it sounded as if the rest of the Peacekeeper ships were equally up to their necks in it. In the wink of an eye the task force had gone from complete control of the situation to a battle for survival. And were losing. "Key missiles for heat-seeking, Rico, and fire the damn things."

"Yes, sir. Salvo one away—"

And an instant later there was a sound like a muffled thunderclap, and the *Kinshasa* lurched beneath Pheylan's chair. "Premature detonation!" Meyers shouted; and even over the crackling of overstressed metal Pheylan could hear the fear in his voice. "Hull integrity gone: forward starboard two, three, and four and aft starboard two."

"Ruptures aren't sealing," Rico called. "Too hot for the sealant to work. Starboard two and four are honeycombing. Starboard three . . . honeycombing has failed."

Pheylan clenched his teeth. There were ten duty stations in that section. Ten people who were now dead. "Chen Ki, give us some motion—any direction," he ordered the helm. If they didn't draw the aliens' lasers away from the ejected honeycombs, those ten casualties were going to have lots of company. "All starboard deck officers are to pull their crews back to central."

"Yes, sir."

"The ship can't handle much more of this, Captain," Rico said grimly from beside him.

Pheylan nodded silently, his eyes flicking between the tactical and ship-status boards. Rico was, if anything, vastly understating the case. With half the *Kinshasa*'s systems failing or vaporized and nothing but the internal collision bulkheads holding it together, the ship had bare minutes of life left to it. But before it died, there might be enough time to get off one final shot at the enemy who was ripping them apart. "Rico, give me a second missile salvo," he ordered. "Fire into our shadow, then curve them over and under to pincer into the middle of the bogie formation. No fusing—just a straight timed detonation."

"I'll try," Rico said, his forehead shiny with sweat as he worked his board. "No guarantees with the ship like this."

"I'll take whatever I can get," Pheylan said. "Fire when ready."

"Yes, sir." Rico finished his programming and jabbed the firing keys, and through the crackling and jolting of the *Kinshasa* writhing beneath him, Pheylan felt the lurch as the missiles launched. "Salvo away," Rico said. "Sir, I recommend we abandon ship while the honeycombs are still functional."

Pheylan looked again at the status board, his stomach twisting with the death-pain of his ship. The *Kinshasa* was effectively dead; and with its destruction he had only one responsibility left. "Agreed," he said heavily. "Hauver, signal all hands: we're abandoning. All sections to honeycomb and eject when ready."

The damage alarm changed pitch and cadence to the ship-abandon signal. Across the bridge, board lights flickered and went dark as the bridge crew hurriedly disconnected their stations from the ship and checked their individual life-support systems.

Pheylan himself, however, still had one task left to perform: to ensure that those alien butchers out there would learn nothing about the Commonwealth from the wreckage of his ship. Getting a grip on the underside of his command board, he broke it open and began throwing the row of switches there. Nav computer destruct, backup nav computer destruct, records computer destruct, library computer destruct—

"Bridge crew reports ready, Captain," Rico said, a note of urgency in his voice. "Shall we honeycomb?"

Pheylan threw the last switch. "Go," he said, pulling his hands back inside the arms of his chair and bracing himself.

And with a thudding ripple that jerked Pheylan against his restraints, the sections of memory metal whipped out from the deck and ceiling, wrapping around his chair and sealing him in an airtight cocoon. A heartbeat later he was jammed into his seat cushion as the bridge disintegrated around him, throwing each of the individual honeycomb escape pods away from the dying hulk that had once been the *Kinshasa*.

"Good-bye," Pheylan murmured to the remains of his ship, fumbling for the viewport shutter-release control. Later, he supposed vaguely, the full emotional impact would hit him. For now, though, survival was uppermost in his mind. Survival for himself, and for his crew.

The shutters retracted, and he pressed his face up to the viewport that looked back on the *Kinshasa*. The other escape pods were dim flickers of light drifting outward from the twisted and blackened hull still being hammered by the aliens' lasers. There was no way to tell how many of the honeycomb pods were intact, but those that were should keep their occupants alive until they could be picked up. Moving carefully in the cramped confines of the pod, he got to the viewport facing the main part of the battle and looked out.

The battle was over. The Peacekeeper task force had lost.

He floated there, his breath leaving patches of fog on the viewport, too stunned to move. The *Piazzi* was blazing brightly, some fluke of leaking oxygen tanks allowing fire even in the vacuum of space. The *Ghana* and *Leekpai* were blackened and silent, as were the

Bombay and *Seagull.* He couldn't find any trace of the *Badger* at all.

And the *Jutland*—the powerful, Rigel-class defense carrier *Jutland*—was twisting slowly in space. Dead.

And the four alien starships were still there. Showing no damage at all.

"No," Pheylan heard himself murmur. It was impossible. Utterly impossible. For a Rigel-class task force to have been defeated in six minutes—*six minutes*—was unheard of.

There was a flicker of laser fire from one of the aliens; then another, and another. Pheylan frowned, wondering what they were shooting at. Some of the *Jutland*'s Dragonfly fighters, perhaps, that were still flying around? The aliens fired again, and again—

And with a jolt of horror Pheylan understood. The aliens were firing on the honeycomb pods. Systematically and painstakingly destroying the survivors of the battle.

He swore viciously under his breath. The pods were no threat to the aliens—they weren't armed, armored, or even equipped with drives. To destroy them like this was to turn a military victory into a cold-blooded slaughter.

And there was nothing that he could do about it except sit here and watch it happen. The pod was little more than a minuscule cone with a power supply, a dioxide/oxygen converter, a backup oxygen tank, an emergency radio beacon, a short-range comm laser, two weeks' worth of rations, a waste-reclaimant system—

He was clawing the equipment access panel open almost before the thought had completely formed in his mind. The aliens out there weren't just blasting every chunk of rubble in sight; they were specifically and deliberately hunting down the pods. And suddenly it was blindingly obvious how they were doing that.

The emergency beacon was a deliberately simple gadget, as unbreakable and foolproof as anything in the Peacekeepers' inventory. But foolproof didn't necessarily mean sabotage proof. A minute later, every wire and circuit line to it cut and the blade of his multitool jabbed into its internal power backup, it had finally been silenced.

Pheylan took a deep breath, feeling the coolness of sweat on his forehead as he turned back to the viewport. The flashes of laser fire were still flickering through the battle debris as the aliens went about their grisly business. One of the ships was working its way his direction, and he wondered tensely whether any of his crew had figured out what was going on and had knocked out their own beacons.

But there was no time to think about that now. That alien ship was coming almost straight toward him, and if they were really determined to be thorough about this, there were other ways besides the beacon to pick him out of the flotsam. Somehow he had to get the pod moving. Preferably in the direction of the watchships that should still be skulking out there somewhere.

He watched the ship's deliberate approach, mentally running through the list of available equipment. But there was really only one possibility, and he knew it. He needed propulsion; ergo, he needed to throw something overboard.

It took longer than he'd expected to get to the oxygen tank release valve on the far side of the narrow equipment bay, and the alien ship was looming large in the viewport by the time he was finally ready. Mentally crossing his fingers, he tweaked the valve release open.

The hiss was loud in the enclosed space of the pod—

as loud, he thought with a macabre shiver, as the hiss of gas in one of those death cells the Commonwealth was forever lodging strong protests about with the Bhurtist governments. It wasn't an irrelevant comparison, either: with the pod's oxygen reserve spewing into space, his life was now solely dependent on the uninterrupted functioning of his dioxide/oxygen converter. If it flicked out on him—and they did so with depressing regularity —he would have only as long as it took the air in the pod to get stale to get it running again.

But so far the plan was working. He was drifting through the wreckage now, slowly but steadily, moving roughly crosswise to the alien ship's approach vector toward the area where the watchships would be if they hadn't already meshed out. Now if he could just make it outside the cone of whatever focused sensor beams the aliens were using . . .

Concentrating on the first ship, he never even saw the second ship's approach. Not until the blue light abruptly flared around him.

"Keller? You still there?"

With an effort Lieutenant Dana Keller pulled her eyes away from the distant flickering of laser light and keyed her comm laser. "I'm here, Beddini," she said. "What do you think? We seen enough?"

"I'd seen enough five minutes ago," Beddini told her bitterly. "Those lousy, f—"

"We'd better get moving," Keller cut him off. Watching Commodore Dyami's task force get sliced to ribbons like that had sickened her, too, but letting Beddini get started on his extensive repertoire of curses wouldn't accomplish anything. "Unless you want to wait and see if they'll come after us next."

She heard the hiss as Beddini exhaled into his mike. "Not really."

"Fine," she said, keying her nav map. Actually, it was unlikely that the aliens even knew they were here—watchships were about as sensor-stealthed as it was theoretically possible to make them. But she wouldn't have bet a day's pay on that, let alone her life. "The book says we split up. I'll take Dorcas; you want Massif or Kalevala?"

"Kalevala. My static bomb or yours?"

"We'll use mine," Keller told him, keying in the sequence to activate and drop the high-intensity tachyon explosive. "You might need yours on the way off Kalevala. Don't start your engines until I give you the word."

"Right."

Behind her Keller felt a whisper of air as the copilot returned from her abrupt visit to the head. "You okay, Gorzynski?" she asked the other.

"Sure," Gorzynski said, sounding embarrassed and still a little sick. "I'm sorry, Lieutenant."

"Forget it," Keller told her, studying the younger woman's tortured face as she maneuvered carefully in zero-gee to her copilot's seat. Younger woman, hell—Gorzynski wasn't much more than a kid. Fresh out of basic, her first real tour . . . and this was how it had ended. "We're heading back. Get the drive sequence ready to go."

"Right," Gorzynski said, getting shakily to work. "What did I miss?"

"Just more of the same," Keller said. "They're still going around icing the survivors."

Gorzynski made a sound in the back of her throat. "I don't understand," she said. "Why are they doing that?"

"I don't know," Keller told her grimly. "But we're going to pay them back with interest. Bet on it."

The board pinged: the static bomb was ready. Keller

touched the primer and the release key, and there was a slight lurch as the bulky cylinder dropped free of the watchship. "Beddini? Static bomb away. Ninety seconds to detonation."

"Acknowledged," Beddini said. "We're out of here. Good luck."

"You, too," Keller said, and keyed off the comm laser. "Let's go, Gorzynski."

They had swung the watchship around and were pulling for deep space when the static bomb blew up behind them, sending out a wide-spectrum saturation burst of tachyons that would blind whatever wake-trail detectors the enemy out there had. Or so went the theory. If it didn't work, the Peacekeeper garrisons on Dorcas and Kalevala had better hope they were ready for company. "Here we go," she told Gorzynski, and pressed the keys.

The sky shimmered, the stars spinning briefly into an illusion of a tunnel as the space around them twisted. And then the twist became a sphere, the stars winked out, and they were on their way.

Keller looked over at Gorzynski. The kid still looked sick, but there was something else there, too. The kind of quiet, dark determination that Keller had seen so often in hardened combat veterans.

She shook her head. What a way for the kid to have to grow up.

The door slid open, and Lieutenant Colonel Castor Holloway stepped into the Dorcas colony's Peacekeeper garrison sensor center. Major Fujita Takara was waiting just inside the door, his face looking somber in the dim red light. "What've we got, Fuji?" Holloway asked.

"Trouble, looks like," Takara told him. "Crane just picked up the leading edge of a static-bomb discharge."

Holloway looked across the room at the tachyon pickup display and the young sergeant sitting stiffly in front of it. "The *Jutland* task force?"

"I don't know what else it could be," Takara said. "You can't really pin down a static bomb from anything but point-blank range, but it's from the right direction."

"Strength?"

"If it's from the same spot where we placed the bogies, it's about the size of a watchship's backstop bomb." Takara's lip twitched. "I don't know if you knew, Cass, but it's only been forty minutes since the task force meshed in out there."

The room, Holloway noted, was very quiet. "I suppose we'd better alert Peacekeeper Command," he said. "We have a skitter ready to fly?"

Takara's forehead creased slightly, and Holloway could tell what he was thinking. There were only two stable stardrive speeds, three light-years per hour and twice that, with only small ships like fighters and skitters able to achieve the higher equilibrium. The problem was it cost nearly five times as much per light-year to fly at the higher speed, which on the Dorcas garrison's budget was a nontrivial consideration. "Number Two can be ready in half an hour," the major said. "I assumed we'd be waiting until we had something more concrete to send them."

Holloway shook his head. "We can't afford the wait. Whatever happened out there, the fact that a watchship dropped its static bomb means there's been serious trouble. Our job is to buy the Commonwealth every minute of prep time that we can. The details of the trouble can wait until later."

"I suppose so," Takara said heavily. "I'll get the skitter crew moving."

He left, the door sliding shut behind him, and Hollo-way stepped over to the tachyon station. "Can you sift anything at all out of that mess, Crane?" he asked.

"No, sir," the young man said. "The tachyon static will blanket everything else in the region for at least another hour. Maybe two."

Which meant that they'd be on Dorcas's doorstep be-fore anyone knew how much of the task force was com-ing back. Or, perhaps more important, if any uninvited guests were following them in. "Keep an eye on it," he told the other. "I want to know the minute the static starts to clear."

"Yes, sir." Crane hesitated. "Sir, what do you think happened?"

Holloway shrugged. "We'll find out in a couple of hours. Until then, I suggest you try to keep your imagi-nation from running away with you."

"Yes, sir," Crane said, a bit too hastily. "I just meant —well—"

"I understand," Holloway assured him. "It's not much fun sitting blind while you wonder what might be com-ing your way. Just bear in mind that the Common-wealth has a long history of winning these little encounters. Whatever's out there, we'll handle it."

"Yes, sir," Crane said. "There's always CIRCE, too."

Holloway grimaced. Yes, that was always the option. The option, and the unspoken threat behind it. There were a lot of people—not all of them nonhumans—who resented living beneath the shadow of CIRCE and the Northern Coordinate Union leaders who held sole pos-session of the weapon's secrets. A lot of people who felt that NorCoord's domination of the Peacekeepers and the political structure of the entire Commonwealth was based on CIRCE and CIRCE alone. But the simple fact was that in the thirty-seven years since that awful dem-onstration off Celadon, the NorCoord military had never again had to fire the weapon. It had kept the peace without ever having to be used.

He looked at the tachyon display, feeling his throat tighten. Perhaps this time it was going to be different. "Yes," he agreed quietly. "There's always CIRCE."

2
The lunch had been served and eaten, the empty dishes cleared away, and the frosted coffee served; and only then did Nikolai Donezal finally ask the question Lord Stewart Cavanagh had known he would eventually get to. "So," Donezal said, sipping carefully at his steaming cup and licking a stray bit of frosting off his upper lip. "Shall we get down to business? Or shall we continue to pretend your visit today has been motivated solely by nostalgia?"

Cavanagh smiled. "That's one of the things I've always liked about you, Nikolai: your unique combination of subtlety and bluntness. Not a single nudge or probe during the meal itself, and now straight between the eyes."

"The ravages of age, I'm afraid," Donezal said regretfully. "I find that I'm useless all afternoon if I ruin my digestion at lunch." He eyed Cavanagh over the edge of his cup. "And turning down favors while eating invariably ruins my digestion."

"Favors?" Cavanagh echoed, giving the other his best innocent look. "What makes you think I'm here to ask for any favors?"

"Long personal experience," Donezal said dryly.

"Coupled with the stories about you which one can still hear being told in parliamentary back offices. If even half of them are true, it would appear you left an impressive trail of wrenched arms behind you during your time here."

"Baseless slander." Cavanagh dismissed the subject with a wave of his hand. "Sprinkled with a bit of jealousy."

Donezal raised an eyebrow. "Perhaps more than just a bit," he said. "Still, you protest more than necessary. I understand that a man cannot create your list of accomplishments without also creating a few enemies along the way."

"Plus a few friends, I hope," Cavanagh said.

"I'm certain you did," Donezal said. "Though the other group is always the louder. Still, the doomsayers we shall always have with us. At any rate, you bought lunch; the least I can do is hear you out."

"Thank you," Cavanagh said, pulling his plate from his inside pocket. He opened it, called up the proper file, and slid it across the table. "My proposal is really quite simple. I'd like to shift a part of my Centauri electronics operation out to Massif."

"Indeed," Donezal said, glancing over the first page and keying for the second. "To be located in the Lorraine and Nivernais states, I see. A good choice—the plunge in iridium prices has hit those two regions particularly hard. An influx of light industry would be welcome." He looked speculatively at Cavanagh. "So tell me what the favor is you need. Free land, or just massive tax breaks?"

"Neither," Cavanagh said, mentally crossing his fingers. Donezal had a good business mind and was, at the core, a decent enough man. But his military tour of duty on the Bhurtist homeworld of Tal during the Peacekeepers' police action there had left some scars where nonhumans were concerned. "What I need is for you to help me get NorCoord's permission to run a pair of satellite facilities in the Duulian and Avuirlian enclaves."

Donezal's face tightened, just noticeably. "I see," he said. "May I ask what Sanduuli and Avuirli have to offer that our human colonists can't match?"

"Frankly, I don't know," Cavanagh said. "That's one of the things I'm hoping to find out."

"Such as whether they can do the work cheaper?" Donezal demanded.

Cavanagh shook his head. "Such as what ideas and improvements nonhuman intelligences and methodology might suggest to us," he corrected. "The satellite facilities would be geared for R and D, not production."

Donezal looked down at the plate again, and Cavanagh could see the strain as he tried to uncouple his judgment from his memories. "You're aware, of course, that five months ago Peacekeeper Command and the Commerce Commission began tightening regulations on nonhuman handling of potential military technology."

"Yes, I know," Cavanagh said. "But the work we'd be doing would be distinctly nonmilitary. All of our Peacekeeper contracts would stay in the existing high-security plants on Avon and Centauri."

Donezal rubbed his cheek. "I don't know, Stewart. Understand, I have nothing personally against either the Sanduuli or Avuirli. And I'd certainly like to see you move a plant onto Massif. But Commerce seems very serious about all this; and to be honest, I'm not sure the term 'nonmilitary' can be applied to anything electronic anymore. There's so much bleed-through between military and civilian equipment, especially with the sort of high-density and semisentient work you do. A great deal of that is still exclusively human property, and many of us would like to keep it that way. Otherwise there could be trouble whenever the next brushfire erupts."

"Possibly," Cavanagh said. "On the other hand, a perception that the Commonwealth is being unreasonably selfish is almost a guarantee that those brushfires will indeed occur."

Donezal made a face. "Well, if that happens, the Peacekeepers will certainly be ready for it," he growled, turning his attention back to the plate. "You should see all the money they've been levering out of the treasury lately. All right, let me look at this again."

Cavanagh sipped at his coffee and looked around the Parliament dining room, memories flickering through his mind as he did so. Certainly he'd come here on business, but Donezal's facetious reference to nostalgia hadn't been completely off the mark. Cavanagh had been less than enthusiastic about serving in the Northern Coordinate Union Parliament when the governor of Grampians on Avon had offered him the job—had argued long and hard, in fact, that there were others in Grampians who wanted the appointment far more. But the governor had persisted; and Cavanagh himself would be the first to admit that the six years he'd spent in Parliament had been among the most interesting of his life. The previous twenty years, spent building up a minor electronics empire from scratch, hadn't prepared him at all for the style and routine of government operation. Everyone had known it, of course, and he suspected there had been a few side bets in the back offices that the new Parlimin from Avon, Grampians state, would never even make it off the landing field.

But he'd surprised them. He'd quickly learned how to adapt his work and people-handling techniques to the strange new environment of politics, and had then proceeded to forge odd but potent coalitions among those who felt the same as he did about a dozen of the most

important issues. None of the coalitions had lasted very
long, but more often than not they'd lasted long enough
to accomplish the goals he'd set for them. He'd become
adept at the art of political arm-twisting, a talent that
had given him a certain notoriety during that first term
and the two subsequent appointments the governor
had talked him into accepting. Apparently, if Donezal
could be believed, some of that notoriety still lingered
in the Parliament chambers.

A movement caught his eye: a young-looking Parlimin gesturing emphatically at the colleagues seated
around him at his table. There were only a few Parlimins still in office who had also served during Cavanagh's stint here, but the current trend among the
national and state governments of the NorCoord Union
was to appoint top business and industrial leaders to
the upper house, and Cavanagh spotted several men
and women he'd locked horns with across tables over
the years. There was Simons of Great Britain, Alexan-
dra Karponov of Kryepost on Nadezhda, Klein of
Neuebund on Prospect . . .

He was looking at Klein when the other's face suddenly went rigid.

Cavanagh looked back at Donezal, to find the same
expression on his face. "Emergency signal?"

"Yes," Donezal told him, fumbling in his pocket and
pulling out his slender whisper-call. "Full-Parliament
alert," he said, peering at the message scrolling across
the display. "Some kind of trouble out at—"

He broke off. "I have to go," he said abruptly, stuffing
the whisper-call back into his pocket and levering himself out of his chair.

"What is it?" Cavanagh asked, standing up himself
and making a quick hand signal. "What kind of trouble?"

"There aren't any details," Donezal said, starting

toward the door. The other Parlimins, Cavanagh noted peripherally, were also heading rapidly for the exits. "Call my office later. Better yet, call your own Parlimin. I'm sure Jacy VanDiver would love to hear from you."

Cavanagh fell into step beside him; and as he did so, the quiet figure of his security chief, Adam Quinn, appeared at his side. "Trouble, sir?" the other asked softly.

"Yes," Cavanagh told him. "Come on, Nikolai, give. I'll owe you one."

Donezal stopped, throwing a sour look at Cavanagh and an only marginally less acidic one at Quinn. "There's a watchship coming in from Dorcas," he bit out. "Apparently, a Peacekeeper task force there has been hit. Badly."

Cavanagh stared at him, an old and all-too-familiar pressure squeezing his chest. "Which task force was it?"

"I don't know," Donezal said, frowning at him. "Does it matter?"

"Very much," Cavanagh murmured. The *Kinshasa*, with Pheylan aboard, was stationed with the *Jutland* in the Dorcas area. If that was the force that had been hit . . . "Let's get over to the chamber," he told Donezal, taking his arm. "They should at least be able to tell us who was involved."

Donezal shook off the grip. "*We* are not going to the chamber," he said. "*I* am going. You're not a Parlimin anymore."

"You can get me in."

"Not for something like this," Donezal insisted. "I'm sorry, Stewart, but you'll just have to wait and find out when the rest of the Commonwealth does."

He turned and joined the general exodus of people now streaming through the dining room's main exits. "Like hell I will," Cavanagh muttered under his breath as he pulled out his phone. "Quinn, where did Kolchin go?"

"I'm right here, sir," the young bodyguard said, appearing magically at Cavanagh's other side. "What stirred up the anthill?"

"A Peacekeeper task force has been hit off Dorcas," Cavanagh told him grimly, punching in a number. "I'm going to see if I can get us some more information."

The phone screen came on, revealing a young woman in Peacekeeper uniform. "Peacekeeper Command."

"General Garcia Alvarez, please," Cavanagh said. "Tell him it's Lord Stewart Cavanagh. And tell him it's urgent."

The cables overhead lengthened and separated, dropping their ski-lift-style chair out of the upper-corridor traffic flow and bringing it to a halt at the floor. Before them, topped by a large Peacekeeper insignia, was the archway into the Peacekeeper Command section of the NorCoord Union government complex. Standing beneath the arch, flanked by the duty guard and a man wearing a major's insignia, was General Alvarez.

"Stewart," Alvarez said in greeting as Cavanagh and his two men came toward him. "I trust you realize how irregular this is."

"I do," Cavanagh said. "And I thank you. I'll try not to be too much trouble."

Alvarez made a face and looked at the officer at his side. "These are my visitors, Major. I'd like them cleared through."

"Yes, sir," the other said. "Hello, Quinn. Long time no see."

"Hello, Anders," Quinn said evenly. "Good to see you. I didn't know you'd moved to Command."

"I'm not surprised," Anders said, an edge of bitterness in the voice. "You haven't exactly kept in touch. So this is him, huh?" he added, throwing a cold look at Cavanagh. "The guy who you helped to dump on the unit?"

"Lord Cavanagh is my employer," Quinn said. "And we didn't dump on the Copperheads. We helped make them stronger and better."

"Yeah, well, that's sure not what it looked like from the inside." Anders looked at Kolchin, and for a moment his eyes seemed to glaze over. "And you're former Peacekeeper commando Mitri Kolchin," he said. "You always stock your payroll with Peacekeeper quitters, Lord Cavanagh?"

Beside him, Cavanagh felt Kolchin stir, and he could imagine what the expression on the young man's face must be. General Alvarez, facing him from a meter away, didn't have to rely on imagination. "You're not here for a discussion of career choices, Major," the general put in. "You're here to authorize temporary clearances for these men. Can you or can't you?"

Anders's lip twitched. "There's nothing in their records to prohibit it, sir," he said. "I can clear them through to the outer briefing room. No farther."

"Good enough," Alvarez grunted. "Thank you. Come on, Stewart—the watchship's records should be here anytime."

"They couldn't transmit from orbit?" Cavanagh asked.

"We didn't want them to," Alvarez said. "There are too many kids out there whose idea of fun is to tie into military transmissions and try to crack the scrambling. The last thing we want is for this to leak out before we're ready." He threw Cavanagh a tight smile. "Which is one reason we're letting you in here. Makes it easier to keep track of you."

"I see," Cavanagh said. He'd already figured that part out, actually. "What do you know so far?"

"Only that a skitter arrived from Dorcas about two hours ago telling us a watchship was probably on its way," Alvarez said. "That all by itself meant bad news."

Cavanagh braced himself. "Do you know which task force it was?"

Alvarez nodded heavily. "It was the *Jutland*'s," he said. "And the *Kinshasa* was definitely there with it. That's the other reason you're here."

"I appreciate it," Cavanagh said, the pressure returning to his chest. "What else do you know?"

"Precious little," Alvarez admitted. "About twenty-five hours ago the tachyon pickup on Dorcas spotted an unfamiliar wake-trail, terminating in the outer rim of a minor system six light-years from Dorcas. They didn't have a tracking baseline, of course, but the *Jutland* and the local garrison commander were able to triangulate a probable endpoint. The force went out to take a look; forty minutes after meshing in, they popped a static bomb. Dorcas picked it up, figured it meant bad news, and fired us off a skitter to give us some advance warning. End of report."

"Forty minutes sounds rather short," Cavanagh said.

Alvarez snorted. "Try frighteningly short. Especially when you consider that Commodore Dyami wouldn't have meshed in right on top of the bogies. Real-space transit time would have eaten up part of that forty minutes. Maybe even most of it."

The briefing room was deserted when they arrived. Alvarez turned on the displays for them, then left to watch the proceedings with his fellow officers in the main command center. Five minutes later the watchship's recordings began.

It was worse than Cavanagh had expected. Worse than he could even have conceived it to be. To watch the entire task force being cut to ribbons was bad enough. To watch the alien ships coldly and systematically destroying the honeycomb pods afterward was horrifying.

And to know that he was watching the death of his son made him feel physically ill. And very, very old.

The battle and its murderous aftermath seemed to take forever. According to the display chrono, the entire episode took barely fourteen and a half minutes.

The record ended, and the display went off, and for a few minutes none of them spoke. Quinn broke the silence first. "We're in trouble," he said quietly. "Big trouble."

Cavanagh took a deep breath, blinking the sudden moisture out of his eyes. It would have been quick, at least. That was something to hold on to. It would have been quick. "Could the force have been taken by surprise?"

"No." Quinn was positive. "Dyami knew to be ready for combat. That's always the assumption when you contact a new race. Besides, the force was fighting— you could see missiles being launched. They just weren't detonating."

"You know if the *Jutland* had any Copperhead fighters aboard, Quinn?" Kolchin asked.

"I doubt it," Quinn said, shaking his head. "Most Copperhead units are stationed aboard Nova- and Supernova-class carriers these days, mostly out in Yycroman space. That's what I've heard, anyway. We could ask Anders on the way out."

"Well, at least that's something new we can try on them next time around." Kolchin paused. "And maybe NorCoord will decide it's time to reassemble CIRCE."

"Perhaps," Cavanagh said. "Quinn, we need to send word to Aric and Melinda about this."

"I can do that, sir," Quinn said. "What should I tell them?"

Cavanagh shook his head. "It doesn't matter," he said through the ache. The ache, and the growing rage that his son had been so cold-bloodedly taken from him. "Just tell them their brother is dead."

3   The Meert was typical of his species: short and stocky, with small greenish-brown overlapping scales and a face that humans almost invariably compared in shape and texture to a peeled orange. He stood stiffly across the desk, his pale-yellow eyes boring into Aric Cavanagh's face, his teeth dripping with saliva.

Decidedly unhappy.

"I want to talk to Cavanagh," he growled, his English coming out mangled but more or less understandable. "I was promised Cavanagh."

"I *am* Cavanagh," Aric told him. "Aric Cavanagh, Lord Stewart Cavanagh's firstborn son. I'm also director of CavTronics operations for this region of space. Whatever your complaint, you may express it to me."

The Meert hissed under his breath. "Human," he growled, making the word a curse. "You care first for yourselves. The Meert-ha are nothing to you but slaves."

"Ah," Aric said, cocking an eyebrow. "Do the Meert-ha care more for humans than for themselves, then?"

The overlapping scales opened slightly, settled back into place. "You insult the Meert-ha?"

"Not at all," Aric assured him. "I merely seek clarification. You accuse humans of caring more for their own kind than for nonhumans. Is it different with the Meertha?"

The Meert was silent a moment, his scales flipping rhythmically up and down. Aric stayed seated, resisting the urge to ease his chair a little farther back from the desk. For a pair of heartbeats he was a teenager again, engaged in his favorite lazy-day pastime of verbally driving his younger brother crazy, when he'd suddenly awakened to the fact that he no longer had thirty centimeters and twelve kilos on the kid. The game had stopped being fun that day . . . and the Meert standing in front of the desk had a lot of the same look about him.

He shook off the memory. He wasn't fifteen anymore, that wasn't Pheylan standing there preparing to pound him, and a nonhuman work foreman in a CavTronics electronics plant surely wouldn't be rash enough to physically attack the owner's son. Still, he was beginning to wish he hadn't left Hill outside with the car. Normally, he didn't feel any need for one of his father's cadre of security guards on these plant tours; but palpitating Meertene scales meant there was a lot of body heat being dumped, and if the Meert was getting overheated, it probably meant he was angry. Aric had thrown in that comment to put the Meert's accusations of species loyalty into perspective, as well as to hopefully knock the approaching tirade off track a little. The whole thing would be rather counterproductive if the Meert tried to break his face instead.

The scales settled back in place. "It is still true that you think of the Meert-ha as slaves," the Meert said.

"Not at all," Aric said, starting to breathe again. "We have always treated our Meertene employees with respect and honor."

"Then why this?" the Meert demanded, pointing two

thick fingers out the window. "Why do you close this workplace?"

Aric sighed. Here it came: the same argument he'd already been through twice on this trip, with two other nonhuman species. He wondered if Commonwealth Commerce had had any idea of the trouble they were creating when they first started dropping these new restrictions through the hopper five months ago. Or if they'd even cared. "In the first place, we aren't closing the plant," he told the Meert. "We're only scaling back some of its operations."

"Meert-ha will no longer work here."

"Some Meert-ha will lose their jobs, yes," Aric conceded. "As will some from the Djadaran enclave, as well."

"Will humans lose jobs?"

"I don't know," Aric said. "That has yet to be decided."

The scales quivered. "When?"

"Whenever we so choose," Aric said. "Would you wish us to rush these decisions? *All* of them?"

The Meert shook his head, the movement scattering droplets of saliva to both sides. In mainstream Meertene culture, shaking the head was often a signal of challenge; Aric could only hope that in this case the Meert was mimicking the human gesture instead. "I speak only of justice," he growled.

"Justice is my goal as well," Aric assured him. "And the goal of my father. Be assured we will both do whatever is possible to achieve it."

The Meert tossed his head. "We will watch and see," he said, crossing the fingers of his hands in the Meertene farewell gesture. "Stay slowly."

Aric returned the gesture. "Go slowly."

The Meert turned and strode out through the office door. "Justice," Aric muttered under his breath, finally

letting go with the grimace he'd been holding back
since the Meert first barged in. His father had warned
the Commissioner of Commerce—had warned him re-
peatedly—that this was both bad politics and bad business. He might as well have tried talking to moss.

The office door slid open again. Aric looked up, muscles tensing and then relaxing as he saw it was just
Hill. "About time," he told the security guard, mock-
severely. "Here I am, risking my life with an angry
Meert, and where are you?"

"Outside," Hill replied calmly. "Keeping out the other
eight who were demanding to get in to see you."

"Really." Aric cocked an eyebrow. "You didn't mention there was a whole delegation out there."

Hill shrugged. "I didn't want to worry you," he said.
"Besides, it didn't seem important, given that I wasn't
going to let more than one of them in anyway. I figured
even you could handle a single Meert."

"I appreciate the confidence," Aric said dryly. At
least that explained why his visitor had been so relatively easy to deal with. Expecting to be part of a nine-
man complaint committee, he'd already been thrown
off stride by having to go it alone. "Have they all left?"

Hill nodded. "This group mad about the layoffs, too?"

"Mad about the threat of layoffs, anyway," Aric said.
Privately, he was still hoping they could persuade
the paranoids at Commerce that no Peacekeeper military secrets were being risked by letting nonhumans
work with CavTronics computer components. "Has the
evening-shift director arrived yet?"

"No, sir," Hill said, stepping over to the desk and
holding out a card. "But this was just transmitted in for
you. Via the skitter from Earth, I think."

"Must be from Dad," Aric said, taking the card and
sliding it into his plate. The two of them had come up
with a little scheme that might create an end-run pre-

cedent around these new restrictions. This might be the word on whether Parlimin Donezal was willing to play ball on it. Keying for the proper decoding algorithm, Aric watched as the message came up.

It was very short.

He read it through twice, a sense of unreality creeping through him. No. It couldn't be.

"Sir? Are you all right?"

With an effort Aric looked up at Hill. "Is the ship back yet?"

"I don't think so, sir," Hill said, frowning at him. "You weren't planning to leave until tomorrow."

Aric took a deep breath, trying to drive away the numbness in his mind and body. "Call the spaceport," he said. "Get me a seat on a liner to Earth. You and the ship can go back to Avon when it gets here."

"Yes, sir," Hill said, pulling out his phone. "May I ask what's wrong?"

Aric leaned back in his chair and closed his eyes. "It's my brother," he said. "He's dead."

"Dr. Cavanagh?"

Melinda Cavanagh looked up from the large high-detail plate and her final run-through of the upcoming operation. "Yes?"

"Dr. Billingsgate is in prep," the nurse said. "Room three."

"Thank you," Melinda said, mentally shaking her head. He could just as easily have paged her or called her on her phone, but instead he'd sent someone else scurrying off to find her. She'd never worked with Billingsgate before, but the Commonwealth's surgical community was by necessity a small and tight-knit group, and she'd heard enough stories to know that this was typical of the man. Opinion was split as to whether it was arrogance, stinginess with his own time, or just a simple preference for human interaction over the more impersonal electronic sort. "Tell him I'll be there in a minute."

She finished tracking through the plan and pulled her card from the plate. Prep Three was just down the corridor, and she entered to find Billingsgate poring over the high-detail plate there. "Ah—Cavanagh," he said distractedly, waving her over. "Ready to suit up?"

"Almost," she said, sitting down in the chair next to him. "There are a couple of minor points I'd like to discuss with you first."

He frowned at her from under bushy eyebrows. "I thought we'd settled everything," he said, his tone dropping half an octave.

"I thought we had, too," she said, sliding her card into his plate and keying for the marked sections. "Number one: I think we should reduce the use of markinine in the third phase. We certainly want to lower blood pressure at that point, but with the shorozine drip only four centimeters away, I think we should consider lowering the dosage by at least ten percent."

The eyebrows frowned a little harder. "A ten percent cut is rather drastic."

"But necessary," Melinda said. "Number two: in phase four you have two separate neurobinders being applied at each of four sites. This one"—she pointed to it on the plate—"strikes me as being just a shade too close to the optic chiasma. Particularly given your revised dosage numbers."

"You think that, do you?" Billingsgate said, his voice starting to shade from annoyed to intimidating. "Tell me, Doctor, have you ever performed this operation yourself?"

"You know I haven't," Melinda said. "But I've consulted on five similar operations."

Billingsgate's eyebrows lifted slightly. "For five different surgeons, no doubt?"

Melinda looked him straight in the eye. "That's unfair," she said. "And you know it. The two operations weren't identical—no two operations are. Trying to bypass me that way and just blindly following the first plan was totally irresponsible. And it could have been fatal."

"It most likely wouldn't have been," Billingsgate pointed out.

"Would you have wanted me to take that chance?" Melinda countered.

Billingsgate's lips pursed tightly together. "You didn't have to humiliate Mueller publicly."

"I tried talking to him privately. He wouldn't listen."

Billingsgate turned back to his plate, and for a minute the room was silent. "So you think we should cut the markinine by ten percent, do you?" he asked.

"Yes," Melinda said. "The lower dosage should do the job perfectly well. Particularly given the patient's metabolic baseline."

"I was going to ask if you'd checked on that," Billingsgate said. "All right; but if the blood pressure doesn't respond properly, we're going to jack the dosage back up. Fair enough?"

"Fair enough," Melinda agreed. "Now, what about the neurobinders?"

The discussion was short and civilized, and in the end he acquiesced with reasonably good grace. Like most surgeons Melinda had dealt with, Billingsgate had strong proprietary feelings toward his operation designs, but he was also experienced enough not to simply ignore the recommendations of a good consultant. With more and more routine operations being handled

by semisentient computerized systems, the only ones
that still required human surgeons were those that
were as much art as they were science. Writing required editors; sculpture required texturers; surgery
required design consultants. Or so the theory went.

"All right, then," Billingsgate said at last. "We cut the
markinine by ten percent and shift the gamma-site
neurobinder three millimeters right-lateral. Is that it?"

"That's it." Melinda closed down the plate. "Is everything else ready?"

"Just about. We just have to—"

He broke off as the door slid open and a nurse
stepped in. "I'm sorry, Dr. Cavanagh, but this just came
for you," she said, holding out a card. "It's marked urgent."

"Thank you," Melinda said, taking it and pulling out
her own plate.

"Make it fast," Billingsgate said.

"I will," Melinda promised, frowning at the scrambled
symbols. She'd expected it to be a job assignment or
something equally official; but this was in one of her
father's private codes. Keying for decoding, she
watched as the lines reformed themselves. . . .

And felt her heart seize up. "No," she whispered.

Halfway to the door, Billingsgate turned back around.
"What is it?"

Wordlessly, she swiveled the plate around to face
him. He stooped to read it. "Oh, my God," he murmured. "Who's Pheylan?"

"My brother," Melinda told him, her voice sounding
distant in her ears. She'd had a chance to see Pheylan
three weeks ago, when they'd both been on Nadezhda.
But she'd been too busy. . . .

Billingsgate was saying something. "I'm sorry," she
said, forcing herself to focus on him. "What did you
say?"

"I said you don't need to stay," he repeated. "The team can handle things without you. Get yourself a flight over to the spaceport and get out of here."

She looked back at the plate, the words dissolving into blurs before her. "No," she said, wiping at her eyes. "I'm the design consultant. I'm supposed to see the operation through."

"That's a recommendation," Billingsgate said. "Not a requirement."

"It's my requirement," Melinda said, standing up. Her mind was starting to function again, spreading out the possibilities and necessities in her usual surgically neat lines. "Give me a minute to get in touch with the Cav-Tronics plant in Kai Ho and I'll be right there."

"All right," Billingsgate said, not sounding convinced. "If you're sure."

"I'm sure," she told him. "I can't bring Pheylan back. Maybe I can help prevent someone else from dying."

She didn't realize until the words were out of her mouth how easily they could be interpreted as a slight on Billingsgate's surgical skills. But the older man didn't even seem to notice. "All right," he said again. "Nurse, tell the team to get suited up. We'll be starting as soon as Dr. Cavanagh is ready."

4 The blue light flared through the honeycomb's viewports, jolting Pheylan out of a troubled sleep. The light faded, flared again, faded again, flared again, faded again—

"All right!" he shouted, slapping the pod wall. "Enough, already!"

The light flared one last time and went out. Pheylan swore under his breath, wincing at the rancid taste in his mouth as he checked his chrono. He felt as if he'd just barely closed his eyes, but he'd actually been asleep for four hours. That made it twenty-two hours since the alien ship had come up behind his pod and swallowed it like a big fish snaring its lunch. Roughly sixty-six light-years, assuming the aliens hadn't discovered a stardrive that ran on a different theory from the Commonwealth's. A long way from home.

The blue light flashed again, twice this time. Reflexively, Pheylan reached for the shutter control, stopped with another curse as his sleep-fogged mind remembered that none of the pod's equipment was functional. They'd done that to him early on, scuffling furtively around the base of the pod where he couldn't see them and knocking out his power supply. He'd been in silent darkness ever since except for the dim light and muffled sounds filtering in from the shuttle-bay-sized room around him.

Without power, of course, his dioxide/oxygen converter was also useless, and there'd been a couple of tense hours when he was debating with himself how close to suffocation he should get before he risked popping the hatch. But while the air inside the pod had slowly grown stale, it hadn't gotten any worse than that. Clearly, the aliens had arranged a supplementary air supply to him, probably funneling it in through the valve he'd weakened earlier when he dumped the pod's reserve oxygen.

For a couple of hours after that he'd worried about bacteria or viruses against which his immune system would have no defense, wondering if his captors had had the foresight to filter such things out. But there was nothing to be gained from such speculation, and eventually he'd abandoned it. Under the circumstances alien variations of influenza were probably going to be the least of his worries.

Outside, the blue light flashed twice more, and as it did so Pheylan noticed that his body was beginning to press into his seat again. Weight was returning; and unless the aliens had belatedly decided to spin the ship, that could mean only one thing.

Wherever they'd been heading, they had arrived.

It was fourteen minutes before the sudden rumbling vibration that indicated they'd made planetfall. The noise and motion died away, and for another fifteen minutes Pheylan sweated in the dim light, his survival-pack flechette pistol gripped in his hand, waiting for his captors' next move.

When it happened, it happened all at once. The pod's exit hatch at his left was abruptly rimmed with light, and with a crackle of superheated metal and a cloud of brilliant sparks the hatch cover blew outward, landing with a muffled clang on the deck below. A cool breeze flowed in through the opening, carrying with it the stink of burned metal. Setting his teeth, Pheylan pointed his gun into the air flow and waited.

No one tried to come in. But then, no one had to. Sooner or later he would have to come out on his own, and waiting until he ran out of ration bars would gain him nothing. Sliding his pistol into the inner pocket of his jacket, he unstrapped from his chair and worked his way through the cramped space of the pod over to the blackened opening. The edges were still warm, but not too hot to touch. Getting a grip on the handholds, he looked cautiously out.

The light outside was too dim to see very well, but he could make out a row of indistinct silhouettes facing him from three or four meters away. Worming through the opening, he dropped to the deck beside what was left of the hatch cover. "I'm Commander Pheylan Cavanagh," he called, hoping the quaver in his voice wasn't as noticeable to them as it was to him. "Captain of the Commonwealth Peacekeeper starship *Kinshasa*. Who are you?"

There was no reply, but one of the shadowy figures left the line and stepped toward him. He stopped a meter away, and Pheylan had the impression that even in the dim light he was having no trouble looking the prisoner over. *"Brracha,"* he said in a deep voice; and as he did so, the lights in the room came up.

And Pheylan finally got a clear look at the creatures who'd destroyed his ship.

They were roughly human in height, with slender torsos and a pair each of arms and legs in more or less human arrangement. Their heads were hairless, the faces roughly triangular in shape as large brow ridges over the deep-set eyes narrowed to hawklike beaks.

They were dressed in tight-fitting footed jumpsuits of a dark shimmery material, with no insignia or other ornamentation that Pheylan could see.

Nor were there any obvious side arms in sight. Pheylan eyed them, wondering if it was possible that the basic concept of hand weapons could somehow have passed them by. If so—if that meant they might miss the flechette pistol in his jacket pocket—

There was a movement to his right, and he turned to see another of the aliens step through an archway into the bay, a long folded towel of what looked like their jumpsuit material draped around the back of his neck. He came up to the alien facing Pheylan, who turned and took the material. Their heads, Pheylan saw now, extended farther back than he'd realized, curving back and under to the neck and to a low spinal ridge that jutted out from their jumpsuits. The ridge terminated just above the legs in a flat, eellike tail that seemed to twirl continually in a tight corkscrewing spiral.

The alien spokesman turned back to Pheylan and held out the material. *"Tarr'ketarr brracha,"* he said in the same deep voice.

Pheylan focused on it and saw that what he'd taken to be a long towel was in fact another of their jumpsuits. "No, thank you," he said, shaking his head and tapping his chest. "I prefer to wear my own uniform."

The alien opened his mouth slightly, and a long dark-red tongue jabbed outward at the jumpsuit in his hands. *"Tarr'ketarr brracha,"* he repeated.

Pheylan grimaced, but it was obvious that they had their minds made up. It was also obvious that unless he wanted to haul out his gun and start shooting, there weren't a lot of options open to him. Stripping off his uniform, he put on the jumpsuit.

It was a perfect fit—amazingly perfect, in fact, right down to the slight but annoying bulge around his waist he'd been promising himself to get rid of for the past two years. Clearly, it had been custom-cut for him; and while that eliminated any potential problems of movement or breathing, it also left him no loose nooks or folds where he might be able to conceal his pistol.

The point turned out to be moot. He was still figuring out how the fastening strip worked when the second alien stooped and collected his uniform and equipment, then turned and disappeared back the way he had come.

The spokesman took a step to the side. *"Brracha,"* he said. Again the tongue snaked out, stiffened to point briefly to the alien's right, then retracted again into his mouth.

Pheylan looked in that direction. There was the outline of a large hexagonal-shaped hatchway on the bulkhead, probably the door his pod had come in through. The request was obvious, and as with the jumpsuit there wasn't anything to do but obey. He headed toward it, the alien spokesman stepping to his side as the rest of the line formed up behind them. As they approached the hatchway, it folded outward, letting in a burst of cool, spicy-pungent air.

The sky outside was blue with a scattering of white clouds. As the hatchway continued to open and Pheylan got closer to it, he saw first the tops of tall graygreen objects—the local equivalent of trees, he decided —and then, between him and the trees, a complex of low, flat buildings. From his angle it was difficult to be sure, but they looked as if they were the same linked-hexagon design as the aliens' ships.

A dozen more of the aliens were waiting for him on the ground, standing in a line facing a flat ramp that had been run up to the edge of the hatchway. Pheylan started down toward them, trying to get a look at everything without being too obvious about it. The building complex seemed to be backed up against the gray-green forest, with a wide-open space between it and the landing area. Here and there a few plants still grew, but most of the ground around the complex was a uniform reddish dirt. An indication that it had been only recently finished, he decided, a hunch supported by the second complex clearly still under construction just off the landing area to his right. At the edge of the forest, midway between the two building complexes, was a small geodesic shape with the ominous look of a weapons dome about it.

He reached the foot of the ramp and stopped. "I'm Commander Pheylan Cavanagh of the NorCoord Union," he identified himself again. "Captain of the Peacekeeper starship *Kinshasa.*"

The middle three aliens in the line stepped forward; and now that he was closer, Pheylan could see that their jumpsuits were a different design from those his shipboard escort were wearing. The two flanking aliens stopped a meter away, while the one in the center took another step toward Pheylan. *"Mirras kryrrea sor zhirrzh har'proov,"* he said. His long tongue extended, curved back beneath the lower beak almost to his neck. *"Svv-selic: Too'rr,"* he said. The tongue swung around to his right to point toward the alien there. *"Nzz-oonaz: Flii'rr."* The tongue swung around to his left—*"Thrr-gilag: Kee'rr."*

"Cavanagh," Pheylan repeated, sticking out his own tongue and trying to point to himself. Not surprisingly, it didn't work very well. "Earth," he added, hoping he was guessing right about what had been said.

"Cavv-ana," the alien repeated. *"Urr't."*

"Close enough," Pheylan said. "Now let me try. Sivseleck: Too-err—"

"Svv-selic: Too'rr," the alien corrected him sharply.

"Right," Pheylan said. "Siv-selick—"

"Svv-selic: Too'rr," the alien insisted.

"Yes, I get it," Pheylan said. He could hear the differences; he just couldn't get his mouth to make the proper sounds. "Sorry, but 'Siv-selick' is as close as I can get. You're not exactly on target with 'Cavv-ana' either, you know."

For a moment Svv-selic gazed at him, as if trying to guess what his prisoner might have said. Pheylan found himself looking at the alien's wide eyes, noticing for the first time that each had what looked like three separate pupils. The two on either end were vertical, catlike slits, while the center pupil of each eye was noticeably wider. It struck him as an odd and rather redundant arrangement.

Though so did the aliens' hands, for that matter, composed of three fingers plus two oppositely placed thumbs. Was the second one a spare? Or did their particular grasping movement require an extra thumb to get a proper grip? Or was the appendage something else entirely?

Long ago, in his second year at the Peacekeeper academy, there'd been a unit on nonhuman physiognomy. He was beginning to wish he'd paid more attention in that class.

The alien stirred, cutting off his musings. *"Brracha,"* he said.

From the chorus line of aliens two approached, each with a small round greenish-yellow ball clutched in one hand. One of them stopped beside the alien on Svv-selic's left—Thrr-gilag, if Pheylan was right about these jawbreaker consonant sounds being names—and handed him the ball. Thrr-gilag took a step forward and, in turn, handed the ball to Svv-selic. At the same time, the other alien handed his ball to Nzz-oonaz, who stepped forward and handed it to Pheylan.

"Thank you," Pheylan said, frowning at it. It was hard

but not too heavy, with a bumpy texture and a strange but not unpleasant aroma. A piece of fruit? He looked back up at Svv-selic, wondering if they intended for him to eat it. Svv-selic, watching him, held up his own piece of fruit—

And suddenly his tongue snapped stiffly out, its edge slashing like a knife blade as it ripped through one side of the fruit.

Pheylan jumped, startled. The tongue retracted and slashed out again, cutting a second deep groove in the other side of the fruit. A thick, clear liquid pooled slowly across the top of Svv-selic's fingers and dripped over them onto the ground. *"Brra'avv rrv nee,"* he said.

Pheylan swallowed hard. As an object lesson, it could hardly have been improved on. It probably also explained why they weren't bothering with hand weapons. "Very impressive," he managed. "Now what?"

"Brracha," Svv-selic said. His tongue slid out, supple and nonknifelike again, and pointed at the fruit in Pheylan's hand.

Pheylan shook his head. "I'm sorry, but I can't," he said, sticking out his tongue again for their inspection. "My tongue doesn't work that way."

For a long, uncomfortable moment Svv-selic just looked at him. Then he turned and handed the lacerated fruit back to Thrr-gilag. As he did so, Nzz-oonaz stepped forward again and took the fruit from Pheylan's hand. *"Brra sev kel't mrrt,"* Svv-selic said.

He turned, the others standing with him following suit, and started toward the building complex. One of the shipboard escort stepped up to Pheylan's side and gestured toward the complex with his tongue. "Right," Pheylan said, and started walking.

They led him to a heavy-looking door in one of the smaller hexagons at the near edge of the complex. Svv-selic swung it open and gestured with his tongue. "Right," Pheylan said again, and stepped inside.

It was a large room, taking up most if not all of the hexagon. Three of the six walls were lined with waist-high consoles, some of them with displays that showed shifting ghosts of hazy luminescence or more sharp-edged patterns of white and gray. A dozen pieces of alien furniture were scattered loosely around two of the other three walls. The sixth wall held the door they'd entered by, itself flanked by another pair of consoles.

And in the center, arranged inside a floor-to-ceiling glass cylinder, was a bed, a chair and fold-down table, a toilet, an open-top shower, and a washbasin.

His cell.

"Nice and cozy," he commented sourly. Actually, it wasn't nearly as bad as he'd expected. Small but adequately appointed, a little short on privacy . . . and, somehow, oddly familiar. He took a step toward it, studying the layout—

And stopped abruptly as a tongue darted out in front of him, pointing to his left.

He looked. Five of the aliens had grouped themselves beside one of the consoles against the wall. A console whose front panel was even now extending a flat, table-like slab into the room.

Pheylan took a deep breath. Alien or not, he knew a medical-examination table when he saw it. "Okay," he said, bracing himself and starting toward it. "Let's get it over with."

It took three hours in all—a long and distinctly unpleasant three hours. Still, he had to admit as the glass door of his glass cell swung shut behind him, it could have been a lot worse.

Maybe that part would come later. After they'd

learned some English and could ask him all the questions prisoners of war were usually asked. He wondered if their culture included the concept of torture.

He took a deep breath, looking around the room and trying to ignore the uncomfortable tingling still running through his muscles from the instruments they'd used in their examination. With three hours to think about it, he'd figured out why the cell arrangement had looked familiar. Except for the missing wall displays and mounted artwork, it was a perfect copy of Commodore Dyami's stateroom aboard the *Jutland*.

He stepped over to the bed and sat down, running a hand over the material. It was noticeably softer than a standard shipboard bunk, and the blanket felt more like plastic than cloth. But they'd gotten the basic style right.

The aliens were still in the outer part of the room, some of them watching him. Swiveling around, he stretched out on the bed and gazed up at the flat, almost featureless ceiling. Wondering if they realized the priceless bit of information this room had given away.

They'd had four ships at the battle: big ships, far too big to use the double-speed skitter stardrive. They'd picked him up at that same battle and flown him here. Presumably directly, and he would have known from the engine sound if they'd stopped along the way. True, they could have had a skitter stashed aboard one of the other ships, which could have arrived here fourteen hours ago. But most of that lead time would have been eaten up by however long it took the aliens to sift through the rubble of the Peacekeeper force. And yet, he'd arrived to find a copy of Commodore Dyami's stateroom already in place for him.

The conclusion was inescapable. The aliens had a method of true instantaneous communication.

It was the breakthrough in tachyonic physics that the

Commonwealth had been looking for for probably the last hundred years. This wasn't just the raw, single-bit information that a ship was passing by a few light-years away or that a tachyon static bomb had just been triggered. This was someone at the battle talking directly to someone here, giving highly detailed instructions as to what kind of environment to set up for the prisoner who was on his way. It was contrary to everything the scientific establishment thought they knew about tachyon physics. And yet here it was.

And the consequences could be devastating. Detailed information from advance scouts, from forward bases, from the height of pitched battles—all of it would be instantly available to the aliens' high command. It would be modern planetary warfare, expanded to interstellar scale.

And he was the only one in the Commonwealth who knew it.

He closed his eyes, unwilling to let his captors see the tears there even if they had no way of understanding their significance. He'd made it through the massacre alive—from the evidence, apparently the only one of the 145 aboard the *Kinshasa* who had. He'd known every one of those men and women, and had been responsible for their lives.

And he'd failed them.

He swallowed, his throat aching with bitterness and guilt. Already he'd replayed the battle a hundred times over in his mind, searching for something—anything— that he could have done differently. Something that he should have done, or shouldn't have done, that would have made a difference.

There was no way for him ever to make up for the people who'd died aboard his ship. The best he could do now was to make sure they hadn't died uselessly.

He opened his eyes again. The aliens were still going

about their business, their tails corkscrewing slowly around as they conversed in small groups or bent over flickering consoles. He would survive, he promised himself silently. No matter what they did to him, he would survive. And as they learned about him, he would learn as much as he could about them.

And when the time was right, he would do whatever it took to escape from this place and get his knowledge back to the Commonwealth.

"Okay, Colonel, we've got us a green light to go in," Lieutenant Alex Williams said, keying the drudgeship's engines off standby. "Where do you want to go?"

"I'm not sure it really matters," Holloway admitted, gazing out the canopy at the brilliantly lit field of debris drifting through space in front of them. "Given Dorcas's location and all, I thought it might be instructive to see what we were up against. I guess I could have saved myself the trip."

"There's not much left to see," Williams agreed. "We've already picked up most of the big pieces and sent them off to the analysis center on Edo. Mostly what we're doing now is picking bodies out of the rubble."

Holloway nodded, his stomach tightening in anger. That part had shown up in exquisitely painful detail in the watchship records. Twenty-eight hundred men and women, most of them slaughtered for no reason. "We're going to have to make them pay for that."

"No argument from me on that one," Williams said grimly. "Odds among my crew are running five to one that we finally bring CIRCE out of retirement."

"Let's just hope they're damn careful when they start putting it back together," Holloway said, looking around at the floating debris. "All we need is for these butchers to get hold of a working CIRCE."

"These, or any other batch," Williams said. "The Pawoles still haven't forgiven us for using it on them. I'll bet the Yycromae wouldn't mind getting their hands on it, either."

"That's certainly a cheery thought." Holloway looked out the viewport at the dim sun of the system, so far away it was hardly distinguishable from the background stars around it. "What were they doing out here, anyway?"

"Probably poking around the cometary halo looking for stuff to mine," Williams said. "Wasting their time— our teams looked the place over about five years ago. Nothing here worth the effort of digging out. Look, Colonel, we've still got a lot of work to do out there. If you want, I can drop you off—wait a minute." He cocked his head slightly, listening intently to his earphone. "Williams here. You sure? Okay, stay with it—I'm on my way."

He keyed the drive, and the drudgeship swung around toward one of the banks of lights. "What is it?" Holloway asked.

"The jackpot, maybe," Williams said. "Someone's spotted what looks like a piece of alien ship outside the scavenger area."

Two other drudgeships were already there when they arrived, their remote analyzers drifting across the fragment's surface. "What have you got, Scotts?" Williams asked, touching a switch and pulling off his headset.

"Looks like a hull plate, Lieutenant," the other's voice came over the cockpit speaker. "A piece of one, anyway. Got some electronic fragments or something on the underside, too."

"What got it, a shrapnel line?"

"Looks more like expansion shock to me," Scotts

said. "Probably flash-heated by a close-in warhead explosion and popped at the seams. I'm picking up some odd dust here, too—could be the same stuff. We'll scoop some of it up."

Holloway peered out at the milky-white plate, only slightly scarred except near the edges where it had broken. "One plate and some dust," he commented. "Must be one very sturdy hull material."

"All that, and more," Scotts said. "I want a copy of the stress-test report when it comes in."

A third remote had drifted in to join the other two now at the hull plate's surface. "What haven't you done yet?" Williams asked.

"Bakst is looking at the edge structure; I'm trying to get an angle on those electronics," Scotts said. "We haven't tried composition yet."

"Okay, I'll run that," Williams said, keying in the program. "The *Jutland* ships took a shot at this before the shooting started," he added to Holloway, leaning over in his seat to peer into the remote's display. "Didn't get 'em anywhere; but then, they were eight klicks away and trying to read through a heat-dump spectrum. Let's see if we can do a little better now . . . well, well. Bingo."

"What?" Holloway asked.

"It's not a metal alloy at all," Williams said, straightening up again. "It's a ceramic."

"A ceramic?" Holloway echoed. "I've never heard of a ceramic this tough."

"Me, neither," Williams said. "I guess we're hearing about it now."

"I guess we are," Holloway agreed. "And that explains why the radar-triggered missiles the force kept throwing never went off. There weren't any large masses of metal for them to lock on to."

"I don't think there were even any small ones," Scotts's voice came from the speaker. "You're going to love this, Lieutenant. These electronics things on the underside? No metal in 'em."

"Not even power lines?"

"If they're here, I can't find them," Scotts said. "All the filaments they've got running in and out are just optical control fibers. No idea how the power's getting in."

"Could they be using a Djadaran electron-tunneling effect?" Holloway asked.

"Not unless they've come up with a way to make it a lot more efficient than the Djadar ever did," Williams said. "How about it, Scotts?"

"I don't think so," Scotts said slowly. "Scan's still running, but so far I'm not reading any semiconductors, either."

"No metals *or* semiconductors?" Williams frowned. "All right, I give: what *is* there?"

"Throw your guess in with mine," Scotts said. "All I'm getting is the optical fibers plus some complex geometric shapes of unknown composition."

"Crystalline?"

"Or amorphous," Scotts said. "The analyzer can't seem to make up its mind on that one, either. We could try taking an interference reading."

"Not worth the effort," Williams said reluctantly. "We're just supposed to find this stuff, anyway—it's up to the geniuses on Edo to figure out what the hell it is. Pull your remotes back and I'll take this piece in. You and Bakst start a search of the area, see if you can find any more pieces. I'll swing a couple more ships over to give you a hand."

"Yes, sir."

Williams keyed the board speaker switch off again

and put his headset back on. "Where are we going?" Holloway asked.

"Back to the *Ganymede* to drop this off," Williams said, looking at the display as he maneuvered the grabber arms out toward the alien plate. "And unless there's something else you want to see, Colonel, I'm going to drop you there with it. We've still got work to do out here. And there's no guarantee the aliens won't come back."

"I understand," Holloway nodded. "I'd better be getting back to Dorcas, anyway."

"I can't say I envy you your post," Williams said candidly. "Playing sitting duck on a rock like Dorcas isn't my idea of a fun tactical stance."

"I could think of better positions myself," Holloway agreed. "Somewhere in Orion Sector springs to mind. You think you'll be able to find all the bodies?"

"Probably," Williams said, the bulk of his attention clearly on the task at hand. "The battle was pretty well localized—it was over too fast for much drift. Why?"

Holloway looked out at the field of junk floating off to their right. "Just wondering if maybe they weren't all killed."

Williams shook his head. "The watchships didn't leave until all the locator beacons had been silenced. And those things don't break down by themselves."

"Yes, I know," Holloway said. "I was just thinking that if I'd just had a run-in with an unknown race, I'd make sure I got at least one live prisoner to take back for study."

Williams shrugged. "You can't count on them thinking like humans."

"It still wouldn't hurt to mention the possibility in your report."

"Frankly, Colonel, I've got better things to do right

now than add stuff to my file work," Williams said. "If you want it put in, write it up yourself."

"Maybe I will," Holloway said, looking out at the lights of the drudgeships moving around against the stars. "Yes. I think I will."

5 **T**he rumors had begun even before they'd left Mees, and for the entire ten-hour trip they seemed to be the sole topic of conversation aboard the liner. There were whispered stories of sudden activity at the Peacekeepers' orbital Bridgehead base; second- and third-hand reports that the governments of the three human enclaves on Mees had been called into emergency session; dark hints that postbattle assessment teams had been activated and been whisked off God only knew where. Through it all Aric had kept to himself, working through the shock and grief of his father's unexpected message as best he could. Wondering how his younger brother had died, and whether the still unknown circumstances surrounding it were to blame for the flurry of nervous hearsay.

It wasn't until he reached the NorCoord Parliament chambers that he had his first inkling that the rumors might for once have been understated. The smiling young pages who normally stood by the doors to the observation balcony had been replaced by a pair of armed and decidedly unsmiling Peacekeeper Marines. They checked Aric's ID carefully, double-checked it against their list, and finally let him in.

He walked down the short entrance corridor to the rear of the balcony proper. Kolchin was waiting there, leaning against the wall with his usual deceptive air of carelessness. A dozen other men and women loitered nearby, all exuding the same aura of alert competence as they gave Aric a thoughtful once-over. Apparently, CavTronics Industries wasn't the only big gun of Commonwealth industry and business represented here today.

"Mr. Cavanagh," Kolchin nodded as Aric came up to him. "Good to see you, sir."

"You too," Aric nodded back, noting peripherally that with Kolchin's identification of him the other bodyguards seemed to lose interest. "Where is he?"

"Down there," Kolchin said, pointing toward one of the lower tiers of seats.

Aric looked. The balcony was barely a quarter full, his father's white hair instantly recognizable in the subdued lighting. He was sitting alone, and even at this distance Aric thought he could see a slump in the older man's shoulders. "Melinda hasn't arrived yet?"

Kolchin shook his head. "No, but she should be here soon. She was doing an operation on Celadon that couldn't be rescheduled and had to catch a ride with one of our transports. They got in to Cheredovat about half an hour ago. Parlan's bringing her in."

Aric nodded. "Okay. Send her down when she gets here, all right?"

"Sure thing."

Parlimin Hurley Maxwell was on the podium down on the floor below, speaking passionately about Peacekeeper preparation and funding as Aric walked down the aisle. "Hi, Dad," he said as he reached his father's row and sat down beside him.

"Aric," the elder Cavanagh said, giving him a poor

attempt at a smile as he gripped his son's hand. "Thanks for coming."

"Sure," Aric assured him, studying the other's face in the subdued light. There were new lines there, lines of fatigue and grief that he hadn't seen three weeks ago. The old man was taking this hard. "How are you doing?"

"No worse than you'd expect," his father said, trying the smile again with the same lack of success. "Of course it's hard; but it's not like we never knew that this day might someday come. Pheylan knew there were risks that came with the uniform, and he accepted them."

"It was more than just acceptance, Dad," Aric reminded him. "He'd wanted to be in the Peacekeepers since before he was seven." He smiled as a stray memory clicked. "Wanted it about as badly as he *didn't* want an office job."

His father threw him a sideways look. "Told you about that fight, did he?"

"We told each other most things," Aric said, swallowing through a suddenly aching throat. He was going to miss Pheylan, too. More than he was willing to admit even to himself. "I remember him storming into my office right after that particular argument and announcing that he'd rather join a pirate gang than disappear like me behind a desk somewhere in CavTronics. It took me half an hour to calm him down."

"That sounds like him," the elder Cavanagh said, shaking his head. "Strange, isn't it. He hated the idea of a desk job; but even in the Peacekeepers that's where he would eventually have wound up. Maybe it's just as well he didn't get that far."

"Maybe," Aric said, looking down at the chamber floor and searching for a way to change the subject. His father was putting up a good front, but beneath the calm words Aric could see an all-too-familiar pattern beginning to form. The downward emotional spirals that followed Aric's mother's sudden death had plagued his father for months afterward, taking a harsh toll on his health and threatening to turn him into a recluse. Now, five years later, Aric suspected he would be even less capable of handling that kind of stress. "What's the big debate down there today?" he asked. "Some fallout from all of this?"

"More than you know," his father said. "I couldn't put it into my message, but your brother didn't just die in an accident or minor skirmish. The *Kinshasa* was destroyed in a full-blown battle. Along with the rest of the *Jutland* task force."

Aric swiveled in his seat. "The *entire* task force?"

The other nodded. "All eight ships. No survivors."

An unpleasant tingle ran through Aric's body. The shipboard rumors had indeed been understated. No wonder the Marines were on guard duty out there. "Where did it happen?"

"Dorcas. A few light-years outside the system, actually."

"Do we know who hit them?"

"All we know is that it's someone new," his father said. "That much was clear from the watchship data. Who they were, or where they come from, we still don't know."

Slowly, Aric turned back and settled again into his seat. A brand-new self-starfaring race . . . and already blood had been drawn. "What's Peacekeeper Command doing about it?"

"Preparing for war." His father gestured toward the chamber floor below. "And I can't say that everyone is upset at the prospect."

Aric focused his attention on the podium. "—and will furthermore cement our position once and for all within the Commonwealth and among the nonhuman worlds," Maxwell was intoning. "For the past decade the policies of the Northern Coordinate Union have been treated with thinly veiled contempt by more and more member states of the Commonwealth. Particularly those policies involving the organization and philosophy of the Peace-keeper forces that protect them. It's high time we demonstrated to the critics that their taxes and young people have not been simply disappearing into some soft, bloated military bureaucracy. The Peacekeepers are hard and lean and ready to fight. It's time they proved it."

He picked up his plate and stepped down from the podium to a ripple of applause from the rest of the chamber. "He's sure ready to go," Aric murmured.

"He's not the worst, either," his father said. "There's a small but vocal faction that's convinced on philosophical grounds that a strong common enemy is exactly what the Commonwealth has been missing lately. Something to pull humanity together, get us all going in the same direction again."

"Under NorCoord leadership, of course."

The elder Cavanagh shrugged. "Some of them genuinely believe that would be better for all of humanity. I'm not sure all of them do."

"Has anyone brought up CIRCE yet?"

"Not yet," the other said grimly. "But it can only be a matter of time."

Aric studied his father's profile. The taut cheeks, the haunted eyes. The memories. "You don't want it reassembled, do you?"

The other sighed. "You see CIRCE as history," he said, gesturing toward the Parliament floor. "Most of the people down there do, too. Even those my age who lived through the events saw CIRCE more as facts and numbers in a news report than anything else. But I was there. I saw what it did."

Aric frowned. "I didn't know you were at Celadon."

"I wasn't at the battle, no," his father shook his head. "But I was with the cleanup crew that went aboard one of the Pawolian warships afterward."

Wandering around a ghost ship . . . "Pretty bad, huh?"

"In its own quiet way it was the most terrifying thing I've ever witnessed," the elder Cavanagh said. "You had to see those ships, Aric, to really appreciate what CIRCE had done to them. The Pawoles knew we were experimenting with ion-beam weapons, and they'd built some awesome ion protection into those five ships. They had multiple layers of superdense metal shielding, high-power dipole field generators, even a liquid-envelope radiation reflector. None of it did a bit of good. Twenty-five thousand Pawoles died in that one shot, radiation-burned right where they stood. A shot, remember, that went straight through the cloud of fighters arrayed between the two lines without even singeing them. That was the eeriest part of all."

Aric shrugged slightly. It was hard to get too worked up over nonhumans who'd died before he'd even been born. Especially when it was the Pawoles who'd picked the fight in the first place. "It ended the war," he pointed out.

"Oh, it ended the war, all right," his father said heavily. "And we were all terrified out of our minds that it would end everything. You know as well as I do that no technology ever remains exclusive property for very long—not nuclear weapons, not the Chabrier stardrive, not anything. If CIRCE's secret had leaked out . . ." He shook his head. "We've been lucky, Aric. Weapons like CIRCE almost always lead in one of two directions: a balance of power where everyone has it, or abuses of power by the exclusive owner. In this case we've had neither."

"Perhaps," Aric murmured noncommittally. It was true enough that CIRCE hadn't been used since the Pawolian war, but not everyone would agree that just because a weapon wasn't fired meant it wasn't being abused. The NorCoord Union had slowly been becoming a secondary voice in Commonwealth politics when the Pawolian war and CIRCE came along. It was hardly a secondary voice now.

A historical fact that was surely not lost on those Parlimins down there. "So how long do you think it'll be before someone finally suggests that NorCoord reassemble the thing and get it ready to use?"

His father nodded toward the floor below. "I'd say right about now."

A Yycroma had taken Maxwell's place at the podium, its furry-scaled crocodilian face almost hidden by the glints of light rippling across the crest and faceted sides of its ceremonial helmet.

Aric frowned. It was hard to tell size and proportion beneath the cloak and helmet, but— "Is that a *male*?"

"It is indeed," the elder Cavanagh said darkly. "A special envoy from the Hierarch, here on some matter concerning the interdiction zone. He took over from the ambassador as soon as they were informed about the Dorcas attack."

"Terrific," Aric growled. A male Yycroma, the heady smell of conflict in his nostrils. Just what they needed.

[I will be brief,] the Yycroma said, his long jaw grinding out the alien words as if chewing small animals. [I have heard long talk today about preparation and political matters. Such things are for the mediation of females. This is not a faction threat or corsair attack that now stands before you. This is an enemy beyond anything you have faced. To use less than your full strength would be the mistake of fools.]

"Typical Yycroman tact," Aric murmured.

"Shh."

[If I speak bluntly, it is because this danger does not threaten only you,] the Yycroma continued sternly. [The prohibition imposed by Peacekeeper fiat upon Yycroman military vessels leaves our worlds and people defenseless against attack from outside should the interdiction zone forces be withdrawn. And such attacks will come. Speak to the Mrachanis—hear their tales of those who once passed through their domain fleeing an enemy they named as the *Mirnacheem-hyeea.*]

He paused, his helmet glinting as he swept his gaze around the chamber. [You have spoken of much today. You have not yet spoken of the CIRCE weapon. Of that you must speak further among yourselves. I say only this. If these are indeed the *Mirnacheem-hyeea,* they will move swiftly to take your worlds from you. If the worlds they seize contain parts of the CIRCE weapon, you will lose by default any ability to use it against them. Think on that.]

He stepped down from the podium and strode back to the observation boxes where the rest of the nonhuman ambassadors sat or squatted. "I guess that makes CIRCE an official part of the discussion," Aric commented.

"Unfortunately, his point's a valid one," his father said. "Scattering CIRCE's components across the Commonwealth might have kept it from being easily abused, but it also makes it vulnerable to precisely that kind of piecemeal seizure."

"I don't see why," Aric said. "The original plans must be still kicking around somewhere. We ought to be able to build an entirely new CIRCE from scratch, let alone manufacture a replacement part or two."

"One would think so," his father said thoughtfully. "But that assumes that it was deliberately designed in the first place."

Aric frowned at him. "Come again?"

"It's just something I've been thinking a great deal about since all this broke. Don't forget that CIRCE came effectively out of nowhere—there weren't even whispered hints about its existence until after it had been used. And in thirty-seven years since then no one else has been able to come up with another working model of it. Either NorCoord's had an incredible run of luck and good security . . . or else there's something about the weapon that can't easily be duplicated."

Aric chewed at the inside of his cheek. Pheylan had gone on a CIRCE kick back in grade school, reading everything he could get his hands on regarding the history and technology of the project. He'd complained at the time how surprisingly little there was available. "So what are you saying?" he asked. "That CIRCE is a nonhuman technology that NorCoord found buried somewhere and figured out how to work?"

His father smiled faintly. "You sound like a second-rate thriller. No, I don't think we've got a nonhuman device here. But research accidents do happen; and I think it's entirely possible that part of CIRCE came from a botched experiment that turned out to be more than anyone expected. Possibly one reason they broke the weapon up, in fact. Scattering the pieces across a dozen planets would make it that much harder for a potential thief to identify and locate the key component."

"But they must have analyzed the whole thing since then," Aric argued. "Surely they know by now what they've got."

"Perhaps. Though I can say from experience that electronic mistakes can sometimes be impossible to reproduce. The larger fact remains, though, that if any part of CIRCE is difficult to replicate, we could be in serious trouble if that component was destroyed or fell into enemy hands."

Aric grimaced. "Peacekeeper Command has presumably thought about that."

"If not, one hopes our Yycroman friend has now reminded them."

Aric nodded. On the floor below, a Dja was waddling its way forward. Apparently, Parliament had decided to give podium time to each of the nonhuman observers. "Did you catch the name he was calling those aliens from the Mrach legend? I couldn't make it out."

"Mirnacheem-hyeea," his father said. "It's a somewhat archaic Mrach phrase that translates roughly as 'conquerors without reason.' One of the few bits of the language I know."

Conquerors without reason. "Sounds ominous."

"Agreed. The real irony of it—and I doubt most of the Parlimins down there know this—is that that's the same term the Mrachanis first used for humans."

There was a rustle of movement in the aisle beside Aric. He looked up—

"Aric," Melinda whispered to him, squeezing his shoulder briefly in greeting as she slid deftly past the two men and sat down on her father's other side. "Hi, Daddy," she said, half turning in her seat to give him a long hug. "How are you doing?"

"I'm all right," he said, hugging her back. "Thanks for coming."

"I'm sorry it took so long," she apologized into his shoulder. Her eyes lifted to Aric's, eyebrows rising in silent question. He shrugged, shook his head fractionally. Only time would tell how well their father was going to weather this new loss.

"Parlan told me all about the battle on the way over,"

Melinda continued, pulling back from the hug but keeping hold of her father's hand. "Do they know yet who did it?"

"Not yet." He eyed her carefully. "How are you holding up?"

"I'm okay," she assured him. "Really. Don't worry about me. How about you, Aric?"

"I'm doing fine," Aric told her. To his own ears he didn't sound nearly as convincing as she had. But then, she'd always been a better straight-faced liar than he had. "How did the operation go?"

"No problems," she said, her tone dismissing it as unimportant. "Has anything new happened since I left Celadon?"

"Nothing we're being let in on," their father said. "Excessive speech making from Parliament, mainly. I presume Peacekeeper Command is making better use of its time."

"They are," Melinda said. "Even before your message arrived, they'd already whisked Dr. Haidar and some others off to Edo. He's one of the best diagnostic surgeons in the Commonwealth."

"Gone to help with the autopsies, no doubt." The elder Cavanagh shook his head, eyes focused on nothing. "There'll be plenty of that sort of work for them to do."

Snugged up against his side in its inside pocket, Aric's phone vibrated silently. "I've got a call coming in," he said, standing up. "Back in a minute."

He had to go out past the Peacekeeper Marines at the door before he was far enough outside the Parliament's transmission shielding to get a clear connection. "Hello?"

"Quinn, sir," the familiar voice and face said. "I thought you ought to know that Peacekeeper Command has begun notifying the families of those killed at

Dorcas. That means the remains should be released soon. Do you want me to contact them and make the arrangements?"

Aric grimaced. A distinctly unpleasant duty; but it was the family's duty, not Quinn's. "Thanks, but I'll do it," he said. "Who do I contact?"

"Mortuary Affairs," Quinn said. "I don't know who the officer in charge is."

"I'll find him," Aric said. "Are you at the ship?"

"Yes, sir. Captain Teva says we'll be ready to head out to Avon whenever your father wants to leave."

"Good. We'll let you know."

"Yes, sir."

Aric keyed off, called up the directory, and punched in the proper number. "Peacekeeper Mortuary Affairs," a young-looking sergeant answered. "Lewis."

"My name is Aric Cavanagh," Aric identified himself. "My brother Pheylan was captain of the *Kinshasa.* I'd like to make arrangements for us to pick up his remains."

"One moment, sir."

The phone went blank. Aric leaned against a convenient wall, gazing around the wide circular lounge that wrapped around the back of the observation balcony. The place was mostly deserted, with the usual swarm of tourists already having been turned away and most of the journalists sniffing around the edges of the story having gone one level down to wait for the Parlimins and aides to come out of the chambers.

"Mr. Cavanagh?" a new voice said.

Aric shifted his attention back to the phone. An older officer had taken Sergeant Lewis's place on the display. "Yes?"

"My name is Captain Rawlins, sir," the other said. "All remains have been released and are in the process of being returned to their home states. However, I don't find any listing here for Commander Cavanagh."

Aric frowned. "I don't understand."

"I don't really understand it myself, sir," Rawlins admitted. "There was a lot of damage out there, and there are several remains that are still only tentatively identified. But Commander Cavanagh is the only one listed simply as missing in action."

"Could they have just missed him out there?"

"Unlikely, sir," Rawlins said. "The cleanup team supposedly got everything worth collecting."

Aric rubbed at his lip. Either someone had messed up, or someone was covering up. Either way, he didn't like it. "Who do I need to talk to?"

"I could transfer you to Civilian Affairs, sir," Rawlins offered. "I doubt they could tell you anything more than I already have, though."

"Don't bother, then," Aric said. "Thank you for your help."

He keyed off, resisting the urge to swear out loud. It wasn't bad enough that he'd lost his brother. Now they couldn't even give him a proper farewell.

Well, he wasn't going to simply sit back and wait. Keying his phone back on, he punched for Quinn. "Yes, sir?"

"Quinn, who's the top Peacekeeper officer who Dad might know personally?" Aric asked him.

"Well, he knows General Garcia Alvarez," Quinn said slowly. "I believe he also has at least a passing acquaintance with Admiral Rudzinski. The admiral was the Fleet's Parliament liaison when Lord Cavanagh was in office."

And now Rudzinski was supreme Fleet commander, one member of the three-man Peacekeeper Command Triad. That could prove useful. "Any idea where Rudzinski is now?"

"I heard he was with the assessment team on Edo. I can check if he's still there."

"Do that," Aric told him. "And then have Teva get the ship ready to fly."

"Yes, sir. I take it we're heading to Edo?"

"You take it right," Aric told him grimly. To Edo, to get his brother back.

Or to find out why he couldn't.

6 **P**heylan had promised himself to do whatever it took to escape from his cell. And for the first four days it looked as though he were going to be leaving on a slab.

It was like no sickness he'd ever had before. Violent stomach cramps without any vomiting; vertigo and light-headedness that left his mind foggy but without any actual pain; fever that came and went almost hourly. It was probably a reaction to some local bacterium or virus, and he would undoubtedly have been much more concerned about it if he'd had any mental energy left for such worries.

He spent most of those four days on his cot, either bundled up to keep warm or with the blankets thrown off and his jumpsuit open to the waist trying to cool himself down. He slept a great deal, too, with strange dreams blending into the equally strange reality of his imprisonment and back again. Occasionally, he would wake up to find some of the aliens standing around him, poking or studying him with dull white instruments. But the memories were foggy. Perhaps they too were dreams.

The fifth day he woke up to find himself healthy.

He lay there for a few minutes, running through a mental checklist and trying to decide whether he really believed it. But the discomfort and confusion were gone, and for the first time since landing he realized he was ravenously hungry.

Carefully, he sat up, aware that four days of dehydration could make him as light-headed as the sickness itself had. On his bed's pullout nightstand was a tall cylinder of some clear liquid and two of his escape pod's ration bars. The liquid proved to be a delicately scented water; the ration bars proved to be just what he needed.

He sat on the edge of his bed, looking around the room as he ate. Three aliens were visible, two of them working at one of the consoles, the third lying on what looked like a sort of stretched-out vaulting horse in the lounge area. None of them seemed to be paying all that much attention to him, but he somehow doubted he was being ignored.

Still, they were aliens; and any excessive sense of privacy he might have once had had been burned out by fifteen years in the Fleet. He finished his breakfast, stripped off his decidedly rancid jumpsuit, and stepped into the shower.

The standard Fleet-shower soap drip was missing, but with some experimentation he discovered that a bumpy section of wall near the shower head was a thick slab of some soapy substance. He scrubbed himself clean and shut off the water, remembering only then that there was no towel out there to dry off with. But that was okay. Simply being able to take a shower had made him feel like a civilized human being again, and if he had to walk around buck naked while he air-dried, it was a small price to pay.

He brushed off the excess water and stepped out. To his mild surprise he discovered that his old jumpsuit was gone, replaced by a new one that had been laid neatly across the bed. "Good maid service," he murmured. He walked across to it, glancing around the room as he did so—

And suddenly felt a surge of adrenaline jolt through him. There, off to his left, a vertical crack was visible in the wall of his cell. A vertical crack that bisected the milky-white lock mechanism set into the wall.

It was the edge of the door to his cell. And it was open.

He continued on to his bed, looking around quickly as he tried to kick his brain cells into activity. Could his captors really have left the door open when they brought in the fresh jumpsuit? No—surely they wouldn't have been that careless. It had to be a test of some sort. A test to see what he would do if they offered him a way to escape.

He sat down on the bed, picking up the jumpsuit and pretending to examine it. On the face of it the whole thing was so blatantly obvious as to be an insult to his intelligence. Here he was, barely recovered from four days of illness, imprisoned on an unknown world with nothing but the clothes they themselves had provided for him; and they expected him to jump at the first hint of a way out?

Or were they expecting a different reaction entirely? A reaction like charging out and trying to kill the aliens in the outer room?

His hand, he noticed suddenly, was dry where he was touching the jumpsuit: the material seemed to have wicked the water away from his skin. Possibly why they hadn't provided him with a towel in the first place. He started to get dressed, watching the aliens out of the corner of his eye as he did so. They were still just going about their business, completely oblivious to the open door.

All right, he told himself as he finished sealing the jumpsuit. It had to be a test, which meant that ignoring the door would tell them only that he was smart enough to be suspicious. But with luck maybe he could use it to plant a few false assumptions. Stuffing the empty water tube awkwardly into the top of his jumpsuit, he mentally crossed his fingers and stepped to the door.

The one time he'd seen them use it, the door had swung open on its own at the touch of a button on a milky-white plate set into the cell wall near the door's edge. It wasn't nearly so easy to push open by hand, but it was also not nearly as hard as Pheylan tried to make it look. Whatever method he used to eventually break out of this place would almost certainly include simple raw strength, and the more the aliens underestimated human muscle power, the better chance he'd have.

So he pushed hard against the door, clenching his teeth as he strained to inch it open, hoping that those who were watching couldn't see that his shoulder was simultaneously pushing against the wall itself. He shifted to a two-handed grip on door and jamb as soon as it was far enough open, grimacing all the more dramatically as he forced tired muscles to strain isometrically against each other and against the skintight material of the jumpsuit. He got it open just far enough and squeezed out.

The three aliens were watching him now, all right. But there was no mad scramble for the door or for hidden weapons. Sacrificial goats, for sure, there to draw the tiger in for the attack.

An attack Pheylan had no intention of making. He'd demonstrated his physical weakness with the door; now it was time to demonstrate his innate innocence and lack of aggression. Stepping up to the nearest alien, he pulled the water tube out of his tunic and held it out.

"Do you suppose," he said, "that I could have some more of this?"

They led him back to his cell, one of them going off to one of the consoles to refill the water tube. This time the door was closed properly behind him.

Apparently, that part of the test was over. Pheylan wondered whether he'd passed or failed.

He drank half the water, then lay down on his side on the cot. Propping his head up with the pillow, resting one hand against the smooth coolness of the cell wall, he gazed out at the aliens as they resumed their work.

Or at least he hoped it looked as if he were watching them. At the moment he was far more interested in the wall of his cell.

His first reaction on seeing it had been to identify it as glass. Later, before succumbing to his illness, he'd changed his mind and decided it was probably a plastic. Now, running his fingertips and nails across the material, he decided he'd been right the first time. An incredibly tough glass, undoubtedly, and a good five centimeters thick on top of it, but a glass nonetheless.

He turned over to lie on his back, trying to think. Glass was a noncrystalline substance, often but not always silicon based. Generally acid resistant, though there were one or two acids that he vaguely remembered would attack it. An old memory drifted up from the past: the time he, Aric, and Melinda had been playing drag ball and he'd driven the ball squarely into the window of his mother's study. The glass itself had survived, but the impact had cracked the framing and popped the pane neatly out onto the desk, knocking over a cup of tea his mother had left there and creating a major mess.

At the corner of his eye, something moved. Pheylan

turned to look; but there was nothing there. Just the wall of his cell and the usual flickering of lights from the consoles on that side.

"Cavv'ana."

Pheylan sat up and looked the other way. Standing just outside his cell were three of the aliens. From the design of their jumpsuits, he tentatively identified them as the three who'd accosted him on the ground outside the ship. "Hello," he said, swinging his legs over the edge of the bed and sitting up. "And how are you today?"

The alien in the center regarded him for a moment, the tip of his tongue flicking in and out of his beak. "I well," he said in a deep voice. "You well?"

For a second the whole thing went straight past Pheylan. Then, abruptly, his mental gears caught with a grinding jerk.

The alien had spoken in English.

"I'm much better," he managed, staring at the creature. "I was sick for a few days."

"Who few days?"

Pheylan frowned. Then he got it. "Not *who; what. What* is a few days," he corrected. "In this case a few is four." He held up four fingers. "Four days."

The alien paused as if digesting that. "I bring your container," he said. He gestured with his tongue to the alien on his left and the pod survival kit gripped in his hand. "You want?"

"Yes, I do," Pheylan said, standing up. "Thank you."

The alien with the bag took a step to the side and knelt down beside the cell door. Three small white squares were set into the glass near the floor, positioned just about right for hinges and a lock. The alien did something with the upper square, and a flat rectangle of the wall swung down. The survival kit turned out to be slightly larger than the opening, but with a little effort he got it through. "Thank you," Pheylan said again as the alien closed the flap.

"You keep alive," the center alien said. Svv-selic, if Pheylan remembered the name right. And if they were standing in the same order as before. "Container necessary?"

"It'll help," Pheylan said, trying to keep the bitterness out of his voice. Such solicitude, all of a sudden, from these things who'd coldly butchered his crew. "But if you want me kept alive, I'm going to need more food than I've got here."

For a minute the aliens conversed softly among themselves. "Food prepare," Svv-selic said.

"Terrific," Pheylan grunted. "So when does the interrogation begin?"

There was another quiet debate on the other side of the glass. "Not understand."

"Don't worry, you'll figure it out," Pheylan assured them sourly. "How'd you learn how to speak English?"

"We later," Svv-selic said. He turned, the others following suit—

"Wait a minute," Pheylan called, scrambling to his feet. For a second, as they'd turned, he'd caught a glimpse of something. . . .

The aliens turned back to face him. "Who?"

"Not *who; what,*" Pheylan corrected again, moving right up to the wall in front of them and thinking quickly. He'd gotten them to turn around as he'd wanted, but now he had to figure out what he'd presumably wanted to say.

Behind the aliens the outer door swung open, spilling a wedge of bright sunshine into the room as another alien came in. Sunshine, and inspiration. "I need more than just food," Pheylan said. "My body needs sunlight every day or two to stay healthy."

For a moment the aliens looked at him. "Not understand," Svv-selic said again.

"Outside," Pheylan said, gesturing to the door, now closed again. "My skin creates chemicals I need to live." He tapped the back of his hand with a finger. "Skin. Chemicals. Vitamin D, melanin—many others."

"Not understand," Svv-selic said. "We speak later."

They turned around again. This time Pheylan knew where to look . . . and at this distance and angle, he saw it clearly.

They went to the door and exited in another brief flood of sunshine. "Sure you don't," Pheylan muttered under his breath, picking up his survival pack and taking it back to the bed. They understood, all right. That pidgin English was nothing but an act, probably designed to lull him into a false sense of security as to how much of what he said they could understand. But it wouldn't work. He'd seen the scars now, nestled there under the overhang at the base of those long skulls of theirs, and he knew what those scars meant.

Svv-selic and his friends were wired.

He sat down on the bed, pulling open the survival bag and dumping the contents onto the blanket beside him. Wired. Probably with wireless transceivers—there hadn't been any sign of a Copperhead-type jack implant, unless that part had been wired in out of sight beneath the jumpsuit material. But they were wired, all right . . . and in retrospect, given the technology, it was foolish to think they wouldn't use it. Everything they saw or heard—his words, his intonation, his expressions and body language—were probably going straight into a computer somewhere on base, a computer that was undoubtedly spitting back to them exactly what they should say. Obvious and inevitable, and the only question left was where they'd gotten the grammar and word base from. Perhaps in his fever he'd done a bit of babbling.

There wasn't much left in the survival bag that they'd decided he could have. He sorted the ration bars in one pile, the vitamin supplements in another, the juice tubes in a third. The medical pack was mostly full, though a check showed tiny indentations in each of the capsules where the aliens had taken a sample for analysis. The tool kit, extra flechette clip, rope, and spare clothing were gone. Pulling out the first of the under-bed drawers, he dumped in the ration bars and juice tubes. The vitamins and med pack went into the second drawer. Wadding up the now empty bag, he opened the third—

And stopped suddenly as the last piece fell into place. Commodore Dyami's stateroom, intact enough for the aliens to make a copy of it for Pheylan's cell. Including the under-bed drawers.

Where Dyami had kept his personal research computer.

Slowly, Pheylan dropped the bag into the drawer and pushed it shut. So that was where the aliens had gotten their word base. Dyami had been one of those secretive paranoiac types who hadn't wanted all his personal records going into his ship's computer system where it could theoretically be accessed by anyone willing to dig through all the security barriers. Keeping a private computer was technically a breach of regulations, but it was an open secret among the task force's senior officers, and Pheylan had never heard of anyone being unduly worried about it. The few concerns he'd heard had focused on what sorts of discomfiting secrets about them Dyami might be compiling in those private records.

He took another sip of scented water and lay back down on the bed. A word base was bad enough; but what else might have been in those files? A detailed map of the Commonwealth, maybe, complete with navigational data? Strength and organizational data on the Peacekeepers, including base and task-force locations?

Or could there even have been something about CIRCE?

Abruptly, Pheylan twisted around. There it was again: something he thought he'd seen, brushing past just at the edge of his vision. But again there was nothing there.

Or at least there wasn't anything there now.

Slowly, he scanned that part of the room, taking a good look at everything and everyone there. There was nothing that could account for the movement he'd seen: no physical movement, no trick of lighting, no reflection. It had to be something else.

Perhaps, like the open door, another test.

He turned again to face the wall. Fine; let them play their little games if they wanted to. Sooner or later he'd find a way to turn one back on them, and then he'd be out of here.

Resting a hand against the wall, he scratched idly with a fingernail, and tried to remember everything he'd ever learned about glass.

7
Edo was the last gasp of the once-proud and ambitious Japanese Hegemony; the last of fifteen colonies still politically united with the home country. Like most other Earth colonies, the others had broken off from their founding nation somewhere along the line, either grouping together with other colonies on the same planet or else joining the Commonwealth directly as independent states. NorCoord's unique political prominence had kept a handful of colonies aligned with it, but union with the Hegemony had had no comparable advantages, and only Edo still remained.

The Peacekeeper base on Edo had been a political compromise, one that critics at the time had roundly criticized. Sixty light-years from Earth, straddling the Lyra and Pegasus Sectors, it was considerably closer to the nonviolent Avuirli than it was to either of the more dangerous Pawolian or Yycroman world groups. As such, the base had long been considered the perfect example of military bureaucratic waste by Peacekeeper opponents. There was no reason, they maintained, to have such an extensive facility out on the fringes near such minor colony worlds as Massif, Bergen, Kalevala, and Dorcas.

For the moment, at least, such criticisms were likely to remain muted.

The base's public waiting room was impressive, too, one that you could be comfortable in for hours. And it was starting to look to Cavanagh as if they might have the chance to put that to the test.

"I'm sorry, Lord Cavanagh," the Marine at the inner door said for probably the tenth time. "Admiral Rudzinski is still in conference. I'm sure he'll contact me when he's ready to speak to you."

"I'm sure he will," Cavanagh said, struggling to contain his irritation. "Can you confirm for me that he has at least been informed I'm here?"

"I'm sure he's been told, sir."

"Can you confirm that?"

"I'm sure he's been told, sir."

"Yes," Cavanagh muttered. Turning his back on the Marine, he strode back to the seats where the other four were waiting.

"Anything?" Aric asked.

"They could replace him with a tape loop," Cavanagh said with a sigh as he sat down between his children. His remaining children. "Rudzinski's still in conference."

"I thought we had an appointment."

"We do. We're almost an hour into it now."

Aric snorted under his breath. "Sounds to me like he's hiding."

Cavanagh glanced at the Marine. "It's starting to look that way, isn't it?"

Beside Aric, Kolchin stirred in his seat. "Maybe we shouldn't wait for official clearance," he said.

Cavanagh looked at him. The young bodyguard was studying the Marine, a thoughtful expression on his face. "Whatever you have in mind, Kolchin, I don't think it would be a good idea."

"It would get us their attention," Kolchin pointed out.

"It would get us thrown off Edo," Cavanagh corrected. "And possibly get you a trip to the hospital."

Kolchin wrinkled his nose. "Hardly."

"Let me try something," Melinda said, pulling out her phone and punching up the directory. "Quinn, do you know the layout of this building?"

"I know some of it," he said.

"Good." She found the number she was looking for and punched it in. "Let's see if this works."

The screen cleared. From Cavanagh's angle the picture wasn't all that good, but it looked like a middle-aged man. "Hello, Dr. Haidar," Melinda said brightly. "This is Melinda Cavanagh. We were on Celadon together last week . . . right, the Billingsgate team. . . . Oh, it went fine. . . . No, actually, I'm right here in the building. My father's here to see someone, but he's in conference and we're stuck waiting. I was poking through the directory and found your name, and thought I'd call and say hello. . . . Why, yes, that would be terrific. . . . I think so; let me check."

She looked up. "We all have Class Three clearances, don't we?"

"Yes," Cavanagh told her, wondering what she was planning. Surely building security wouldn't be fooled by anything this transparent.

"Yes, we're all clear," she confirmed, turning back to the phone. "Great. We'll be waiting."

She closed down the phone. "He'll be here in a couple of minutes. We're going to get a tour of the medical facilities."

"That sounds wonderful," Cavanagh said, frowning at her. "We will, you realize, have an escort all the way there and back."

"We're not here to see Admiral Rudzinski," she reminded him. "We're here to find out about Pheylan."

She looked across at Quinn. "And every Peacekeeper medical lab I've ever seen has had at least one terminal with a Mindlink jack."

Cavanagh looked at Quinn, too. "I don't think that would be a good idea, Melinda."

"No, sir, she's right," Quinn said. His face was tight, but his voice was firm. "It's our best bet."

"Can you can handle it?"

Quinn gave a short nod. "No problem."

"All right. If you're sure." Cavanagh stood up. "Let's get ready."

He stepped toward the guard; and as he did so, the door behind the Marine slid open. Admiral Rudzinski stood there, flanked by two more Marines. "That won't be necessary, Lord Cavanagh," the admiral said quietly. "All of you, please: come with me."

The admiral led them down the maze of corridors, his two Marines following closely behind. Aric walked beside Kolchin, keeping a careful eye on the bodyguard's face. Kolchin had that coiled-spring look about him, and if he decided that Rudzinski was taking them to detention instead of an office, he was likely to object rather strenuously. Aric wanted to be ready to hit the floor if that happened.

They reached a door with Rudzinski's name and a number three on it. "You two wait here," the admiral instructed the Marines as he palmed it open. "The rest of you: inside, please."

It was a conference room, small but impressive even by the corporate standards Aric was used to. A holographic map of the Commonwealth and nonhuman worlds dominated one wall, with a corresponding tactical map on the wall opposite it. Filling most of the room was a stylish French curve–shaped table equipped with a central display spine and surrounded by a dozen comfortable-looking chairs.

Seated in one of those chairs, looking like a cross between a thundercloud and an extremely sour lemon, was Parlimin Jacy VanDiver.

He opened his mouth to speak; Aric decided to get in the first word. "Well, well," he commented lightly. "Old-home week on Edo, I see. At least now we know what the delay was."

"One more time, Admiral," VanDiver warned, clearly intent on ignoring Aric completely. "This is both ill-advised and unnecessary."

"Would you rather they find out another way?" Rudzinski countered.

"They have no right—"

"They have every right, Parlimin," Rudzinski cut him off. "They are Commander Cavanagh's family."

"None of whom have clearance for Class One information," VanDiver snapped. "Or any official standing in either the Peacekeepers or the NorCoord government."

"Are you suggesting that I'm a security risk?" the elder Cavanagh asked quietly.

VanDiver looked him straight in the eye. "I'm saying, *Lord* Cavanagh, that contrary to what you seem to believe, you're no longer the Parlimin from Grampians on Avon. You're a private citizen. You don't rate any special treatment."

"Thank you for reminding us of that." Deliberately, the elder Cavanagh turned back to Rudzinski. "You have information for me about my son, Admiral?"

"To be perfectly honest, Lord Cavanagh, we don't have anything solid enough to qualify as information," the other said, gesturing them to seats around the table as he sat down at the inner-curve chair. "What we have comes more properly under the heading of vague speculation."

He touched a key on the control board, and a field of slow-moving points of light appeared on the spine displays. "A section of the battle scene near Dorcas," Rudzinski identified it.

Aric glanced at his father's face. The pain was back, but buried so deeply that he doubted anyone else in the room except he and Melinda could see it. No surprise there: showing that kind of emotion in front of Jacy VanDiver would be the last thing he would want to do.

"It was taken a few hours afterward," Rudzinski continued. "Here"—a large circle appeared, filling most of the display— "is where the *Kinshasa* was during the battle. We know that both from the watchship data and from the fact that all the honeycomb pod debris retrieved from inside that sphere came from the *Kinshasa*." He paused. "And here"—a hazy and slightly distorted white cone appeared near one edge of the circle—"is a stream of oxygen molecules."

He paused. Aric glanced at the others, looking for some indication that any of them had the slightest clue as to what that was supposed to mean. If the blank expressions were anything to go on, they were as mystified as he was. "You said that as if it was important," he prompted.

"We're not sure whether it is or not," Rudzinski said. "What we do know is that it didn't occur during the battle itself. The conical shape's too well preserved for that, and the momentum-vector map too uniform."

"So where did it come from?" Aric asked.

Rudzinski glanced at VanDiver. "There's no way to know for certain," he said, the words coming out with obvious reluctance. "But it's not inconsistent with a deliberate, controlled leak from a honeycomb pod's oxygen tank."

For a long minute the room was silent. "You said you'd identified some of the pods from the *Kinshasa*," the elder Cavanagh said at last. "Did you find any pieces from Pheylan's?"

VanDiver slapped the table. "There you go," he said, glowering at Rudzinski. "I told you he'd jump to this conclusion, Admiral. I told you he would."

"We haven't identified any specific pieces, no," Rudzinski shook his head. "But bear in mind that that doesn't necessarily mean anything. Not with the kind of destruction we're dealing with here."

"But you clearly suspected something," the elder Cavanagh persisted. "Otherwise, why the investigation?"

Rudzinski made a face. "Blame it on the commander of the Dorcas Peacekeeper garrison," he said. "He took a fact-finding joyride out to the battle site and then filed a recommendation that an effort be made to confirm no prisoners had been taken. One of the analysis team picked up on the suggestion and took it seriously." He waved at the display. "That's what dropped out."

Quinn stirred. "Those momentum vectors you mentioned," he said. "What direction were they pointing?"

"Away from the apex of the cone," Rudzinski said. "And, possibly coincidentally, away from the watchship positions."

"As if someone was using his reserve oxygen supply to get his pod moving toward safety?"

"There is no evidence that anyone survived the battle," VanDiver snapped. "Not Pheylan Cavanagh; not anyone."

Quinn ignored him. "Admiral?"

"It's not inconsistent with that scenario," the other conceded. "It's also not inconsistent with a simple leak."

"He's dead, Cavanagh," VanDiver insisted. "They all

are. The Conquerors didn't stop shooting until every single beacon was silenced."

"Beacons can fail," the elder Cavanagh countered. "Or can be shut off." He looked at Rudzinski, a new fire in his eyes. "Or can be blocked."

"No," Rudzinski said, shaking his head. "We've already run that simulation. An operating beacon being pulled inside another ship would show a distinctive fade curve before dropping below detection threshold. There's no sign of anything like that in the watchship records."

"That doesn't prove anything."

"Neither does wishful thinking," VanDiver said, climbing to his feet. "All right, Admiral, you've done your duty. Now if you're quite ready, the rest of the Parliament observation group is waiting for us."

"Just a minute," Aric said as Rudzinski also stood up. "You haven't said what the Peacekeepers are going to do about finding Pheylan and getting him back."

Rudzinski's face seemed to sag a little. "I'm sorry," he said, looking at the elder Cavanagh. "There's nothing we can do. Without some kind of solid evidence that Commander Cavanagh is still alive, we can't risk sending out a search party."

"Why not?" Aric demanded. "He's out there somewhere—"

"You don't have any proof of that," VanDiver cut him off.

"And *you* don't have any—"

"Enough!" Rudzinski barked.

Aric broke off in midsentence. Rudzinski glared at him, then at VanDiver, and finally turned back to the elder Cavanagh. "In the first place," he said, his voice quiet again, "we wouldn't have any idea even where to start looking. Their exit vector was masked by the watchship static bomb, and without a baseline heat-dump profile for their hulls we can only make a guess as to how far they came. But that's not the crucial point. The crucial point is that if we go charging around out there playing blindman's buff, they're going to pick up on our tachyon wake-trails and follow the search parties straight back to the Commonwealth. And if there's anything certain about all this, it's that we're a long way from being ready to deal with a full-scale invasion."

So you're just going to abandon him. With an effort Aric kept his mouth shut. An insulting accusation like that wouldn't help solve anything; and besides, he knew it wasn't true. Rudzinski's primary responsibility was to defend the Commonwealth, and he couldn't put twenty-four worlds into unnecessary danger for a single man.

The elder Cavanagh put it into words first. "We understand, Admiral," he said, standing up and offering his hand. "I appreciate your time. And your honesty."

"I'm sorry I couldn't do more," Rudzinski said, gripping the proffered hand. He glanced at VanDiver— "And I presume I don't have to insult you by reminding you that everything we've said today comes under the Official Secrets Regulations."

"None of it will leave this room," the elder Cavanagh promised.

Rudzinski nodded. "The Marines outside will escort you to the exit. I wish I could do more."

"Thank you, Admiral," the other said softly. "I think you've done enough."

Across the room the door chimed softly. "Come in," Cavanagh called.

The panel slid open. "You wanted to see me, sir?" Quinn said.

"Yes." Cavanagh gestured to the chair beside his desk. "I need your professional opinion on something."

"Certainly," Quinn said, coming in and sitting down.

Cavanagh swiveled the desk plate around toward him. "Take a look. Tell me what you think."

He watched as Quinn's eyes flicked down the text. "Are you serious about this?"

"Very serious." Cavanagh cocked an eyebrow. "You don't seem surprised."

Quinn shrugged slightly. "Kolchin's call, not mine. Said you were practically broadcasting it on the drive back to the ship." He gestured to the plate. "But this isn't the way to do it."

"Why not?"

"Because freighters aren't designed for military activity," Quinn told him. "They're not warships, no matter how many missiles and particle cannon you cram into them. You send them out against our aliens out there, and they'll be cut to scrap."

"All right," Cavanagh said. "So how do we bring them up to fighting trim?"

Quinn shook his head. "We don't. It can't be done. Freighters don't maneuver well, they handle in gravity wells like helium-filled bricks, and their acceleration/mass ratio is a couple orders of magnitude lower than what you need for combat. And they're damn big targets."

Cavanagh grimaced. He'd sweated for nearly two hours trying to work up a halfway respectable task force from the ships and crews in the CavTronics merchant fleet. Two wasted hours, apparently. "Let me put it this way: I'm going to go look for Pheylan. What can you do to give me a fighting chance?"

Quinn sighed. "Look, sir, I know how you feel. But this doesn't make any sense. You haven't got the weaponry or the experience. And you don't know where he is."

"We've got the vector they came in on," Cavanagh said. "I'll start with that."

"He may not even be alive, sir," Quinn said quietly. "Odds are he isn't."

Cavanagh looked away from him, toward the wall with the inset pictures of his children and his late wife. "Then at least I'll know that for certain," he told Quinn. "Either way, I'm going."

He could feel the other's eyes on him. "We can't do it with freighters," Quinn said at last. "We need warships. Six attack fighters—Axehead- or Adamant-class, if we can get them. Plus crews. Plus a stardrive-equipped fueler to carry them."

"Really," Cavanagh said, slightly taken aback by the sudden shift in attitude. "Where do you propose we get them?"

"We steal them, of course," Quinn said.

Cavanagh felt his mouth drop open. "You're not serious."

Quinn returned his gaze without flinching. "As serious as you are about going."

For a half-dozen heartbeats Cavanagh just stared at him. The man meant it, all right . . . and the challenge was now squarely on Cavanagh's side of the table. Just how far *was* he willing to go to find his son?

The door chimed, jolting into his thoughts. "Come in," he said, reaching over and swiveling the plate back around to face him.

"Dad." Aric nodded in greeting as he and Melinda walked into the room. "We interrupting anything?"

"Not really," he assured them. "How are you two doing?"

"We're holding up." Aric glanced at Melinda. "We wanted to talk to you about Pheylan."

Cavanagh glanced at Quinn, got a fractional shake of the head in return. "What about him?"

Aric's face changed; not much, but enough. He looked at Quinn, back at his father. "We were wondering if there was anything we could do to help get him back," he said, strolling behind Quinn and around the side of Cavanagh's desk. "Some kind of pressure we could bring to bear on Rudzinski or the Parliament."

"We don't know if he's even still alive," Cavanagh said, watching his son's all-too-casual approach. He'd picked up on the mood, all right, and he was aiming for a look at the plate. "But that's a good idea," he added, reaching over and blanking the screen. "Why don't you and Melinda go work up a list of Parlimins who owe me favors."

"Sure," Aric said, measuring his father with his eyes. "You want to tell us first what's going on?"

"What do you mean?"

"Come on, Dad," Aric said. "This is no time for playing games. You and Quinn are planning something. What is it?"

Cavanagh looked at Melinda. She was watching him, too, her expression firm and alert. He'd never noticed before how much there was of Sara in her face when she looked like that. "All right," he told them. "I'm going after Pheylan."

"I see." Aric looked at his sister. "When?"

"Wait a minute," Melinda said. "Personnel before timetable, Aric. You're not talking about going yourself, are you, Dad?"

"Yes, I am," Cavanagh said. "And I don't want to hear any arguments about it."

"Too bad," she said. "Because you're going to get some. This is not some little joyride out to—"

"Melinda." Aric held up his hand. "Let's hear it from the top first, okay? Dad?"

"There isn't much yet to tell," Cavanagh said, waving them both to chairs. He should have known that he couldn't keep this from them for very long. Though to be honest, he hadn't really wanted to. "I was planning to take four of our armed freighters and go look for him, but Quinn tells me that won't work. He thinks we ought to borrow some Peacekeeper attack fighters instead."

"Does he, now," Aric said, giving Quinn a long, speculative look. "And how does he intend to perform this interesting feat of prestidigitation? Especially in the middle of war preparations?"

"Actually, the mobilization will work in our favor," Quinn said. "A lot of Peacekeeper ships and personnel are being rushed back and forth across the Commonwealth right now. A couple extra transfer orders slipped into the stack will hardly be noticed."

"How many transfer orders are we talking about?" Aric asked.

"Not many," he said. "We'd need to get hold of a deep-space fueler and half a wing of Axeheads." He hesitated. "And one Copperhead fighter."

Cavanagh looked at Aric, saw his own surprise mirrored in his son's face. "I appreciate the offer, Quinn," he told his security chief. "But this is my responsibility. Mine and my family's. I'm not inviting you along."

"You don't have a choice," Quinn said bluntly. "You're going to need someone with military experience in command of those fighters—that's not even open to question. Don't worry, there should still be a few Counterpunches lying around that I can get my hands on."

Cavanagh looked again at Aric, searching for something to say. Locating and getting hold of a Copperhead fighter hadn't been the part he was worried about, and both he and Quinn knew it. But finding a diplomatic way of putting it . . .

He was still searching when Melinda jumped into the gap. "I still want to know, Dad, when it was decided that you personally would be going on this trip."

"About two hours before you and Aric crashed the party," Cavanagh told her. "And it's not open to debate."

"Dad—"

"I said it's not open to debate, Melinda," Cavanagh repeated, putting some warning in his voice.

"Really," she said, not shriveling in the slightest under his glare. "I'd like to hear that from Quinn."

"Quinn has nothing to do with the decision."

"He most certainly does," she countered. "He's in charge of the expedition."

Cavanagh blinked at her. "Since when?"

"It's standard company policy, Dad," Aric put in. "You pick the right people for the job, then get out of their way. You told me that my first day."

Cavanagh shifted his glare to his son. He didn't shrivel, either. "Of all the things I've said to you over the years," he growled, "you had to remember that one. All right, Quinn, your turn. Let's hear your two cents' worth."

"Actually, sir, they're right," Quinn said. "You can't go."

Cavanagh tried the glare one last time, with the same results. "Why not?"

"To be perfectly honest, because you're too old," the other said. "The fighter pilots we get aren't going to go along with this unless they're convinced we're legitimate Peacekeeper officers. Fifty-seven-year-old men aren't generally in line-officer positions, and there's no reason why a senior officer would go on a search/rescue mission like this."

"We can find a reason."

"Not one that'll hold up long enough." Quinn looked

at Melinda. "Unfortunately, Dr. Cavanagh, that also leaves you out."

Melinda frowned. "Why?"

"Because there aren't a lot of female attack fighter pilots or tail officers," he said. "Chances are good that whoever we get will know most or all of them, at least by name."

"Why can't I be a special envoy from Peacekeeper Command?" Melinda asked. "Or from Parliament? A specialist in captives or something?"

"Because I'd then have to explain why I'm flying a fighter without a tail," Quinn said. "This is going to be fragile enough without pushing things more than we have to."

Aric stirred in his chair. "Process of elimination," he said. "I guess that leaves me."

For a moment no one spoke. "I guess it does," Quinn agreed at last. "When do you want to leave?"

Aric's lip twitched. "The sooner the better, I suppose. What do we do first?"

"Head to Earth. I have an old associate at Peacekeeper Command who might be willing to put me onto a mothballed Counterpunch and some Axeheads that aren't doing anything."

"Okay," Aric said. "What about the deep-space fuel ship?"

"I can get that," Cavanagh said. "I know of a couple of older ones that have been decommissioned and converted to civilian use. I presume you'll be jumping off from Dorcas?"

"Right," Quinn said. "We'll need some other supplies, too—I'll make up a list. You can probably address them to me, care of the Dorcas Peacekeeper garrison."

"Or he could address them to me there," Melinda suggested. "I could go ahead and get everything set up.

That way you'll be ready to go as soon as you get there with the fighters."

"That would save time," Quinn agreed, standing up. "All right, we'll do it that way. If you'll excuse me, I'll go get started on the supply list."

"Anything I can do to help?" Aric asked.

Quinn shook his head. "Just be ready to go when I am. I'll let you know."

He left. "Well," Melinda said into the sudden silence. "And to think all we came in to talk about was putting political pressure on Parliament."

Cavanagh nodded, studying his son and daughter and marveling once again at the wide range of personalities he and Sara had created together. Aric, quiet and thoughtful, master manipulator of words but about as nonphysical as it was possible to get. Pheylan, three years younger, forever struggling to escape Aric's prestigious scholastic reputation and spending as much time fighting with his brother as he did defending him from schoolyard bullies. Melinda, midway between them in both age and abilities, skilled in the exacting physical art of surgery but with a lot of Aric's ability to use words as weapons when she chose, often to her detriment.

Pheylan had left home to join the Peacekeepers. Melinda had gone away, too, to the less hazardous but no less nomadic career of surgical design consultant. Only Aric had opted for the safe and familiar life of his father's business.

And so, naturally, it was Aric whom he was sending out into the unknown.

Melinda stirred and got to her feet. "I think I'll go watch Quinn work up his list," she said. "Maybe I can get some orders placed before you leave. You'll say good-bye before you go, won't you?"

"Sure," Aric assured her. "See you later."

She smiled at her father and left. "So," Aric said, cocking an eyebrow. "I trust you're as impressed by the irony of all this as I am."

"You don't have to go, Aric," Cavanagh said. "We can still concoct some story as to why a fossil my age is out on a mission like this. Better yet, we could send Kolchin or Hill along."

Aric shook his head. "Like you said before, Dad, this is family business. Besides, we can't tell Hill or anyone else about this. VanDiver would have your head on a platter if we broke the Official Secrets Regulations."

"I'm willing to risk that."

"I'm not." Aric smiled tightly. "Besides, think of the look on Pheylan's face when he sees his stick-at-home brother coming out of the blue to rescue him." His smile faded. "More important, someone has to be there who can keep an eye on Quinn. And can order him to unplug from that fighter if things get awkward."

Cavanagh sighed. "Good luck on that one," he advised his son. "Quinn considers his security duties to extend to the family, not just the corporation. And he takes those responsibilities very seriously."

"Yes, well, even he ought to be willing to concede that his duties don't extend to damn-fool stunts like this," Aric said.

Cavanagh nodded, feeling his chest tightening. The enormity of what they were planning was beginning to sink in now . . . and with it were coming the doubts and fears. They weren't just talking about skirting some outdated regulation here, or of pushing the edge of accepted business practice. This bordered on treason. "Aric—"

"We don't have any other choice, Dad," the other said softly. "Not if we want to get Pheylan back. You know it; I know it; Quinn and Melinda know it. In fact, I'd bet money that Admiral Rudzinski knows it. It's our family. Our risk."

"Except that we're hardly the only ones at risk anymore," Cavanagh reminded him soberly. "There are those six Axeheads of Quinn's, for starters. That's twelve men right there. But the real danger is the one Rudzinski brought up back in the meeting. If we lead the aliens back to the Commonwealth, we could be responsible for murdering millions of people."

"No," Aric said emphatically. "You can't take the blame for that one. We've got thousands of ships crisscrossing the Commonwealth every day, every one of them laying out a tachyon wake-trail. If the aliens really want to find us, they aren't going to need a fueler and half a dozen fighters to do it. As long as we're careful and spread a few static bombs judiciously around, that shouldn't be a real threat."

"I hope you're right," Cavanagh said.

"I hope so, too." Aric took a deep breath, exhaled it noisily. "Anyway. I'm glad we had this little talk, Dad. Better go to my cabin, I guess, and get ready to go."

"You'll say good-bye before you and Quinn leave, won't you?"

"Melinda would kill me if I didn't," Aric said wryly. "Don't worry, I will."

He stepped to the door . . . and paused. "By the way," he said over his shoulder, his voice sounding odd. "Did you notice what VanDiver called them today?"

"Yes," Cavanagh said. "He called them the Conquerors."

Aric nodded. "Sounds like someone's been taking that Mrach legend seriously."

"Legends often have a basis in fact."

"Yes. Might be worth sending someone out to Mrach territory to look into that. Well . . . see you later."

The door opened and closed behind him. "Yes, indeed," Cavanagh murmured to the empty room. "It might be worthwhile, at that."

For a moment he sat there, listening to the background hum of his ship. Then, stirring, he turned on his plate again. He had a fueler to locate and arrange purchase for. After that he would have Quinn's list of supplies to order.

And after that perhaps he would take that little trip to Mra that Aric had suggested. To hear firsthand this Mrach legend of the Conquerors.

8 There was a new assortment of aromas drifting through his cell when Pheylan awoke; and he opened his eyes to discover that breakfast had been served.

It consisted of six flattened hemispheres sitting on a contoured tray just inside the dog flap they'd stuffed his survival pack through the previous day. Each of the lumps was a slightly different shade of tan paste, with chunks of brightly colored food items of different sorts embedded in them. The overall effect was that of holiday cheese balls assembled by color-blind children, and Pheylan wasn't at all sure it was something he really wanted to face first thing in the morning. But his ration-bar stock was being steadily depleted, and he wanted to save at least a couple of days' worth for whatever escape attempt he wound up making. And after all, the Peacekeeper recruiter *had* promised him new and exotic experiences.

Figuring out the utensil they'd supplied with the meal was the first challenge. The main part was shaped basically like a half-melted spoon, but it had a spring-loaded textured stick attached at the back end that worked against the edge of the spoon bowl like something midway between tongs and chopsticks. Probably a breeze to use with that extra opposing thumb of theirs, Pheylan decided, but his human hands couldn't seem to get the hang of it. The whole thing was made of a soft, rubbery material, and eventually he just gave up on the chopstick attachment and bent it back out of his way.

The aliens' first attempt at a home-cooked human meal was, not surprisingly, a decidedly mixed achievement. Only one of the six food lumps tasted genuinely good, the rest ranging from so-so to nearly tasteless to a near-perfect reenactment of the time he'd misread the heat setting on the oven and turned his mother's roast into charcoal. He ate all of them, though, except the last, starting with the best-tasting and working his way down the scale. It would be interesting to see if his observers took note of the order and adjusted the menu accordingly for his next meal. He rather thought they would.

His three interrogators arrived near the end of the meal, and this time he spotted the unobtrusive door they came in by. It was sandwiched between two consoles, one of which blocked any view of what lay beyond. A prep room, maybe, with no guarantee of another exit from it. Still, something to keep in mind.

"Greeting, Cavv-ana," Svv-selic said as Pheylan laid the tray aside. "You well?"

"Reasonably well," Pheylan said, dropping the tong-spoon on the tray and taking a last sip of water. Svv-selic's proficiency with English seemed to be improving, though perhaps not as quickly as Pheylan would have expected of someone equipped with the aliens' version of Mindlink connections. Either they were having trouble deciphering the data in Commodore Dyami's computer, or else their translators weren't as sophisticated as the equivalent Peacekeeper programs. He hoped it was the latter; it would be nice if humanity was ahead of them in at least one area. "And you?"

"We well." Svv-selic motioned, and the shortest of the three—Thrr-gilag, if Pheylan remembered right—stepped forward with what looked like a folded jumpsuit under his arm. He opened the dog flap and stuffed it into the cell. Pheylan watched the operation closely, counting off the seconds and trying to gauge whether or not he would have time to leap forward and grab a wrist before the alien could withdraw it. It would be barely possible, he decided, though how useful it would be he wasn't sure.

"You wear this," Svv-selic said as Thrr-gilag closed the dog flap again.

Pheylan stepped forward and picked it up. It was a jumpsuit, all right, made of the same material as the one he was wearing but with a stiffened and slightly thickened ring around the upper arms, forearms, midthighs, and ankles. There were also rings around the chest and waist, their placements corresponding to that of the arm rings. Scattered across the suit, on the chest, back, and arms, were a number of small glassy disks embedded in the material. "What's this?" he asked.

"Wear," Svv-selic said. "We go outside."

Pheylan frowned at him. "Outside?" he repeated. "As in, outside this room?"

The other seemed to consider, or maybe was waiting for the translation to catch up. "You need outside. We go."

"Yes, sir," Pheylan muttered, stripping off his clothes and climbing into the new jumpsuit. The thicker rings weren't particularly heavy and didn't seem to constrict his movements any. "All right," he said, patting the fastening strip closed. "I'm ready."

"You not leave we," Svv-selic warned as Thrr-gilag stepped to the door and opened it. "Do, punish."

"I understand," Pheylan agreed. That must be what the rings were for: some mechanism for keeping him in line. Under the circumstances, certainly a reasonable precaution.

Unfortunately, he couldn't just leave it at that. At some point along the way he was going to have to find out what exactly the mechanism consisted of. He hoped it wouldn't hurt too much.

The third interrogator, Nzz-oonaz, stayed well back as Svv-selic and Thrr-gilag moved into step on either side of him. That made Nzz-oonaz the backup, which implied that he was the one with the obedience-suit trigger. The one to be watching, then, when Pheylan made his break.

They moved across the room to the door. Svv-selic did something to one of the consoles flanking it, and the door swung open; and for the first time since his arrival nearly a week ago Pheylan stepped outside.

The weather was much as it had been the day he landed: blue skies and white clouds, a cool but not uncomfortable temperature, light breezes. At the far end of the landing area sat a small ship about the size of a Peacekeeper courier, with a handful of the aliens working busily around it. The second complex he'd seen under construction at that end of the landing area was coming along nicely, and two more of the low weapons-style domes had joined the first.

And in the center of the triangle formed by the three domes was something else that hadn't been there before. A small pyramid shape sparkled in the sunlight, perhaps three meters high, brilliant white but with dozens of dark spots scattered irregularly across the top two meters of its surface.

"Good?"

Pheylan looked at Svv-selic, trying to decipher the other's economical use of the language. Then he got it: he'd told them humans needed sunlight to survive. "It's helping," he nodded, opening the neck of his jumpsuit a few centimeters and turning his face to the sun. "Though it's going to take a while, dressed like this. Not much exposed skin area. It would go a lot faster if I could take off this suit."

Svv-selic's tongue flicked out. "You not do."

"Okay." Pheylan shrugged. "I was just asking." He took a deep breath, stretching his arms out to the side. "Do you suppose I could run a little? Humans need exercise, too."

The tongue flicked out again. "You not leave we."

"Can we at least walk, then?" Pheylan persisted, pointing over to the forest about sixty degrees to the left of the domes and pyramid. "I'd like to take a look at those trees."

There was the usual pause as the translation came through, and another moment as Svv-selic and Thrr-gilag consulted among themselves. "We go," Svv-selic said at last. "You not leave we."

They started off toward the trees, crunching through the loose red dirt surrounding the complex and raising small clouds of dust with each step. Thrr-gilag and Svv-selic stayed close beside him, with Nzz-oonaz still hanging back. "You—Thrr-gilag," Pheylan said.

The shorter alien looked up at him. "Speak."

"How come you never talk to me?"

Thrr-gilag's corkscrew tail picked up its pace a little. "Not understand."

"You never talk to me," Pheylan repeated, throwing a glance toward the domes and pyramid and shifting his path a couple of degrees in that direction. "Neither does Nzz-oonaz, for that matter. It's always Svv-selic who does the talking. Don't you two want to be here?"

Thrr-gilag looked past him to Svv-selic. "Too'rr rights," he said.

"Who or what is Too'rr?" Pheylan asked.

"Svv-selic Too'rr," Thrr-gilag said.

Svv-selic Too'rr? Pheylan ran the two words around his mind a couple of times. Was Too'rr a family name? A title? A military rank? A caste designation? "I don't understand," he said, easing a couple more degrees toward the domes and pyramid. "Is Svv-selic an expert at this type of alien interrogation?"

A pause. "Not understand."

"Is he expert at talking to non—what do you call yourselves, anyway?"

Another pause, and another short conversation between the two aliens. "We Zhirrzh," Svv-selic said at last.

Pheylan tried it out. It wasn't as hard to pronounce as their names, actually, though the word tended to buzz unpleasantly against his tongue. "So is Svv-selic the resident expert at talking to non-Zhirrzh?" he asked again.

Abruptly, Svv-selic's hand snaked over to grip Pheylan's upper arm. "Not go," he said.

"What?" Pheylan frowned as he stopped.

"Not go," Svv-selic repeated. His tongue jabbed out to point at the domes and pyramid Pheylan had been easing them toward.

"What do you mean, not go?" Pheylan asked. So his gut feeling had been right: the domes and pyramid were something important. "I just want to look at the trees."

"We go," Svv-selic said, pointing with his tongue at a group of trees ninety degrees away from the domes.

"I want to see *those* trees," Pheylan insisted, pointing again near the domes. Sneakiness hadn't worked; time to try bluster. If it didn't work, it would at least give him the chance to test out his obedience suit's capabilities. He hoped that they hadn't overestimated human physique when they'd designed the thing. "I'm going, and you can come with me or not. Your choice."

He started off toward the trees, watching Nzz-oonaz out of the corner of his eye. The Zhirrzh had raised one hand toward him, and he could see a small black device nestled in the curled fingers. The obedience trigger, or else a weapon. "Not go," Svv-selic said.

"Don't worry, I'm not running away," Pheylan called over his shoulder. "Where would I go? I just want a closer look at those trees."

"Not go," Svv-selic repeated, more insistently this time.

Pheylan ignored him. Nzz-oonaz was still pointing his black gadget at him, but so far nothing seemed to have happened. Setting his teeth together, Pheylan took another step, wondering whether it would be an injection or an electric shock and wishing irritably that whichever it was they would get on with it. He took another step—

"Nzz-oonaz: kasar!" Svv-selic called.

It was indeed painful, but not in any way Pheylan had anticipated. From somewhere over his shoulder came a faint hum; and suddenly his legs jerked together and his arms were yanked to his sides and he toppled forward to slam face first into the ground.

For a long minute he lay there, feeling the feathery stalks of the local grass-equivalent prodding against his cheek and fighting to get some air back into his stunned lungs. So that was what they'd come up with. No risky drugs, no potentially dangerous electrodes, just a few strategically placed electromagnets designed to completely immobilize him. Simple, elegant, and very safe, provided he didn't break his neck when he fell. Carefully, trying not to let the effort show, he tested the magnets' strength. He might as well have saved himself the effort.

The humming behind him stopped, and he was once again free to move. Laboriously, he got his feet under him and stood up again. "You not go," Svv-selic said.

"I get the message," Pheylan agreed, rubbing his cheek and jaw where they'd hit the ground. "I wasn't going to do anything, you know. I just wanted to look."

"Why go?" Svv-selic asked.

"Because I was curious," Pheylan told him. "We humans are curious people. It's probably our most distinguishing characteristic."

Svv-selic jabbed out his tongue toward the domes. "Curious not good," he said emphatically.

Pheylan looked. A triangular-shaped door had opened in each of the three domes, and a Zhirrzh was now standing just outside each opening. All of them held long gray sticks with thin rectangular muzzle openings and lots of small but sharp-looking edges arranged around the business end.

And all three of the sticks were pointed at Pheylan.

"You not go," Svv-selic said again.

"You're getting repetitious," Pheylan grumbled. There seemed to be a strange shimmering deep inside the muzzles, like some kind of eerie pilot light. Maybe it was just his imagination. "But you make your point. All right. We'll go look at the trees over there instead."

Pheylan had hoped for a chance to examine his new obedience suit more closely, but the Zhirrzh weren't naive enough to leave him alone with it any longer than they had to. They escorted him back to his cell after the brief exercise period and Svv-selic ordered him to strip the thing off. Pheylan did so, they opened the dog flap for him to put it outside, and then they and it disappeared back through the back door.

Pheylan put his old jumpsuit back on, trying to make sense of what he'd just seen. It was clear now that the three domes out there were guardhouses, not the weapons clusters he'd first thought. Their arrangement, furthermore, made it equally clear that what they were guarding was the white pyramid.

The question was, why?

It was too small to be a house, at least for anyone the size of a Zhirrzh. Could it be a tomb? But again, the proportions were wrong for a Zhirrzh, and there was no reason why a tomb should be guarded that way in the first place. A monument? Again, he couldn't think of any reason why a monument would need a three-man guard on it.

Except that they were aliens. There were no guarantees that they would think or behave anything at all like humans. No guarantees that Pheylan could even hope to understand their reasons and motivations.

He shook the thought away. No. They were vicious, cold-blooded killers; but they'd brought him here, given him food and clothing, and so far seemed to be doing all they could to keep him alive. Whatever alien quirks their psychology and culture might have, there was enough overlap here for him to figure out what was going on.

Something flickered at the edge of his vision. Pheylan turned, but as always he was too slow to see anything. Outside the glass wall of the cell one of the Zhirrzh techs, attracted by his movement, looked over at him. Pheylan looked back, and the alien turned back to his work.

So what was the pyramid? If not a monument, could it be something technical? A transceiver, maybe, for that instantaneous communications system of theirs?

Or something even more esoteric?—a terminal, say, for some kind of broadcast power?

But, then, why wasn't it taller? Or inside a building or protective shell where it would be out of the elements? The Commonwealth's experiments with broadcast power, he knew, had been notoriously finicky with regard to atmospheric factors. Unless the pyramid shape *was* its protective shell.

Pheylan shook his head. On the face of it, he had to admit, this was a pretty ridiculous waste of mental energy. The pyramid could be any of a thousand different things, from a planetary communications beacon to a traffic-control signal for the landing area. It could be the Zhirrzh equivalent of a torus music system, a wind-powered computer, a piece of government-mandated artwork—

Or a weapon.

Pheylan looked out at the Zhirrzh working at their consoles, his mouth suddenly dry. An unknown, guarded device in the middle of a Zhirrzh base. A base with no obvious ground-to-space or ground-to-air weapons clusters.

He went over to his bed and lay down on his side, folding his arms across his chest. There had been innumerable late-night bull sessions back at the Peacekeeper academy centering on the possible science and technology of the mysterious CIRCE weapon. One of the more intriguing ideas Pheylan had heard had been that it was a field-effect gadget of some sort, requiring two to five electromagnetic poles and an equal number of resonant-locked tachyon generators. The resultant radiation cascade was theorized to occur at certain specific intersection points between the field contours, supposedly unaffected by any matter elsewhere in the area.

Such as the fighter squadrons at Celadon. Or the atmosphere of a planet.

Did the Zhirrzh have a version of CIRCE? Was that white pyramid one of its poles?

All right, Cavanagh, settle down. First question to ask was whether this place was a forward military base or a colony or a major Zhirrzh world. Presumably they wouldn't bother setting up a CIRCE on just any old world they happened to land on. Second question was whether the pyramid out there was unique or whether it had lots of brothers nearby. Third question was whether the pyramid was fixed in place or had mechanisms for transport or aiming.

Good questions, all of them. Problem was, he couldn't think of any way to get any answers.

Outside the glass wall two of the Zhirrzh had gotten together and were consulting on something. Pheylan watched them, wishing that Aric were here. He, Pheylan, had always been the physical one of the family; Aric, in contrast, had been much better at manipulating words. More than once Pheylan had watched in secret awe as Aric had finessed information out of their father that he'd flat-out said he wasn't going to tell them.

Pheylan had admired that ability. Admired and envied it both, though he'd been careful to hide that from his brother. In their youth Aric would simply have taken such an admission and found a place for it in his arsenal of verbal abuse, a sport he already got far too much pleasure out of. And after they'd both become adults, the subject had somehow never come up.

Pheylan wished now that he'd said something. Now that it was very likely too late.

He swore under his breath. Thoughts like that weren't going to do him any good here. So he wasn't a wizard with words? Fine. He'd get out of here without them. He had a brain, eyes, and muscles, and it was time he started using them.

And the first step was to learn every square centimeter of this place. Every square centimeter, and every move his captors out there made.

His arms still folded across his chest, Pheylan got started on a set of what he hoped were indiscernible isometric exercises, and began to memorize the room.

9 **T**he narrow Granparra street was about as crowded and noisy a place as Aric had ever seen before in his life. Hundreds of pedestrians in rough, colorful fabrics were crammed into the area, pushing and jostling their way along in both directions and in and out of side streets. The flow eddied back and forth, with parts of it sometimes coming briefly to a complete halt as someone paused to examine the wares displayed in the window-front shops or stopped to greet a friend or neighbor. The cacophony of shouts and shouted conversations assaulting Aric's eardrums included at least three different languages; the odors coming from stoves and shops were varied and exotic and made him want to sneeze.

"How much farther?" he called to Quinn ahead of him.

"I don't know," the other called back over his shoulder. A few heads turned at the sound of English words, and Aric noted with some uneasiness that not all of the expressions on those faces were friendly. "The numbering system here isn't always as clear as it could be."

There was a blood-chilling shriek from above him. Reflexively, Aric ducked, glancing up just as a troop of monkey-sized grooma scampered past on the living vine lattice that covered the entire city a few meters above their heads.

Covered the city, and most of the rest of the island. "What do you think of the mesh?" Aric asked, moving up close behind Quinn where he wouldn't have to shout. "Sentient, or not?"

"Not," Quinn said firmly. "The Parra's a plant. Plants aren't sentient. Period."

"I'm not so sure," Aric said, looking up at the vine mesh uneasily. Had anyone ever established whether or not the thing had auditory senses? He couldn't remember. "It does seem able to sense what goes on around it."

"So do sunflowers, if you want to get technical," Quinn said. "There are a lot of other plants that react on a chemical level if you poke or cut them. No one claims those are sentient."

"Except that the same reaction doesn't occur when the vine is cut naturally by lightning strikes," Aric pointed out. "The chemicals in the outer skin don't change, and the grooma don't go nuts. It's only when someone tries cutting the vine back that it counterattacks that way."

"Could be a chemical reaction to the metal in the cutting tools," Quinn said. "Or a reaction by the grooma themselves to the noise and commotion. The point is that no one's ever come up with even a candidate for a nervous system. Let alone enough of one for sentience."

Overhead, another chattering troop of grooma passed by, their claws digging small air and sunlight punctures through the tough outer surface of the vine as they traveled. The Parra seemed to need those punctures, just as it also needed the mineral-rich body oils the grooma paws left behind. In return, the grooma ate

the large red buds that the Parra seemed to grow specifically for their benefit.

For their benefit alone. Any other herbivore that
started eating sections of the vine would quickly be met
by crazed troops of grooma that would usually drive off
the intruder in short order. Whether or not it was
chemical changes in the red buds that drove the frenzy
was still being hotly debated in high academic circles,
as was the whole question of Parra sentience.

For the people who lived here, of course, the subject
was far from academic.

"Here's our street," Quinn said, breaking into Aric's
musings. "Bokamba's place should be at the end of it."

"I'm right behind you," Aric assured him. Following
Quinn, he eased his way out of the traffic flow and into
the narrow street.

And nearly bumped into Quinn as the other came to
an abrupt halt five steps later. "What—?"

He strangled off the question. Ten meters ahead four
tough-looking young men were drifting from the sides
of the street to positions blocking their path. Four men
with expressions set in black stone. "Uh-oh," Aric murmured.

"Fair assessment," Quinn murmured back. "Let's
wander back to the main street and try it from the
other direction."

Aric glanced over his shoulder. Just inside their side
street three more men had appeared, cut in the same
mold as the four ahead of them. "Too late," he told
Quinn. "I think it might be time to call for help."

"Going for your phone wouldn't be a good idea right
now," Quinn said. "The police couldn't get here in time.
If they came at all."

Aric swallowed. Quinn had warned him before they
landed that the people of Granparra had no love for
NorCoord or NorCoord citizens. It was starting to look

as if he'd understated the case a bit. "So what do we do?"

Quinn shrugged fractionally. "We see what they want."

He started walking toward the four men now standing in a line across the street in front of them. "Hello," he nodded. "Nice day."

The two men in the middle glanced at each other, but aside from that there was no reaction. Quinn kept going, aiming for the gap in the middle; the four men responded by pulling closer together to block it. Quinn walked to within a meter of the group and stopped. "I wonder if my friend and I might pass," he said. "We have an appointment with a gentleman farther down the street."

"NorCoord," one of the men said, his English thickly accented. "That is right, is it not? You are NorCoord."

"Why do you ask?" Quinn countered.

One of the men spat on the ground. "You are NorCoord. Don't deny it."

"I'm not denying it," Quinn said. "I just want to know why you care."

Another of the men growled something in a fluid-sounding language. Aric eased a little to the side, not wanting to get too far away from Quinn but also not wanting to get in his way if this thing exploded. He glanced back at the three men still blocking their escape, hoping fervently that the Peacekeepers had found time to teach their elite Copperhead pilots something in the way of hand-to-hand fighting.

The four men stepped forward, hands bunched into fists. Quinn stood his guard, swiveling slightly on one foot to turn his right side toward the others. He lifted his hands into a loose ready position Aric had seen Kolchin use on the sparring mat—

"Savva!" a new voice barked.

Aric shifted his attention to the street behind the youths. A middle-aged man was standing there, a few meters back, his arms folded across his chest. "What do you do here?" he demanded.

One of the youths growled something over his shoulder. The middle-aged man growled something back, punctuating the comment with a jabbing finger. For a minute or two the debate went back and forth, with both sides sounding angrier with each exchange. But from the body language Aric could tell that the older man was winning; and even before the youth spat one final expletive and moved reluctantly out of the way, his heartbeat had returned more or less to normal. Together he and Quinn passed between the scowling faces and stepped up to the middle-aged man. "So," the man said, eying Quinn with an expression that seemed to be a mixture of curiosity, hospitality, and distaste. "You came. I wasn't really sure you would."

"My word that much in question these days?" Quinn asked.

The older man smiled wryly, and as he did so, the distaste seemed to fade away. "Perhaps it's merely Anders's opinion of your word that is in question. My apologies." His eyes flicked to Aric. "And this, I take it, is the other gentleman Anders spoke of?"

"Yes," Quinn nodded. "This is Aric Cavanagh, son of my employer. Mr. Cavanagh, I'd like you to meet Reserve Wing Commander Iniko Bokamba. My former commander in the Copperheads."

"So what do you think of Granparra's famous hospitality to strangers?" Bokamba asked as he poured a little honey into the steaming liquid in Aric's mug. "A bit disappointing, perhaps?"

Aric glanced at Quinn, but the other was staring

meditatively into his own mug. "I've occasionally seen warmer welcomes," he conceded. "I get the impression it was more than just our nonresidency status they were objecting to."

For a brief moment Bokamba's eyes bored into his. "You're NorCoord," he said, turning away and setting the honey vase down on the side table. "The Granparri have a long and deep resentment against the NorCoord nations."

"NorCoord is just one member of the Commonwealth," Aric said. "The Granparri have an equal voice."

Bokamba smiled tightly. "And did the Granparri put a weapons platform above Earth and the NorCoord nations, as well?"

Aric frowned. "The Myrmidon Platform wasn't put there as a threat. It was put there to protect you."

"Was it?" Bokamba demanded. "Or was its purpose merely to exact vengeance when Granparra was destroyed?"

Quinn stirred in his seat. "We didn't come here to talk politics, Iniko."

"He needs to hear this, Adam," Bokamba insisted. "He is a son of privilege, with beliefs that have been created and nurtured by other sons of privilege."

"I'm not a son of privilege," Aric said. "My father wasn't given the title of lord until he left Parliament six years ago."

"I do not refer to titles or ranks," Bokamba said. "I refer to your citizenship in the Northern Coordinate Union. *That* is where your privileges arise from."

"The NorCoord people have worked hard for what we've achieved, Commander Bokamba," Aric said. "And those achievements have benefited all of the Commonwealth."

"Kindly do not lecture me on the obvious," Bokamba said coldly. "Despite the technological limitations which the Parra imposes on us, we are not ignorant savages. Certainly the people of the NorCoord nations have worked hard, and certainly they have accomplished great things. But their time has passed."

"I don't know how you can say that," Aric said. "Why shouldn't NorCoord have as much right to survive as, say, Centauri?"

"I do not speak of survival," Bokamba countered. "I speak rather of the unnatural extension of power. All empires have a fixed life span, Mr. Cavanagh, a time after which their part in history is over. The empire of Rome rose and fell; so too did the domination of the Mongolians, the British, the Soviets, and the Americans. The Japanese Hegemony and Pan-Arab Caliphate have both come and gone. Only the empire of NorCoord remains. And it should not."

"Except that it's not an empire," Aric insisted. "NorCoord has no more power than any other Commonwealth member."

Bokamba shook his head. "You see it from the inside, Mr. Cavanagh. No empire looks oppressive to those in power. On paper, perhaps, all Commonwealth states are equal. But in reality it is NorCoord who dominates all that is said and done. It is the NorCoord military who commands the Peacekeepers; it is the NorCoord Parliament who makes laws that all will eventually live by; it is the administration of the NorCoord chancellor which dictates how commerce and business will be done across the Commonwealth and even in the nonhuman worlds." He waved a hand, encompassing the room with the gesture. "You have seen how the Granparri live. Tell me why we are here."

Aric took a sip from his mug, trying to remember what he'd learned about minor-world Commonwealth history back in college. Granparra had been claimed by Mexico some fifty years ago after a few other nations had taken a look and decided not to bother with it. The Mexicans had planted a colony here on Puerto Simone Island, the one place on the planet where Parra vine domination had choked out most of the rest of the planet's lethal vegetation, a colony that had then struggled on for a few years before they finally gave up on it. The place had remained essentially abandoned for the next twenty years until the current population had arrived under a Commonwealth incentive program to provide some of the perpetually dispossessed peoples of Earth with land of their own. "Because you wanted a world of your own," he said. "And because you weren't willing to take anyone else's word that Granparra couldn't be conquered."

Bokamba smiled grimly. "Yes, that is the reason why many of us came. But that is not the reason why we were sent here."

"I don't understand."

"What happened twenty-five years ago?" Bokamba asked. "Out there, barely thirty light-years away?"

Aric grimaced. He could see where Bokamba was going with this now. "We ran into the Yycromae."

"Exactly," Bokamba nodded. "And NorCoord saw in them the greatest threat to humanity since the Pawoles. And so"—he waved his hand again—"they brought us here. To provide an excuse to station a Peacekeeper force over our world." A muscle in his cheek twitched. "And to provide a target the Yycromae couldn't ignore."

Aric looked at Quinn. The other shrugged. Apparently, he'd been over this territory before with Bokamba. "I guess it's a good thing the Yycromae *were* able to ignore it," he said. "I suggest that you might be reading a little more malice into the situation than really existed."

"Am I?" Bokamba retorted. "Is it merely coincidence

that the recolonization of Granparra began at the height of the Commonwealth's tension with the Yycroman Hierarch? Is it coincidence that the Myrmidon Platform was transported here from Bergen, which was itself clamoring for more protection from possible Yycroman strikes? And is it coincidence that not a single NorCoord citizen was given authorization to travel to Granparra until after the Pacification had ended and the interdiction zones established?"

"There were a lot of NorCoord citizens who were serving on the Myrmidon," Quinn reminded him quietly. "As well as taking part in the Pacification."

"The NorCoord people fancy themselves as the wolves," Bokamba snorted. "They have no interest in playing the role of bait."

"Very soon now they're likely to be both," Aric said.

Bokamba looked back at him, some of the fire fading from his face. "Yes," he murmured. "The Conquerors. For once, it appears that there will be enough death to go around for everyone."

He muttered something under his breath and drank from his mug, and for a minute his eyes were distant with memory. Then, taking a deep breath, he returned to the present. "Anders's message said you needed my help, Adam. What is it you want?"

Aric could see Quinn brace himself. "Anders said you still had one of our old Counterpunch fighters in working condition. I'd like to borrow it."

"Would you, now. And who would be flying it?"

A muscle in Quinn's cheek twitched. "I will."

Bokamba's eyebrows lifted. "Really. Well, that alone was worth chasing Savva and his bullies away to hear." He looked at Aric. "And what exactly is this private mission that has enticed Adam Quinn back into the cockpit?"

Aric took a deep breath. He'd worked out a whole

speech on the trip here from Earth, using every trick of language and every persuasive technique he knew. Looking into Bokamba's face, he realized all of that had been a waste of time. "My brother was captain of the *Kinshasa*," he said. "We think he might have been captured by the Conquerors. We want to go find him and get him back."

Bokamba looked at Quinn, back at Aric. "Have you any proof he was taken captive?"

"We have indications," Aric said. "Nothing solid enough for the Peacekeepers to move on."

Bokamba looked down into his cup. "Going to do it alone?"

"I was hoping to borrow a half squadron of Axeheads," Quinn said. "Mr. Cavanagh's father is arranging for a long-range fueler for us."

"How do you intend to borrow these Axeheads?"

"Fake myself some orders," Quinn told him evenly. "I was hoping you could get me the unit operation numbers for a fighter wing somewhere, preferably some unit that's so far been left out of the mobilization. If I can get a look at one of their current orders, I should be able to construct a more or less legitimate orders code."

Bokamba stood up and went over to the honey vase, pouring another dribble of honey into his cup. "I could get you the unit numbers," he said as he returned to his seat. "But it would gain you nothing. Even in a crisis situation they run a check over all incoming orders. You're not active—you're not even reserve. You wouldn't get past the first level."

Quinn looked at Aric. "Then we'll go out alone. Assuming you'll lend me your fighter."

Bokamba gazed into his cup again, lips pursed tightly together. Aric listened to the muffled sounds from the city outside, trying without much success to read the older man's face. Even to be sitting here discussing this could mean trouble for Bokamba down the line, and the man surely knew that. "I'll make a deal with you, Adam," he said at last. "You can take my Counterpunch . . . provided the half squadron of fighters you take with you are also Copperheads."

Aric threw Quinn a startled look, got an equally surprised one in return. "We appreciate the offer, Commander—" he began.

"Adam?" Bokamba asked, his eyes on Quinn.

"As Mr. Cavanagh said, we appreciate the offer," Quinn said slowly. "But we can't accept it."

"You don't have a choice," Bokamba told him. "You haven't a hope in hell of getting orders like that through on your own. I do. But I'm Copperhead reserve, and if I try requisitioning anything but Copperheads I'll light red flares from here to Earth and back again. So it's Copperheads or nothing."

"I can't do it," Quinn said, shaking his head. "It would put your head in the chopper, too. That wasn't why we came here."

Bokamba's face twisted in a lopsided smile. "My head's already well inside the chopper. If you walk out of here and I don't report this—and I won't—I'll be in as much trouble as you when you get caught. On the other hand, if you succeed and find Commander Cavanagh, they won't be able to touch any of us. Heroes, you know. It's therefore to all our benefits for you to go out as well equipped as possible."

Quinn studied him. "And there's nothing more to this?"

Bokamba's smile faded. "Of course there's more," he said quietly. "We're facing war here, Adam—understand that. Not some small police action like the Yycroman Pacification or troubles with the Bhurtala or Djadar. This is full-scale war, against a powerful and vicious enemy. You were one of the best Copperhead pilots who ever flew. Possibly *the* best. Against an enemy like the Conquerors, we need to have the best."

Quinn looked away. "You don't understand why I left."

"I think I do," Bokamba disagreed. "And despite what your resignation did to the unit, I don't really blame you for leaving. But those problems have been corrected. I think that if you get the chance to watch the new generation of Copperheads in action, perhaps we can entice you permanently back into the cockpit."

There was another long silence. "I can't promise anything," Quinn said at last.

"I wouldn't want you to," Bokamba assured him. "All I'm asking is for you to give us another chance."

Quinn looked at Aric. "Trying to borrow Copperheads instead of regular fighters will get us in worse trouble if we're caught," he pointed out.

"I'm willing to risk it," Aric said, silently releasing the breath he'd been holding. Personally, getting into official trouble was the last thing he was worried about in all this. The chance to have some of the Commonwealth's premier fighter pilots along was an opportunity he was ready and willing to grab with both hands.

"All right, Iniko," Quinn said, looking back at Bokamba. "We accept. And thank you."

"No thanks needed," Bokamba said, smiling grimly as he stepped over to Quinn and gripped his hand. "Whatever you decide about the Copperheads, Commander Cavanagh is a Peacekeeper. It's only right to try to get back one of our own. Come, let me take you to where my Counterpunch is stored."

The door slid open. "Parlimin VanDiver?" the young aide said hesitantly.

Jacy VanDiver looked up, annoyed. Couldn't the man see he was busy? "What is it, Peters?"

"A report's come in from a Mr. Taurin Lee on Avon," the aide said, holding up a card. "You said you wanted to be kept informed."

VanDiver frowned. What was Lee doing on Avon . . . ? Oh, right. He'd assigned the man to keep an eye on Cavanagh and his family after that irresponsible fool Rudzinski had caved in and given them all that soap-bubble nothing the Peacekeepers had collected. "So inform me," he said.

Peters took a step forward, holding out the card—"No; *you* tell me," VanDiver said. "Summarize."

"Yes, sir." Peters fumbled out his plate, cringing a little under VanDiver's glare. As well he should. The man was young and new to the staff, but even he ought to know that a NorCoord Parlimin didn't have time to read everything that came across his desk. That was what staff members were for in the first place.

"Yes, sir," Peters said again as he found the place. "Lord Stewart Cavanagh left Edo for Avon shortly after Mr. Lee began his surveillance. Aric Cavanagh—that's Lord Cavanagh's eldest son—"

"I know who he is," VanDiver cut him off coldly. "Get on with it."

"Yes, sir. Aric Cavanagh left for Earth aboard a CavTronics freighter. Dr. Melinda Cavanagh also left on a CavTronics freighter, destination unknown."

"What do you mean, destination unknown?" VanDiver demanded. "They filed a flight schedule, didn't they?"

"Uh . . ." Peters skimmed frantically through the report. "Mr. Lee doesn't say. Maybe the schedule wasn't filed through the normal Edo spaceport. That's sometimes done with freighters."

"Or else Cavanagh's playing it cute," VanDiver

growled. He'd called it, all right—Cavanagh was up to something. And whatever it was, it was going to be trouble. He could call that one with his eyes closed. "Send Lee a message," he ordered Peters. "Tell him to find out where that freighter went and get one of his people following the daughter. Ditto for the son. That's always been a cozy little family—I want to know why they've suddenly split up this way. Lee himself is to stay on the father. I want to know everywhere the family goes and everything they do. Got that?"

"Yes, sir," Peters said, scribbling madly on the plate. "Anything else, sir?"

VanDiver glowered at his desk. He didn't know yet what Cavanagh had up his sleeve; but whatever it was, it would undoubtedly be flamboyant. The man thrived on that sort of thing. "Tell Lee to instruct his people that if any of the Cavanaghs even goes near a net or media journalist, he's to have them arrested."

Peters's stylus paused in midstroke. "Sir?"

"You heard me," VanDiver snapped. "Lee can invent something, use my name, invoke Commonwealth security—whatever he has to. But the Cavanaghs are not to talk to journalists."

"Yes, sir," Peters said, his stylus moving again. He finished his notes and looked up. "Will there be anything else, sir?"

For a moment VanDiver studied him. The young man's lips looked uncomfortably tight, and it occurred to VanDiver that he'd probably heard stories about Cavanagh from the other staffers. "Just bear in mind this has nothing to do with the so-called feud between Cavanagh and me," he told the other. "Yes, we were business rivals once; yes, the governor of Grampians passed me over three times to appoint him to the NorCoord Parliament. But that's all water under the bridge. What this is about"—he jabbed two fingers on the desktop for emphasis—"is military security. The Cavanagh family has information about that run-in with the Conquerors that they shouldn't have, and which could disturb the proper focus of the government and the Peacekeepers if it was released to the public. I intend to make sure that doesn't happen."

"Yes, sir." Peters still didn't look entirely happy, but the tension lines had smoothed out a little. "I'll get this out on the next skitter to Avon."

He left; and as the door slid shut behind him, VanDiver snarled out an old street curse he had carefully avoided using for the past thirty years. The Peacekeepers were scrambling to get to battle readiness, rumors of all sorts were shooting across the Commonwealth like tachyon static bursts, Parliament had barely an hour ago finally released the official version of the slaughter off Dorcas; and here he was, Parlimin Jacy VanDiver, having his time and attention wasted by Stewart Cavanagh. The sort of thing that always happened when he locked horns with the man.

Well, no more. This time, with a little luck and a little planning, he would sink Cavanagh for good.

The skitter to Avon wouldn't be leaving for another half hour. Pulling out an official records card, VanDiver punched for one of the more obscure and unused forms in the Parliament catalog. Depending on where Cavanagh chose to make his big play, Lee might have trouble enlisting the help of local law-enforcement officers fast enough to silence him. But with an official NorCoord Parliament carte blanche in hand, that would no longer be a problem. Wherever Cavanagh went, there would always be Peacekeeper forces somewhere nearby.

Smiling grimly to himself, VanDiver began to fill out the form.

10

The *Cavatina*'s hatchway slid open, and as the cool air flowed into the ship's entrance foyer, so too did the exotic aromas of the Mrach world of Mra-mig. Stepping out onto the top of the ramp, Cavanagh took a deep breath of the chilly air. It had been a long time since he'd been on any of the five Mrach worlds, and the intervening years had dulled his sense of smell somewhat. But the aroma was still pleasant, evoking memories and that sense of mystery and counterpoint the Mrachanis so carefully cultivated.

A counterpoint underlined in the view from the *Cavatina*'s ramp. Overhead a group of Mrach courier ships shot past, their flowing-metal design glinting like white gold in the sunlight, followed closely by a flock of dark birdlike flurries flying in an identical formation. Beyond them, rising up over the long marbled-tan spaceport terminal building and the rooftops of Mig-Ka City beyond, a distant range of white-capped black mountains thrust up into the blue sky. Mystery, counterpoint, and consummate civilization—that was the Mrach image.

An image that was starting to show the strains of the looming Conqueror threat. Those couriers flying overhead had been wobbling slightly with the unaccustomed drag of hastily mounted rocket launchers, the distinctive twittering drone of their engines laboring noticeably under the extra weight. The vast parking field, designed to accommodate a hundred commercial ships the size of the *Cavatina*, was two-thirds empty, with the majority of the ships still parked there of the same flowing-metal Mrach design as the aircars. And according to Captain Teva, the *Cavatina* was the only ship since they'd entered the system to be landing on the sloped runways instead of departing from them.

The Commonwealth had finally released the news about the Conquerors' attack . . . and all over the Mrach worlds, Mrachanis and visitors alike were looking fearfully at the sky. Many of those visitors were leaving.

"Sort of ironic, isn't it," Kolchin commented from Cavanagh's side. "The Mrachanis were gearing up to get stomped by the Yycroman Empire when we conveniently showed up and shoveled sand on the fire for them. Now here they are again, smack in the Conquerors' probable approach cone, looking to get stomped again."

" 'Ironic' isn't exactly the word that I'd use," Cavanagh told him. " 'Tragic' is more like it."

"No, that's not what I meant," Kolchin shook his head. "I meant that if we hadn't interfered back then, they wouldn't have had any choice but to build themselves some defenses and learn how to use them. But we came along and made the Yycromae go back home. So they didn't have to. And they didn't."

Cavanagh nodded, understanding now. "Yes, I see. And so now they're stuck having to play catch-up."

"Right," Kolchin said, shading his eyes with one hand as he looked up at the aircars. "And I'll tell you one thing: war isn't something you learn on the fly."

A motion to the left caught Cavanagh's eye: the *Cavatina*'s groundcar, being maneuvered carefully out of its aft storage hold. "You spent some time in Mig-Ka City a few years back, didn't you?" he asked Kolchin as the two of them started down the ramp to meet it.

"It was just a couple of weeks," the other said. "The Yycromae were complaining about the interdiction again, and the Mrachanis asked Command to send some of us to each of their worlds to discuss urban defenses."

"What did you think of them?"

"I don't know," Kolchin said slowly. "They seemed nice enough—polite and friendly and all that. But . . . I don't know. They seemed to do an awful lot of talking sometimes without really saying anything. Whenever guys in the military do that, you figure they don't know what they're talking about. I don't know. Some days I thought they'd be worth defending to the death; other days I was ready to ice the whole planet myself and be done with it."

Cavanagh thought back to his own infrequent dealings with Mrachanis. "I know what you mean. They have a knack for pushing buttons over the whole emotional spectrum. Probably without the slightest idea that they're even doing it."

Kolchin grinned. "Well, we wound up pushing a few buttons right back at them. We had two guys in the unit from Modendina on Palisades who liked to talk Italian to each other when they were off duty, and three more from Edo who always started jabbering in Japanese whenever the Italians started up. Plus there was Crazy Ray, who could swear in twenty different languages, with gestures to match. The Mrachanis couldn't figure out what to make of any of those guys, and you could tell it drove them nuts."

Hill was waiting in the driver's seat as they got into the car. "Captain Teva's already checked clearance, sir," he told Cavanagh. "We can go straight through."

"No customs?" Kolchin asked, frowning.

"Apparently not inbound," Hill shrugged. "Teva said he got the feeling the Mrachanis are delighted to have a few more humans hanging around the city."

"Probably want us in the line of fire if the Yycromae decide to take a poke at them," Kolchin muttered. "Get the Peacekeepers here that much faster."

"Could be," Hill agreed. "Teva said he's heard rumors that the interdiction units are already starting to be reassigned to border and planetary-defense positions in other parts of Lyra and Pegasus Sectors." He looked at Cavanagh. "Where to, sir?"

"Information Agency," Cavanagh told him. "I think that's our best bet."

"Yes, sir." Hill punched it into the console, glanced briefly at the map and location, and turned into one of the vehicle lanes between the ship-parking areas. "By the way, the port people assigned us to the Mrapiratta Hotel," he said over his shoulder. "Just northeast of the port."

Cavanagh frowned. "I told Teva we didn't want accommodations."

"Yes, sir. The Mrachanis insisted on reserving us a suite anyway."

Cavanagh shook his head in annoyance. One of the more irritating Mrach characteristics was their insistence on treating all non-Mrach visitors as if they were attending youth summer camp, including assigning quarters for them at the various hotels in the spaceport and central-city areas. Most human visitors were willing to put up with the procedure, especially once they discovered that more often than not they were being booked into luxury hotels at a fraction of what the equivalent would cost on a Commonwealth world.

What other alien species thought about it Cavanagh didn't know. Certainly the times he'd been to Mrach worlds there hadn't been many nonhumans staying in his hotel. Somehow he'd never gotten around to inquiring as to where those other races were being lodged.

"Hill, do we have any binoculars?" Kolchin asked suddenly, looking out and up through the rear window.

"Right-hand under-seat drawer," Hill told him. "Why?"

"Something's coming in," Kolchin said, getting out the binoculars and turning them on as Hill let the car coast to a stop. Twisting half to the side, Kolchin braced his left elbow against the rear hatchway and focused through the window.

Cavanagh turned, searching the sky and finally locating the fuzzy dot moving toward the spaceport. "Trouble?" he asked.

"I don't know," Kolchin said, adjusting the binoculars. "It's a human design—courier-class ship, looks like. Flashy type, too. The kind NorCoord Parlimins and top Peacekeeper brass like to use."

"A fact-finding tour?" Hill hazarded.

Kolchin snorted. "In a potential war zone? Not likely. If that's a Parlimin in there, it has to be something pretty important." He lowered the binoculars and looked at Cavanagh. "Like maybe informing the Mrachanis the Yycroman interdiction is about to end."

For a moment the car was silent as each of them apparently considered the possible repercussions of being in Mrach space at the moment when restrictions on traffic in and out of Yycroman worlds were suddenly lifted. "Let's not jump to conclusions," Cavanagh said at last. "A Parlimin might not want to visit a war zone himself, but there are plenty who wouldn't mind risking an aide or two to come out and take a look. Anyway, the Commonwealth would be more likely to send news like that directly to Mra and let the Mrach government handle the job of passing the word on to their other worlds."

"Maybe," Kolchin said, shutting off the binoculars. "I suggest, sir, that you might want to have Captain Teva keep the ship on standby. Just in case we have to get off in a hurry."

Cavanagh looked back out at the ship rapidly nearing the field. The only ship, aside from theirs, to land since the *Cavatina* entered the system. "Yes," he said. "I think we'll do that."

The Mrachani's mouselike face seemed to flatten, the iridescent crewcut-length hair covering his neck and shoulders stiffening briefly before settling down into place again. "You surely joke, Lord Cavanagh," he said, his melodious tenor's voice making an odd contrast with his alien appearance. "Folklore? Old spacer stories?" The hair stiffened again. "Rumors and stories are hardly the things from which lucid decisions are made."

"That's an interesting point of view," Cavanagh said. "Especially considering that it was apparently from those same legends that the NorCoord Parliament adopted the name 'Conquerors' for our new enemy."

The body hair flattened a little tighter against the skin beneath it. "Was it the Mrachanis who spoke of those legends?" he asked, an edge of bitterness creeping into his voice. "Was it the Mrachanis who gave any credence to them at all? No. It was the Yycromae who did so."

"I understand that," Cavanagh nodded. "But I don't see what difference it makes who brought the subject up. The fact is that you ran into an unknown alien race out there—"

"So the Yycromae say," the Mrachani interrupted. "The Yycromae say many things which are not true.

Forever they seek to weaken the resolve of the Human Commonwealth to protect the Mrachanis against their aggression."

"The Commonwealth has no intention of abandoning the Mrachanis," Cavanagh assured him. "But—"

"Has it not?" the Mrachani interrupted again. "Even now we hear tales that Human Commonwealth forces will soon be withdrawn from around Yycroman worlds."

"I thought rumors weren't the stuff of lucid decisions," Kolchin reminded him mildly.

"But even the Yycroman peril pales in the face of the new danger waiting beyond the air of our homes," the Mrachani continued, ignoring Kolchin's comment. "The Mrachanis have put their trust in the strength of arm and mind of the Human Commonwealth. Have you the resolve to protect our worlds from that threat as well?"

"As I said, I don't expect the Commonwealth to abandon you," Cavanagh said, letting his voice go a little sterner. "But the Commonwealth's strength and resolve will depend on how much we know about the threat we face. Anything you hold back from us, even rumors or stories, could affect that strength."

The Mrachani seemed to shrink back into its skin. "Do you threaten us?" he whined. "We trust the Human Commonwealth with our lives."

"I'm not threatening you," Cavanagh sighed, feeling irritated and guilty both. Kolchin was right; you could like the Mrachanis and at the same time want to wring their necks. "I'm trying to point out that this is no time to be coy. The humans and Mrachanis are in this together, and anything you can tell us could turn out to be important. No matter how trivial it seems."

The Mrachani looked at Kolchin, back at Cavanagh. "I will order these rumors searched out," he said at last, lifting a delicate arm and letting it fall again in a gesture of weary defeat. "If they exist, they will be delivered to you. Where do you stay on Mra-mig?"

"We'll be in our ship," Cavanagh told him. "The *Cavatina*, in docking slot—"

"A private ship?"

"Yes," Cavanagh said. "The *Cavatina*, registered on Avon. It's in docking slot—"

"It cannot be done," the clerk interrupted again. "Data cannot be delivered to a non-Mrach ship. You must be in a hotel."

Cavanagh frowned. "What are you talking about? I get data transfers to my ship all the time."

"We cannot do it," the clerk insisted. "All areas are shorthanded as we prepare to defend our homes. Data can only be delivered to Mrach ships or buildings."

It could be legitimate, Cavanagh supposed; data transfers outside a net did take a minuscule bit more effort to arrange than transfers within one. But it could also be more along the lines Captain Teva had suggested: that the Mrachanis wanted as many humans between them and the Yycromae as they could possibly get.

Unfortunately, either way there wasn't much he could do about it. Not if he wanted a look at those records. "Fine," he told the clerk. "You can send the information to us at the Mrapiratta Hotel." He lifted an eyebrow. "And we're in something of a hurry."

"I will order the rumors searched out," the Mrachani repeated. "I can promise no more than that. As I have said already, we are shorthanded. But whatever is possible will be done."

"I appreciate your efforts," Cavanagh said. "And I'll again remind you that any information we can gather about the Conquerors will help us all."

The Mrachani eyed him another minute. Then, without replying, he turned away and busied himself at his computer terminal.

The appointment, apparently, was over. Cavanagh caught Kolchin's eye and nodded toward the door. Kolchin nodded back, and together they left the office.

"What do you think?" Cavanagh asked as they hit the street again.

"He wasn't very happy about it," Kolchin said. "I get the distinct feeling he thinks we're wasting his time."

"There's a good chance we are," Cavanagh conceded. Somehow he'd expected that this legend would be something every Mrachani would at least have heard of, even if they didn't give it much credence. Now he was beginning to wonder if he was wasting everyone's time, his as well as theirs. Wasting time, and looking rather like a fool on top of it.

He forced the thought away, feeling a flash of annoyance at himself for having thought it in the first place. He'd never yet let the risk of looking like a fool stop him before. Now, with Pheylan's life on the line, was no time to start.

Pheylan's and Aric's both. "We'll give them one night," he decided, looking down the street and raising his hand. Fifty meters away, their car pulled away from its parking space and headed toward them. "If they haven't come up with anything by tomorrow morning, we'll assume they haven't got it."

"So we're going to take the hotel room after all?" Kolchin asked as Hill pulled up to the carved curbstone in front of them and popped the doors.

"We're going to have to start there, anyway," Cavanagh said as they got into the car. "But if we don't have anything by dinnertime, it might be worth trying a different tack. Hitting one of the spaceport clusterings, say, and seeing if we can find an old Mrach spacer we could get talking."

"I'm not sure I'd recommend that, sir," Kolchin said guardedly. "A lot of non-Mrachanis hang around spaceport clusterings, too. Could be risky."

"I doubt that you and Hill would have any trouble handling the odd Pawolian drunk," Cavanagh said. "Change in plans, Hill: we're going to the Mrapiratta Hotel, after all."

"Yes, sir," Hill said, his attention on the rearview display. "Before we go, sir, I wonder if you'd have a look out to your left. Across the street, beneath that triangular overhang a little ways back."

Cavanagh turned. Seated with its back against a building, being generally ignored by the Mrach pedestrians passing by, was the hairy and angular shape of a Sanduul—a female, he guessed, from the height and general build. Propped against her bent knees was a small trapezoidal wooden frame with a piece of cloth stretched across it. "Looks like she's doing a threading," he said.

"Yes, sir, that's what I thought," Hill agreed. "Now take a look at that alleyway two buildings farther back."

Cavanagh craned his neck. In the alleyway were three Mrachanis, young adults by the looks of them, muffled comfortably against the cool temperatures. "What about them?"

"They've been there since I parked the car," Hill said. "I'm not absolutely sure, but I think they're watching the Sanduul."

Cavanagh frowned. "Why would anyone do that?"

"I don't know," Hill said. "But I can't see any other reason why they'd just be standing there."

"Maybe they're waiting for someone," Kolchin suggested.

"Why not wait inside one of the buildings, then?" Hill countered.

"Maybe it's not someone who lives here," Kolchin

said. "Maybe they're just using the alley as a meeting point."

"Could be." Hill nodded to their immediate left. "So is that group doing the same thing?"

Cavanagh looked. There, standing in a sheltered entryway one building to the Sanduul's other side, were two more young Mrachanis. Mrachanis, furthermore, with the look of people who'd been there awhile and who weren't planning to move on anytime soon.

And they were indeed looking in the Sanduul's direction.

"They're not waiting for transportation, either," Hill added. "I called up the schedule, and there's nothing coming by here for another hour."

"Interesting," Cavanagh murmured, rubbing thoughtfully at his cheek. "Especially after all that moaning about how shorthanded everyone in Mig-Ka City is. I wonder what they're up to."

"If you want, Hill and I could go ask them," Kolchin offered.

Cavanagh looked at the two groups of Mrachanis again. "Yes, let's go take a closer look," he decided. "But you and I will go, Kolchin. We'll take that group in the alleyway, I think. Hill, is there any way for you to get the car around behind them?"

"Yes, there's a clear path back into the alley," Hill said. "You sure you wouldn't rather have me out here where I can back you up?"

Cavanagh lifted an eyebrow. "Against what, five Mrachanis? Anyway, I'd rather have you back there blocking their exit when they realize we're heading their direction. We'll give you a couple of minutes to get in position."

He and Kolchin got out of the car, and Hill drove off. "In general, sir, I have to say that this isn't such a good idea," Kolchin said. "In the future, I'd rather you sit in a locked car and let us handle situations like this. You never know how nonhumans are going to react."

"In general, I fully agree with you," Cavanagh agreed. "But we're talking Mrachanis and a Sanduul here. You'd be hard-pressed to find a less violent group."

"Maybe," Kolchin said, still clearly not convinced. "You planning to talk to the Sanduul?"

"It's as good a way as any to give Hill his couple of minutes," Cavanagh said. "Besides, I've always wanted to see a Duulian threader at work."

They crossed the street, passed the two Mrachanis in the building entryway without looking at them, and headed toward the Sanduul. From this angle Cavanagh could see that her only protection against the cool air was a flimsy-looking serape wrapped tightly around her thorax. The threading board was braced against the makeshift easel of her folded legs, and as they got closer Cavanagh could see that her hands were shaking slightly with cold.

Kolchin noticed it, too. "Kind of out of her element here, isn't she?" he commented.

"It gets colder than this in parts of Ulu," Cavanagh said. "But they wear more clothing there than this one's got on."

They reached the Sanduul and stopped. "Hello," Cavanagh said.

The Sanduul looked up, her hands pausing in their work. "Good day, kind sirs," she said, the slightly distorted words accompanied by the odd hum characteristic of Duulian pharynxes. "Do you come to see my threading?"

"Yes, we do," Cavanagh told her. "May I hold it?"

"My honor," she said, lifting her hands away from the threading. For a moment one of the tendrils of silk from her under-claw spinnerets stretched out between fingertip and cloth before snapping off and dropping flat against the cloth.

Carefully, Cavanagh picked up the frame by its edges. It was a picture of the Information Agency, but with the distant mountains towering over the building as if they were directly behind it. The sun was half-visible, rising between two of the mountain peaks into a blue sky peppered with white cirrus clouds. "Turn it; just so," the Sanduul suggested, twitching her head a fraction to the side.

Cavanagh did so; and suddenly the scene was somehow different. Everything was still there, but the mood had been subtly changed. Instead of a cheery sunrise, it had somehow become a brooding sunset, the optimistic promise of a fresh new morning turning into the sadness-tinged end of a wasted day. He turned the picture back again and the sunrise returned, complete with its upbeat mood. "Extraordinary," he told the Sanduul as he handed it back. "Absolutely unique. I've never seen anything like it."

The Sanduul opened her mouth wide, displaying the razor-sharp teeth that had so unnerved the first humans who landed on Ulu. "You honor my talent," she said, closing the teeth back in again. "Fibbit u Bibrit u Tabli ak Prib-Ulu offers her thanks."

"Cavanagh of Hamilton of Townsend from Grampians-Avon assures her the gratitude is all his," Cavanagh said, hoping he was getting the ritual order of his lineage right. "I've seen Duulian threadings before, but never one with such an inventive approach. May I ask why you're working here instead of on Ulu?"

The spidery face turned away as she arranged the frame again against her legs. "The Mrachanis also admired my talent," she said. "They invited me to study on Mra-mig. For this I was given a gift of money and a promise of schooling with Mrach artists."

Cavanagh looked down at the thin serape rippling in the breezes. "What happened?"

"I do not know," she said, whistling softly through her pharynx in the Duulian equivalent of a sigh. "When I arrived, I was told there had been a mistake. My gift of money had been withdrawn. But I had not enough for the traveling home. So I am still here."

"Couldn't you get help from someone?" Cavanagh asked. "The Duulian embassy, perhaps?"

"There is no advocate of the Sanduuli on Mra-mig," Fibbit said. "I have tried to send messages to Ulu, but the cost has been too high."

Cavanagh frowned. She must be living right on the edge not to be able to afford to send a simple letter. Even messages sent by skitter didn't cost *that* much. "How long have you been here?"

"Half a year." She rubbed a fingertip claw across her serape. "It has become cold."

"It has indeed," Cavanagh said. "How have you survived?"

She stroked her artwork gently. "I do threadings," she said. "Sometimes I am hired by a Mrachani, as now. Other times I make portraits of Mrachanis or others and offer them for sale."

"Others?"

"There are others in Mig-Ka City besides the Mrachanis. Some are humans." She displayed her razor teeth again in another smile. "I like threading humans. You have such depth of faces. But there are few living here."

"I'm surprised there are any at all," Cavanagh commented, trying to make sense of this increasingly nonsensical situation. As far as he could tell, Fibbit was a completely harmless representative of the equally innocuous Duulian race. So why did the Mrachanis have her under surveillance? Especially when they could get rid of her simply by buying her a ticket to Ulu?

"There are several," Fibbit assured him. "One human has been here twice since this threading began. His face is most depthful."

Cavanagh frowned, a quiet bell going off in the back of his mind. "You mean here to the Information Agency?"

"Yes," Fibbit said. "Four days ago, and six days ago."

Cavanagh looked at Kolchin, got a slight shrug in return. "It's where any non-Mrachani would come if he wanted to find out anything," the bodyguard pointed out.

"True," Cavanagh agreed. But if the human was someone important or dangerous, it might explain the surveillance on Fibbit. "Did you speak to this human, Fibbit?"

"No," she said. "He passed me, but did not speak. His face was most depthful."

"How well do you remember it?" Cavanagh asked. "Well enough to do a threading?"

"There is no need," Fibbit said. "I have already threaded him."

"Really," Cavanagh said, looking down at the threading again. This was, of course, none of his business, with no connection whatsoever to his reason for coming to Mra-mig. But he'd already gotten the ball rolling for the Conquerors information, and this situation of Fibbit's was becoming more and more intriguing. "I wonder if I might be allowed to take a look at it."

"It would be my honor," Fibbit said. "It is at my home, only a short distance from—"

"We've got company," Kolchin interrupted.

Cavanagh turned. Three Mrachanis were crossing the street from the direction of the Information Agency.　　•

Clearly headed their way. "Do you know any of those Mrachanis, Fibbit?"

"The one of the center selected me to create this threading," the Sanduul said. "Perhaps he is coming again to check on my progress. Or perhaps not. Mrach faces do not have the depth of human faces."

Cavanagh looked at them. Their faces *were* hard to read, he realized suddenly, even compared to other nonhuman species. Odd that he'd never noticed that before. "It'll be all right," he soothed Fibbit. "Let's see what they want."

"Lord Cavanagh," the center Mrachani said as the group came up. "I confess surprise at finding you here. I was under the impression you had returned to your hotel to await our information package."

"My driver noticed Fibbit while he was waiting for us," Cavanagh explained, looking the Mrachani over. It definitely wasn't the clerk he and Kolchin had talked to inside the Agency; this one was taller, older, with far more poise and verbal polish. "I've always been interested in Duulian threadings."

There might have been a reaction to the mention of Fibbit's name. With all the breezes blowing at the Mrachanis' body hair, Cavanagh couldn't be certain. "Yes, she is a master artist," the Mrachani agreed. "The Mrachanis have purchased several of her threadings; perhaps you would be interested in contemplating them. I have a listing of their current locations in my office."

"Perhaps later," Cavanagh said. "Is that all you came to tell me?"

The Mrachani seemed surprised. "My intent was not to speak with you at all," he said, taking a sidling step around Kolchin toward Fibbit. "As I already stated, I was surprised to find you here. My purpose was merely to inspect the threading's progress."

Wordlessly, Fibbit handed him the frame. The Mrachani looked at it, then offered a view to each of his companions. "It is excellent," he told Fibbit. "Precisely as I desired. Come with me, and I will arrange for your payment."

"Now?" Fibbit asked, her head tilting with surprise. "But it is not yet finished."

"It is precisely as I desired," the Mrachani repeated, in a tone that somehow discouraged further argument. "Your payment awaits inside. Come."

"I come." Fibbit stood up, rising to an amazing height as she unfolded herself to vertical. "I am ready," she said, gripping her serape tighter around her thorax.

The Mrachani looked back at Cavanagh. "Your information will be ready soon, Lord Cavanagh," he said. "I trust you will find it useful."

"I trust so, too," Cavanagh said.

The nonhumans headed back across the street, Fibbit's spidery physique towering over the much shorter Mrachanis. "We haven't checked into the hotel yet," Kolchin reminded him. "If that package arrives before we do, it'll get bounced back here."

"I know," Cavanagh said, watching the group heading back to the Information Agency. It all seemed perfectly reasonable and straightforward . . . and yet, there was something about it that seemed a little bit skew. Something he couldn't put his finger on. "I think just Hill and I will go to the hotel for now," he told Kolchin. "I'd like you to stay here a little longer. Make sure Fibbit comes out all right."

Kolchin frowned. "Fibbit?"

"Yes," Cavanagh said. "They slipped her away from us just a little bit too neatly."

Kolchin seemed to consider that. "Maybe," he said at last. "I don't see what it has to do with us, though."

"Neither do I," Cavanagh admitted. "Call it a hunch.

"Yes, sir," Kolchin said. "You want me to have a talk with those Mrachanis down the alleyway while I'm waiting?"

A motion to his right caught Cavanagh's eye, and he turned as their car pulled to the curb in front of them. "They must have spotted me," Hill said through the open window. "They all suddenly took off a minute ago." He glanced behind them at the spot where Fibbit had been. "The Sanduul left?"

"They took her into the Information Agency," Cavanagh said. "Allegedly to buy her threading. Which way did our loiterers go?"

"Opposite direction," Hill said, nodding behind him. "Though they could have circled back around."

"We'd better get moving," Kolchin put in. "If they're watching us, this can't help but look suspicious. You can drop me off a block away. Hill, we've got a break-apart scooter in back, don't we?"

"We should have," Hill said. "What's going on?"

"I'll tell you on the way," Cavanagh said. "You just be careful, Kolchin." He looked out the window at the Information Agency as they drove off. "You're armed, aren't you?"

"I'm always armed, sir," Kolchin said quietly. "Don't worry. Whatever's going on, I can handle it."

11 They dropped Kolchin off and then headed back to the spaceport and their assigned hotel. The staff was expecting them, though the front clerk seemed mildly upset that only two of the three he'd been promised were here. Cavanagh checked them in, assured the clerk that the third of their party would officially check in when he arrived, and went up to their suite to await the Information Agency's package.

The wait turned out to be surprisingly short. Hill hadn't even finished his security sweep of the rooms when a trilling from the suite's computer announced that the package had arrived.

"That was fast," Hill commented as Cavanagh inserted a card and keyed the computer for acceptance.

"Amazingly fast," Cavanagh agreed. "Especially considering that the clerk wasn't expecting to find anything at all."

The computer beeped again and shut down. Withdrawing the card, Cavanagh slid it into his plate. The translator was already loaded, and by the time he'd seated himself in one of the plush conversation-pit chairs surrounding the corner-mounted flame sculpture, the five pages of flowing Mrach script had con-

densed their way down to three pages of English.
Settling back, mentally crossing his fingers, he started
to read.

It was short, and it was very disappointing. According to the records, an unknown alien ship had passed
through the Mra system two centuries earlier, shortly
after the Mrachanis' first tentative steps into space. The
aliens had made contact with a manned Mrach probe
on its long way to one of the nearer planets of the
system, stopping just long enough to learn the Mrach
language from the crew before moving on. Among other
things, the aliens had told the Mrachanis they were
running from a powerful race currently in the process
of destroying and conquering their own homeworld.
But they'd said other things, as well, some of which had
later proved to be untrue. They'd left no physical evidence behind when they'd departed, either, a fact that
had later led to thinly veiled allegations that the whole
"visitation" had been nothing more than an elaborate
hoax dreamed up by bored crew members to stir up the
expedition's organizers. The report ended with an ap-
pended note that the search for more information was
still under way, and that anything further would similarly be forwarded to the hotel.

He shut the plate off and laid it aside. "Anything?"
Hill asked from the door to one of the two bedrooms.

"Not really," Cavanagh told him. "We could have
saved ourselves the trip out here. How's the suite
look?"

"It's clean," Hill said, eyeing his employer. "You
know, sir—and not to be presumptuous—it might help
if I knew what exactly you were looking for. And why
you were looking for it."

"No presumption inferred," Cavanagh assured him.
"I'm looking for information about the Conquerors.
What they're like, where they might have come from—

that sort of thing. The 'why' of it, unfortunately, is restricted information at the moment."

"I understand," Hill nodded. "If I may make a suggestion, then, perhaps we should try the main government archives on Mra."

Cavanagh shook his head. "Actually, I doubt they would be any more complete than the records here. The Mrachanis take special pride in their efficiency at disseminating information among themselves. That's why we came here instead of going on to Mra in the first place: access to the same data without spending the extra five hours of travel time each direction."

"We're on that tight of a schedule?"

Cavanagh ran through the numbers. Melinda would be on Dorcas by now, as should the fueler he'd sent out to her there. He hadn't heard anything from Aric, but if they were still on Quinn's timetable, they shouldn't be more than a couple of days behind her. Figure twenty hours for the *Cavatina* to reach Dorcas from here . . .

And then what? The whole purpose of this side trip had been to get some idea of where Aric should start searching for his brother. Now he had nothing.

In his pocket his phone vibrated. Pulling it out, he keyed it on. "Yes?"

The view on the display was a surprise: a distorted, shadowy image that looked nothing at all like a face or anything else. "Kolchin, sir," the bodyguard's voice murmured, barely louder than the background hum behind it. "That Sanduul—Fibbit. Did you want to talk to her, or just see that she got out of the Information Agency okay?"

"The latter, mostly," Cavanagh said, frowning at the question. The image on the display shifted slightly, and suddenly he realized that what he was seeing was a close-up of Kolchin's jacket. The other was holding the phone close to his chest, just below chin height. "I could probably find a few questions to ask her, though," he added, "if you're looking for an excuse to bring her here."

"It's not a question of excuses, sir," Kolchin said. "But if you want to see her, you'd better get over here to the spaceport. Looks like the Mrachanis are kicking her off the planet."

It was a fast five-minute drive to the port from the hotel. Hill didn't bother parking the car but simply left it at the entrance, and they hurried inside.

Kolchin was waiting for them across the mostly empty outer lobby by one of the corridors leading to the gates. "Where is she?" Cavanagh asked as they came up to him.

"Heading toward exit customs," Kolchin said. "Better hurry—once they get her through, we won't be able to get to her without a lot of trouble."

"Right," Cavanagh said as they set off down the gently curving corridor. "Tell me what happened."

"I threw the scooter together and circled back to the Agency," Kolchin said. "They were just bringing her out —the same three Mrachanis plus an extra one. A big government-style car pulled up and they all got inside. I got a chaser planted on the car before they took off and paralleled them a few blocks away to a kind of run-down part of town. Mostly non-Mrachanis hanging around, looked like."

Cavanagh frowned. "I didn't think there were any non-Mrach enclaves anywhere near Mig-Ka City."

"It's not listed as an enclave on the map," Kolchin said. "Though if I were them, I'd keep this place quiet no matter who was living there. It's more like a fifth-world slum than anything else. Anyway, they all went inside one of the rats' nests, stayed there a few minutes, and then all came out again. The Sanduul was wearing a big backpack sort of thing, and the Mrachanis were each carrying a stack of threading frames. They threw everything in the car and hightailed it straight here."

"Was the Sanduul cuffed?" Hill asked.

"Didn't look like it," Kolchin said. "Near as I could tell, she was going along with whatever was happening."

"Any idea which flight they're headed for?" Hill asked.

"Not really," Kolchin said. "I checked the schedule, and the next ship to Ulu doesn't leave for another six hours. Doesn't make much sense for them to be rushing around like this."

They rounded a final curve in the corridor; and there, at a low customs table twenty meters ahead, were Fibbit and a half-dozen Mrachanis, two of them wearing the bright-blue tamlike caps of customs officials. "Maybe they've got a good reason," Cavanagh said. "Let's find out."

The Mrachanis saw them coming, of course; but if Cavanagh had been hoping for signs of surprise or guilt, he didn't get them. One or two at a time the Mrachanis turned calmly to look at the newcomers, until Fibbit noticed and turned herself. "Cavanagh!" she called, her mouth opening wide in that ferocious-looking Duulian smile. "Be honored for me. I am going home!"

"That's great, Fibbit," Cavanagh said, throwing a quick look around at the Mrachanis. "But I thought you couldn't afford a ticket."

"I have been honored with a gift," she said happily. "An unnamed but very honorable benefactor. I am going home."

"I'm honored for you," Cavanagh said, taking a step to the side for a closer look at the customs table. The backpack Kolchin had mentioned was lying there opened, its contents laid out in neat rows across the scanners. On the far side of the table, already checked through, were twin stacks of the trapezoidal threading frames. "I was hoping to see one of your threadings, though," he reminded her, nodding toward the stacks. "Would you mind if I took a quick look?"

"Those have been passed through already," one of the blue-capped Mrachanis spoke up.

"Can't we get them out?" Cavanagh asked. "Just long enough to look at them?"

"That is not proper procedure," the Mrachani huffed. "Once items have passed through customs screening—"

"Please," another Mrachani interrupted smoothly. "That will not be a problem. For Lord Stewart Cavanagh, former official of the Northern Coordinate Parliament, certain exceptions can be made."

Cavanagh focused on him. Older than either the customs officials or the three who'd hustled Fibbit off into the Information Agency earlier, he had an almost tangible air of experience and quiet confidence about him. Clearly, this was the newcomer Kolchin had mentioned. "Thank you," he said to the other. "And you are . . . ?"

"Paallikko," the Mrachani said with a slight bow. "Department of Guest Relations. Tell me, Lord Cavanagh, what is it in Fibbit's work you wish to see?"

"She told me about a threading she'd done of another human," Cavanagh said. "Someone she'd seen visiting the Information Agency recently."

"I see," Paallikko said. "Do you know this human personally?"

Cavanagh shrugged. "I doubt it. Fibbit didn't get his name."

"Yet you wish now to see his face."

"I want to see how well Fibbit does with human threadings," Cavanagh told him. "I like her style, and I was thinking of hiring her to do a threading of me."

"And for this you follow her and accost her at the spaceport?" He wrinkled his forehead in a parody of a human raising his eyebrows. "Most unusual behavior."

"We former NorCoord officials are full of eccentricities," Cavanagh countered. "Among other things, we sometimes worry about inadequately clothed and fed artists, of all races and species. Part of our heritage, you know."

"Ah," Paallikko said, nodding. "The ancient Avon tradition of—what is it called? Noble benevolence?"

"Chivalry," Cavanagh corrected. "And it dates back considerably before the colonization of Avon. Fibbit was in trouble, and I wanted to see if there was anything I could do for her once I'd finished my errand."

"Most honorable," Paallikko said. "And yet, as you see, there is no need for your assistance. Fibbit is going home."

"I'm glad," Cavanagh said. "I would still beg the indulgence of seeing her threading before she leaves."

"Chivalry," Paallikko said as if trying the word on for size. "Yes. Yet now I must confess to confusion, Lord Cavanagh. Is the valuing of privacy not also an ancient tradition? Guests of the Mrachanis do not come to Mig-Ka City to have their faces shown openly to strangers."

Cavanagh cocked an eyebrow. This was an argument he hadn't expected. "The man was walking around in public," he reminded Paallikko. "It doesn't sound like he had anything to hide. If I'd been here, I'd have seen him myself."

"But you were not here," Paallikko said. "For what reason, then, should I allow you to impose on his privacy?"

Cavanagh looked at Fibbit. "To be honest, Paallikko,

I'm not sure it really requires your permission. The threading is Fibbit's property. The decision on whether to show it to me should be hers."

"It has already cleared customs—" the customs official began.

"Please," Paallikko again cut him off. "You make a good point, Lord Cavanagh. What is your wish, Fibbit u Bibrit u Tabli ak Prib-Ulu?"

For a second the Sanduul just stood there. Then, suddenly, it seemed to dawn on her that she was being asked into this conversation. "Yes," she said. "Cavanagh may of course see the threading."

"Then it is decided." Paallikko looked at the two customs officials. "Bring the threadings here to me."

Silently, they complied, each bringing one of the stacks of frames back to the customs table. "It is here," Fibbit assured Cavanagh, lifting the frames one at a time to peer at the threading beneath. "I remember him well, and it was just a few days . . ."

She trailed off, holding up the top three frames and staring down at the fourth. "What is it?" Cavanagh asked.

Slowly, Fibbit set the three frames down on the customs table and held up the fourth.

Once, clearly, it had been a threading. Now it was nothing but a tangled mass of broken Duulian silk threads. "What happened?" Cavanagh asked.

"I don't know," Fibbit said, her voice almost too low to hear. "I don't know."

"A shame, indeed," Paallikko said.

Cavanagh looked at him, then stepped around Fibbit to the three threading frames she had removed. Picking up the top two, he set them aside and then turned the third one over. The wood on the underside seemed smooth enough; but at one corner one of the nails holding the frame together was protruding a couple of millimeters. "I think I see what happened, Fibbit," he said, showing her the nail. "It must have somehow raked across the threading beneath it while they were all being brought here."

"Yes," Fibbit said, her voice still mournful.

"Could you redo it?" Kolchin asked. "Make a new one, I mean?"

"It doesn't matter," Cavanagh said, throwing a warning look at the bodyguard. "I can see enough of your style from these other threadings, Fibbit. Would you be willing to do a threading of me?"

For a moment Fibbit's attention stayed on the ruined threading. Then, with a whistling sigh, she placed it back on the stack. "Certainly I would be willing, Cavanagh," she said. "Do you ride this ship with me?"

Cavanagh looked at Paallikko. "I thought perhaps we could do it at my hotel before you leave," he said. "Your flight is still six hours away."

Fibbit turned her head to one side. "Six hours? But I was told I would be leaving now."

"You will be," Paallikko said. "The commercial liner Lord Cavanagh refers to is indeed not leaving for six hours. Your place is aboard a Mrach diplomatic courier which will be departing immediately."

"Ah." Fibbit looked back at Cavanagh. "I am sorry, Cavanagh. But I could give you my locator at Prib-Ulu. Perhaps you could see me in the future."

"Perhaps," Cavanagh said. "But on the other hand, the future is always so uncertain. The demands of my business often interfere with other, more personal desires; and you, too, Fibbit, might travel again such that I would have trouble finding you."

"Surely you could make time, Lord Cavanagh," Paallikko said. "There is always time for that which is truly important to us."

"Is there?" Cavanagh countered. "Is there always?"

For a moment Paallikko gazed at him. "If you have a point, Lord Cavanagh, I would request you arrive at it."

"I do indeed have a point," Cavanagh acknowledged. "The point is that a certainty today is worth two promises for tomorrow. Put another way, I would like to have Fibbit do my threading now."

"But I cannot, Cavanagh," the Sanduul said, waving her arms helplessly. "Please do not ask me. How, then, would I reach my home?"

"We would take you there ourselves, of course," Cavanagh said. "As soon as my errand here is complete. My ship has more than enough room for you."

"But my unnamed benefactor," Fibbit protested, her eyes flicking guiltily from Cavanagh to Paallikko and back again. "He might be offended or hurt if I refused this gift."

"I don't think so," Cavanagh assured her. "True benefactors seek a noble result, not the glory of creating that result themselves. I'm sure he will be pleased if you reach home as he desires, no matter how that result is achieved." He looked at Paallikko. "I trust the Mrach government has no objections to Fibbit staying an extra day on Mra-mig?"

"Truthfully, it is somewhat awkward," Paallikko said hesitantly. "Her exit order has already been approved and time-marked for this night. To extend her residence would be improper."

"I thought certain exceptions could be made," Kolchin spoke up, "for former NorCoord Parlimins."

Deliberately, Paallikko turned to look at him. "I was under the impression, Lord Cavanagh, that human custom was for subordinates to remain silent unless invited to speak."

"We humans have many different customs," Cavanagh said. "They add a richness to our various cultures."

"Anarchy," Paallikko hissed contemptuously. "That is what your so-named cultures truly are. Anarchy."

"Sometimes it does look that way," Cavanagh conceded. "Still, we make do."

For a long minute no one spoke. Then Paallikko hissed again. "An exception will be made," he said reluctantly. "But for one day only, until sunset tomorrow. If that is not acceptable, the Sanduul must leave now."

"It's quite acceptable," Cavanagh said, trying to ignore the twinge of guilt whispering in his ear. His errand here was finished—he should be on his way to Dorcas right now to help Aric and Quinn with their preparations. He had no business spending even an extra day here chasing shadows or tilting at windmills or whatever in blazes he was doing. "We'll probably be off Mra-mig well before that."

"Then it is so ordered," Paallikko said, pointing to one of the customs officials. *"Kavva mron ce gan ce mrash."*

The other nodded. *"Ba mrash,"* he said, and hurried off.

Paallikko looked back at Cavanagh. "The records will be altered," he said. "Will you need assistance with accommodations, Lord Cavanagh? Or with the threading frames?"

"Our suite is large enough for all of us," Cavanagh assured him. "And as for the frames, we'll only need to take this damaged one with us. The rest have already passed customs; presumably they can be taken directly over to the *Cavatina*."

One of the blue-capped Mrachanis glanced at Paallikko and then nodded. "It will be done," he said.

"Good," Cavanagh nodded. "Come with us, Fibbit. And thank you, Paallikko, for your assistance and your time."

"It is ever an honor to serve those of the Human Commonwealth," the other said softly. "Good evening to you, Lord Cavanagh. May you enjoy your threading."

Cavanagh smiled. "Thank you," he said. "I'm sure I will."

12

The last tube of emergency sealant had been located, the last replacement electronics module checked and resealed, the last ration box counted; and with a sigh of relief Melinda Cavanagh shut off her plate and dropped it on the crate beside her. "That's it," she said aloud. "All present and accounted for."

There was, predictably, no answer. Standing up, gingerly easing her back into a more or less vertical position, she let her gaze sweep across the piles of crates and cylinders stacked against the wall of her borrowed warehouse. There was a lot of material here, and through the distant pounding in her temples she permitted herself a brief moment of mildly smug satisfaction. She'd thrown this whole thing together in what had to be record time, and she'd done it well. Everything a fourteen-man expedition should need for a few weeks away from home, and all right here in this room.

Now all she needed was the big box that was supposed to go around it.

"Hello?" a voice called from somewhere behind her. "Anyone home?"

Melinda turned, frowning. That didn't sound like the

man who'd rented her this space. "Over here," she called. "Back by the rear doors."

There was the sound of footsteps . . . and then, coming around someone else's pile of crates, a youngish man in a Peacekeeper uniform emerged into view. "Hello," he said again. He walked toward her, sweeping his gaze across the supplies she'd just finished inventorying. "Quite a stockpile you have here."

"I'm glad you like it," Melinda said, trying without success to read the black combat-style insignia on his collar. "Can I help you with something?"

"Probably," he said, still examining the crates as he continued toward her. "I heard about this impressive cache of yours and wanted to come take a look for myself."

"I had no idea it would become a tourist attraction," Melinda said dryly. "I don't mean to be rude, but I'm rather busy at the moment. And this *is* private property."

"I'm afraid that distinction doesn't mean much at the moment," he said. "Dorcas is about half a wink away from martial law. Whether or not that wink happens will likely depend on the level of cooperation we get."

"Really," she said, letting her tone drop into frostbite range. "Does your commanding officer encourage this sort of strong-arm language with visiting civilians?"

The man stepped over to her and stopped; and for the first time he turned his full attention on her. "That's not strong-arm language, Dr. Cavanagh," he said, his voice as cold as hers. "It's a statement of fact. We're facing a possible attack here—a probable attack, in my personal estimation. Visiting civilian or not, you're in a war zone and under my authority. I have both the right and the responsibility to do whatever it takes to protect the citizens of Dorcas."

Melinda swallowed hard. Now, a meter away and no

longer moving, she could finally make out the hawk-and-star insignia of a lieutenant colonel on his collar. "I'm sorry," she said, and meant it. "I didn't mean that the way it sounded."

For a moment he just stood there and let her flounder. Then—almost reluctantly, she thought—his lip twitched in a half smile. "Apology accepted," he said. "I'll meet you halfway: my choice of words could have been better, too. Let's try it again from the top, shall we? Welcome to Dorcas, Dr. Cavanagh. I'm Lieutenant Colonel Castor Holloway, commander of the Peacekeeper garrison here. My logistics officer tells me you came in with half a freighter load of supplies." He waved at the stacks of crates. "Obviously, he was correct. You can probably guess my next question."

"What's it all doing here?" Melinda suggested.

He smiled again. "Very good. And?"

Melinda studied him. Up close she could see he wasn't quite as young as she'd first thought. Somewhere in his late thirties, she decided, with eyes that looked considerably older than that. "I don't suppose I could tell you it was a private matter and that we should leave it at that."

Holloway shook his head. "Afraid not. You see, I pulled the record of your entry before I came down here. Apparently, you wanted permission to leave your freighter in orbit for a few days instead of bringing all this stuff down. That tells me that you don't intend any of these goodies for the fine citizens of our colony, but are simply using Dorcas as a transfer point."

Melinda nodded. He was sharp, all right. She would have to watch her words carefully. "You're right, we are," she said. "I'm meeting my brother Aric and some other men here in a day or two. All this is to be transferred to them." She fixed him with a stern look. "A task that would have been considerably easier if I'd been allowed to stay in orbit as I requested."

"An orbiting ship would also have instantly identified Dorcas as an inhabited planet if a Conqueror scout happened to mesh into the system," Holloway pointed out. "Or orbiting hardware of any sort—you may have noticed the absence of any communications or nav/weather satellites on your way in. I'm sorry if you were inconvenienced; but as I've already mentioned, this is a war zone. There's no point in being more of a sitting duck than we already are." He cocked an eyebrow. "All of which leads to another obvious question. Why Dorcas?"

Melinda shook her head. "I'm afraid I can't tell you that."

"I'm afraid you'll have to," Holloway countered. "Midspace freight transfers might be a common sight at Earth or Bergen, but not at out-of-the-way spots like Dorcas. One might suppose you had some, shall we say, less than legal transaction in mind."

"Oh, come on," Melinda scoffed. "There are a million and a half cubic light-years of empty space out there for people to shuffle ships around in. Why in the world would anyone choose an inhabited planet to transfer illegal goods at? Especially a planet in the middle of a major Peacekeeper operation?"

"That's a good question," Holloway agreed. "That, along with the time crunch in general, is what's kept this supply dump of yours intact instead of disassembled and run through an extra-fine sand sifter. I'll ask it again: why Dorcas?"

Melinda sighed. "All right," she said. "The truth is that Aric and I are assisting a high-ranking Peacekeeper officer with a somewhat delicate and rather unofficial operation. It involves the space near Dorcas; hence, this is where we rendezvous."

"Very impressive words," Holloway said. "You have any substance to go along with them?"

"If you mean official authorizations, I'm afraid not," Melinda said, trying to keep the hesitation tearing at her throat from showing in her voice. Making up lies on the fly wasn't something a surgical design consultant's career had adequately prepared her for. "As I said, the operation is somewhat delicate. I was told that as long as we didn't request assistance from local Peacekeeper forces, we wouldn't have any trouble with them."

"Were you, now," Holloway said. "Rather naive thinking on someone's part. Have you any documents at all? Of any type?"

"No." She hesitated; but she could think of only one card she could still play. "If you want confirmation, you'll have to contact Peacekeeper Command directly."

He cocked an eyebrow. "Peacekeeper Command. As high as that?"

Melinda nodded. "Possibly even higher."

Holloway bowed his head slightly. "You've piqued my interest, Doctor. I believe I'll take you up on your suggestion. Anyone in particular I should direct the message to?"

The point of no return was well behind her. Bracing herself, Melinda took the plunge. "Send it directly to Admiral Rudzinski's office."

Holloway's eyebrows lifted. "Rudzinski himself, eh? You're definitely running in a higher circle than I would have guessed."

"Just make the message brief," Melinda said, sternly ordering her stomach to behave itself. If Holloway called her bluff and actually sent an inquiry to Earth, she was going to be in a swirl of trouble about seventy hours from now. But the option was to be in the equivalent depth of trouble right now . . . and in seventy hours Aric and Quinn, at least, should be safely off Dorcas and out of reach of official wrath. "The admiral has a lot of other matters to deal with."

"I shall be the soul of brevity," Holloway promised in what he probably intended to be a seventeenth-century Shakespearian British accent. "As well as the soul of discretion. In case it turns out that Rudzinski actually has heard of you."

"Will that be all, then?" Melinda asked, ignoring the not-very-veiled suggestion that she was in fact lying through her teeth about all this.

"For now," Holloway said. "Oh, there's one other thing. About half an hour ago now, we had a freighter mesh in that was piggybacking what seems to be an old Moray-class long-range battle fueler. Yours?"

From his tone it was pretty clear he already knew the answer. "Probably," she said. "Didn't they transmit a destination invoice?"

"Of course," Holloway said calmly. "I was just looking for confirmation." He nodded toward the crates. "I presume all this will be going aboard. I'll give orders for it to land as close to you as possible."

"Thank you," Melinda said.

"No charge." Holloway glanced at his watch. "If you'll excuse me, I have a great deal of other work to do. Be sure to bring your brother around when he arrives, Dr. Cavanagh. I'd very much like to meet him."

He nodded again and, executing a neat about-face, made his way out the way he'd come. "Right," Melinda murmured under her breath. "I'm sure he'd love to meet you, too."

The fueler came down alone, moving awkwardly in the unaccustomed environment of a planetary atmosphere and gravity well. Melinda held her breath as it wobbled its way toward the landing field, but the pilot evidently knew what he was doing and made it without turning stern up and driving into the ground. Bypassing the usual runways—the fueler had no landing gear to speak of—it curved up into half a loop, and with a roar and splash of Icefire dropped neatly onto its stern at the edge of the field closest to Melinda's rented warehouse.

The Icefire dissipated, and the twisting coronal glow around the edge-effect airfoils faded away, and Melinda started breathing again as she looked it over. The ship was a model of simplicity, little more than a large, slightly flattened cylinder with eight docking ports along its sides and a coupling port at the bow that enabled it to link up with larger ships or other fuelers. The space-normal Icefire drive at the stern was complemented by a Chabrier stardrive at the bow, with the compressed living quarters and control section in the center. Halfway up along the side facing her was a hatchway with an open-air lift-cage track running the length of the ship beside it, and as Melinda walked toward the fueler, a storage compartment near the hatchway opened and the lift cage rotated out and onto the track. It started down, arriving at the base of the fueler the same time she did.

She got in, and the cage started back up. Up close the fueler seemed smaller than she had expected it to be, especially considering that it was supposed to serve as both living quarters and mobile supply dump for sixteen men and their fighters. She wondered if Aric, who had once loudly complained about having to share a hotel room with his brother, really understood what he was getting himself into.

Like the rest of the ship, the hatchway and narrow corridors beyond it had been designed for free fall. Negotiating them in full gravity was something of a challenge, but with some stretching and ingenuity Melinda managed it without too much trouble. Passing through the cracker-box wardroom and half-cracker-box galley, she reached the control room.

It was empty.

She frowned. The pilot ought to be here, running through the check-down procedure. "Hello?" she called.

"Hello, Dr. Cavanagh," a disembodied voice replied from a section of the control board. "My name is Max. Welcome aboard."

"Thank you," Melinda said. So that was why the fueler was two days behind the tentative schedule her father had set for its arrival here. The old fox had thrown her a little twist. "Excuse my surprise. I was expecting to find a human pilot."

"I was apparently an afterthought of Lord Cavanagh's," the computer said. "It occurred to him that having someone of my capabilities aboard might prove beneficial to the mission."

"I'm sure it will be," Melinda agreed. "I'm afraid I'm a little unfamiliar with the CavTronics line of semisentients. May I ask which series you are?"

"I'm one of the Carthage-Ivy group," he said. "Carthage-Ivy-Gamma, if you need the full database designation."

"That's with, what, Class Six decision-making capabilities?"

"Class Seven," he corrected her. "I understand—"

"How about logic structures?"

"Modified Korngold-Che decay-driven randomized," Max said. "If you're truly interested, Dr. Cavanagh, all my specifications are on file. I understand you've brought the supplies for the expedition?"

"Yes," Melinda said, trying to hide a smile. That was a CavTronics computer, all right. Perpetually driven crazy by what he saw as self-absorbed conceit on the part of other companies' parasentient computers, her father had deliberately programmed the Carthage series with a strong reluctance to talk about themselves.

She glanced across the control board, her smile fading. The computer wasn't the only alteration her father had made in the fueler's original equipment. There, to the side of the main display, was a newly installed Mindlink jack for Quinn to use. Quinn, who had once stated at NorCoord Parliament hearings that he never again wanted to use the Mindlink that the Copperhead surgeons had built into his brain.

"Dr. Cavanagh?" Max prompted.

With an effort Melinda brought her attention back to the immediate task at hand. It made sense, of course, under the circumstances. But still, somehow, it seemed out of character with the quiet respect for other people she'd always associated with her father. Perhaps he was capable of a more hard-edged pragmatism than she'd ever realized. "Everything's over in that warehouse just to the north of here," she told Max.

"I trust you brought plenty of fuel," the computer said. "I wasn't expecting to have to land and take off again from here."

"Neither was I," Melinda said. "We'll just have to hope there's enough for what Aric and Quinn need."

"There is an alternative," he suggested. "My accompanying freighter is presumably carrying fuel reserves. Lord Cavanagh instructed its captain to withdraw from Dorcas as soon as I was in position, but under the circumstances you could presumably countermand that order."

"No, you'd better let him go," Melinda said. "The local Peacekeeper commander doesn't want ships sitting in orbit any longer than they have to."

"You could order it to land."

"And have the crew sitting around where Colonel

Holloway can pump them for information?" Melinda shook her head. "No, thanks."

"I understand." There was a brief pause. "The freighter has been instructed to carry out its previous orders."

"All right," Melinda said, glancing around the control room and locating the spare module storage compartments. "I can handle most of the small stuff myself. For the crates and tanks, we'll need lifters and people to operate them. I'll get back to the warehouse and start the ball rolling." She turned to go—

"Just a moment," Max said suddenly. "I'm picking up a signal that appears to be in one of Lord Cavanagh's private codes."

"Is it Dad?" Melinda asked, squeezing through the cramped space to the command chair. His errand on Mra-mig must have gone faster than he'd expected.

"No," Max said. "It's Mr. Aric Cavanagh. I've answered his hail and set the decoder. Here he is."

The soft hum of a carrier signal came on. "Melinda?" Aric's voice came.

"I'm here, Aric," she called. "Welcome to Dorcas."

"Pleased to be here," he said dryly. "After twenty-six hours in a fighter, it's going to be nice to be able to turn around without bumping into something."

"Don't get too used to it," she warned him. "This fueler hasn't got a lot more room than that cockpit has."

"Dr. Cavanagh, this is Quinn," a new voice cut in. "I read you as moving away from the planet. Is something wrong?"

"That's not me," Melinda said. "That's the freighter that brought the fueler in. The fueler and supplies are here on the ground."

"On the *ground*?" Quinn repeated. "I wanted them in orbit."

"I wasn't given that option," she told him. "No ships are allowed to stay in orbit longer than two hours. Peacekeeper orders."

There was a long moment of silence. "Not good," Quinn said at last. "Not good at all."

"What's the matter?" Aric asked. "Can't the fueler lift off the ground?"

"It can lift just fine," Quinn said grimly. "That's not the problem. With it sitting on the ground like that, we won't be able to stencil on the proper insignia and numbers without everyone around seeing us do it."

"Ouch," Aric said. "You're right. And if we don't get it painted, those incoming Copperheads are going to ask some awkward questions."

"Which we don't have answers for," Quinn said. "We'll have to think of something to do about that. Dr. Cavanagh, did you get everything on the list I gave you?"

"Yes, it's all here," Melinda said, frowning. "Did you say incoming *Copperheads*?"

"We'll explain later," Quinn said. "Our first job is to get the supplies aboard the fueler. You get started, Doctor; we'll be down in about an hour to give you a hand. We need to be finished by morning—the rest of the fighters could be here as early as noon tomorrow."

"I'll get right on it," Melinda promised. "Watch out for the local Peacekeeper commander—a Lieutenant Colonel Holloway. He's not stupid, and he's already halfway to locking this whole thing down on general principles."

"Don't worry, I know how to handle officers like that," Quinn assured her. "You just get the loading started."

"All right. I'll see you soon."

The carrier went dead. "I have the local communication frequencies identified, Dr. Cavanagh," Max said. "Would you like me to contact someone about hiring workers?"

"Thank you, but no," Melinda said, prying herself out of the chair and clawing her way to the control-room door. "We're drawing enough attention as it is without people finding out we've got a Carthage-Ivy here. You just stay quiet and run some checks on the fueler's systems. We may have to get this thing off the ground on ten minutes' notice."

"Now, here's the north end of the canyon, coming in low from the east," Major Takara said, keying the tactical display for the next view. "If you look closely—right there—you can see where we've burned the softer rock out from under that granite crest. Shredder gun nests here, here, and here; rocket launchers under these overhangs; dazzler projectors up on the crest here and over here."

Holloway nodded. It wasn't anything like an ideal textbook defensive setup, but it was light-years better than anything they'd had when that watchship had burned through on its way to Earth sixteen days ago. "You've done good work, Fuji," he said.

"Thanks, but we've still got a long way to go," Takara said. "I just hope the Conquerors are considerate enough to actually invade. I'd hate to have gone to all this effort and then have to sit there while they fry the planet from orbit."

"If you're going to wish for something, wish for them to miss the Commonwealth completely," Holloway said tartly. "All right, what's left to do?"

"Here, not much. We've just about finished with that soft rock layer—everything else seems to be solid granite. I figure we'll have enough room for the command post and medical facilities, plus as much of the supply cache as we can squeeze in."

"Leaving the bulk of the civilians out in the cold."

"And the bulk of the garrison, too," Takara conceded. "That geologist group is still hunting for more of those soft rock intrusions or whatever they're called, and if they find any, we'll be happy to burn out more of these half-cave things. But chances are everyone's going to have to make do with tents and shelters.

Holloway looked out the window as another aircar convoy lifted off with supplies for the canyon. "Assuming we have any civilians left by the time the Conquerors hit."

"Actually, I think most of the exodus is over," Takara said. "Everyone who's still here seems ready to stick it out. Colonist types, you know."

"Yeah—proud, brave, and stubborn. Personally, I'd rather they all tucked their tails and ran like craven puppies. Guerrilla warfare is grim enough without having twenty-five thousand civilians underfoot."

"Don't sell them short, Cass," Takara warned. "Even civilians can be dangerous when they get their backs up."

"As long as they're dangerous to the Conquerors and not to each other. Or to us." Holloway keyed for an overview of the canyon. "All right. The north end looks about as secure as we can make it. Let's see what we can do with this gap over here on the eastern wall."

His comm buzzed. "Colonel, this is Sergeant Crane. You asked to be informed if any unusual spacecraft came into the system."

The hairs on the back of Holloway's neck pricked up. "How unusual is it?"

"Oh, no, sir, it's not *that* unusual," Crane hastened to assure him. "It's just that fighter wake-trail we picked up half an hour ago. Turns out it's an old Counterpunch."

Holloway looked at Takara. "A Counterpunch?"

"Yes, sir. They've just meshed in, and they seem to be having a coded conversation with someone down here."

Takara was already halfway to the door. "Find the other end," Holloway called as he circled his desk. "I'll be right there."

They reached the sensor center to find Crane and another operator hunched over the main board. "It's not a standard Peacekeeper code, sir," Crane reported as they came up to him. "Also doesn't appear to be any of the ones the nonhumans use. We're still sectoring for the other end—haven't found it yet."

"Could it be an industrial code?" Takara asked.

Crane shrugged. "I suppose so. Who on Dorcas would bother with anything like that?"

"Dr. Melinda Cavanagh, that's who," Holloway said. "Three days' leave time says the other end is in or near that fueler that just came down."

The operator fiddled with his board. "I'll be damned," he muttered. "You're right, sir, it is."

"Want me to get some people over there?" Takara asked.

"Transmission's ended, sir," the operator said before Holloway could answer. "Wait a minute. The Counterpunch is hailing us now."

"Put it on speaker," Holloway ordered. "Unidentified Counterpunch fighter, this is Dorcas Control. Please identify yourselves."

"Dorcas Control, this is Wing Commander Adam Quinn," a voice with distinct military crispness said. "Requesting permission to land."

"Commander, this is Lieutenant Colonel Holloway," Holloway said. "May I have your assignment authorization number, please?"

"I'm not being assigned to your garrison, Colonel," Quinn said. "I'm just passing through."

"Sorry to hear that," Holloway said. "We could certainly use you. I'd like the number anyway."

There was a short pause. "It's six seven four two four nine five five," Quinn said. "MSC code Foxtrot Lima Victor Victor."

"Thank you, Commander," Holloway said. "Landing control will give you instructions for vector insertion. I'd like you to report to my office when you get down."

"Certainly, Colonel. Thank you."

"Carry on, Sergeant," Holloway nodded to Crane. "Fuji, a word with you, please."

They stepped over to an unoccupied corner of the room. "What do you think?" Holloway asked.

Takara shrugged. "The authorization code sounded legitimate enough."

"It had the right number of numbers and letters, anyway," Holloway said. "That's about all we can tell from here."

Takara looked back across the room. "Well, we can check up right now on Wing Commander Quinn," he pointed out. "He should be listed in the general personnel file."

"If not, I certainly want to meet this civilian who can fly a Copperhead fighter," Holloway said. "Yes, go ahead and check him out." He pursed his lips. "And while you're at it, I want anything and everything you can find on Dr. Melinda Cavanagh."

Takara frowned. "I thought she said she was associated with CavTronics Industries."

"That's what she said, yes. I want to find out if it's true."

Crane looked up. "All set, Colonel," he said. "They should be down in about forty-five minutes. Shall I arrange billeting?"

"Not yet," Holloway said. "Let's see if he's made

other arrangements. Did you get the name of Quinn's tail?"

"Ah—" Crane blinked. "No, actually, I didn't. He didn't offer, and I didn't think to ask. Shall I call him back?"

"Don't bother," Holloway shook his head. "I'd lay long odds that it's Dr. Cavanagh's brother Aric. Throw his name into the hopper, too, Fuji, while you're at it."

"I'll just go ahead and run the whole family," Takara said. "It'll probably save time in the long run."

"Thanks," Holloway said, throwing the other a wry smile. "Get that started, and then report back to my office. I still want to see what you've got in mind for that gap in the east wall."

The office door slid open with its usual gentle hiss; and with a jerk Holloway snapped upright in his chair. "Yes?"

"Sorry, Cass," Takara apologized from the doorway. "I didn't realize you were asleep."

"Didn't realize it myself," Holloway admitted, rubbing at his eyes and glancing at his watch. Near as he could figure, he'd lost about half an hour. Minor loss of time, major loss of pride. "What are you doing here?" he asked the other. "You're supposed to be off duty."

"Like you, you mean?" Takara said pointedly as he stepped into the room. "Still working on that gap?"

"Still banging my head against it, anyway," Holloway said, looking over the multiple aerial views he'd mapped out on his display. "We can't just let it sit there wide open like that, Fuji. It's an open invitation for high-speed fighter-strafing attacks."

"I'd suggest sleeping on it," Takara said with a straight face. "Sorry; you've already tried that, haven't you?"

"That's cute," Holloway growled. "You have a reason to be here insulting your commanding officer instead of in your quarters where you belong?"

"Two things," Takara said, pulling over a chair and sitting down. "We got a skitter in from Edo about half an hour ago. Apparently, we're finally going to get ourselves a fleet."

"About time," Holloway said. "It's only been, what, two weeks since they promised it to us? When's it supposed to arrive?"

"It'll be another three or four days. I gather they're still in the process of putting it together."

"Terrific," Holloway said. "What are we getting, converted barges?"

"They didn't specify," Takara said. "I doubt we'll rate higher than a Vega-class, though. Maybe a Rigel, if they're feeling really generous that day."

"They won't be," Holloway sighed. "Not with every planet in Lyra and Pegasus Sectors screaming for more protection. The Conquerors *would* pick the most spread-out Commonwealth sectors to come at."

"Maybe on purpose." Takara held up a card. "And here's the other bit of news. Hobson finally got around to pulling that stuff together on Commander Quinn and the Cavanagh family. If you're still interested."

"I don't have much choice," Holloway grumbled, taking the card. "They're here, they're temporarily my responsibility . . . and I'll bet money they're up to something improper."

Takara shrugged. "The problem is figuring out what that is."

Holloway slapped the card into his display, stifling a curse. There was a vicious and powerful alien race out there gathering like storm clouds to launch an attack on the Commonwealth. Even now an assault force could be driving toward Dorcas. He had barely three hundred trained military personnel to help him prepare for that attack, plus twenty-five thousand civilians his troops would have to move on two hours' notice and ultimately wind up playing nursemaid to. That was if they were lucky. The last thing he had time for was whatever this stupid game was the Cavanaghs were playing. "They still loading that fueler out there?"

"They were when I came across the quad," Takara said. "Had some kind of canvac barrier rigged up on one side of it, too. Did Quinn happen to say anything about that when you two had your little talk?"

"Quinn didn't say much of *anything* when we had our little talk," Holloway said. "Maybe they're resealing some seams." He glanced over the material Hobson had put together—

And paused. Read it more carefully . . . "You look at any of this?" he asked Takara.

"Haven't had a chance. Interesting?"

"You could say so, yes. Aric and Melinda's daddy is Lord Stewart Cavanagh, former NorCoord Parlimin from Grampians on Avon. That name strike any bells?"

"It does indeed," Takara said slowly. "Wasn't he the one who took on the whole Copperhead command structure a few years back? Got their rear ends in hot water with Parliament?"

"Try dipped them in molten lead," Holloway said. "He's the one who pushed through the hearings that concluded they were letting people into the Copperheads who weren't even close to being emotionally fit for the job." He cocked an eyebrow. "Want to take a stab at who his keystone witness was?"

Takara's eyes narrowed. "Don't tell me. Wing Commander Adam Quinn."

"You got it," Holloway nodded. "We've got us a celebrity out there, Fuji."

"Terrific," Takara said sourly. "You know, Cass, I'm

starting to think that maybe we ought to check up on
Dr. Cavanagh's credentials, after all."

"I'd like nothing better," Holloway said. "Unfortunately, I have a strong suspicion that it would turn out
to be a waste of time. Figure eighteen hours to Earth by
skitter, another hour or two to get word to Admiral
Rudzinski and find out he's never heard of Melinda Cavanagh or any top-secret Peacekeeper mission, then another eighteen hours to get back here." He waved in
the general direction of the landing field. "You really
think it's going to take them another thirty-seven hours
to load that fueler and grab themselves some atmosphere?"

"Not at the rate they're going," Takara agreed. "But
unless you want to lock up the whole bunch of them on
general suspicion, I don't see what we can do about it.
Of course, once they're gone they're someone else's responsibility."

"That's one way to look at it," Holloway said. "Not
going to earn you any commendations, though. But I
don't see any alternatives myself."

He stopped suddenly. "Yes, I do," he said. "Yes, of
course I do."

"What?"

Holloway favored him with a tight smile. "Melinda
Cavanagh has no documentation, and we'd have to go
to Earth to check up on her story. Obviously, they've
already thought of that. What they may *not* have
thought of is the fact that she's no longer the only
player in the game. Enter Wing Commander Quinn
. . . and he *does* have documentation. An official
Peacekeeper authorization number."

Slowly, Takara matched Holloway's smile. "Which will
be on update file at any of a number of places. Such as
the Peacekeeper base on Edo."

"Which is only a seventeen-hour round trip," Holloway nodded, pulling his plate over and punching up an order. "It's worth taking a shot at. Go alert the crew— I'll have the order cut by the time they're ready to lift."

"Right," Takara said, heading for the door.

"And then hit the sack," Holloway added. "We've got a busy day tomorrow."

"There's another kind?" Takara paused at the doorway. "What do you think they're up to, anyway? Quinn and the Cavanaghs?"

"No idea," Holloway said, gesturing at the display. "But there's one other interesting point here I didn't mention. Aric and Melinda have another brother—had another brother—name of Pheylan. Until recently commander of the Peacekeeper ship *Kinshasa.*"

"The *Kinshasa,* huh?" Takara said thoughtfully. "Yes. That could explain all this."

Holloway frowned at him. "Really? How?"

"No idea," Takara shrugged. "I'm just saying it *could* explain it."

"Thanks," Holloway said dryly. "You're so helpful sometimes. I just hope to God that whatever this is, it's something minor. Something we can just lock them up for."

Takara's lip twitched. "I hadn't thought about that. But we are officially a war zone now, aren't we?"

"That we are," Holloway nodded. "With all the peripheral fun stuff that comes along with it."

"Like summary trials."

"And summary executions."

Takara exhaled noisily. "You're right," he said. "Let's hope real hard it's something minor."

13 The three Zhirrzh interrogators didn't come back to see Pheylan the day after that first trip outside his prison. Nor did they come the day after, or the day after that. On the fourth day they finally reappeared.

With Svv-selic no longer in charge.

It was obvious from the moment they entered the outer room through their private door. Svv-selic had always been the one in the middle of the group whenever they all stood or walked together, with Thrr-gilag and Nzz-oonaz flanking him and generally keeping their mouths shut. This time, it was Thrr-gilag, the short one, who held center position as they walked over to the glass wall of his cell.

And it was Thrr-gilag who spoke. "Good day, Cavvana," he said. "You well?"

"Reasonably well," Pheylan replied, wondering if he should comment on Thrr-gilag's new status and deciding it was probably best to ignore it. "I could use some sunlight, though. It's been a long time since I was outside."

For a moment Thrr-gilag seemed to study him. "That

your doing," he said. "You must not go where forbidden."

"I didn't mean to do anything wrong," Pheylan assured him. Just one more bit of evidence, if he'd needed it, that that white pyramid thing out there was extremely important to these people. Apparently, Svv-selic had been demoted because of it. "We humans are curious, that's all."

"So you said," Thrr-gilag said. "Do you want go outside?"

Pheylan looked at Nzz-oonaz, standing near the dog flap with the obedience suit across one arm. "Yes, I do," he said cautiously. There was something about the way they were all just standing there that he didn't care for.

"We have question," Thrr-gilag said. "You answer question, you go outside."

So they were finally getting around to the inevitable interrogation. "Let me go outside first," Pheylan said. "Then I'll answer your questions."

"Question first," Thrr-gilag said. "If you refuse, no go outside."

Pheylan pursed his lips. "Compromise," he suggested. "I'll answer your questions while we're outside."

For a moment Thrr-gilag stood there, apparently considering the offer. Pheylan held his gaze, mentally crossing his fingers. The more he could get them to back down—on anything—the more potentially useful precedents he would have set for future negotiations.

And to his mild surprise Thrr-gilag did indeed back down. "You answer question outside," he agreed. "If not, you not go outside again."

"All right," Pheylan nodded. "But remember that if you do that, I'll die."

"You not die," Thrr-gilag said. "We not allow." He gestured, and Nzz-oonaz knelt down and stuffed the obedience suit through the dog flap.

They watched as Pheylan changed clothes. "Do as we say," Thrr-gilag warned as he opened the cell door. "Else punish again."

The weather outside wasn't nearly as pleasant this time as it had been four days earlier. The sky was completely covered with gloomy bands of gray and dirty-white clouds, and a moderate increase in the earlier cool temperatures was more than offset by the gusty winds that swept restlessly across the landing area, kicking up clouds of red dust. "This isn't going to help me very much," Pheylan warned Thrr-gilag. "Not much sunlight getting through those clouds."

"Tomorrow come back outside," Thrr-gilag said. "Unless you refuse answer question."

"Ah," Pheylan said, grimacing to himself. So that was why Thrr-gilag had backed down on the question of an open-air interrogation. He'd seen the weather and had known full well that they weren't giving anything away for free. "Fine," he grunted. "Let's hear these questions."

"One question only," Thrr-gilag said. "Tell everything about weapon CIRCE."

Pheylan's stomach tightened into a hard knot. So there it was: the dark fear that had been lurking at the back of his mind ever since he'd first realized that Commodore Dyami's personal computer had been captured intact.

The Zhirrzh knew about CIRCE.

"I don't understand," he stalled. "What do you mean?"

"CIRCE," Thrr-gilag repeated. "Do you refuse tell?"

Pheylan looked over at the white pyramid and its three surrounding domes, trying to figure out what the hell he was supposed to do now. The survival of humanity might well hinge on NorCoord's ability to use CIRCE against the Zhirrzh and those invulnerable warships of theirs. The more the Zhirrzh knew about the weapon, the better their chances of coming up with a defense against it.

But he'd made a deal with Thrr-gilag. If he reneged on that promise, he'd lose any chance of making future bargains. Besides which, there was probably nothing he could tell them that they hadn't already gotten from Dyami's computer. "No, I didn't mean that," he assured Thrr-gilag. "I was trying to ask what you wanted to know. I don't really know anything about CIRCE except its history."

From behind Thrr-gilag, Svv-selic muttered something in their own language. "You command human spacecraft," Thrr-gilag pointed out. "You know human weapons."

Pheylan shrugged. "Commanding a ship doesn't have anything to do with it," he said, starting to walk toward the woods behind the base. "Not with CIRCE."

"But CIRCE is human weapon," Thrr-gilag persisted, taking a couple of quick steps to catch up to him.

Pheylan glanced at him . . . and looked back again. Close up, he could see for the first time that there was a small button the same color as Zhirrzh skin nestled beneath a shallow horizontal ridge on the side of Thrr-gilag's head. It was hard to tell for sure, but it looked as if there were four thin appendages extending from the button into the four parallel slits curving across the skin beneath the ridge. "What's that thing?" he asked, pointing to it.

"This?" Thrr-gilag asked, his tongue snaking out around the side of his head to point at the button. Pheylan twitched his hand back a little; he'd almost forgotten Zhirrzh tongues could do that. "It connect to interpreter."

"To an interpreter?" Pheylan repeated. "You mean a mechanical interpreter? A computer?"

"Yes."

"But I thought . . . never mind."

"Explain."

"I said never mind," Pheylan said, starting to turn away.

Thrr-gilag's hand snaked out, its three fingers and two thumbs wrapping around Pheylan's upper arm. "Explain," he demanded.

Pheylan looked at the audio link again, threw a quick glance over his shoulder at Svv-selic and Nzz-oonaz. Now that he knew what to look for, he could see that each of them was wearing one, as well.

So then what was that scar all of them had at the base of their skulls? The scar he'd assumed was the mark of a Copperhead-type Mindlink implant?

Thrr-gilag was still waiting. "I assumed you were connected to a computer translator in a more permanent way," Pheylan told him. "These scars back here." He reached out toward the back of Thrr-gilag's head—

He didn't fall flat on his face this time, but only because he was more or less balanced when Nzz-oonaz triggered the magnets in his obedience suit. His right elbow did crack painfully against his rib cage, however, as his arms were yanked to his sides. "Hey!" he snapped, bending violently back and forth at the waist as he fought to keep his balance. "I was just trying to point to it."

Thrr-gilag said something, and the magnets shut off. "Explain word 'scars,' " Thrr-gilag said.

"Scars are marks of surgery," Pheylan told him, throwing a glare at Nzz-oonaz as he rubbed his elbow. "Cutting into someone's body to take something out or put something in. All three of you have them, right at the base of your skulls." He started to point, changed his mind, and indicated the spot on the back of his own neck. "Right here."

For a long moment the three Zhirrzh just looked at him, their nonhuman faces unreadable. Nzz-oonaz muttered something to Thrr-gilag, who replied in the same tone. Svv-selic joined in, and for a minute they held a quiet three-way discussion. Pheylan waited, blinking against the dusty wind blowing across his face and surveying the landscape around them. The last time they'd been out here, he'd spotted what had seemed to be a path leading back into the woods from a corner of the building where his cell was located. He was hoping today to get a closer look at that area.

"Humans not have *fsss* organ?"

Pheylan shifted his attention back to Thrr-gilag. "What?"

"Scar mark of *fsss* organ," Thrr-gilag said. "Humans have here?" His tongue darted out to point to the right side of Pheylan's abdomen.

Pheylan frowned. There was nothing noteworthy there except the small keyhole mark where he'd had his appendix removed when he was ten.

A mark which, now that he thought about it, the Zhirrzh examiners had paid an unusual amount of attention to during that long physical exam his first day here. "I don't know," he told Thrr-gilag. "We don't have the same names for organs that you do. What does a *fsss* organ do?"

Svv-selic growled something, his tongue flicking restlessly in and out of his mouth. Thrr-gilag replied—reluctantly, Pheylan thought—and then turned back to Pheylan. "Not proper subject," Thrr-gilag said. "You tell about CIRCE."

"There's not much more to tell," Pheylan said. So Thrr-gilag was changing the subject; and in a suspiciously abrupt way. Was this *fsss* thing something taboo to discuss in polite conversation? Or was it something they didn't want humans to know about? Either way, one more bit of information to tuck away for future reference. "The name CIRCE is supposed to be an acronym—that means it's short for the full name of Collimated Ion Resonance Cannon, Ephemeral. Everything else I know is just the history that's in the public record. Only a few humans know what CIRCE really is or how it works."

"Tell history."

Pheylan took a deep breath, an unexpected shiver running up his back. They must have shown the cadets that old watchship recording fifty times back at the academy . . . and it had been as eerie the fiftieth time as it had the first. "It was an ambush," he told Thrrgilag. "Five top-of-the-line Pawolian warships were hanging off Celadon system's innermost planet, hiding in the umbra—the shadow. They headed straight out toward the three NorCoord ships, none of which was more than half the size of theirs. They launched their fighters ahead of them, we launched ours, and they had at it."

"You see?"

Pheylan shook his head. "This was thirty-seven years ago. I wasn't even born yet. I've just seen the record."

"Tell more."

"There's not much more to tell," Pheylan said. "The fighters met between the converging warship lines, and the battle was getting started when the Pawoles' tactical structure suddenly just collapsed. They started retreating, with the NorCoord fighters in pursuit . . . and on the record you can see that the warships behind them have started drifting out of formation. CIRCE had killed everyone aboard."

There was a moment of silence, followed by another three-way conference. Pheylan kept walking, watching the forest off to his left. It hadn't been just a trick of angle and lighting: there was a path there, all right.

More or less straight, heading back into the trees and underbrush behind the complex. Altering his direction a few degrees, he headed toward it.

The conference behind him ended. "How?" Thrr-gilag asked.

"How what? How did CIRCE kill them?" Pheylan shook his head. "Radiation burns of some kind. Beyond that I haven't the foggiest."

Thrr-gilag seemed to consider that. Or else was listening to their computer floundering over the word "foggiest." "Why CIRCE not used in attack against Zhirrzh?" he asked at last.

Pheylan glared into his alien face. "Get your facts straight, Zhirrzh. We didn't attack first. You did."

"Not true," Thrr-gilag said. "Commanders and Elders say. Human ships attack first."

"Were you there?" Pheylan demanded. "You personally?"

Thrr-gilag's tongue flicked out a couple of times. "No. Kee'rr clan Elder speak—"

"I *was* there," Pheylan cut him off. "And I don't care what your Elders or your commanders or anyone else tells you. Your ships fired first."

He turned his back on the Zhirrzh, the faces of his murdered crew flickering across his vision. Rico, Hauver, Meyers, Chen Ki—

"You not speak words against Elders," Svv-selic admonished him. "Too'rr clan Elder say same."

"As say Flii'rr clan Elder," Nzz-oonaz chimed in.

"I don't care what your Elders say—"

"No more!" Svv-selic snarled, taking a step toward him. "You speak no more words against Elders. Or punish."

Pheylan felt his lip twist. So that was how it worked here. The official line was that the *Jutland* task force had been the aggressor, and that was how it was going to be. And Svv-selic and Nzz-oonaz were going to fall dutifully into line like loyal party functionaries. Unwilling to question the supreme Zhirrzh authority, or even to listen to anything that might conflict with the official version of the truth. Their minds already made up.

Absolute control, coupled with absolute subservience . . . and yet, even as the contempt bubbled in Pheylan's throat, he recognized that here, finally, was a chink in the Zhirrzh armor plate. A potentially devastating chink. Human history had demonstrated time and again the basic instability of autocratic, information-manipulating governments, from Nazi Germany to the Soviet Empire to the Chinese Domination to Celadon's Quadarch regime. All it took was the right spark to set it off.

The truth that their government was lying in order to justify a war could be that spark. And with a sudden surge of adrenaline, Pheylan realized that the necessary tinder might be standing right there in front of him.

Thrr-gilag hadn't joined in the quick chorus of reproach that had come from the other two Zhirrzh. On the contrary, he was being noticeably quiet. "I was there," Pheylan repeated, looking directly at him. "I know what happened."

"You not speak against Elders," Thrr-gilag said. But to Pheylan's ears the words sounded hesitant and unsure, and there'd been just a slight pause before he said them. "Not proper subject. Tell why CIRCE not used against Zhirrzh."

Pheylan turned away and started walking toward the forest path again. "CIRCE isn't standard-issue equipment aboard human ships," he said. "Contrary to what your leaders have probably told you, we humans don't kill just for the hell of it. Only when it's absolutely necessary."

"CIRCE used against others."

"It was used against the Pawoles." Pheylan threw them a grim smile. "But, then, the Pawoles attacked first."

They had reached the edge of the forest before Thrr-gilag spoke again. "How often CIRCE used?"

"Just that one time," Pheylan said. "The Pawoles were smart enough to capitulate before we had to use it again." He looked Thrr-gilag straight in those three-pupiled eyes. "Other nonhumans we locked horns with were smart enough not to make us use it at all."

He turned back to the forest. "Looks like a path here," he commented, gesturing to it. "Where does it lead?"

"Not go there," Thrr-gilag said.

"I won't," Pheylan assured him, taking another step toward it. The feathery grasslike ground-cover plants were worn away from the center of the path, he could see now, exposing the familiar reddish dirt and mixed with bits of leaves and twigs.

And a handful of flat, finger-sized gray stones.

"I just wanted to know where it went," he continued as he took another step toward the path. His knowledge of geology ranked near the bottom of his expertise list, but those stones sure looked like slivers of flint. With sharp edges . . .

"Not go there," Thrr-gilag insisted.

"Is more of the complex that direction?" Pheylan continued as if he hadn't spoken, taking another step. Eventually, Nzz-oonaz was going to wake up to the fact that he wasn't stopping and trigger the obedience suit. He had to be in position in front of those stones before that happened. "Will you be putting a real road through to it?" he added over his shoulder. One more step . . . two . . . three . . .

"Kasar!" Thrr-gilag called.

Even braced and ready for it, the obedience suit still packed a terrific wallop. Arms glued to his sides, Pheylan winced as he toppled helplessly over to slam chest first to the ground. "Hey, you didn't need to do that," he snapped indignantly, twisting his head around to glare at the three Zhirrzh. "I wasn't going to go in there."

"You did not stop," Thrr-gilag said.

"You didn't tell me to," Pheylan countered. They were moving toward him; but from their angle, for another second or two, his left hand would be partially hidden from their view. Carefully, keeping the movements as inconspicuous as possible, he searched across the ground with his fingers. "All you said was not to go in there. I didn't."

Thrr-gilag paused, his face twisting slightly in something that might have been a moment of uncertainty . . . and as the alien stood there, Pheylan's fingers found what they'd been looking for. Easing the stone beneath his palm, he closed his hand halfway around it.

"Say not go there," Thrr-gilag said. "Mean you stop."

"I'll try to remember that for the next time," Pheylan growled. "Can I get up now?"

Thrr-gilag made a gesture. Nzz-oonaz lifted the black trigger gadget and pointed it at Pheylan, and the magnets shut off. "Thank you," Pheylan said, pulling himself to his feet and rubbing his elbow where it had cracked into his ribs again. Nzz-oonaz had pointed the trigger at him, just as he had the first time they had used the suit. Did that mean the trigger worked with a directional signal, like infrared or a tight sonic, instead of radio? "Some kind of warning might be nice in the future," he added, rubbing his chin where the ground-cover plants had scratched it and then tugging his jumpsuit collar open another couple of centimeters.

Under cover of the motion he dropped the stone into the neck of the suit.

"You go back inside now," Thrr-gilag said.

Pheylan looked back along the path, cutting along the shrubbery to disappear among the trees. Whatever was down there, he couldn't see it. Probably nothing more useful than the Zhirrzh equivalent of an outhouse, anyway. "Suits me," he told Thrr-gilag. "Let's go in."

It took some doing to sneak the stone out of the obedience suit as he undressed, what with all three Zhirrzh watching him like misshapen hawks. But he managed it, palming the stone in his left hand as he pushed the suit back out through the dog flap, and then smuggling it into the shower with him.

The ventilation system, operating through a series of small slits in the ceiling, was pretty good; but while Pheylan had never been able to steam up the cell's outer glass wall, the open-topped shower stall itself was another matter. He got the hot water going . . . and under the temporary cover he examined his new prize.

It was a small treasure, as treasures went, perhaps five centimeters long and three wide. It was thin, too, no more than three millimeters thick, and while the edges weren't pleasant for human fingers to handle, they were a long way from being sharp enough to cut either obedience-suit material or Zhirrzh skin.

Still, it was something; and just having a solid, potentially dangerous object in his hand again was an immense boost to his morale. If he could successfully hide it, and then find a way to sharpen one of the edges without his captors catching on, it would open up a whole range of new options for him.

What those options were, he wasn't exactly sure yet. But he'd think of something.

He washed and got out of the shower, rubbing vigorously at his hair with the stone again concealed in one hand. He still wasn't sure why he was getting away so easily with this, but the more he thought about it, the more he realized that the design of the Zhirrzh hand probably didn't allow this kind of undetectable palming. His original plan had been to conceal it in his jumpsuit boot, snuggled up beneath his toes, but the difficulty of retrieving it quickly had made him change his mind. Sitting on his bed as he pulled on his jumpsuit, he slid the right-most of the under-bed storage drawers open a centimeter and dropped the stone inside, sliding it down between the drawer itself and the crumpled survival pack that filled most of the space.

He spent the rest of the day in his by-now-familiar routine, dividing his time between isometric exercises, his memorization of the outside room, and the continual contemplation of how he might escape this place. Several times he found himself wanting to ease the drawer open and touch the stone, to feel its edges and reassure himself that it was still there. But he resisted the temptation. He'd already noticed that their surveillance of him seemed to ease up after he turned in for the night. That would be the proper moment to move the stone to a more permanent hiding place.

The moment never came. He was lying on his bed, drowsily watching the Zhirrzh techs puttering around, when suddenly the outer door flew open and six of the aliens stormed in and headed straight for his cell. Two of the Zhirrzh were carrying the same long gray sticks he'd seen earlier in the hands of the pyramid guards on his first trip outside; two others were holding stubby flashlight-sized devices. The last two appeared to be unarmed.

"What's going on?" Pheylan demanded as they took up military-precise positions around his cell, the two unencumbered Zhirrzh moving to the door, the other four flanking them on either side. All four weapons, Pheylan noted uneasily, were pointed straight at his face through the glass . . . and up close, those long sticks looked even nastier than they did at a distance. "What's going on?" he asked again, less aggressively this time. Unlike the projectile and missile weapons used by the Peacekeepers, the Zhirrzh ships had used high-energy lasers. If the sticks and flashlights pointed at him were scaled-down versions of those, they could burn him to ash right through the cell wall. Possibly one reason they'd made it out of glass in the first place.

"You stand away," a voice came from behind him.

Pheylan turned. Thrr-gilag was standing there, his tongue flicking in and out of his mouth, the corkscrewing tail going at double-time rate. "What?" he asked the Zhirrzh.

"You stand away," Thrr-gilag repeated. His tongue stiffened to point across the cell at the shower. "Stand there."

Wordlessly, Pheylan stood up and walked over to the shower, the weapons tracking him the whole way. The outer door swung open and the two unarmed Zhirrzh stepped inside. One stood beside the open door as the other walked to Pheylan's bed. Pulling open the drawer, he pushed the survival pack out of his way and retrieved the stone.

Pheylan looked at Thrr-gilag. "Not proper," the Zhirrzh said. "Not keep."

"I see," Pheylan said, the words coming out mechanically through a dry mouth. So he'd been wrong. All the cleverness, all the subterfuge—all wasted. They'd known about the stone, probably from the second he picked it up.

No. That was wrong. It had been sitting in that drawer for a good twelve hours now. If they'd known about it from the beginning, they would surely have taken it away from him before now.

He looked back at the two Zhirrzh as they stepped back through the door and swung it shut. And yet, they'd known where it was. Exactly where it was, in fact—that Zhirrzh had gone straight for it, without any hesitation or groping around. And from the way they'd burst in here like that, he would swear that they'd just that moment found out about it.

So how?

The first Zhirrzh circled around the cell to where Thrr-gilag was still standing, and for a minute they conversed quietly between themselves, turning the stone over in their fingers as they examined it. Pheylan watched them, possibilities swirling through his mind like leaves in an aircar backwash. They were slightly telepathic, and they'd only just figured out that he had the stone. They were very telepathic, but only some of them, and the one with the power had just gotten into town that night. They'd just completed some nightly scan of his cell, a scan sensitive enough to pick up a five-cubic-centimeter chunk of flint and place it precisely in the proper corner of the proper drawer. They had a direct pipeline to God, and God didn't want Pheylan leaving just yet.

Or more likely, they'd known about it all along and had just been playing with him. Letting him have twelve hours of false confidence and hoping like blazes that he didn't plan to use the stone before they could get it away from him.

Thrr-gilag looked up at him. "Not proper," he said again. "Tomorrow not go outside."

"That's not fair," Pheylan protested, knowing full well that argument was useless but also knowing that he had to try. "You never said something like this wasn't allowed. Besides, I need to go out. I need the sunlight."

"You punish," Thrr-gilag said. "Not do again."

He turned away and strode back toward his private door. On the other side of the cell, the Zhirrzh commander collected his troops and led them out the other way. The techs in the outer room, the incident over, went back to their tasks.

Slowly, feeling numb, Pheylan walked back to his bed. All right. He'd lost the stone; but then, realistically, he shouldn't have really expected to get away with it in the first place. He'd lost the stone, but in its place he had another bit of information to take back to the Commonwealth when he escaped.

Lying back down again, he closed his eyes. And tried to figure out just what that bit of information was.

14

"Lord Cavanagh?"

Cavanagh awoke with a start, to find a shadowy figure standing beside his bed in the darkened room, gently shaking his shoulder. "Who's there?" he croaked through a sleep-dried mouth.

"It's Kolchin, sir," the figure said quietly. "We've got visitors."

"Really." With some difficulty Cavanagh focused on the bedside clock. The glowing numbers read 4:37. "Bit early for casual conversation, isn't it?"

"There's nothing casual about this group," Kolchin said. "They're an assistant liaison and three heavies from the Commonwealth consulate over on Mra-ect."

"From Mra-ect, eh?" Cavanagh said, sitting up and reaching for his robe. "Nine light-years, just to see us. How flattering. What do they want?"

"I'm not exactly sure," Kolchin said. "But I think they're after Fibbit."

Cavanagh paused halfway into his robe. "Fibbit? What on Earth for?"

"No idea," Kolchin said. "They keep skating around the issue—say they want to talk to you personally. But they keep looking around like they're hunting for something."

"What do you mean, looking around?" Cavanagh asked, getting his robe in place and pulling on his house shoes. "They're not already in, are they?"

"No, Hill's got them pinned in the foyer," Kolchin assured him. "But they keep trying to look through the privacy glass into the hallway and social room. Seemed pretty annoyed I wouldn't let them in any farther."

"Let them be annoyed," Cavanagh grunted. At four-thirty in the morning he was capable of considerable annoyance himself. "Where is Fibbit, anyway?"

"Actually, I don't know," Kolchin admitted. "She was working on that threading you asked her to do for a couple of hours after you went to bed. But after that I sort of lost track of her. She didn't leave, and she's not in your room here. That's all I know."

"Probably asleep in a corner somewhere," Cavanagh said, giving his robe sash a final tug. "Let's go see what's going on."

The four visitors were visible only as vague shapes through the smoked privacy glass divider that separated the foyer from the rest of the suite, with Hill another vague shape facing them. "I'm Lord Cavanagh," Cavanagh said, coming around the divider into the foyer behind Hill. "What can I do for you?"

"I'm sorry to bother you, Lord Cavanagh," a burly middle-aged man in the middle of the group said, taking a short step forward. He looked tired and grumpy, but not particularly sorry. "I'm Assistant Commonwealth Liaison Petr Bronski." His eyes flicked over Cavanagh's shoulder. "May we come in?"

"State your business and I'll consider it," Cavanagh said.

One of the young men flanking Bronski muttered something under his breath and stepped forward to join his boss. Hill shifted position in response to block his path, and out of the corner of his eye Cavanagh saw Kolchin move up a pace as well. All four of the visitors had a brittle, no-nonsense air about them, the sort of men the Commonwealth would naturally post to a former Yycroman colony world only recently awarded to the Mrachanis. Still, even at two-to-one odds, if they decided to get rough, Cavanagh's money was on Kolchin and Hill.

Maybe Bronski saw that, too. He lifted a hand; reluctantly, his subordinate stepped back again. "I'd advise cooperation, Lord Cavanagh," he said, pulling a wallet folder from his pocket. "I don't really need your permission to come in."

Cavanagh took the folder and opened it. Bronski's diplomatic ID was impressive, but here in Mrach territory it didn't carry much weight. The temporary Mrach government red card beside it, though, was something else again. "In that case, come in," he said, showing the red card to Kolchin as he stepped aside. "Hill, show these gentlemen to some seats."

"That won't be necessary," Bronski said, stepping in around the privacy glass. "All we want is the Sanduul, then we'll be on our way."

"The Sanduul?" Cavanagh echoed as Bronski's three men brushed past Hill and headed toward the social room.

"Yes, the Sanduul," Bronski said, falling into step behind his men. "Fibbit u something u something from somewhere on Ulu. You know who I mean."

"What do you want with her?"

Bronski reached the center of the social room and stopped. "Not that it's any of your business," he said, looking around, "but she's being deported."

"She was given a one-day extension."

"I guess it must have been revoked," Bronski said. "Where is she?"

Cavanagh looked around. The social room was furnished Mrach-style, with odd bits of furniture and hanging artwork scattered around, all of which focused attention and traffic toward the sunken lounge that took up a quarter of the room in the far corner. Long, narrow couches and soft contour chairs alternated around the rim of the lounge area, focusing attention still further onto the gently undulating glow of the fire sculpture in the corner itself. Leaning against one of the couches near the fire sculpture was the threading frame Fibbit had been working on. Fibbit herself was nowhere to be seen. "Are you sure they're deporting her?" he asked Bronski.

"I asked where she was, Cavanagh," Bronski said, ignoring the question as he walked over to the lounge and stepped down the two light-edged steps. His three men were already tromping down the hallway that led to the dinery and bedroom areas of the suite. Hill looked as if he was planning to stop them; Cavanagh caught his eye and shook his head. The Mrach government was big on authority, and a red card was the top of the food chain as far as non-Mrachanis went. Whatever they wanted with Fibbit, they wanted it pretty badly.

"What's this?" Bronski asked from the lounge.

Cavanagh turned to find him glaring down at the threading frame propped against the couch. "It's a threading I commissioned from Fibbit," he said.

Bronski peered over at him, looked back at the threading. "Doesn't look a thing like you. Is it yours or the Sanduul's?"

"Mine."

"Let's see the receipt."

"I don't have one yet."

"Then it's the Sanduul's," Bronski said with a brisk nod. "It'll go with her."

"Wait a minute," Cavanagh said, stepping over to the lounge as Bronski picked up the frame. "This isn't making any sense at all. Can't you at least tell me what's going on here?"

For a moment Bronski seemed to study him. "Sure, I'll tell you what's going on," he growled. "What's going on is that my chief hauled my rear end out of bed four hours ago with two items of news: one, that the Mrachanis were having trouble with a Sanduul who wouldn't leave Mra-mig; and two, that there was some human running around poking his nose where it didn't belong. We'll get to you soon enough; right now we'll just take the Sanduul. You going to turn her over to us, or not?"

"To be perfectly honest, I don't know where she is," Cavanagh said. "If she's not here, then she must have gone out after I went to bed."

Bronski snorted. "With those two sharp-eyed bodyguards of yours standing around?" he demanded, dropping the frame onto the couch. "Sure she did."

"My men have to sleep, too," Cavanagh countered, trying to remain patient. "Her things are still here—I'm sure she'll be back. And if you don't mind my saying so, this whole thing is a colossal waste of everyone's time and energy. I was going to take Fibbit off Mra-mig in the morning anyway."

"Maybe that's why she's disappeared," Bronski suggested acidly. "I know you ex-Parliament types don't like to believe it, but occasionally things do go on in this universe you don't know anything about." He shifted his attention past Cavanagh. "Well?"

Cavanagh turned to see the three men file back into the social room. There was no sign of Fibbit. "Not here," one of the men reported, stepping past the others to join Cavanagh and Bronski in the lounge. "I think he's right—she must have slipped out while everyone was sleeping. Pretty sloppy, if you ask me." He turned his head to squint down at the threading on the couch. "Who's this guy, Cavanagh?"

"Just someone Fibbit saw recently," Cavanagh told him. "Her other threading of the man was ruined at the spaceport. I suggested she might want to reproduce it while her memory of his face was still fresh."

"Really." The man looked hard at Cavanagh, then back at the threading. "Saw him here in Mig-Ka City, you say?"

"I didn't say," Cavanagh said. "As it happens, she did. Do you recognize him, Mr., ah . . . ?"

"Lee," the other supplied. "Taurin Lee."

"Do you recognize him, Mr. Lee?" Cavanagh repeated.

Lee was studying the threading, his forehead wrinkled in thought. "Not at the moment," he said. "But that can be remedied." He looked at Bronski. "I presume we're taking this with us."

Bronski opened his mouth to answer . . . and stopped as, across the room, the doorbell chimed.

For a moment everyone froze. Cavanagh recovered first, throwing a glance at Kolchin. The other nodded fractionally and started for the door.

The motion seemed to unfreeze the others. "Hold it, bodyguard," Lee snapped, dropping the threading and darting across the social room to catch up. Bronski's other two men were moving now, too, with Hill close behind them. Grimacing, Cavanagh joined the parade, wishing Fibbit's timing could have been a little better.

And again reminding himself that none of this was any of his business. Lee and Kolchin reached the edge of the privacy glass together and circled around it, and there was a half-felt puff of air as the door opened.

Cavanagh had expected either a shout of triumph
from Lee or a squawk of surprise from Fibbit. But there
was only the muffled sound of a quiet voice.

He reached the privacy glass just as Kolchin reappeared at the edge. "It's a Mrachani, sir," he said. "He
says he needs to talk to you."

Something about Fibbit? "Ask him to step in."

Kolchin turned to the door and nodded, taking a step
back to let the Mrachani past.

As with most nonhumans, Mrach faces were a bit
tricky for humans to tell apart, but Cavanagh was
pretty sure this wasn't anyone they'd spoken to at either the Information Agency or at the spaceport.
"Which is Lord Cavanagh?" the Mrachani asked, easing
somewhat uncertainly through the crowd around him.

"I am," Cavanagh identified himself. "And you
are . . . ?"

The Mrachani's body hair flattened. "No names," he
hissed. "And only a little time. I bear a private message
from my superior. He has learned of your search and is
willing to help."

Cavanagh felt his heartbeat speed up. So there *was*
something more to those legends. "You have information about the Conquerors?" he asked.

Bronski threw a sharp look at him, but the Mrachani
seemed merely taken aback. "Conquerors? No. The human. The one the Sanduul threaded. The one you have
been seeking. You will find him among the Yycromae in
the Northern Wooded Steppes of the planet Phormbi."

The hairs on the back of Cavanagh's neck stiffened.
"What's he doing there? Is he in trouble?"

"I can say no more," the Mrachani hissed, backing
toward the edge of the privacy glass. "I must go, lest I
am discovered by the others. Seek well."

He scuttled back around the privacy glass, his silhouette crossing quickly and disappearing out the door.

"Interesting," Bronski said as the silhouette that was Lee closed the door behind their departing visitor. "You still want to claim this is just some random person your Sanduul threaded, Lord Cavanagh?"

"I never said it was a random person," Cavanagh said. "I said I didn't know who he was. I still don't."

"Sure," Bronski said, hooking a thumb back toward the social room. "Garcia, go get that threading."

"Wait a minute," Cavanagh said as one of Bronski's men headed back. "That threading is my property. You have no right to take it."

"You got a receipt?"

"I don't need one," Cavanagh said. "Fibbit is currently in my employ. As long as she's not present, Mrach law says all her property is legally mine."

Bronski snorted. "Nice try. But you're not a Mrachani."

"According to that I am," Cavanagh said, pointing to Bronski's pocket. "You're using a red card. That implicitly puts me under Mrach law."

Bronski's eyes narrowed. Apparently, that wasn't something that had occurred to him before. "That's ridiculous."

"Not at all," Cavanagh said. "You're operating under Mrach law, and Mrach law is very serious on the subject of property seizure. Unless you choose to put me under arrest, my property and I stay right here."

"So maybe I should arrest you," Bronski shot back.

"Unfortunately, you can't," Lee said quietly, coming back around the privacy glass. "We have no charges sufficient to warrant such an action. Not yet, anyway."

"How about harboring a fugitive?" Bronski demanded.

"The Sanduul isn't listed as a fugitive," Lee said, eyeing Cavanagh coldly. "Besides the obvious problem that she's not here."

Bronski swore under his breath. "That's typical," he growled. "Really typical. About the only thing you NorCoord Parliament types churn out more than helpful advice is paper turning that advice into law. Fine. You keep the threading, Cavanagh, and I hope you strangle yourself on it. Garcia, make a recording of the damn thing and let's get the hell out of here."

"But don't think this is more than a temporary respite," Lee warned. "At the moment, we're limited; but that's not going to last. The minute you leave Mrach space, you'll be under Commonwealth authority again."

Cavanagh sent him a brittle smile. "If that's supposed to frighten me, Mr. Lee, it doesn't. I'm well equipped to deal with Commonwealth authority."

"Are you?" Lee countered. "Perhaps. But perhaps not. You've had a very cozy ride on the NorCoord government, Lord Cavanagh, one that has lasted far longer than it should have. But all rides eventually come to an end . . . and while NorCoord is a very useful friend, you'll find we can also be a highly dangerous enemy. I suggest you think long and hard about that before you decide to take us on."

"I'll keep that in mind," Cavanagh promised.

Garcia rejoined them. "Got it from three different angles, sir," he told Bronski. "Want me to record anything else?"

"No, that'll do for now," Bronski said. "We can always come back later. I trust you're not planning to go anywhere, Cavanagh?"

"Just back to bed," Cavanagh said. "That all right with you?"

"Help yourself," Bronski said. "Get all the sleep you want. We'll have lots more questions for you in the morning."

"I'll look forward to them."

"So will I. Good night, Lord Cavanagh. Sleep well."

With one last sardonic smile Bronski passed around the privacy glass and left, his men following behind him. There was another puff of air, and Kolchin came back around the divider. "All clear," he reported. "Privacy seal's back in place."

"Thank you," Cavanagh said, plodding back across the social room and dropping tiredly onto the couch beside the threading. This whole thing was rapidly being blown way out of proportion. "I don't suppose they've gone very far, though."

"Probably not," Kolchin agreed. "Bronski was saying something about covering the entrances as they left. What's all this about, anyway?"

"I haven't the slightest idea," Cavanagh shook his head. He felt old and tired and was starting to wish he'd never seen Fibbit or her threadings. "The way they're acting, you'd think we were sitting on the CIRCE schematics. Let's back up: does anyone have any idea where Fibbit went?"

"I am here," a trembling Duulian voice came from directly beneath him.

Cavanagh jerked, startled, and looked down. From beneath the narrow couch a thin Duulian arm had appeared, the claws scrabbling around for a grip on the thick carpet. "Fibbit!" Cavanagh said, jumping up and crouching down to look. She was there, all right, folded and wedged into an impossibly compact space. "You startled me."

"Greatest apologies, Cavanagh," Fibbit said, her voice still trembling. "I did not plan to rudely listen in on the private conversation."

"It wasn't exactly private," Cavanagh told her, watching in fascination as she unfolded in stages and pulled herself out from under the couch. He'd never even heard of Sanduuli having the ability to do that. "I'm just glad you had the sense to stay quiet while they were here."

"There was no choice," Fibbit sighed, standing upright and stretching her long limbs. "I was in cold-sleep. Not easy to break. What do they want of me, Cavanagh?"

"I wish I knew," Cavanagh said, reaching over and picking up the threading frame. "But at a guess, I'd say it has to do with this human. So he's the one you saw going into the Information Agency?"

"Yes," Fibbit said, and even through her nervousness Cavanagh could hear the pride in her voice. "Do you like it?"

Cavanagh held it up to the light. It was the first close look he'd had at the portrait; and as with Fibbit's other threading, it was extraordinarily good. The face was that of an older man, probably in his mid-seventies, white-haired but alert, with a keen intelligence in his eyes. He was wearing a tan-and-brown arc-striped jacket, with an intricately knotted scarf keeping the wind off his neck.

And he looked familiar. Somehow, he looked familiar.

"I like it very much," Cavanagh said, tilting the threading slightly. Fibbit had incorporated the same technique here that she'd used in her Information Agency threading, the technique that had allowed her to create that mood shift between cheerful sunrise and a melancholy sunset. Here, as with that one, the face still looked the same as Cavanagh shifted the frame back and forth; but at the same time, there was something significantly different about it. He turned it back, then back again—

And suddenly he had it. "His emotions are changing," he said, tilting the threading again. "He's going from basically calm to—" He tilted the frame, a shiver running up his back. "From calm to terrified. Genuinely terrified."

"Yes," Fibbit said. "He walked twice past me. The first time seven days ago, the second two days later."

Cavanagh gazed at the threading, trying to work through the conversion calculation. But it was more than his brain was up to at five in the morning. "Kolchin, I'm too foggy. Can you get it?"

"Yes, sir," Kolchin said. "The first time was just before the news would have broken publicly here about the Conqueror attack at Dorcas. The second would have been right after it."

"Explains the mood change, anyway," Hill put in.

Cavanagh tilted the threading again and for a long minute stared at the frightened version of the face. "No," he said slowly. "No, there's more to it. There's fear here, all right, but it's much more complex than just that. There's an element of—I don't know. Guilt or shame or a sense of unfulfilled accountability. Something like that. Fibbit, are you sure you don't know who this human is?"

"I do not know him," Fibbit insisted.

"I think Lee does, though," Kolchin said. "Or at least he's got an idea."

Cavanagh shook his head. "Lee's welcome to him," he said, setting the threading firmly back down on the couch. "We have more pressing business, and we've spent too much time here already. Hill, give Teva a call and tell him to get the ship ready to fly; Kolchin, go scout us out a route that'll get us past whoever Bronski's left behind. We're leaving."

He crossed the social room back toward his bedroom. "What of me?" Fibbit asked, coming up tentatively behind him.

"That's up to you," Cavanagh told her, half closing the bedroom door behind him and pulling off his robe.

"We have an errand on Dorcas, but afterward we'll be happy to take you back to Ulu. Otherwise, you can wait here for Bronski or the Mrachanis to send you home directly. It's your choice."

The Sanduul shook her head violently. "I do not trust Bronski," she said emphatically. "And I am now afraid of the Mrachanis. Yet I will put you in danger with all of them if I accompany you."

"Don't worry about it," Cavanagh assured her, passing up the clothing he'd worn yesterday in favor of a simple mechanic's jumpsuit they'd brought up from the car's storage case when they'd checked in. Not exactly the sort of thing a former NorCoord Parlimin usually wore, but it was comfortable and went on quickly, and for the moment that was more important than fashion. "Bronski can make veiled threats until the moose go over the mountain, but the simple fact is that he hasn't got a legal leg to kick with. And he knows it."

"But—"

"Sir?" Kolchin said, stepping to the half-open doorway. In the dim light his expression looked grim. "We've got trouble. I took a look out the door, and there seems to be an argument going on down the hall by the elevators. Bronski's people and a pair of Bhurtala."

Cavanagh whistled soundlessly between his lips. "Bhurtala?"

Kolchin nodded. "The argument seems to be getting louder, too. We ought to try and get out of here before the shooting starts."

"Indeed," Cavanagh agreed, sitting down on the bed and starting to pull on his half boots. Confrontations between humans and Bhurtala had a bad tendency to end in violence. Especially when the human side of the confrontation had people like Bronski aboard. "Any thoughts on how best to get off the floor?"

"Well, we're not going by elevator, that's for sure,"

Kolchin said. "We could try for the stairs, but I think we'd do better to take the emergency drop chutes. Probably set off an alarm, but it'll be a lot faster. There's also a better chance Bronski won't have people watching the other end, like he might have at the stairways."

"Sounds good," Cavanagh said, feeling his stomach tighten. Drop chutes, like most emergency equipment, were something one never expected to actually use. He'd never used one, or even known anyone who had, and he wasn't really anxious to start now. "Where are the chutes?"

"The nearest is about three meters down the hall. Should be easy to make, even if Bronski and the Bhurtala stop arguing long enough to notice us."

A spidery hand touched Cavanagh's arm. "Is this bad, Cavanagh?" Fibbit asked hesitantly. "What are Bhurtala?"

"Big, strong creatures with a rather violent dislike for humans," Cavanagh told her. "Don't worry, though, we'll be all right."

"They dislike humans?" Fibbit repeated, her face a mirror of astonishment.

"Intensely," Cavanagh said. "Comes of our trying once too often to remake their culture to suit the more self-righteous and meddlesome of our leaders."

"It's not just humans," Kolchin added. "They don't like anyone else much, either. I don't know what the Mrachanis are thinking, letting them wander loose around Mig-Ka City like this."

"Fortunately, that's not our problem," Cavanagh said, getting to his feet. "Let's go."

Hill had cracked open the door and was waiting there with his gun at the ready as the others came up. Through the narrow gap, Cavanagh could hear the indistinct sound of voices coming from the end of the hall. "They still at it?" he asked.

"Yes, and they're getting louder," Hill said. "Sounds like the Bhurtala have gotten it into their thick heads that humans shouldn't be leaving the hotel at this hour. Bronski's arguing the point with them."

"Any sign of hotel security?"

"Not yet."

"Probably staying out of it on purpose," Kolchin said. "All right, I'll go out first and secure the chute area. Lord Cavanagh, you and Fibbit will follow at my signal. Hill will backstop from the doorway; if the thing breaks, I'll lay down cover fire. Everyone got it? Okay, Hill, give me some door."

Hill let the door open all the way, dropping down to one knee in the opening, his gun gripped ready in his left hand as he peered out toward the sounds of argument coming from their right. Sliding past him, Kolchin slipped silently out to the left. Cavanagh eased forward and craned his neck for a look.

They were there, all right, barely fifteen meters away: Bronski and his three men arrayed in a line opposite a pair of squat, meter-wide Bhurtala who had planted themselves squarely in front of the elevator bank. Three of the humans—all but Lee—had small flechette guns pointed at their challengers, a move that struck Cavanagh as more provocative than it was prudent. Bhurtala skin had elephantine thickness and density, and standard-load flechettes didn't do a lot of good against it.

From behind him came a soft double snap of fingers. "Okay," Hill said, dropping the muzzle of his gun into ready position. "Go."

Clenching his teeth, Cavanagh sidled out into the hall, Fibbit almost walking on his heels as she huddled close behind him. Kolchin was waiting by the shallow alcove that marked the chute doorway entrance, his eyes focused past them at the elevators. Cavanagh got one step—two—

"Hey!" someone shouted from behind him. "There's the Sanduul—"

And abruptly, the hall lit up like the inside of a firecracker as a thunderclap of sound slammed into Cavanagh, picking him up and throwing him toward the floor.

A hand caught his arm before he made it all the way down, hauling him upright again and half dragging him another step forward. "Come on!" a voice—Kolchin's? —shouted through the ringing in his ears. "Here's the door—go!"

There was another explosion, this one sounding more distant in his stunned hearing. In the accompanying flash of light he saw that Kolchin was shoving him toward one of the three slender poles of the drop chute, and he got his hands out in front of him just in time to grab it as his stumbling feet hit the small foot platform.

And then the memory-metal safety cage had whipped into position around him and he was dropping nearly free fall through the darkness. Beneath him came the rush of air and the distant wail of emergency sirens; above him, closer but still sounding distant, was what sounded like a shrill whine of fear or exhilaration. Far overhead now came the sound and dim flash of a third explosion—

And a heartbeat later his weight suddenly came back as the platform began its breakneck deceleration. He gripped the pole tightly, not trusting the safety cage enough to lean his weight against it, wondering just how fail-safe these things really were. . . .

With a last-second jolt and a brief metallic squeak the platform surged to a halt. A dark, moaning shape dropped to the floor beside him as the safety cage retracted once again. Straight ahead, outlined by flashing red lights, was a door; prying his hands off the pole, Cavanagh headed that direction, staggering slightly from the vertigo of the ride down and the sonic-shock aftereffects of the multiple explosions up above. The sections of the door split smoothly apart as his shoulder hit it, dumping him unceremoniously outside. Catching his balance, he looked around.

He was in the narrow alleyway that ran between the hotel and the covered entrance ramp of the parking/ storage building beside it. At this hour of the morning it was only dimly lit, and as near as he could tell, it was deserted.

"Cavanagh?" a shaking Duulian voice called weakly from the doorway. "Where are you?"

"I'm right here, Fibbit," Cavanagh said, stepping back to take the arm groping blindly through the split doorway. He'd forgotten what poor night vision Sanduuli had; no wonder she'd been wailing so loudly on the way down. He pulled the door open a little more, half helping, half pulling Fibbit through—

With a whoosh and squeak of metal, another figure dropped to the floor back by the drop poles. "Kolchin?" Cavanagh asked.

"Yes, sir," the other acknowledged. "Is Fibbit there?"

"She's right here. Where's Hill?"

His answer was another whoosh of air as Hill's platform arrived. "You all right?" Kolchin asked.

"Fine," Hill said, sounding a little winded. "We'd better get moving—I dropped a misty, but that won't stop them for long."

"Right," Kolchin said as they joined Cavanagh and Fibbit in the alleyway. "I'm going to try to get to our car. You take Lord Cavanagh across the street and find some cover."

"Got it," Hill said, his gun in his hand again. "Come on, sir."

They started down the alleyway at a quick jog. "What happened back there?" Cavanagh asked, not entirely sure he wanted to hear the answer.

"We didn't hurt anyone, if that's what you mean," Hill assured him. "Just blew out some sections of floor and ceiling for visual cover."

They reached the end of the alleyway, and Hill paused to throw a careful look both ways down the deserted cross street. "Looks clear," he said. "That doorway over there—the one with the overhang? We'll try for there."

They made it across the street and into the doorway without attracting any obvious notice. "You think it's safe for me to call the ship?" Cavanagh asked, pulling out his phone.

"Put it on scramble," Hill said, crouching at the edge of the doorway and looking again down the street. "And keep it short."

"Right."

He punched in the number; and Teva himself answered on the first buzz. "Lord Cavanagh," he said, his voice tense. "Where are you, sir?"

"We're on our way," Cavanagh said. "We should be there in ten minutes."

Teva glanced at something past the phone screen. "I'm not sure you've got that long, sir," he said. "We just got a call from someone named Petr Bronski who says he's a Commonwealth assistant diplomatic liaison. He's ordering us to secure from launch prep and prepare to receive him."

"What are the Mrachanis saying?"

"The Mrachanis? Nothing."

Cavanagh frowned. "Nothing?"

"Well, nothing since they gave us lift clearance a couple of minutes ago. That was just before Bronski called."

"And the clearance hasn't been revoked?"

"No, sir."

Cavanagh looked out into the deserted street, chewing his lip. This didn't make any sense at all. If Bronski wanted the *Cavatina* grounded, his first call should have been to the spaceport tower, not to the ship. After all, he was acting under the auspices of the Mrach government.

Or at least that was what he claimed. . . .

"New orders," he told Teva. "Lift now, while you still have clearance."

Teva's jaw dropped a centimeter. "Now, sir?"

"Now," Cavanagh repeated firmly. "Don't wait for us; and don't be there when Bronski arrives."

"Lord Cavanagh, I have a responsibility to you."

"Your responsibility is to the ship and to the family," Cavanagh said firmly. "And to obey all family orders. Go to Dorcas as scheduled and tell Aric that the vector search came up dry. He'll understand. After that you're to head back home. We'll find our own way back or else contact you there."

Teva took a deep and obviously painful breath. "Yes, sir," he gritted. "Good luck, sir."

The screen blanked. "Any sign of Kolchin?" Cavanagh asked, putting the phone away.

"Not yet," Hill said, throwing Cavanagh an odd look. "Sir, I'm not sure sending the *Cavatina* away was a good idea."

"I don't like it either," Cavanagh conceded. "But if they don't get off now, they might not get the chance. I've had a few minutes to think; and there's only one reason I can think of as to why those Bhurtala were at our elevators. They have to be working for the Mrachanis. Or rather, one group of Mrachanis."

Hill frowned. "Passing over the whole question of their working for any non-Bhurt boss, I thought the Mrach hierarchy was pretty much monolithic."

"That's what I've always heard, too," Cavanagh agreed. "But remember that visitor we had, the one who was worried about being caught talking to us? You'll notice he showed up and disappeared just ahead of the Bhurtala. Bhurtala who seemed anxious to keep any humans from leaving the area."

"Which would put the Bhurtala and Bronski on different sides," Hill said slowly. "Unless they both work for the same people and just got their wires crossed."

"That's a possibility," Cavanagh nodded, looking over at Fibbit. The Sanduul was pressed into deep shadow, probably somewhere between bewildered and terrified by all this. "Either way, the implication I get is that the man in Fibbit's threading is more important than anyone's letting on."

"Whoever he is," Hill grunted. "Here comes Kolchin."

"Good," Cavanagh said, beckoning to Fibbit. "Come on."

The car pulled to the curb, and the three of them quickly piled in. "Any trouble?" Cavanagh asked as Kolchin pulled away and headed down the street.

"None," the other said. "Whoever hired those Bhurtala seems to be a little slow on the uptake."

So Kolchin was working on the same line of thought that Cavanagh was. "They might be, but Bronski isn't," he said. "He called the *Cavatina* and ordered them to secure from launch prep."

"And?"

"And I ordered Teva to go ahead and lift."

"I see," Kolchin said, his voice not giving anything away. "What about us?"

"I'm not sure," Cavanagh conceded. "I was hoping

you might have an idea where we might be able to buy ourselves a ship."

He peered into the front seat in time to catch Kolchin's tight smile. "Actually, sir, I might be able to do a bit better than that. You remember I told you I was here once to advise the Mrachanis on urban warfare?"

"Yes."

"One of our recommendations was to stash some fighters and courier ships way out in mountain caves where they wouldn't be caught in whatever fighting happened over Mig-Ka and other cities. That way they wouldn't be caught completely without out-system communication capabilities."

"Sounds like a good plan. You wouldn't happen to know where these ships are hidden, would you?"

"As a matter of fact, we helped supervise their hiding," Kolchin said with a sort of grim satisfaction. "We'll be there in a couple of hours."

Beside him Hill snorted gently. "Assuming the Mrachanis don't get their act together and come after us, of course."

They reached a long-distance highway and turned onto it. "Yes," Kolchin said as they started toward the distant mountains, dark shapes against the pale pre-dawn sky. "Always assuming that."

15 The tachyon wake-trails showed up on the pickup display at precisely one o'clock the next afternoon; and it was a tense ten minutes before the sensor chief was finally able to identify them.

"You sure, Gasperi?" Holloway asked, frowning at the display. "That doesn't look like any fighter baseline I've ever seen."

"It's fighters, all right, Colonel," Gasperi assured him. He touched a key, and six images appeared across the ident screen. "What threw me was that they're flying in a nonstandard formation," he said, fiddling with the controls. "Very close, with a partial overlap and interference cancellation in the baseline signatures. Watch as I bring them together."

The images on the screen moved inward; and the corresponding baseline schematic rippled and convulsed into a copy of the one showing on the tachyon pickup. "Like that."

"Makes for a much smaller footprint than a standard formation," Takara observed. "Harder for any snooping Conqueror scouts to pick up. Pretty fancy flying, though."

"Fancy or stupid," Holloway agreed. "Any idea yet who they are?"

"With that kind of formation?" Gasperi shrugged. "Have to be Copperheads. Corvines, probably."

Takara looked at Holloway. "The rest of Commander Quinn's contingent?"

"Probably," Holloway said. "What are we looking at, about an hour to mesh and another to groundfall?"

"About that," Gasperi nodded.

Holloway looked at his watch. Almost exactly the same time the skitter was due back from Edo, assuming the desk pilots there had been halfway efficient at pulling up Quinn's orders. Or the lack of them.

Takara was obviously following the same line of thought. "Going to be close," he murmured. "You suppose he planned the timing deliberately?"

"Probably depends on whether or not he's legitimate." And if he wasn't, Holloway very much wanted to read the interrogation record of someone who'd managed to beg, borrow, or steal a half squadron of Copperhead fighters. A man like that would have to be smart, devious, and extremely brazen.

The sort of man who wouldn't leave anything to chance.

He stepped over to a terminal and keyed for entry. "Something?" Takara asked.

"A hunch," Holloway said, punching up a listing of the traffic into Dorcas since Melinda Cavanagh had come in with that private supply depot of hers. If they were pulling some con here, they almost certainly would have been smart enough to include a quiet backstop in their plans. . . .

And there he was, nestled in among the legitimate supply and logistics flights of the past few days. A small, private courier ship, with a single person aboard, logged in barely four hours behind Quinn and Aric Cavanagh. "What do we know about this one?" he asked Takara, indicating the entry.

"Don't think there's anything special about him," Takara said, squinting at the screen. "He logged in just before I went off duty yesterday. Name's McPhee—forward man for a shipload of nonperishables that should be coming in sometime in the next couple of days. His ID and documents seemed legit enough."

"He's with the Peacekeepers?"

"No, he's a civilian," Takara shook his head. "Working directly out of—" He looked sharply at Holloway. "Out of the NorCoord Parliament."

Holloway nodded sourly. "The same NorCoord Parliament our friend Lord Stewart Cavanagh served three terms in. Any bets on this being just some wild coincidence?"

"Not from me," Takara said. "You know, Cass, we really don't have time for this."

"Agreed. Unfortunately, we can't afford to ignore it, either."

"So what do we do?"

Holloway rubbed at his cheek. All right. Quinn and the Cavanaghs had a tanker and Counterpunch on the ground, with six Corvines on their way in. Highly visible, the whole bunch of them. Which meant that whatever sleight of hand was in the works, the silent backup would likely be the keystone to it. "We split them up," he said. "You were planning to take a survey team out to Site B soon, weren't you?"

"I could head out anytime," Takara nodded. "You want me to take one of them along and keep him there for a couple of hours?"

"You got it," Holloway said. "Make it McPhee—the others should be easier to keep track of."

"What if he refuses to go?"

Holloway cocked an eyebrow. "How can he? He's

here to assist in preparations for an incoming supply shipment, isn't he? Well, then, he needs to see what we're doing at Site B."

"Of course," Takara said dryly. "Silly of me."

Holloway looked at the tachyon pickup. "Just be careful," he said quietly. "We don't know what they're up to or what stakes they're playing for. It could get messy."

"Don't worry," Takara promised. "We're Peacekeepers, remember? We'll take care of him."

With one final push the last of the ration boxes finally cleared the inner lip of the storage-compartment hatch. Trying to hold everything in place at once with one hand, Aric eased the rolling cover down across the compartment with the other. He held his breath; but this time, to his relief, the latch clicked shut without jamming. "I'm finished here," he called. "You need any help?"

"No," Quinn's voice drifted in from somewhere in one of the fueler's other rooms. "I should be done in a minute, and Max can handle the check-through on his own. Why don't you go see how Dr. Cavanagh is doing."

"Right," Aric grunted as he began working his way backward out of the galley storage alcove. Melinda had been right: stuff twelve more people in this fueler, and it was going to be real cozy. He could only hope that getting the fueler into zero-gee would make all these cramped spaces feel larger.

Melinda was waiting on the ground by the time he reached the base of the fueler. "How's it going?" she asked.

"It's all in," he told her. "And contrary to my original expectations, it all fits. You?"

She nodded. "All the external compartments are

loaded, and I've got the last fuel canister going in now. How's Quinn doing?"

"Sounded like he was about finished loading the backup cells," Aric said. "All we'll have to do then is have Max fire up the electronics and make sure everything works. And we'll be ready to go." He looked up at the canvac barrier still shrouding one side of the fueler. "You check the paint job lately?"

"About ten minutes ago. Still feels a little sticky."

Awkward, but hardly surprising. They'd expected to be doing all this lettering and insignia work in orbit, and paints formulated for vacuum couldn't be expected to perform well in atmosphere. "Well, chances are we've still got a few hours before Dad and the Corvines show up. Maybe it'll be dry enough by then to get through the atmosphere without streaking."

"I hope so," Melinda said, looking up at the fueler. "Personally, I think the sooner you get out of here, the better. I get the feeling that Colonel Holloway is still flipping a coin as to whether to simply ground the project and haul the three of us in for questioning."

A motion across the parking field caught Aric's eye: a military groundcar had emerged from between two of the warehouses and was heading their way. "Looks like he may have finished his toss," he said, stepping to the intercom beside the base of the lift-cage track. "Quinn? We've got company. Peacekeeper car on its way."

There was a moment of silence. "How many men in it?"

Aric squinted. "Four, including the driver. Looks like Colonel Holloway's one of them."

"I'll be down in a couple of minutes," Quinn said. "Play it by ear until I get there. Just remember that as far as they know, we're completely legitimate."

"Right," Aric said, taking a deep breath. Like any other trade negotiation, he told himself firmly. That's all it was. Just a normal trade negotiation, with exceptionally high stakes.

The car pulled to a halt beside them. "Good afternoon," Holloway said as he and two of the other men got out. "How's the loading going?"

"We're just about finished," Aric told him, giving Holloway's two companions a surreptitious once-over. Big, competent-looking men, with Peacekeeper Marine insignia on their collars and big, no-nonsense handguns in quick-draw holsters at their sides. "Just need to finish transferring our fuel and run an electronics-and-sensor test and we'll be ready to go."

"After the rest of your fighters get here, of course," Holloway said, looking up at the canvac barrier. "I take it you've finished your welding?"

"We weren't doing any welding," Aric said, something in Holloway's tone warning him not to simply concur with the other's statement.

"Didn't think it smelled like sealant primer," Holloway agreed calmly. "What *were* you doing?"

"There was some minor damage to one of the airfoil surfaces," Aric told him. "We replaced it and then repainted around it."

"I see," Holloway said, his face not giving away whether he bought that or not. "I wonder if I might speak with Commander Quinn."

"He's up in the ship," Aric told him. "He should be down in a few minutes."

"I'd appreciate it if you'd ask him to come down now," Holloway said.

Courteous phrasing, polite tone. An order nonetheless. "Certainly," Aric said, keying the intercom and relaying the message.

A minute later Quinn had joined them. "Colonel," he nodded to Holloway. "What can I do for you?"

"I just stopped by to tell you that the rest of your

force is on its way into the system," Holloway said. "We're expecting them to mesh in at any minute. I thought you might like to use the relay in my car to give them any updated information or orders."

Aric felt his lip twitch. The original plan had been to let the Corvines contact the Peacekeeper garrison as per standard approach procedure, and then to take over the communication from orbit, giving the fighters their instructions via a directional signal that the garrison's ground receivers wouldn't be able to pick up. With the fueler stuck on the surface instead, Quinn had warned him that such a scheme would be problematic at best. Clearly, Holloway wasn't going to allow them even that much of a chance at getting around him.

"Thank you, sir," Quinn said, stepping past Holloway toward the car and accepting the microphone the driver handed him. "This is Commander Quinn."

"Stand by, Commander," a voice said. "We've just made contact with the Corvines." There was a click—

"Copperhead Task Force Omicron Four to Dorcas ground control," a new voice said crisply. "This is Commander Thomas Masefield. Request permission to speak with Wing Commander Adam Quinn."

"This is Wing Commander Quinn," Quinn said. "Welcome to Dorcas, Commander."

"Thank you, sir. Have you any updated orders for us?"

"No new orders, but the rendezvous schedule's been altered a bit," Quinn said. "You'll need to get an orbit insertion vector from ground control and come in."

There was a short silence. "I understood we were in something of a hurry, sir," Masefield said.

"We are," Quinn agreed. "But we're waiting on one more arrival. I'm hoping he'll be here in time for us to meet you in orbit; if not, you'll have to come all the way down."

"Acknowledged, sir. Reading about forty-five minutes to orbit from here, sixty minutes to ground."

"Good. Carry on, and we'll see you shortly."

"Yes, sir. Copperhead Omicron Four out."

Quinn clicked off the mike and handed it back to the driver. "Thank you, Colonel," he nodded to Holloway. "Was there anything else you wanted?"

"As a matter of fact, there was," Holloway said, taking the mike again from the driver and flicking it back on. "Lieutenant Gasperi? Report on the incoming skitter."

"We've got a firm track on it now, Colonel," a voice came. "Getting data transmission."

"Good. Stand by." Holloway looked at Quinn. "It's a skitter from Edo, Commander, in case you were wondering. We sent a confirmation inquiry to the Peacekeeper base there about your assignment authorization number."

Carefully, Aric avoided looking at either of the others. Melinda had warned them when they'd first arrived that Holloway was suspicious of the story she'd spun for him. But they'd dismissed her fears, knowing full well that there wouldn't be time for him to get a skitter to Earth and back before they would all be gone from Dorcas. The possibility that Holloway would focus instead on the mission's authorization number—and thereby cut twenty hours out of the round-trip loop—had somehow never occurred to him.

Which made it polished-plate clear why this sudden burst of cooperation and courtesy on Holloway's part. He'd called their bluff; and now that the blade was on its way down, he intended to be in on the kill personally.

Casually, Aric threw a glance at the two Marines. They were between the group and the fueler, standing well apart, their hands resting casually on their holstered guns.

"Colonel?"

Holloway lifted the mike. "Go ahead, Lieutenant."

"Data transmission from Edo," Gasperi said. "Quote: Regarding your inquiry, Peacekeeper AAN 67424955/ MSC Foxtrot Lima Victor Victor. Copperhead Fighter Unit Omicron Four assigned to Reserve Wing Commander Iniko Bokamba for unspecified patrol mission. Transfer via Dorcas. AAN confirmed, 4/7/03, 15:07:39 LMT, Station 33, Peacekeeper Command Processing Center, Edo. Unquote."

"I see," Holloway said. "No mention of Commander Quinn?"

"No, sir. But there's an addendum that says there was a private communication attached for Omicron Four's commander. Edo doesn't have a copy of that."

Holloway cocked an eyebrow. "Interesting. Would you care to comment on that, Commander?"

"I'm not sure what comment is necessary, Colonel," Quinn said evenly.

"We could start with why Commander Masefield seems to think you're in charge of this mission instead of Bokamba," Holloway said.

"I assume it was part of the private communication."

"You assume? Don't you know?"

"I really don't see what the problem is, Colonel," Melinda put in. "The whole idea of this was to confirm Quinn's orders, wasn't it?"

"Except that we haven't confirmed his orders," Holloway told her. "We've confirmed Wing Commander Bokamba's orders. How that relates to any of you is still unexplained."

"Then I suggest you ask Wing Commander Bokamba personally about it," Aric said. "Assuming, of course, he's willing to tell you."

For the first time Holloway seemed taken aback. "Bokamba is here?"

"He will be shortly," Aric said. "You heard Quinn tell Masefield that we were still waiting for someone, didn't you?"

"Indeed," Holloway murmured, looking thoughtfully at each of them in turn. "Any idea when he'll arrive?"

"Not really," Quinn said. "Soon, I hope."

"I'm sure you do," Holloway said, stepping back to the car door. "All right, then. We'll await his arrival and see what he has to say. Until then, good day."

He got into the car and closed the door behind him. The two Marines silently joined him, and the vehicle turned around and headed back across the field.

Aric took a deep breath and looked over at Melinda. "What do you think?"

"He's not fooled," she said. "Not a bit. He knows there's something off-key about all this. He just doesn't know what."

"I agree," Quinn said. "And I'm afraid it forces our hand. The minute those Corvines get close enough, we're taking off."

"What about Dad?" Melinda asked.

"We can't afford to wait for him," Quinn shook his head. "Stopping to refit the fueler with that Carthage-Ivy computer has already thrown him off our original schedule. If the Mrachanis are slow about dredging up that Conquerors legend, it could be another six to twelve hours before he arrives. There's no guarantee another skitter from Edo or Earth won't get here first with an update on the authorization number."

"It's worse than that, actually," Aric said. "Holloway's never going to believe a Copperhead wing commander will be coming into the system aboard a civilian yacht."

"And, of course, as soon as they mesh in, Holloway will make contact and ask to speak to Bokamba," Quinn said grimly. "Teva will have no idea what he's talking about; and then we really will be in the soup."

"I understand all that," Melinda said. "But as it stands now, you don't have any idea where to start looking."

Quinn shrugged. "We'll just have to make do with the data from the original attack."

Melinda sighed. "I don't like it," she said. "But I don't see any alternative. What do you want me to do?"

Quinn looked up at the fueler. "You can start by telling Max to skip the sensor and nonessentials check and go directly to launch prep. Can he get the fueler up to orbit alone?"

"He landed it alone," Melinda said. "I presume he won't have any trouble lifting."

"All right," Quinn nodded. "Mr. Cavanagh and I will both go up in the Counterpunch, then. After that, the only other thing left for you to do will be to lie low until the *Cavatina* gets here." His lip twitched. "Unless you want to see if you can distract Holloway for us while we lift."

Melinda blinked. "Distract him?" she echoed. "How do you propose I do that?"

"You'll think of something," Aric assured her. "Come on, Quinn, let's get started."

"Got it, Colonel," Hobson called from across the room. "Bokamba, Iniko Ilom."

Holloway stepped to his side and ran an eye over the record. Bokamba was a Copperhead reserve wing commander, all right, with a pretty impressive record to boot. Still listed as inactive, but with all the other activity going on at Peacekeeper bases, the records updates reaching Dorcas were falling further and further behind. "What about that cross-check with Quinn?" he asked Hobson. "You find anything?"

"Yes, sir," the other said, pulling up a new record. "Turns out Quinn was in Bokamba's squadron for a little over a year. Just before he resigned his commission."

And went on to become Lord Stewart Cavanagh's star witness at the Parliament hearings on the Copperheads. "Okay," Holloway said. "At least that part's legit. You find anything else?"

"Actually, sir, I did." Hobson keyed his board again. "The system was a little quiet at the moment, so I went ahead and did a global cross-search. That McPhee fellow who came in right after Quinn? Turns out his flight plan originated from Granparra, which happens to be Bokamba's residence."

"Mm." More proof, if Holloway had needed it, that McPhee was in with the Cavanaghs on this. "Thank you."

"Just a second, sir," Hobson interrupted, lifting a finger. "I don't know if you were aware of this, Colonel, but McPhee got his ship refueled and prepped at Granparra at the Myrmidon Weapons Platform."

"How do you figure that?"

"It's right here." Hobson pointed at one of the multidigit numbers in McPhee's flight schedule. "This section here—the last five digits—are the service-classification code. It's very definitely a Peacekeeper base, and the only base in the Granparra system is the Myrmidon Platform."

"Interesting," Holloway said, frowning at the number. "Has someone changed the rules on civilian use of Peacekeeper facilities?"

"If they have, I haven't heard about it," Hobson said.

Holloway shifted his gaze across the room. "Gasperi, has Major Takara checked back in yet?"

"His team's just landed, sir," Gasperi called back. "He should be here in another minute or two."

"Give him a call," Holloway ordered. "Tell him I want to see him and McPhee in my office."

"Yes, sir," Gasperi said. "Oh, and Colonel?—Dr. Melinda Cavanagh's here to see you."

Good; that saved them the trouble of going out and finding her. "Have Duggen and Spaulding escort her to my office," he told Gasperi. "Have them tell her I'll be there shortly."

"Yes, sir."

He stepped to a terminal and sat down, permitting himself a tight smile as he got to work. Finally—finally —he had the hook he'd been looking for since Melinda Cavanagh first dropped her private variety store into the middle of his base. NorCoord political hack or not, McPhee was now officially in violation of a whole raft of Peacekeeper regulations, with the proof right there in his flight record. Together with his obvious connections to Quinn and the Cavanaghs, that gave Holloway enough justification to lock the whole bunch of them up. At least long enough to sort out what was going on here.

He chewed his lower lip, feeling the unpleasant tingle of acid swirling against the base of his esophagus. Somewhere deep inside him, he knew, he was still clinging to the hope that whatever they were up to was something minor. But with six top-line Corvine fighters now involved, that hope was becoming increasingly hard to hold on to. And with the possibility of a summary military trial and judgment looming ever more likely down the road . . .

He shook his head firmly. His job was to uncover the truth, and let the ax fall wherever it fell. And that was what he was going to do.

They were all waiting when he arrived at his office: Takara, McPhee, and Melinda Cavanagh, with Duggen and Spaulding flanking the door. "Good afternoon,"

Holloway said as he rounded the corner of his desk and sat down. "As I'm sure you're all aware, we're extremely busy here, so I'll get right to the point. Mr. McPhee, you've stated you're a forward man for a supply shipment which is supposed to be on its way to Dorcas. Who exactly is in charge of this shipment, and where is it coming from?"

McPhee shrugged. "I'm working under the auspices of the NorCoord Parliament. I thought you knew that."

"Yes, I did," Holloway said, gazing at the other's stony expression and wishing he'd been able to get here before the two groups arrived. In the first surprise at being brought face-to-face with Dr. Cavanagh, McPhee's expression might have been interesting to observe. "But so far all you've given us have been vague generalities. Let's hear some specifics. Who and from where?"

McPhee's face hardened a little more. "I don't care much for your tone, Colonel," he said.

"I'm sorry to hear that, Mr. McPhee," Holloway countered. "*I* don't care much for civilians who illegally use facilities at a Peacekeeper weapons platform."

"Weapons platform?" Takara asked. "Where did he do that?"

"At Granparra," Holloway told him, watching McPhee closely. If the other was worried, he wasn't showing it. "He got his ship refueled and serviced at the Myrmidon Platform. I just found out myself a few minutes ago."

"What makes you think it was done illegally?" McPhee asked.

"You're a civilian," Holloway said. "On civilian business." He held up the card he'd just finished compiling. "I have a list of the regulations here. They're very clear on such matters."

"There are exceptions."

Holloway leaned back in his chair. "I'm listening," he invited.

McPhee dropped his gaze, and Holloway caught his surreptitious glance to where Melinda Cavanagh was sitting quietly taking it all in. His lip twitched once; and when he raised his eyes again, they were unexpectedly burning with an icy anger. "I'm sorry to disappoint you, Colonel," he said. "But as it happens, I have full and total authority to requisition any Peacekeeper facilities, equipment, or personnel I want. Up to and including you and your garrison."

"Impressive words," Holloway said, an odd feeling starting to tingle against the back of his neck. "You have any substance to go along with them?"

"I think this will suffice," McPhee said, pulling a card from his pocket. "Even for you." With careless accuracy he flipped it through the air to land in the middle of Holloway's desk. "You're welcome to check it, of course."

Holloway picked up the card. "A NorCoord Parliament carte blanche," he commented, trying to keep his voice casual. So Melinda Cavanagh's story had been true all along. These people really were involved in some top-secret under-the-counter operation.

And if this Parlimin Jacy VanDiver—or Admiral Rudzinski himself—chose to be upset that an overzealous lieutenant colonel on a minor-colony world had stuck his nose into the matter . . .

He pursed his lips. No. First things first. "Thank you, Mr. McPhee," he said. "I believe we'll do that." He glanced at his desk, at the spot where his terminal had been before being moved out to Site A an hour ago. "Fuji, get out to the sensor center and check this out," he said, holding the carte blanche out to Takara. "You know how to do it?"

"Yes, sir," Takara said, suddenly sounding crisp and formal as he bounded from his chair and took the card. "I confirm the overall form and style of the text, then locate and compare the confirmation encoding that'll have been buried in the standard data file updates within forty-eight hours of issuance."

"Right," Holloway said. "Make sure no one looks over your shoulder while you're doing it."

"Yes, sir," Takara said, and headed out at a brisk walk.

Holloway watched him go, noticing that Duggen and Spaulding had suddenly become Peacekeeper recruits again, standing with a parade-ground stiffness that was usually dispensed with in the garrison's more informal surroundings. Apparently, even a distant whiff of that carte blanche was potent stuff. "At ease, gentlemen," he suggested. "We're not passing in review."

The Marines shifted into at-ease position, Spaulding reddening slightly as they did so. "An intriguing situation, Mr. McPhee," Holloway said, turning back to the other. "It's rare to see a parliamentary carte blanche these days."

"Save your breath, Colonel," McPhee advised coldly. "And your excuses, before you bother making any. Whatever fallout comes from this, it's going to land squarely in your face."

Holloway locked eyes with him. "If I were you, Mr. McPhee," he said quietly, "I wouldn't be too quick to start shoveling blame. People who suddenly appear in a war zone with absurd cover stories shouldn't be surprised when they attract official scrutiny. Whatever this imagined fallout of yours might be—"

"*Imagined* fallout?" McPhee cut him off. "You know, that's just the sort of asinine statement that shows you really haven't the faintest idea what's going on here."

"I'm acutely aware of that," Holloway countered, trying hard to hold on to his temper. He could put up with politicians who fumbled around in military circles without a clue what they were doing. Politicians who insisted on frosting their ignorance with arrogance drove him nearly homicidal. "I trust *you* are aware that if you'd presented your credentials at the outset, my officers and I would have made every attempt to cooperate with you."

"Oh, certainly," McPhee shot back. "Present my credentials, and have the whole garrison buzzing with rumors. That would certainly have been helpful."

Holloway took a careful breath, putting all his strength into not saying what he so badly wanted to say. To suggest that his men had nothing better to do than sit around discussing what some hotshot datapusher from Earth might be up to . . . "If you don't mind," he said, "I think we'll put the rest of this conversation on hold until Major Takara has finished his examination of your credentials. I'm sure Parlimin VanDiver would prefer we handle things by the book."

McPhee didn't answer, but the look on his face promised that he would remember this when the time came for reprimands. Sitting in the middle of a war zone, Holloway found it difficult to care.

The awkward silence seemed much longer than the few minutes it actually took Takara to return. "It's genuine, sir," he told Holloway, handing the carte blanche back across the desk. "There are five separate confirmations; all five checked out."

"Thank you," Holloway said, resisting the temptation to flip the card back across to McPhee the way the other had thrown it to him. "All right, Mr. McPhee, you are who you say. Now, what exactly is it you want from us?"

"What I *wanted* was for you to stick to your own work and leave me alone," the other said stiffly. "But since you've now effectively shredded my mission, I'll just have to settle for your confiscating that Counterpunch and fueler out there."

Holloway threw a glance at Melinda Cavanagh, sitting there quietly, her face unreadable. "I don't understand."

"What part didn't I make clear?" McPhee asked sardonically. "The part about confiscation, or the specific ships involved?"

Takara half rose from his seat. "Colonel—"

Holloway waved him back down. "Just a minute, Major."

"Colonel, this is important—"

"You heard the Colonel," McPhee snapped, throwing him a glare. "Shut up." He swiveled the glare onto Holloway. "I was ordered by Parlimin Jacy VanDiver to look into allegations that the Cavanagh family was conspiring to commit illegal activities. I'd originally hoped to ferret out what specifically they were up to, but thanks to your meddling that chance is gone. Still, illegal possession of Peacekeeper property ought to be enough to put the whole bunch of them under arrest."

"It's not Peacekeeper property," Melinda Cavanagh spoke up, her first words since the meeting had began. "Both ships and all the supplies are privately owned."

"What about the Corvines on their way in?" Holloway asked her.

"Corvines?" McPhee demanded. "Where? How many?"

"Colonel, they're gone," Takara called, clearly determined this time to make himself heard. "Both of them."

"Both?" Holloway frowned. "I thought there were six of them."

"Not the Corvines," Takara gritted. "Cavanagh and Quinn and their ships. They lifted while I was checking Mr. McPhee's credentials."

For a heartbeat McPhee just sat there, his mouth half-open. "What?" he breathed.

And then, abruptly, he bounded from his chair. "What?" he all but screamed. "What blithering—?" He jabbed a finger at Holloway. "Get them back. *Now.*"

Holloway had already keyed his comm. "Gasperi, what's the status on that Counterpunch and fueler that just lifted?"

"Lift was clean, Colonel," Gasperi said, his gaze flicking across the status board outside the range of Holloway's display. "No problems."

"Are you in contact with them?"

"No, sir, they've already cleared the horizon. Should be back in range in about an hour."

"What about the Corvines?" McPhee demanded at Holloway's side. "Can you raise them?"

"No, they're also out of sight line," Gasperi said, frowning uncertainly at McPhee. "Colonel, Major Takara okayed the lift."

"Yes, I know," Holloway assured him, thinking hard. "What about the incoming skitter? Is it in sight line with either the Corvines or the Counterpunch?"

"Not sight line, no," Gasperi said. "Might have enough diffraction bend to get a signal to them, though."

"Give it a try," Holloway said. "Have them inform Commander Quinn and Aric Cavanagh that they're to bring their ships back to ground immediately and to make themselves available for questioning."

McPhee snorted. "You don't really expect them to comply, do you?"

Holloway ignored him. "And get Number Two crash-prepped to fly. I want it in the sky in fifteen minutes."

"Yes, sir," Gasperi said, keying in the order. "Sir, we've also just picked up a new tachyon wake-trail coming in toward the system. Baseline identifies it as an Effenzeal-Royce star yacht. ETA about two hours."

Holloway looked at Melinda Cavanagh. "Yours?"

"My father's."

He nodded and looked back at the comm. "Keep an eye on it," he told Gasperi. "And get that skitter in the air."

"Yes, sir."

"You'll be wasting your time," Melinda Cavanagh advised as he keyed off the comm. "They'll be gone before the skitter can reach them."

"It's our time to waste, thank you," Holloway said. "I take it there's not much chance we'll find Wing Commander Bokamba aboard that ship?"

She shook her head silently. "Terrific," Holloway growled, keying the comm back on. "Gasperi, what's the status on that skitter relay?"

"Sorry, sir," the other said. "There's no response. The signal's probably not getting to them."

"What about Number Two?"

"Still being prepped, sir. It'll be another few minutes."

Holloway clenched his fist beneath the desk. "We may not have a few minutes," he said. "Move it."

"Yes, sir," Gasperi said, starting to look a little frazzled. "I'll have the—"

He broke off, turning his head to the side. Another voice said something, and Holloway saw Gasperi wince. "What?" he demanded.

"Sorry, sir," Gasperi said, turning back. "The fueler's just meshed out. From the wake-trail it looks like the Corvines went with it."

"And the Counterpunch, too, no doubt," Holloway sighed. "All right. Secure from launch prep on Number Two. Everyone back to normal."

"Yes, sir."

Holloway keyed off the comm and turned to Melinda

Cavanagh. "Congratulations," he said, hearing an edge of bitterness in his voice. "You and your brother seem to have gotten away with it. Whatever 'it' is."

He had the minor satisfaction of seeing a flicker of pain cross her face. "I'm sorry, Colonel," she said. "Our intention wasn't to get you or anyone else in trouble."

"Well, you've succeeded in that, too," he told her. "Under the circumstances I think you owe me an explanation as to what's going on."

"Again, I'm sorry," she said, looking at McPhee. "Under the Official Secrets Regulations I'm not allowed to talk about it." A faint smile twitched at her lips. "All I can say is that you're partly to blame for getting the whole thing started."

Holloway frowned. "What's that supposed to mean?"

"That's enough," McPhee said sharply. "Colonel, I don't know what's going on, either. But if she's not lying —if this does come under the Official Secrets Regulations—then the conversation is now over. Just lock her up somewhere until I get my ship ready, and I'll take her off your hands."

Holloway looked up at him. "I'm afraid you're jumping the gun a bit. If you want her arrested, you'll have to wait until we've done a proper interrogation."

McPhee's eyes narrowed. "Are you deaf, Colonel? I said the conversation was over. You're officially out of the circle."

"I suggest you brush up on your military law, Mr. McPhee," Holloway said, standing up and looking McPhee straight in the eye. "This woman is on my planet. She's in my garrison. She's under my jurisdiction. If I want to interrogate her, I can do that."

McPhee glanced at Takara, the first signs of uncertainty beginning to crack into that arrogant surface. "You're exceeding your authority, Colonel."

"On the contrary," Holloway said. "In case you

missed it, we're in a war zone here. I can declare full martial law anytime I choose; and the minute I do, your magic carte blanche becomes nothing but a moderately interesting souvenir."

"Are you declaring full martial law, then?" McPhee demanded.

There was a beep from the comm before Holloway could answer. Leaning over, he swiped at the key. "What?" he demanded.

It was Gasperi again . . . and his face had gone white. "Colonel, we've just picked up a new group of wake-trails," he said, his voice hoarse. "Same baseline as the others. The first ones."

Holloway felt his stomach tighten. "You're sure it's not a resonance between the fueler and that incoming yacht?"

"I'm positive, sir. It's the Conquerors."

Holloway glanced at Takara. He couldn't hear the other end of the conversation, but it was clear from his expression he'd already guessed what was happening. "How many?"

"It's hard to tell," Gasperi said. "Looks like five. Maybe six."

And it had taken only four Conqueror ships to demolish the *Jutland* task force. "And they are incoming?" he asked, just to be sure.

"Yes, sir," Gasperi breathed. "I think so. I'd say two hours before they hit the system."

"Understood," Holloway said. "Give the colony-evacuation order. All ships and vehicles to be prepped at once; senior officers to meet me in the command room in five minutes. And start prep on Number Two again. When it's ready, get it out to Edo with the news."

"Yes, sir."

Holloway keyed off the comm. "The Conquerors?"

Takara asked, his voice sounding like someone walking through a graveyard.

Holloway nodded. "Two hours out. Five ships, maybe six." He looked at McPhee. "The answer is yes, Mr. McPhee. As of now, Dorcas is under full martial law."

16

The last red light on the fighter-status board winked orange and then turned to green. "This is Shrike," a heavily Russian-accented voice came over the fueler's speaker. "I show positive docking."

"Confirmed," Quinn said, glancing at the course setting and then at the status boards. "Final check; all fighters."

One by one the six pilots checked in. "Acknowledged," Quinn said. "Stand by for mesh-out."

He keyed off the intercom. "All right, Max," he said. "Let's go."

"Yes, Commander," the computer answered. "The Peacekeeper base appears to be attempting communication. Do you wish an orbit plot that will bring us into full contact range?"

"Negative," Quinn said. "We don't have the time. Kick it."

"Acknowledged." There was a flicker from the boards, a creak of metal from some uncompensated stress line, and they were off.

Aric took a deep breath. "Well," he said. "Here we go."

"I guess so," Quinn said, doing something with the board. "You ready for this?"

In the distance, from all around them, came a series of dull thuds as fueler/fighter interface hatchways were sprung. "I hope so," Aric said. "You're Hydra and I'm El Dorado, right?"

"Right," Quinn nodded. "When I was a pilot, fighter crews always used tag names when they were together and away from other personnel, which would mean pretty much from now on. I suppose that could have changed in the past few years, though. Masefield will introduce us to the others; listen to see what he calls them and take your cue from that."

There was a flicker of a shadow outside the control room, and a slender young man with close-cropped sandy hair appeared at the doorway. "Commander Quinn?" he said, offering his hand. "I'm Tom Masefield; Clipper. Good to meet you, sir."

"Same here," Quinn said, taking the other's hand. "This is my tail, Cavanagh—El Dorado. I'm Hydra."

Clipper cocked an eyebrow. "Really. I understood it was Maestro."

Quinn glanced at Aric. "It was. Once. What else did Bokamba say in that private message?"

"Not much," Clipper said, giving Aric a speculative look. "All I know is who you are and that Bokamba has transferred this command to you. Unofficially, I presume?"

"Quite unofficially," Quinn agreed. "Did he say anything about the mission?"

Clipper shook his head. "He just said to trust him. And you."

He broke off and moved aside as a second man, dark in hair and complexion, floated into view beside him. "Hydra, El Dorado, this is my tail," he introduced the man. "Lieutenant Sieyes; Delphi."

"Honored, sir," Delphi said, offering his hand to Quinn. "I noticed on my way in that the others were assembling in the wardroom."

"Good," Quinn said. "Let's go get acquainted."

The last of the other ten men were squeezing their way in as Aric and his group arrived. Even empty, the wardroom had always struck Aric as being pretty small. With fourteen men filling it from floor to ceiling, it was long past the borderline into claustrophobic.

"All right, men, dress it up," Clipper called, easing past Quinn into the wardroom as the others deftly repositioned themselves to line up with their commander's definition of vertical. "In descending seniority order. Khirkov and Asquith: Shrike and Crackajack. Bethmann and Marlowe: Jaeger and Watchdog. Vanbrugh and Hodgson: Wraith and Augur. Atkinson and Young: Paladin and Dazzler. And Kempis and Savile: Harlequin and Bookmaker. Don't ask about that last one, by the way. Gentlemen: this is Quinn, our temporary commander, and Cavanagh. Hydra and El Dorado."

"Good to meet you all," Quinn said. "Let's get right down to business. If you'll look at the display there—"

"A question, first, if I may, sir," Jaeger spoke up. "I'd like to know what exactly our authorization is on this."

"You saw our orders, Jaeger," Clipper reminded him.

"Yes, sir, I did," Jaeger nodded, his eyes still on Quinn. "I don't recall any mention of a Commander Quinn in them. Watchdog also noticed something else unusual as we were bringing the fighter into dock. The Peacekeeper markings on the side of the fueler seemed to be a bit smeared."

"You're very observant, Watchdog," Quinn complimented him. "You're right, the markings are fresh. This ship has only recently been recommissioned into service."

"I see," Jaeger said, his voice studiously neutral. "Have you official orders confirming that, sir?"

Quinn glanced at Clipper. "Let's go ahead and cut through the noise here," he said to Jaeger. "This is not, in fact, a sanctioned Peacekeeper mission. I have no orders; I'm not even a reserve officer anymore. I needed an escort on an unofficial but important mission into unknown space. Bokamba offered to get me one. You're it."

Aric looked around the tiny room, his mouth dry. He'd known this moment would eventually come, but he'd hoped they would be too far along for anyone to turn back easily when they learned the truth. Here, barely minutes out, Quinn was not only inviting them to leave, but to arrest the two of them in the bargain and haul them straight back to Dorcas.

"Quinn," Wraith said suddenly. "Of course. Maestro."

A murmur of surprise rippled through the room. "Maestro?" Dazzler said. "*The* Maestro?"

"There was only one," Clipper said, his voice and face both a little pinched. Small wonder; with Bokamba's private message to him, he was effectively an accessory before the fact here. The team could haul him in, too.

"I see," Dazzler said, pushing himself gently away from the wall to drift toward Quinn. "You're the one who made all the noise that forced the Peacekeepers to reevaluate their screening procedure. Kept a lot of people out of the Copperheads. Including my brother."

"That's enough, Dazzler," Clipper said. "Get back to your position."

"No, that's all right," Quinn said, his voice sounding tired. "Let him have his say."

"Thank you, sir," Dazzler said, maneuvering to a stop directly in front of Quinn. "It was my older brother, sir. Charleston; four years older than me. He'd wanted to be a Copperhead since he was fifteen. The day after his eighteenth birthday he went down and enlisted. He went through the tests, the preliminary pilot training— the whole slate. He was two weeks from getting his Mindlink implant when the NorCoord hearings forced everyone to undergo new certification. He didn't make the new cut."

"I'm sorry," Quinn said.

Dazzler shook his head. "Don't be," he said. "It took him six months to get over it; but at that point he realized that going into the Copperheads would have been the worst mistake of his life. He wasn't anywhere near to having what it took to be a professional warrior."

And to Aric's surprise Dazzler held out his hand. "A long time ago he told me that if I ever ran into you, I was to thank you for saving him from the rashness of youth. His words."

For a pair of heartbeats Quinn didn't move. Then, looking as if he didn't quite believe it, he reached out and took the other's hand. "Thank you," he said quietly.

"No thanks needed," Dazzler said, releasing Quinn's hand and floating back toward his place in the group. "You helped take some of the glamour out of being a Copperhead. Speaking strictly for myself, I'd rather not fly with people who came in looking for glamour. I want the best. You helped make sure that's what we got."

For a long minute the room was silent. "You were going to tell us about the mission," Clipper said.

"Yes." Quinn took a deep breath, and Aric could see the effort in his face as he forced the ghosts of the past back down where they belonged. "You all know about the Conqueror attack on the *Jutland* task force," he said. "What you don't know is that the body count came up one short. Commander Pheylan Cavanagh, captain of the *Kinshasa.*"

"Cavanagh?" Harlequin asked, looking at Aric.

"My younger brother," Aric said.

"Ah," Augur said knowingly. "So that's why we're going off half-cocked this way?"

"It's nothing of the sort," Aric said, keeping his voice level. "We tried to get the Peacekeepers to mount a proper rescue mission. Admiral Rudzinski turned us down."

"All the more reason we shouldn't be here," Jaeger said. "This is well past just being unsanctioned, Maestro. It's been effectively forbidden."

"Is there any evidence Cavanagh's still alive?" Delphi asked.

"Nothing positive," Quinn said. "Just the fact of no body and no debris from his escape pod. And the reasonable assumption that the Conquerors would want to take at least one live prisoner for examination."

"I watched those recordings very carefully," Shrike said, his finger fidgeting through his beard. "It was my understanding that all pod emergency beacons had been silenced before the watchships left the scene."

"That's true," Clipper put in. "But there's been some speculation that the Conquerors were using the beacons to locate and destroy the pods. It's possible Commander Cavanagh figured that out and shut his off before they got to him."

"And had his prudence rewarded by being taken prisoner," Crackajack said. "Some deal. You have any idea where to start looking?"

"We have the incoming vector that the *Jutland* and Dorcas garrison computed," Quinn said. "My plan was to look for likely systems that direction and check them out."

"That will take time," Jaeger pointed out. "And meanwhile the worlds of the Commonwealth are open to enemy attack."

Crackajack snorted. "After what happened to the

Jutland, I hardly think six Corvines are going to make a lot of difference."

"That's irrelevant," Jaeger said sharply. "Our job is not to decide whether our presence is important or not. Nor is it to take our ships wherever we ourselves think proper. Our job is to go where ordered and to do there whatever needs to be done." He looked at Quinn, then at Clipper. "We have no legitimate reason to be here, Commander. I respectfully but strongly suggest we turn around and go back."

A muscle in Clipper's cheek twitched. "Maestro?"

"You're welcome to go back, Jaeger," Quinn said. "All of you are, in fact, if you don't want to continue. El Dorado and I are going on, whether you stay or not."

"I'm staying," Dazzler said. "You're going to need a tail, anyway."

"Sorry, Dazzler, but you can't lose me that easily," his partner Paladin said. "Looks like you've got yourself a wingman, Maestro."

"Delphi and I are in, too," Clipper said. "Call me old-fashioned, but I don't much care for the idea of Command simply abandoning Cavanagh to the Conquerors. Our people deserve better than that."

"So do all the people of the Commonwealth," Wraith said. "We're wasting time, Jaeger."

"Yes," Jaeger said, looking around. "Who else is coming back with us?"

"And if you want to leave, this is the time to do it," Clipper added. "If you don't go now, you're in for the duration."

Aric looked around the group. None of them looked especially comfortable, but none of them spoke up, either. "I guess it's you two, then," Clipper said at last to Jaeger and Wraith. "You'd better get going before you lose any more distance. Maestro, you want to go back to control and mesh us in?"

"That won't be necessary," Wraith said, pushing off a wall toward the wardroom doorway, his partner Augur following him. "We can disengage in mesh." His lip twitched in an almost reluctant half smile. "Besides, right now you need all the distance you can get. The farther you are from Dorcas when we blow the whistle, the less likely they'll send someone chasing after you."

"You're probably right," Quinn agreed. "Thank you."

"Consider it our contribution to the cause." Wraith nodded to Clipper. "Good luck, sir. We'll see you at the court-martial."

"Thank you," Clipper said dryly. "We'll bring you back a piece of Conqueror ship as a souvenir."

The four men left the room, disappearing into the complex of small rooms between them and the hull. "All right, Maestro," Clipper said. "What's the plan?"

"As I said, it's going to have to be a physical search," Quinn said, floating over to the wardroom repeater board. A tactical star map was displayed there, with several colored lines, circles, and a slender cone superimposed on it. "Here's where the Conquerors hit the *Jutland* force," he said, indicating the tip of the cone. "Dorcas didn't have a baseline, so the incoming vector's a little vague. Clipper, I asked Bokamba to see if the lab people had come up with an estimate of how far the ships had come. Was there anything in his message about that?"

"No," Clipper said. "I've heard from other sources that they're still having trouble getting zero-point friction and heat-capacity readings from that piece of hull they found."

"Okay," Quinn said, studying the map. "In that case I guess we take potshots and hope for warrior's luck. With a twenty-degree uncertainty on the vector and assuming a hundred-light-year range, we wind up with eighteen systems to check out. If we don't find anything, we'll try expanding the cone."

"What happens when we find them?" Bookmaker asked.

"You four Corvines will fly cover while El Dorado and I go in for a closer look," Quinn told him. "I trust you haven't neglected your atmospheric combat work."

"The rust rubs off quickly," Clipper assured him. "I don't suppose this fueler is armed?"

"As a matter of fact, it is," Quinn said. "We've got two shredder guns and a bank of five space/space missiles."

Clipper gave Aric a speculative look. "You ever had experience with military hardware, El Dorado?"

"No," Aric said. "But I won't be the one using it. Max, say hello to everyone."

"Good day, gentlemen," Max's voice said smoothly. "My name is Max. I'll be handling all shipboard functions for the duration of the trip."

"Interesting," Bookmaker said, cocking an eyebrow at Aric. "Is that a parasentient?"

Aric nodded. "A Carthage-Ivy-Gamma. Class Seven DM capabilities."

"Decay-driven randomized, right?"

"Right," Aric said. "Modified Korngold-Che."

Bookmaker looked at Clipper. "Well, old man Cavanagh didn't scrimp on equipment, anyway. Carthage-Ivys are the current top of the line, a couple of notches above anything else on the market. Expensive as hell, too."

"He probably cut himself a discount," Clipper said. "How will it do in combat?"

"About as well as any parasentient would," Bookmaker said. "Much faster than any human, naturally, but a little short on combat imagination."

"That's all right," Clipper said. "Two shredder guns

and five missiles aren't likely to strain its capabilities. Max, how does the ship itself look?"

"All systems are working properly," Max said. "It seems to have been kept in good repair. We have an extensive assortment of replacement modules aboard, too, should something go wrong."

Clipper shifted his attention to Quinn. "You ever worked with this computer before?"

"No," Quinn said. "But Lord Cavanagh handled the installation personally. I would presume he chose the best."

"Bookmaker seems to agree," Clipper said. "All right, then. How are we fixed for supplies?"

"We had about three weeks' worth," Quinn said. "With two fewer ships and four fewer men, we can stretch that out a bit."

Clipper pursed his lips. "We can," he said. "But I'm not sure we should. Jaeger and Wraith had a valid point: our sworn duty is to the Commonwealth. In fact, the more I think of it, the more I think you're pushing things as it is. Eighteen systems—you're talking something close to a month there."

Quinn glanced around at the other Copperheads. "How many systems would you feel comfortable with?" he asked Clipper.

Clipper gazed at the display, a pained look in his eyes. "I don't think we can afford to do more than five," he said bluntly. "If we haven't found Commander Cavanagh by then, we should turn back."

Aric felt his stomach tighten. "Five systems? That's—"

He broke off at Quinn's gesture. "You realize, of course," Quinn said to Clipper, "that if we don't bring Commander Cavanagh back, we're going to be in that much more trouble."

"I'm extremely aware of that," Clipper said, looking

him straight in the eye. "Don't forget that as accessory before the fact, my head's on the block right next to yours."

Quinn grimaced. "You're right, of course," he agreed soberly. "My apologies. Very well: five systems it is. And we hope for warrior's luck."

"That we do." Clipper turned to the others. "All right, gentlemen. Briefing's over, and we've got gear to stow and fighters to deprep. Let's get to it."

There was a noisy but organized exodus from the wardroom until only Aric and Quinn were left. "Went better than I expected," Quinn commented.

Aric nodded mechanically, his eyes on the display. Five systems. Out of the billions of stars in the galaxy, they had just five to look at. It was like a roll of the dice, with Pheylan's life and the careers of a lot of good men on the table.

A lot of good men, and one good woman. "Max, was that the *Cavatina* you were picking up just before we meshed out?" he asked.

"The wake-trail registered as an Effenzeal-Royce star yacht," the computer replied. "No further identification was possible."

"No, of course not," Aric murmured. "Thank you."

"We knew she was going to be in trouble the minute the *Cavatina* arrived," Quinn reminded him.

"She was already in trouble," Aric said. "Those attempts to contact us weren't just Holloway calling to say good-bye. I just hope there's something Dad can do to calm him down."

"I'm sure there is," Quinn said. "Your father still has quite a few high-level contacts in both Parliament and Peacekeeper Command. He can probably arrange some kind of house arrest for her back on Avon until we get back."

"I hope so," Aric said. "I'd hate for her to be stuck in the brig on Dorcas."

"Stockade," Quinn corrected. "Or guardhouse, if she's a temporary prisoner. Brigs are aboard ships."

Aric snorted gently. "Thank you."

"Don't worry, she'll be fine," Quinn said. "If you're going to worry about anyone's safety, I suggest you worry about ours."

Five two-man fighter ships, against possibly the entire Conqueror battle force. "You're right," Aric said. "I'll try to keep my priorities straight."

17 It was impossible to slam a sliding door open; but as Colonel Holloway came stalking into the room, Melinda had the distinct impression that he'd tried to do so anyway. "I don't have time for this, Cavanagh," he bit out. "McPhee and his ship are ready to lift. Get aboard."

"We can't leave yet," she said, trying not to flinch before that glare. "The *Cavatina*'s only going to be a few minutes ahead of that Conqueror force. If I don't warn them away as soon as they mesh in, they're dead."

"We can chase them away without your help," Holloway said, sounding fractionally less angry. "They'll be fine. Now get on that ship and get out of here."

Mclinda shook her head. "He won't listen to you, Colonel," she said. "I know my father. He knows I'm here, and he'll argue the point with you. You won't be able to convince him fast enough."

Holloway exhaled noisily. "Look, Doctor, I understand your concern. But you're worrying about nothing. Yes, they're only a couple of minutes apart; but the odds of their both picking the same area to mesh in are practically nonexistent. Your father will see what's happening and scramble out of here."

"Can you guarantee that?"

"Of course not," Holloway shot back. "I also can't guarantee that they'll mesh in far enough away for you and McPhee to get past them if I let you wait around here any longer. I'm sorry, but that's the way it has to be."

Melinda took a deep breath. The logic, unfortunately, was irrefutable. And it left her with only one option. "Then let McPhee go," she said. "I'll stay."

Holloway's eyes narrowed. "What?"

"I'll stay here," she repeated, trying to ignore the painful thudding in her chest. "Chances are you're going to need all the medical expertise you can get. I'm a doctor, and I'm offering my services."

"In case you've forgotten, you're also a prisoner," he pointed out.

"You've placed Dorcas under martial law. You can temporarily suspend the charges if you want to."

His eyes locked on to hers like twin laser scalpels. "You understand what you're offering?" he asked.

"Yes," she said quietly. "Which isn't to say I'm thrilled by the whole idea."

For a half dozen of her accelerated heartbeats he continued to study her. "I'd be worried about you if you were," he said at last, pulling out his comm. "All right, you've got yourself a deal. Duggen? Cavanagh's staying here. Tell McPhee to seal up and get moving." He got an acknowledgment and shoved the comm back into its belt pouch. "Come on."

The landing area was an anthill of furious activity, with Peacekeepers shoving last-minute civilian survival bags into aircar storage compartments as the civilians themselves crowded aboard. Melinda watched their faces as Holloway eased his car through the chaos toward the command complex, marveling that amid all the haste she was seeing no signs of hysteria or panic.

On the contrary, everyone seemed grimly ready for whatever was on its way. "They seem well prepared," she commented.

"We've had a couple of weeks," Holloway reminded her. "Those who didn't want to stay left a long time ago."

"How many are left?"

"More than I like. About twenty-five thousand, out of an original population of forty-seven."

Melinda glanced up at the clear blue sky, wishing irrationally that there were some clouds up there to hide them from unfriendly eyes. "Where are you taking them?"

"There's a narrow canyon in the mountains about seventy kilometers east of the settlement," he said. "It's got a river for water and about as much shelter as we're going to find anywhere nearby. We've prepped it as best we could in the time we had."

"What about food and medical supplies?"

"We've got everything we could pack up and move out there. The question will be how well we can defend it if the Conquerors decide they want to root us out."

And whether they cared enough about the surrounding real estate to nuke the place, Melinda added to herself. But that line of reasoning was too unproductive and unpleasant to bring up. Holloway had undoubtedly already thought of it, anyway.

With all the activity going on outside, Melinda had expected to find the command complex in more or less the same state, with troops busily dismantling and moving equipment out to the aircars. To her surprise the place was already nearly empty, with only a handful of Peacekeepers still monitoring what was left of the equipment. "You work fast," she commented.

"Like I said, we prepped as best we could," Holloway said, moving across the empty room to a console with a half-dozen displays showing complicated-looking patterns. "Crane, what's the latest on our visitors?"

"Still incoming," the young man said, his voice quavering a little. "The yacht and Conquerors both. And we picked up a new signal just a couple of minutes ago. Looks like two of the Corvines are coming back."

Holloway frowned. "Just two of them?"

"That's what the baseline says," Crane said. "The fueler's still outgoing; I assume the other fighters are still with it."

Holloway looked at Melinda. "Did the fueler have a tachyon detector built into the hull? Never mind," he waved the question away before she could answer. "They left before the Conqueror wake-trails showed up. Means those two Corvines don't know what they're flying into. Crane, what's their ETA?"

"If they do a standard mesh, a couple of minutes before the yacht and Conquerors are due in," Crane said.

"Doesn't rain but it pours," Holloway commented. "All right, get a laser trained on their vector. We'll want to give them as much warning as we can."

"Yes, sir," the other said, keying his board.

"It should just be a couple more minutes before the yacht meshes in," Holloway said to Melinda. "You know what you're going to say?"

Melinda nodded, wishing she knew how to read the patterns on those displays. It was like sitting in pitch-darkness, listening to the breathing of some unknown animal. Not knowing when or how it was going to strike.

Something on the console pinged, making Melinda jump. "Colonel, the Corvines have meshed in," Crane said. "We've got laser contact."

"Corvines, this is Colonel Holloway," Holloway said. "We've got a red-alert situation here: five or more bogies incoming, probable Conqueror warships. What's your current status?"

There was a moment of silence, punctuated by what might have been an under-the-breath curse. "This is Lieutenant Bethmann, Colonel," a voice said. "I'd say as of right now our status is that of support units under your command. What are your orders?"

"Get down here as fast as you can. You have a grid location for the colony?"

"We've got it, yes, sir."

"We're evacuating to a canyon in the mountains seventy-two klicks due east of the settlement," Holloway told him. "Come in from the north, and we'll guide you down."

"Acknowledged," Bethmann said. "On our way."

Holloway keyed off. "Well, at least we may now have a way to plug that gap in the eastern wall," he commented. "What's ETA on the yacht, Crane?"

"Forty-five seconds, sir," Crane said.

"Good. You ready, Doctor?"

"Yes," Melinda said, conscious again of the thudding of her heart. "Colonel, how soon after the Conquerors mesh in can they get to the surface?"

Holloway shrugged. "Depends on how far out they do their mesh. We usually run an eight-thousand-klick safety margin ourselves, but there's no reason you can't come in a lot closer. If I were commanding an attack force, I'd bring us in as tight as I could without getting into serious magnetic-field conduction problems. I'm guessing they'll mesh a couple thousand klicks out. Maybe only a thousand, if their commander is a little nuts. We'll know soon enough."

"I see," Melinda murmured.

"Don't worry, we should have plenty of time to get to the canyon before they get here." He threw her a measuring look. "Sorry you stayed?"

She looked at the enigmatic patterns on the displays. "I'm fine."

The console pinged again. "Yacht's meshed," Crane announced. "Go ahead, Doctor."

"*Cavatina*, this is Melinda Cavanagh," Melinda called. "Dad, you have to get out of here right away. There's a Conqueror force coming in right behind you."

"Dr. Cavanagh, this is Captain Teva," the familiar voice of the *Cavatina*'s commander came back. "We confirm the wake-trail; you sure it's a Conqueror force?"

"Quite sure," Melinda told him, her eyes on the displays. Wishing she knew what they were telling her. "Is my father there?"

There was a brief pause. "I'm afraid he's not with us," Teva said. "But he said to tell your brother that the vector search had come up dry."

So he hadn't been able to get anything about the Conquerors from the Mrach legends. Just as well Aric and Quinn hadn't waited. "I understand," she told Teva. "Now get out of here."

"Doctor, if a Conqueror force is coming in—"

"There's nothing you can do," Melinda cut him off. "You can't get to me in time; and if you try, you'll fly right into them. Don't worry about me—I'm with the Peacekeeper force here. You just get out of here and sound the alarm."

"Doctor, I have a responsibility to you."

"Your responsibility is to the ship and to the family," Melinda said, enunciating the words carefully. "And to obey all family orders. Is that clear?"

She could picture the pinched look on Teva's face. But the coded phrasing was precise and unequivocal . . . and Teva *did* know his responsibilities. "Clear, Dr. Cavanagh," he sighed. "Good luck."

"You too."

Holloway motioned, and Crane keyed off the transmitter. "Does he mean it?"

"Yes," Melinda said. So that was it. She was here, and she was in for the duration. "Shouldn't we be getting out of here ourselves?"

"Go ahead," Holloway said, his attention on the displays again. "I want to wait and see what size force we're up against. Get on any of the aircars out there that has room for you."

"All right." Melinda turned and started for the door. She was nearly there when the console pinged a third time—

"Colonel!" Crane yelped.

Melinda spun back around. "What?"

"They're right on top of us," Holloway gritted, slapping Crane's shoulder and racing toward Melinda. "This is Holloway," he barked into his comm. "Full alert—the bogies have meshed at atmosphere level—five hundred klicks up. All personnel and vehicles, get out of the settlement immediately."

The words were barely out of his mouth when a violent thunderclap rocked the building. Melinda fought for balance, dimly aware that Crane was shouting something through the ringing in her ears.

And then Holloway was beside her, steadying her with a firm grip on her upper arm. "What happened?" she shouted.

"They hit the main transmitter," he shouted back, turning her back toward the door again. "Laser blast. Let's go."

They ran outside, Crane right behind them. Melinda looked up—"Colonel!" she gasped, jerking back against him. Overhead a dozen air vehicles were hovering all around them—

"What are you doing?" he demanded, grabbing her

arm again and hauling her bodily away from the complex. "Those are ours. Come on."

She let him lead her toward the last aircar still waiting on the ground, feeling a hot flush of mortification rush across her face as she watched the vehicles overhead swing out of their vertical ascents and head east. A second later the embarrassment was forgotten as a brilliant flash lit up the hills to the west. "Another shot," Holloway shouted, his grip on her arm tightening. "Brace yourself—"

The thunderclap seemed quieter this time; but to her surprise the ground tilted wildly beneath her as the sound seemed to drive straight through her head. She fought for balance, felt a second hand on her other arm—

And then, suddenly, she was being pulled up a short ramp into a low-ceilinged metal compartment. "Sit down," Holloway ordered, pushing her down into one of a pair of empty seats just behind the cockpit area and dropping into the other one himself. "Bremmer—go!"

The aircar lurched upward and swung around. Her head still throbbing, Melinda fumbled with the unfamiliar military-style restraints, getting them fastened just as the pilot opened the throttle and sent them roaring eastward.

"You all right?" Holloway asked.

"Fine," Melinda said, blinking her eyes a couple of times and stretching her jaw experimentally. She wasn't quite fine, not yet, but she was definitely headed that direction. "What happened? Sonic shock?"

"Probably." Holloway took her face in his hands, turning it toward him and peering into her eyes. "Your pupils look okay," he said, letting go again. "Must have just shaken up your inner ear a little."

"Yes," she agreed, looking around with some surprise. From the size of the aircar she'd expected it to be a passenger design, with room for forty or fifty people. But aside from the pilot and copilot, the cabin was equipped with only six other seats. Crane was in one; the remaining three held grim-faced men in civilian clothing.

"It's a cargo carrier," Holloway explained, ducking his head slightly to look past the pilot's shoulder at the foothills rolling past beneath them. "Bremmer, you picking up any bogies yet?"

"No, sir," the pilot said. "But the range on this thing isn't very good. Shall I call the array at the canyon?"

"You wouldn't get through," Holloway said. "Cash to crinkles that second shot took out the backup transmitter. Just keep her low and fast."

The minutes crept by. Melinda leaned close to Holloway, trying to get as good a view as she could out the cockpit canopy, the only windows on the aircar. The plains and low hills began to give way to taller mountains, some covered with squat, rubbery-looking trees, others craggy and bare except for occasional patches of ground cover. The aircar hugged the ground, staying no more than a few meters above treetop level, dipping and rising with the terrain. As they ducked over some of the higher passes, she could see snow-covered peaks in the distance, and she wondered how high up in those mountains Holloway's canyon was situated. If they were going to have to deal with frostbite and hypothermia—

"We're picking up something, Colonel," the copilot said suddenly. "Coming into detection range behind us—"

He was cut off by a brilliant flash to their right. Reflexively, Melinda twisted her head away, just in time to catch Holloway's shoulder with her forehead as the aircar lurched to the side. She rocked back again as the pilot straightened out; and then the crash webbing whipped out, wrapping protectively around her and pinning her in place. "How bad?" Holloway shouted over the suddenly shrill engine noise.

"Bad," the pilot shouted back. "Starboard stub's gone —airfoils inoperative. We're going down."

Melinda set her teeth together to protect them, straining against the grip of the crash webbing to look ahead out the canopy. The wooded hills, still shooting past underneath, were rising toward them at an alarming pace. An unusually tall tree suddenly appeared in front of them, twisting to the side at the last second as the pilot managed to veer around it. They dropped to treetop level, and the whine of the engine was drowned out by the cacophony of branches scraping across the underside of the aircar. Farther down, and suddenly Melinda was being thrown back and forth inside the webbing as the aircar twisted furiously between the trees like a crazed snake. She squinted her eyes half-shut against the shaking as they fell, not wanting to watch but unable to look away. The screech of branches against metal was all around them now, a banshee scream of imminent death—

And with a horrendous crash, they hit.

"You all right?" Holloway asked.

Melinda blinked her eyes open. The aircar was down, the whine of the engines had stopped, and aside from an unpleasant tingle where her skin was pressed tightly against the crash webbing, she seemed to be unhurt. "Yes," she said. "How long was I out?"

"Minute or so," Holloway said. He'd already freed himself from his webbing; forcing a hand through the mesh at her side, he triggered her release. "We've got to make tracks," he said as the webbing retracted. "There's a camo suit under your seat. Get it out and put it on."

Melinda obeyed, pulling out the heavy package and unfolding it. It consisted of a hooded serape and a thick belt connected together by a slender tube. Sliding forward in her seat, she got the belt on and pulled the serape over her head. The material was heavy and thick, with an odd texture to it.

"Ever fired an Oberon assault gun?"

"I've shot rifles a few times," Melinda said, getting shakily to her feet and looking around. The last of the other passengers, also wearing a camo serape, was just easing past the torn and twisted metal where the door had been, a thick and thoroughly nasty-looking double-barreled military rifle clutched in his hand. Crane was standing next to the gash, pulling two more of the assault guns from an open storage rack. "It was nothing like that, though."

"Then this isn't the time to learn," Holloway decided, accepting one of the assault guns from Crane and ushering Melinda toward the exit. "First-aid kit's under the pilot seat—grab it. We've got to get to cover before a follow-up ship gets here."

The crash had gouged a surprisingly wide gash through the surrounding landscape, probably much of the damage caused by trees knocking each other down as the aircar plowed its way through. Ahead Melinda could see the three civilians picking their way carefully across the rubble toward the nearest edge of standing timber, their serapes rippling in the breeze. The pilot and copilot were angling to either side of the civilians' direction, the copilot limping heavily.

"This way, Doctor," Holloway said, pointing toward the copilot. "Crane, you go with Bremmer. Find some cover and dig in. Stay off the comm—the Conquerors like to track radios. Whistles and hand signals only."

"Right."

Holloway and Melinda reached the edge of the trees the same time as the copilot. "That looks good over there," Holloway said, pointing to a low rock formation. "Wei, how's the ankle?"

"Not too bad, Colonel," the copilot said, his voice soft and polite. "I don't think it's broken."

"We'll find out soon enough," Holloway said, taking his arm and helping him to the cover of the rock. "Did you get a Mayday out before we hit?"

"Yes, sir," Wei said, wincing as he sat down on the ground. "But there was no response. We're still eight klicks out—they probably didn't pick us up."

"One of the other aircars might have, though," Holloway said, unslinging his assault gun. "Check his ankle, Doctor. No, hold it—let me get your suit going first."

Melinda held still as he reached under her serape and slid a switch forward on her belt. Faintly, from the hood, she heard a gentle hissing. "What's that?" she asked.

"Liquid nitrogen from the belt tanks," he said, reaching under his own serape. "Works with the reflective layering to erase your infrared signature. Here's the other half of the mirage," he added, pulling a fat disk from under his serape. Working his right arm free from the serape, he clicked a switch on the disk and threw it through the trees to land about twenty meters away from them, roughly opposite the aircar's nose. "If the thing works—for a change—it should now look more like a human being than we do."

"Of course, it's all a waste of time if they don't have IR detectors," Wei pointed out. "Or don't know what a human signature looks like."

"We can but try," Holloway agreed. "Okay, Doctor, go ahead and check his ankle."

Carefully, Melinda got Wei's boot off, feeling a drop of sweat trickle down the middle of her back despite the cooling effect of the serape against it. She was a doctor, certainly, and had had the whole spectrum of medical training. But theory and simulation work were a far cry from working on living patients. What actual surgery she'd done was years in her past, and she wasn't at all sure how well she was going to be able to dust off those skills.

But for the moment, at least, it wasn't a challenge she had to face. "It's just a sprain," she assured Wei, opening the first-aid kit and digging out a pressure bandage. "It should be all right in a few—"

"Quiet," Holloway cut her off. "Something's coming."

Melinda froze, listening. In the distance she could hear a faint humming sound. "One of ours?" she whispered.

"Doesn't sound like it," Holloway said grimly, working a pair of slides on his assault gun. "Wei, signal Bremmer and Crane to get ready."

"Yes, sir," Wei said, digging a slender tube from his tunic pocket and looping the attached chain around his neck. Lifting the tube to his lips, he blew three short oddly pitched trills and then one long one. The answer came immediately: one long and one short.

"I think I see them," Holloway said, peering up through the trees. "Cavanagh, get as much of you under your serape as you can and stay put."

Melinda hunched down behind the edge of the rock formation, pulling her legs up beneath the edge of the serape and tightening the hood a little closer around her face. The humming was getting louder, and she caught a flicker of something white as it shot past a gap in the tree canopy above. Clenching her teeth, she braced herself—

And suddenly it was there, swooping across the gap gouged by the crashing aircar: a milky-white dragonfly-like vehicle, topped with a circular haze of whirling rotors. It made a tight loop around the crushed nose of the aircar and then moved around behind it. For a moment it hovered there, sending up a cloud of dust from the freshly turned earth, swiveling its nose gently back and forth as if deliberately inviting anyone nearby to attack. Melinda tensed, but the Peacekeepers held their fire, and a minute later the ship settled to the ground. On both sides doors popped open.

And from them two aliens stepped out.

Melinda squinted across the dusty clearing, her fear momentarily forgotten in sudden clinical interest. The aliens were like nothing she'd ever seen before: roughly human in height, with slender bipedal builds and thin, narrow heads that extended well behind them. Good cranial capacity, with enough brain size for mental capability plus strong manipulative control. They were too far away for her to get a good look at the hands, but from the way they gripped the gray sticks they were holding, they clearly had opposable thumbs. Possibly two per hand, in fact. They had tails, too, short flat things that extended from low dorsal ridges just above the juncture of the legs and continually twirled around in a corkscrewing motion that reminded her of a water creature she'd seen once. A heat radiator, possibly, or perhaps some sort of atmospheric sampler like those in snake tongues. One of the aliens turned in her direction, giving her a clear view of a triangular face, deep-set eyes beneath brow ridges, and a pointed snout reminiscent of a bird's beak. They walked slightly bent forward, their feet appearing to have something of the same splayfooted design of seagull feet except without any webbing between the toes.

"Colonel?" Wei whispered urgently.

"Hold your fire," Holloway murmured. "Maybe they'll be happy with wrecking the aircar and go away."

Melinda swallowed, jolted back to the deadly realities of the situation. These weren't just a new species of self-starfaring aliens come here for her to examine.

These were the Conquerors. They were here to kill.

Four more of the aliens had joined the first two, the newcomers waiting beside the craft as the first pair picked their way across the rubble to the side of the aircar. They looked inside, and through the pulsating wind from the rotors Melinda could hear them saying something. An amplified voice answered back. "Well, they know we got out," Holloway murmured beside her. "Let's see how badly they want to find us."

The answer was quick and decisive. Within a few seconds the vehicle had lifted smoothly back into the sky, rising ten meters before coming to a halt. Fanning out, the six Conquerors on the ground started toward the trees where Holloway had thrown the decoy disk.

"Shouldn't we open fire?" Wei asked tensely, his knuckles tight where he gripped his assault gun.

"All in good time," Holloway told him, squinting upward at the hovering vehicle. "You and I will try to take out the copter. Set for full antiarmor, then whistle Crane and Bremmer that they're to hit the ground troops when we open fire."

"Yes, sir," Wei said, lifting his whistle and launching into a short series of blasts.

The Conquerors stopped, dropping down into half-crouched stances, their heads darting back and forth as they searched for the source of the sound. Melinda tensed, but the odd pitch of the whistle seemed to defeat their efforts to locate it. Wei finished his message, and for a moment the Conquerors remained where they were—again, Melinda thought, almost as if deliberately inviting attack. But again Holloway held his fire, and after a moment they straightened up and continued their cautious march toward the trees.

"Sir?" Wei hissed nervously.

"Get ready," Holloway said. He threw a glance at Melinda, and she was struck by the underlying calmness in his face. "Brace yourself, Doctor; this is going to be noisy. Wei, on zero. Three, two, one, zero."

The two assault guns erupted in unison, shattering the quiet of the forest with the vicious stutter-bark of explosive shells cycled together with what sounded like small missiles. An instant later the sound was echoed from across the woods as the other Peacekeepers and civilians opened fire.

Melinda pressed closer to the ground, squeezing her eyes shut, cringing as the multiple thunderclaps of explosions pounded against her ears and head. Through the noise she could faintly hear shouts; through her closed eyelids she could see flickers and flashes of brilliant light—

And then there was a violent crash that picked her up and slammed her to the ground again.

And silence.

Cautiously, she opened her eyes and lifted her head a few centimeters. Sprawled on the ground in her line of sight were the unmoving forms of the nearest Conquerors, their jumpsuits spattered with very humanlike red blood. Beyond them the crumpled form of the copter lay canted and burning against the ground perhaps thirty meters behind their wrecked aircar. Crane and Bremmer, along with the three civilians, were making their way across the open land toward the copter. "Is it over?" she asked, not realizing until she said it how inane the question probably sounded.

But if Holloway agreed with that assessment, he didn't say so. "For the moment," he said. "No, stay put —we're holding backstop position. You hurt?"

"Just a little shaken," she said, coughing on the words. The air was thick with acrid smoke from the explosions and fire, burning her nose and lungs. "What happens now?"

"If they're all dead, we head for the canyon," Holloway told her. "They might have backup on the way; and if they didn't before, they probably do now."

Melinda looked over at the pressure bandage on Wei's sprained ankle. "It's going to be a long walk."

"The alternatives aren't any more pleasant," Holloway countered. "Keep quiet, and watch."

Across the clearing the Peacekeepers and civilians had reached the downed Conqueror copter. Much of the smoke had blown away now, and Melinda could see dozens of what looked like thin cracks crisscrossing the milky-white surface. One of the Peacekeepers—the pilot Bremmer, Melinda tentatively identified him—fired a short burst at the side of the craft, blowing the door off. "Take it careful," Holloway muttered under his breath. "Slow and careful." Lowering his assault gun slightly, Bremmer stepped to the hatchway and eased his head in for a look inside—

And with a shout jumped back away from the copter as a Conqueror staggered out.

Melinda gasped. But even as the Conqueror grabbed the edge of the doorway and pulled himself upright, Bremmer took a step forward and jabbed the muzzle of his assault gun hard into the alien's upper torso. The Conqueror might have gasped—Melinda couldn't tell for sure—and staggered backward. One of the civilians jumped in behind him, bringing his weapon over the alien's head into a choke hold against his neck. The Conqueror reached up to the gun, but for all his obvious straining was unable to budge it.

"Watch it," Holloway muttered. "Real careful. Get him on the ground before you search him." Across the way Bremmer handed his weapon to Crane and stepped up to the alien—

And in that instant the Conqueror struck.

Melinda didn't see clearly what happened, only that

Bremmer abruptly jerked back and to the side, his neck erupting into a spray of blood as he fell to the ground.

"Get away from him!" Holloway shouted, snapping up his assault gun.

But too late. Even as someone screamed—even as Crane dropped the second weapon that was encumbering him—the Conqueror twisted his head to the side beneath the pressure against his neck . . . and this time Melinda had a horrifyingly clear view of the attack. From the alien's mouth something knifelike lanced out, slicing cleanly through the neck of the man behind him. There was another scream, this one gurgling horribly, as he collapsed into a heap. The Conqueror grabbed for the assault gun now sliding loosely down his torso—

And then Crane opened fire, and the Conqueror seemed to explode into fragments and a spray of blood.

Melinda stared at the scene, her whole body shaking violently, her stomach twisting and sick as it hadn't been since her first year of medical school. She'd seen the documentaries on the wars the Peacekeepers had been involved in over the past thirty-seven years—the wars and the police actions and the pacifications. But neither that nor her medical training had prepared her for this. This was dangerous, bloody, and real.

And in the deepest core of her being she understood, perhaps for the first time, that she was truly and genuinely in the middle of a war.

She took a shuddering breath. Yes, she was in a war. But she was also a doctor in a war, with all the responsibilities that went along with that. Including her promise to Holloway. "I'm going over there," she said, standing up. "There might be something I can do."

"Sure," Holloway said, his voice angry and bitter and not believing for a second that there was any hope at all for the two men. "Wei, stay here. Keep a sharp eye."

They made it across the scarred ground without incident. To discover that there had indeed been no urgent need for the trip.

"Dead?" Holloway asked.

Melinda nodded, standing up again. Her heart was still pounding, but at least her stomach was settling down a little. The trick was to try to think of this as clinically as possible. To see them as medical subjects, not as murdered men. "Slashed carotid arteries," she said. "Both of them." She looked at Crane. "Did you see what happened?"

He shook his head. "Happened too fast. Some kind of weapon—came out of his mouth—"

"Hold it," Holloway cut him off, his eyes gazing hard at nothing in particular.

Melinda frowned. And then she heard it too: an all-too-familiar humming sound—

"Cover!" Holloway barked, grabbing her arm and pulling hard. Yanked off balance, Melinda fell to the ground, rolling partway over to bump her shoulder into the side of the downed copter. Holloway threw himself protectively on top of her as the others hit the scorched ground beside them.

And with an angry blast of hurricane wind three more Conqueror copters shot past overhead.

From the trees came the stutter-bark of an assault gun as Wei opened fire. One of the copters twisted to the side, shivering under the barrage as multiple explosions scattered bits of white from its underside. Above her Melinda could hear Holloway shouting something, his weight shifting and his elbow digging painfully into her ribs as he swung up his assault gun. All three copters were firing now, brilliant flickering bursts of laser fire tracking toward Wei's position in the trees. Melinda shrank back against the hot side of the downed copter as, all around her, Holloway and the others also began firing. One of the copters swung back around toward this new threat, ignoring the explosive shells raking across its side, its lasers lancing across the ground toward them. Melinda half closed her eyes, wondering how it would feel to die—

And with a flash of blue-white fire, the side of the copter blew out. Twisting over like a wounded animal, it plunged to a shattering impact on the ground. The other two copters abandoned their attack on Wei, swinging around just as twin blurs of black and white screamed past overhead.

The two Corvines had arrived.

The copters swung around again, their lasers trying to track the fighters. But the Corvines had already cut into impossibly tight turns and were coming back around again in some kind of double flanking maneuver. The copters fired, missed, fired again—

And disintegrated together in twin bursts of flame as the Corvines roared past.

The fragments hit the ground, the thunder of the explosions faded away, and then there was silence except for the ringing in Melinda's ears. "You all right?" Holloway asked, his voice sounding faint and distant despite the fact that she could feel the warmth of his breath on her cheek.

"You keep asking me that," she chided, her own voice sounding no clearer than his did. Considering all her eardrums had been through, she was probably lucky she could hear anything at all. "What now?"

"We get out of here," he said, rolling off her and getting to his feet. "Crane, go check on Wei. The rest of you—"

"Colonel Holloway?" a voice called.

Holloway looked to the left. "Over here," he called back.

Melinda stood up as a man in Peacekeeper uniform came around the side of their protective copter, his assault gun held ready. "Colonel," he said, and even through her dazed ears Melinda could hear the relief in his voice. "Thank God, sir—we thought they'd iced you. We've got an aircar around back that way."

"Thanks," Holloway said. "Any status reports yet?"

"I haven't heard anything, sir," the other said. "Everyone's keeping off the radio. I know the Conquerors have taken the settlement, though, and that some of the other transports in that last batch are overdue. The Corvines have gone off to run cover for the search ships."

"All right," Holloway said grimly. "Let's get going before they need to bail us out again. Send someone to go give Crane a hand." He glanced at Melinda. "And have someone pick up one of those Conqueror bodies over there—grab whichever's in the best shape. Get a couple of their weapons, too."

Three minutes later they were in the air again. Melinda found herself looking past the dirty, powder-stained men to stare at the body bags that had been hastily piled in the rear of the craft. The war had indeed begun . . . and she was indeed here in the middle of it.

"Sorry you didn't leave when you had the chance?" Holloway asked quietly from beside her.

She turned to look at him. Those cool brown eyes were studying her closely. Maybe trying to decide if she was going to be more trouble than she was worth in the coming days. "I'm sorry any of this had to happen at all," she said. "I wish we could all have started by talking instead of shooting."

"*We* did," he reminded her bluntly. "It was the Conquerors who came out shooting."

"Maybe we scared them."

"Or maybe they just aren't interested in talking," Holloway countered. "There are all sorts of people, Doctor, humans and nonhumans alike, for whom talking just slows down the process of taking whatever it is they want. You run into one of them . . . well, you're a doctor. You know that sometimes there's only one way to stop a rabid animal."

He looked past her at the body bags. "Let's just hope the politicians have the guts to do it before anyone else has to die."

Melinda looked at the body bags again, a shiver running up her back. "You're talking about CIRCE."

"Damn right I am," he said. "I don't know what the geniuses at NorCoord are waiting for, anyway. I'd have started reassembling the thing the day the *Jutland* force was hit."

"Political considerations, probably," Melinda said. Pheylan had gone into a CIRCE kick, she remembered, when he was a child. Something he'd said then . . .

"You'd know more about that than I would," Holloway grunted. "Maybe this will finally get them off their soft seats and doing something."

"Maybe," Melinda said. "Colonel, you were in supreme command of the Peacekeeper forces on Dorcas, weren't you?"

"Still am," he said. "For whatever it's worth. Why?—you want the job?"

"No," Melinda said. "I was just wondering if you'd have known if any of the CIRCE components were being stored here."

For a long moment Holloway just stared at the body bags, his face rigid. "Oh, hell," he murmured at last.

Melinda's heart seemed to skip a beat. "*Is* one of them here?"

"I don't know," Holloway said, his face still tight. "Local commanders never do. But if it is, there's only one likely place it could be."

"Back at the garrison?"

"Not quite that bad," he said. "But bad enough. There's a small automated tectonic-monitoring station in the hills just north of the settlement that some NorCoord agency put in a few years back. At least, that's what they told me it was. If it's really the storage point for a CIRCE component—" He shook his head. "The good part is that it's well enough snugged in underground that the Conquerors probably won't know anything's there. The bad part is that we can't get to it without having to practically walk into their arms."

"So what do we do?"

"I don't know," Holloway conceded. "But it's not exactly a priority. First job for us is to dig in and get ready for whatever the Conquerors decide to throw at us. If we survive . . . well, we'll see then what we can do."

18 **F**rom the strangely shaped control board wrapped around Hill came a shrill warble, jarring Cavanagh out of a light and troubled doze. "What is it?" he asked, straining to see in the dim light of the indicators and subsidiary displays. "Hill?"

The warbling cut off. "It's all right, sir," Hill said, his silhouette moving across the tiny colored lights as he shifted in his seat. "Just a proximity warning, Mrach style. We're coming up on Phormbi."

Cavanagh squinted at his watch. Seven hours, approximately, since that mad scramble out of Mig-Ka City. "Do we know where we're going?"

"Yes, sir, the Northern Wooded Steppes. There's a map and a little bit about the place on the computer here. With your permission I'm going to key the auto-entry to bring us in on the night side. Try to avoid whatever they've got in the way of a traffic pattern."

"Fine," Cavanagh said, rubbing his eyes. Between the interrupted sleep on Mra-mig and all the adrenaline surges since then, he was feeling desperately tired. "Kolchin? You awake?"

"Yes, sir," the other's voice came softly. "I think Fibbit's still in that cold-sleep of hers. You want me to try to wake her?"

"Don't bother," Cavanagh said, his ears still ringing from that proximity alarm. Either that cold-sleep was incredibly hard to break, or else Duulian hearing was on a par with Duulian night vision. "Hill, do you have any idea what the landing procedure's going to be like?"

"None at all, sir," Hill said. "I've never been to a Yycroman world before. But I'm sure one of the interdiction ships will be able to tell us."

"Let's hope it's short and quick," Kolchin said. "Could be awkward if word of our departure from Mra-mig arrives while we're still up here chatting."

"At least we know the news couldn't have beaten us here," Hill pointed out. "That's something."

"Yes," Kolchin said. "Lord Cavanagh, I've been thinking about what happened back there at the hotel. Your suggestion that what we saw was a power struggle between Mrach factions?"

"Yes. And?"

"Another possibility's occurred to me. That red card Bronski showed you—could it have been a forgery?"

Cavanagh frowned into the darkness. "Interesting thought," he agreed. "I've never seen one up close before, and I didn't take the time to examine this one."

"Same here," Kolchin said. "But that might explain why the Mrachanis didn't send a representative up with him. And why he didn't haul us away when he had the numbers on his side."

"And perhaps explain the incident at the elevators," Cavanagh added slowly. "If Faction A issues official red cards, but Bronski was actually working for Faction B, Faction A might have sent the Bhurtala to bring him in."

"But why would a NorCoord diplomat be working for the Mrachanis?" Hill objected.

"We only have Bronski's word that he's a NorCoord diplomat," Kolchin reminded him. "If he can forge a red card, a diplomatic ID isn't going to be a problem."

"All of which brings us back to the man in Fibbit's threading," Cavanagh said. An odd and not entirely pleasant thought had suddenly occurred to him. "New line of thought, Kolchin. What are the chances that the whole Bhurtala thing at the hotel was a setup? That the Mrachanis fed us this tip about Phormbi and then deliberately let us escape?"

For a moment the only noise in the cabin was the twittering drone of the drive beneath them. "If they wanted us to escape, why didn't they let Bronski pass?" Kolchin asked.

"All they were guarding was the elevators," Cavanagh pointed out. "I didn't see anyone at the stairway down the hall, and there was certainly no one by the emergency drop shaft. Maybe if Bronski had turned around and taken the stairs instead of arguing, they'd have let him go."

"I suppose that's possible," Kolchin said thoughtfully. "Bronski sure wasn't the type to back down. All right, let's assume they wanted us to leave there and go to Phormbi. Why?"

"All I can think of is that we're on a wild-snipe chase," Cavanagh said. "Maybe they know who the man in Fibbit's threading is and don't want us talking to him. Or maybe there's something more to those Conqueror legends they don't want us to find out."

Kolchin seemed to ponder that. "Sounds pretty complicated for Mrachanis," he said. "They're not supposed to be that good at chicanery."

Cavanagh shrugged. "Most people I've met have been perfectly capable of becoming chicanerous when important interests were at stake. What differs is their abilities to do a good job at it."

"Maybe that's why the Mrachanis pointed us to Phormbi instead of someplace a lot farther away," Hill suggested dryly. "It would be days before we'd know Fibbit's friend isn't on Nadezhda."

"If you want, sir, we could turn around and head back," Kolchin said. "We've got plenty of fuel."

Cavanagh shook his head. "No point to that now. As long as we're already here, we might as well stay long enough to ask a few questions."

There was another brief warble from the control board. "We're here," Hill announced. "Stand by. . . ."

From somewhere behind them came the dull multiple thud of relays snapping open. The blackness through the canopy turned to the brief illusion of a tunnel, and then the stars flowed back into their proper positions around the large green-blue crescent hanging in space before them. "Right on target," Hill said approvingly. "Good autoentry on this thing."

"Mrach efficiency," Cavanagh told him, peering out at the specks of light moving in the planet's vicinity. "Which ones are the Peacekeeper ships?"

Hill leaned over his displays. "Actually . . . none of them."

Cavanagh frowned. "None of them?"

"No, sir. I'm picking up about thirty merchant-class, but they're all Yycroman design and registry. No Commonwealth ships of any kind."

Cavanagh rubbed at the stubble on his cheek. No Peacekeepers . . . and here they were flying a Mrach courier ship in Yycroman space. Not a smart move, by anyone's standards. "How soon before we're in laser range?"

"Searching for a satellite or ground station now," Hill said. "Couple more minutes."

Cavanagh nodded, looked out at the dark planetary surface ahead. If the sporadic clusters of lights scattered across it were anything to go by, Phormbi was not exactly a heavily populated world. "Maybe we should go ahead and contact one of those ships first. At least that would let someone know who we are."

"I don't think it'll be a problem," Kolchin soothed him. "They haven't got any ground- or orbit-based weapons anymore."

"I wouldn't bet money on that if I were you," Hill said, his voice suddenly odd. "Lord Cavanagh, you'd better have a look." The canopy shimmered, altering from viewport to display mode—

And there, looming out of the darkness behind them, was a dark shape. A shape splashed with lights and strangely curved luminescent edges. A shape out of the history records; a shape that no longer existed.

A shape that was rapidly overtaking them.

"That's a Yycroman warship," Cavanagh breathed, his voice seeming to come from a long distance away.

"Yes," Hill said. "And I'm not sure . . . but I think they want to talk with us."

After the sparsely furnished style of their Mrach hotel suite, the Yycroman room they were taken into was something of a shock. Large and ornate, packed almost too full of furniture and artwork to be comfortable, it felt to Cavanagh more like a museum with seats than an office or waiting room. Fibbit, in fact, seemed to treat it in exactly that way, flitting around the room from painting to sculpture to clothwork to scroll, studying everything in sight, apparently oblivious to the pair of Yycroman guards at each of the room's three doors.

The guards, of course, were not oblivious to her. Cavanagh could see their eyes moving beneath the glitter of their helmets as they watched every twitch of her long limbs. Or any twitch from the rest of them, for that matter.

Finally, after nearly two hours of waiting, they had a visitor.

A high-level visitor, too, judging from the elaborate ceremonial helmet and tooled cloak. [Which is Lord Stewart Cavanagh?] the Yycroma demanded, striding toward the ornately carved chair facing the prisoners.

"I'm Lord Cavanagh," Cavanagh said, standing up. "May I ask whom I have the honor of addressing?"

[I am Klyveress ci Yyatoor,] the Yycroma said, brushing the cloak to one side and sitting down. [Twelfth Counsel to the Hierarch.]

A female name, plus a title and position that traditionally went to a female. "Honored to meet you, ci Yyatoor," Cavanagh said, bowing low, a little of the tension leaving his throat. There was nothing good about this situation, but at least he wouldn't have to worry about sparking the hair-trigger male Yycroman temper. "I'd like to apologize for any problems our sudden appearance here may have caused," he continued. "I hope we can quickly resolve any misunderstandings that might still remain."

[Three of you carry passports of the Northern Coordinate Union,] Klyveress said, her eyes raking each of the three humans and then flicking to where Fibbit was now standing stock-still among the artifacts. [The Duulian has no passport at all. Yet you arrived here aboard a sensor-stealthed Mrach courier ship. Explain.]

"I admit it's an unusual situation," Cavanagh conceded. "As I explained to the ship's captain, we were forced by circumstances to borrow a Mrach courier when we left Mra-mig."

[Would a human fleeing the Mrach not seek out other humans?] Klyveress countered. [Yet you came to

Phormbi instead of to a world of humans or the human ambassadorhold on Kammis. Explain.]

"We were looking for someone," Cavanagh said. "A human who we were told was somewhere in the Northern Wooded Steppes region of Phormbi."

Klyveress's gaze seemed to sharpen. [Who told you this?]

"A Mrachani who came to our hotel room a few minutes before we had to leave."

[His name? Position? Title?]

"I'm sorry," Cavanagh shook his head. "I don't know anything at all about him."

[Yet you believed this Mrach whom you knew nothing at all about?]

Cavanagh grimaced. Put that way, it did sound pretty ridiculous. "We didn't have any other leads," he said. "I thought it would be worth a try."

[Who is this man you seek?]

"I'm afraid I don't know that, either."

The Yycroma cocked her crocodilian head. [Yet you follow him. Have you no better uses for your time?]

Cavanagh felt his lip twitch. This was starting to get sticky. Klyveress clearly suspected them of being agents of the Mrachanis; and given the highly illegal existence of that Yycroman warship they'd run into out there, she had good reason to be hostile toward potential spies. "We went to Mra-mig looking for information about the Mrachanis' supposed contact with the Conquerors," he told Klyveress.

Klyveress hissed gently through her long snout. [It is not supposed. It is real.]

"Are you sure?" Cavanagh asked, frowning.

[We are quite certain. Continue your story.]

"There's not much more to tell," Cavanagh shrugged, wondering how on Earth the Yycromae would know anything about two-hundred-year-old Mrach legends.

Had they already been in space by then? "We saw Fibbit—the Duulian—threading on the street and observed what seemed to be several Mrachanis watching her from concealment. That caught our interest, and so we went over and talked to her. Among other things she told us about a human who'd passed her a couple of times, and offered to show us the threading she'd made of him. Shortly after that the Mrachanis suddenly seemed to be trying to get her away from us and off the planet. That aroused my curiosity even further, and when the Mrachani I mentioned came to our suite and told us the man was on Phormbi, we decided to come here and see if we could find him."

[And if you could not?]

"We'd probably have just gone on to Avon," Cavanagh said. "Left the courier ship with the Mrach embassy there and taken Fibbit back to Ulu once the *Cavatina* caught up with us."

Klyveress hissed again; a long, thoughtful sound. [I have read your record, Lord Cavanagh,] she said. [You were not an ally of the Yycromae during your service to the hierarchy of NorCoord. But neither were you an ally of the Mrach.]

"My goal was to be an ally only of justice and truth."

[A noble ambition,] Klyveress said. [One which the Yycromae understand and honor. But when truth is hidden, such intentions can quickly be twisted into injustice. In this event I have no doubt that is what has happened.]

Cavanagh frowned. "What do you mean? What truth was hidden?"

[Many truths were hidden,] Klyveress said, standing up. [Perhaps later will be time for me to detail the full twistings of Mrach deceit. But for now I must leave you.]

Cavanagh looked at the guards at the doors. "What about us?"

[You wished to see the Northern Wooded Steppes,] she said, twitching her cloak back into position around her. [You shall see them now. You shall be our guests there for the following few days.]

"Your guests?" Cavanagh asked pointedly. "Or your prisoners."

[We do not wish to do this to you, Lord Cavanagh,] Klyveress said evenly. [I have little doubt that you are here at the manipulation of the Mrach. But for a few days you cannot be permitted to speak of what you have seen. The Peacekeeper ships are gone, and the path is open. The Yycromae must act now, before the time has passed.]

"And what exactly are you proposing to do?"

Klyveress gestured. The six guards at the doors left their posts and came forward, one of them bringing Fibbit with him. [We will make the wrongs right,] she said.

The guards came to a halt in a semicircle around them. "And do you include the Commonwealth in these corrections?" Cavanagh asked quietly.

She studied him. [You do not understand, Lord Cavanagh,] she said. [Someday, perhaps, you will. Come; your transport is waiting.]

The Northern Wooded Steppes were a series of flat plains in the northern section of Phormbi's second-largest continent. Despite the arid climate, the steppes were nevertheless covered with forests of huge fan trees, forests that had apparently been there since before the centuries-past climate changes that had killed off all the smaller and less deeply rooted vegetation. Tall and smooth-barked, with a single wide spread of leafy branches at the top, the fan trees had been thought in the ancient legends of the region to be the pillars that held up the sky. With the contrast of the shadowy-green canopy above and the totally barren ground below, the silent sentinels standing aloof from one other in the permanent twilight made for an impressive sight.

A sight that was even more impressive at the moment. In all directions, almost as far as they could see from their third-floor window, the ground between the tree trunks was covered with spaceships, cables, support equipment, and a city's worth of Yycromae working furiously among it all.

After twenty-five years of forced peace, the Yycromae were once again preparing for war.

"It's insane," Cavanagh murmured, staring out at all the activity. "Don't we all have enough trouble with the Conquerors sitting out there ready to attack?"

"Maybe that's why they're doing it now," Hill said from across the room. He'd been pacing restlessly around the suite since they'd arrived here. Why, Cavanagh didn't know; he surely wasn't going to locate any surveillance devices with his bare hands. "Maybe they figure the Peacekeepers will have their hands too full to have time to come after them."

"Then they're fools," Cavanagh bit out. "There's no way in hell that the Commonwealth can just sit back and ignore an attempt at genocide."

On the other side of the room, Fibbit looked up from her morose contemplation of the floor. "What?" she said, sounding startled. "Genocide? What?"

Cavanagh looked at her, a surge of irritation rising into his throat. Didn't Fibbit have any idea at all as to what was going on here?

With an effort he forced the annoyance away. No, probably she didn't. For all their artistic genius, the

Sanduuli were about as politically sophisticated as an average four-year-old human. "It's all right," Cavanagh soothed her. Under the circumstances she was probably feeling even more helpless than the rest of them. "It's all right. Don't worry, we'll handle things."

"Yes," Fibbit said, not looking particularly convinced. "I believe you."

Cavanagh sighed. Great. Nothing like having a little extra burden of trust to pile on top of the rest of the guilt he was lugging around for having gotten them into this mess in the first place. Why on Earth hadn't he just gone on to Avon instead of dragging everyone out here? "Look, why don't you go do a threading or something?" he suggested to her. "There's no sense in just sitting around worrying."

Fibbit looked around helplessly. "But I have no threading material. Also no frame."

"Hill will improvise something for you," Cavanagh said, looking over at the other. "Hill?"

"Yes, sir," Hill said, not quite suppressing a grimace. "Come on, Fibbit, let's see what we can find."

Fibbit unfolded herself from her seat, and together she and Hill went into one of the suite's other rooms. Sighing again, Cavanagh turned back to the window. "We're all going to go crazy if we have to stay here very long," he told Kolchin. "You'd better start finding us a way out of here."

Kolchin held up a finger. "Just a minute, sir."

Cavanagh frowned, leaning forward for a closer look. Kolchin's eyes were tracking methodically across the scene outside, his lips moving silently as he did so.

Whatever he was doing, a minute later he was done. "Well?" Cavanagh prompted.

"I'm not sure," Kolchin said slowly. "Looks to me like what they're doing is just fitting external weapons pods onto those ships down there. Newer merchant types, most of them, probably designed with this kind of quick military conversion in mind."

"They haven't been at this very long, then?"

"Not more than a week," Kolchin said. "Probably not even that long—the interdiction ships couldn't have been pulled out more than a couple of days ago."

"And when they did, the Hierarch decided this was their chance to pick up the war where they'd left off," Cavanagh growled.

"Well, that's just it, sir," Kolchin said. "They haven't been at this very long; and from the way Klyveress talked, it sounded like they weren't going to be at it much longer. And I doubt they'd risk trying to run an operation this size on any of their other worlds— they're much more populated, too close to major trade routes, with far too many non-Yycroman ships coming in and out. Best guess is that this is it."

"Isn't it enough?"

"No, sir," Kolchin shook his head. "That's just the point. It's not."

Cavanagh frowned at him. This wasn't just some intellectual game Kolchin was playing, he realized suddenly. "What do you mean?"

"Well, look at them," Kolchin said, gesturing. "There's a lot of stuff out there, but most of what you see is actually support and operations equipment. There aren't more than thirty or forty actual ships that we can see. Even if the whole steppe region is crammed this full, we're only talking maybe a thousand ships. And these are converted freighters, not real warships."

Cavanagh pursed his lips, thinking back to what Quinn had said about converting freighters to combat ships. "Perhaps this is only the support fleet," he suggested. "The actual battle force could be made up of ships like the one out there that caught us."

"No, I don't think so," Kolchin said. "We took their

war fleet down pretty thoroughly after the Pacification. They couldn't have hidden more than a couple of ships that size from the inspectors. And there's no way they could have built another shipyard since then. Not with the interdiction zone and the limitations on what goes in and comes out of their worlds."

Cavanagh nodded. Kolchin was right on that point, anyway. He'd seen the inside of the interdiction-zone operation when he was in the NorCoord Parliament. "So where does that leave us?"

Kolchin shrugged. "It leaves us with a thousand ships' worth of strap-on weaponry setting out to take or destroy three major and two minor planets. It can't be done, and the Yycromae have to know that. Not in a single strike, anyway, which is all they're going to get before the Peacekeepers come down on them."

Cavanagh looked out at the ships below, his chest suddenly feeling tight. "Unless they're not planning to rely on just missiles and particle beams," he said quietly.

He could feel Kolchin's eyes on him. "You're not serious."

"No?" Cavanagh countered. "Tell me it's impossible. Especially now, when NorCoord is presumably digging the components out of wherever they've been stored all these years and bringing them together for reassembly."

"I hadn't thought about that part," Kolchin murmured. "God in heaven. If the Yycromae have got it, we're in big trouble."

Cavanagh took a deep breath, trying to ease the tightness in his chest. CIRCE in the hands of vengeful Yycromae . . . "Well, let's not jump to conclusions," he said. "There could be some perfectly legitimate tactical scheme where a thousand ships are all they need."

Kolchin shook his head. "I wish Quinn were here.

They didn't teach us much about line-ship warfare in the commandos." He turned his back on the window. "By the way—for what it's worth—this shows you were right about the Mrachanis letting us escape. Ten to one they knew all about this place and wanted us to come blow the whistle on it."

Cavanagh had forgotten all about that conversation. "Certainly looks that way," he said. "What did the ci Yyatoor call it? A sensor-stealthed courier ship?"

"Right," Kolchin said. "All that means is that it's harder to locate once it meshes in. Same sort of stuff we do with watchships. There's some field-baffling on the tachyon emissions, too, so that you can get a little closer before the wake-trail detectors pick you up. But even with a ship the size and speed of a courier, they're going to have half an hour's warning that you're on your way in."

"It's still something the Yycromae would assume was a spy ship."

"Can't say I blame them," Kolchin conceded. "What I don't get is why the Mrachanis would bother sending us here. Why not j   call in the Peacekeepers directly?"

"I don't know," Cavanagh said. "Maybe they didn't want to answer any awkward questions about how they knew the buildup was going on. Or maybe they were trying for a two-for-one deal: we blow the whistle on the Yycromae, plus we get distracted from our hunt for the man in Fibbit's threading. Or we blow the whistle and forget about the Mrach Conqueror legends. Take your pick."

Kolchin shook his head. "This is starting to sound way too complicated for Mrachanis."

Cavanagh snorted. "I'm beginning to get the feeling Mrachanis aren't nearly as simple and ingenuous as they'd like us to believe." There was the sound of a movement behind them, and he turned to see Hill come up. "You get Fibbit settled down?"

"More or less," Hill nodded, looking slightly disgusted. "I improvised a threading frame from a plastic sorting box I found in one of the armoires and a towel from the cleansing room. She wasn't happy with the texture, but I told her to consider it a challenge. She said she was going to try to thread that man from Mig-Ka City for you again."

"How's the room look?" Kolchin asked him.

Hill shrugged. "Well, there's no sign of any recent installations. They could be running bouncers off the windows, of course, but with all the noise and vibration out there they're not going to get much that way."

"Any idea what this place is?" Cavanagh asked. "It looks like a hotel."

"That's exactly what it is," Hill agreed. "Put up about twenty years ago by a joint Swiss-Yycroman consortium."

"Strange place to stick a hotel," Kolchin commented.

"It had a strange clientele, too," Hill said. "Most of them were bored rock climbers who wanted to tackle something different."

Kolchin stared at him. "You're kidding."

"No joke," Hill said. "The Joint Interstellar Climbing Club declared the trees here to be Class Sevens or Eights or something, and within days the climbers started to deluge the place. I guess the place was still humming until about six months ago, when the Yycroman government decided they were tired of burying the failures and declared the place closed."

Cavanagh frowned. "Six months ago?"

"That's what the skitter's records said," Hill said. "Why, is the number significant?"

"Probably not," Cavanagh said slowly. "It just struck me that that was almost exactly the same time that the

Commerce Commissioner suddenly started restricting nonhuman access to Commonwealth military technology."

"You think there's a connection?" Kolchin asked.

Cavanagh looked out the window at all the military activity outside. "Probably just a coincidence."

For a long minute no one spoke. Kolchin broke the silence first. "I suppose the next step is to find a way out of here."

"I think we should sleep on it," Cavanagh said, rubbing at his eyes. "I don't know about either of you, but I'm just about dead on my feet."

"I understand, sir," Kolchin said. "You and Hill go ahead and get some sleep."

"What about you?"

"I'm all right," Kolchin assured him. "I slept some on the skitter." He glanced out the window. "Besides, there's a little something I'd like to try."

"Fine," Cavanagh said, too tired to argue. "Whatever you do, just be quiet about it."

"Don't worry, sir," Kolchin assured him. "You won't hear a thing."

19 The three interrogators didn't come again for seven full days. But that was all right, because it took Pheylan that long to come up with another plan. By the time they arrived, he was ready to give it a try.

"I was starting to wonder if you weren't going to come back," he commented as the four of them walked out into the bright sunshine. "This would be better for me if I could go out every couple of days, you know."

"Pleased you go out at all," Thrr-gilag said. "You try take that stone."

Pheylan shrugged. Actually, under the circumstances, he was a little surprised that Thrr-gilag hadn't been summarily demoted from his spokesman duties the way Svv-selic had been earlier. Did that imply Thrr-gilag had more clout in the Zhirrzh hierarchy? Or was it because this latest incident hadn't involved that mysterious white pyramid? "I didn't mean anything by that," he told them.

"Perhaps," Thrr-gilag said. "Or not. But no purpose. We walk this way today." His tongue snaked out, pointing directly away from the pyramid toward a clump of turquoise-tinted bushes at the edge of the forest.

"Fine," Pheylan said, heading obediently in the indicated direction. He'd been wanting to take a look in this area, anyway.

"Explain to us about weapon called Copperhead."

Deliberately, Pheylan counted to two before turning to look at Thrr-gilag. "What?"

"Copperhead," the Zhirrzh repeated. "Explain to us."

Pheylan shrugged. "It's a snake from our homeworld. Venomous, lives mostly in the Confederate region of North America—"

"It is weapon of war," Thrr-gilag interrupted. "Explain about Copperhead. Or go inside."

Pheylan grimaced, but there really wasn't any way around it. "The Copperheads are humans like me," he said. "Specially equipped to handle a particular type of attack fighter."

"How equipped?"

"They have direct brain-to-computer linkages," Pheylan said, feeling his forehead wrinkling. As far as he knew, there hadn't been any Copperheads aboard the *Jutland.* Had the Zhirrzh found some reference to them in Commodore Dyami's computer? "That gives them faster response time and better control of their ships. Why the sudden interest?"

"Zhirrzh interested in all things human," Thrr-gilag said.

"You've run into some of them, haven't you?" Pheylan accused him. "Where? What happened?"

"I ask questions," Thrr-gilag said. "What more about Copperhead?"

"I don't know anything more than that," Pheylan said, fighting back a fresh surge of frustration with this situation he was in. Either the war had started in earnest, or it hadn't, and either way emotion wasn't going to do him any good.

"Where Copperhead located?" Thrr-gilag asked.

"I don't know that, either," Pheylan said, squinting at the bushes ahead. Were those long thorns nestled in among the blue-green leaves? "Peacekeeper Command's undoubtedly been shifting men and ships around like crazy since you attacked the *Jutland*."

They had reached the bushes now, and Pheylan discovered that he'd been right: their branches were indeed covered with thorns. Big ones, too. "Interesting plant," he commented, stepping toward it. Out of the corner of his eye he saw Nzz-oonaz half lift the black trigger gadget warningly. "We've got thorn bushes back on some of our worlds, too," he added, crouching down for a closer look. "You have any on your world?"

"Thorns common plant defense," Thrr-gilag said.

"Ah," Pheylan said, shifting his weight and easing his left hand carefully into the limited space between the thorns. His attention, though, was not on his hand, but on his upper left arm. Specifically, on the small glassy disk embedded in the material of his obedience suit halfway between elbow and shoulder. He'd been planning to find a sharp stick to use for this gambit, but if he could get it to work with these thorns, so much the better. "Are any of your thorn bushes poisonous?" he asked Thrr-gilag. "Some of ours are, though they're mostly just irritants. Barbed points, mildly acidic chemicals—that sort of thing."

"We have both kinds," Thrr-gilag said, and Pheylan could imagine he could hear a note of uneasiness in the alien voice. "We do not know about this plant."

"It's okay, I'm being careful," Pheylan assured him. He was in position now: his hand with a more or less clear path back out of the bush, an inward-pointing thorn pressing a millimeter or so into the material of his suit just beneath the edge of the glass disk. "I used to play around this sort of bush when I was a—ouch!"

He yanked his hand out of the bush, feeling a slight

jab in his upper arm as the thorn there poked briefly into the material before being torn from its stem. Rocking back on his heels, he gripped his hand, cursing under his breath.

"What?" Thrr-gilag demanded, stepping closer.

"Got me a little," Pheylan growled, making a show of rubbing his hand as he surreptitiously glanced at his upper arm. It had worked: the thorn had pried the glass disk a millimeter or so out of its niche in the suit material. Enough, maybe, for him to get his fingernails under the edge.

"Where hurt?" Thrr-gilag asked.

"Here," Pheylan said, uncovering the hand and peering closely at it. "Right there," he added, pointing to the white indentation he'd just made with his fingernail as he brought his hand away. "Looks like it didn't break the skin. Sure hurt, though."

Thrr-gilag jabbered something in the Zhirrzh language, and Svv-selic stepped forward. "Svv-selic take sample of thorn," Thrr-gilag said. "Examine for poison."

"Thank you," Pheylan said. So they *didn't* know anything about the plant. That implied that this was probably some kind of forward base, without a full-fledged colony attached to it. A potentially useful bit of information.

"Feel ill?" Thrr-gilag persisted.

"No, I'm fine," Pheylan said, focusing his attention for a moment on the pinprick he'd taken in his upper arm and belatedly recognizing the risk he had in fact taken here. If these thorns *were* poisoned, he could be in trouble. "Seems a little odd that the plant has thorns at all," he added, to change the subject. "Usually that sort of thing is a defense against plant-eating animals. But there don't seem to be animals of any sort around here."

"There many animals," Thrr-gilag said. "They kept away by outer fence."

"Kept away?" Pheylan asked pointedly. "Or attacked and killed?"

All six pupils in Thrr-gilag's eyes seemed to contract a little. "Zhirrzh not attack first, Cavv'ana," he said.

But to Pheylan's ears the response lacked any real conviction. "Of course," he said, putting as much sarcasm into his voice as he could manage. "I forgot. Your Elders told you that. And of course, your Elders wouldn't lie."

"You not speak evil against Elders," Svv-selic snapped. "You warned before: not speak evil."

"Perhaps the Elders are wrong," Pheylan countered. "Or were themselves lied to."

"Not possible," Svv-selic insisted. "All Elders present."

Pheylan cocked an eyebrow. "*All* the Elders were there?"

"Not all Elders of Zhirrzh," Thrr-gilag said. "Elders of Kee'rr and Too'rr and Flii'rr clans there."

"Then they were lied to," Pheylan said. "I was there, remember—"

"Elders not lied to," Svv-selic insisted. "Elders there."

"But the commanders of the fleet—"

"Elders there."

Pheylan sighed, recognizing a dead end when he was on one. Clearly, clan loyalty was going to prevent the Zhirrzh from asking awkward questions about the *Jutland* battle, even in the face of clear evidence to the contrary. Probably why these particular three had been given the job of interrogators in the first place.

But even the most monolithic lie could be broken if you hit it hard enough and often enough. And in Thrr-gilag the cracks were already beginning to show.

"Fine," Pheylan said. "You believe whatever you want to." He pointed past the bushes toward the edge of the forest. "Is it okay if we walk over there?"

It was by no means easy to pry the tiny disk out of the arm of his obedience suit; and doing so while in the process of removing the suit—and under a half-dozen Zhirrzh gazes, yet—was even trickier. But Pheylan managed it. Possibly he was starting to get good at this skulduggery stuff; more likely, the fact that the Zhirrzh had no fingernails had left a blind spot where this sort of thing was concerned.

He set the shower for hotter than usual and waited until he had a thick coating of condensation on the walls before examining his prize. The disk's upper surface, as he'd already noted, was composed of a dark glassy substance. The underside was lighter-colored, with what looked like a tiny patch of circuitry in the center, and a short pair of trailing wires that ended where he had torn them out of the suit.

No. He squinted closely at the disk as he rubbed soap across his forehead. No, they weren't wires, but another glassy substance. Optical fibers, then, unless the Zhirrzh had developed some sort of exotic field-effect or tunneling-control circuitry.

Which meant that he'd been right about the trigger gadget that Nzz-oonaz carried. Glassy sensors—and, moreover, glassy sensors scattered around different parts of the obedience suit—meant that the Zhirrzh were using a directional signal to trigger the thing. Almost certainly an infrared or ultraviolet pulse, though it was possible they could have drifted into the X-ray bands of the spectrum. Not that it mattered.

He frowned, palming the disk again as he scrubbed soap into his hair. No, he was wrong. The type of signal they were using was not simply of academic interest. If he could block enough of the sensors on his suit without the Zhirrzh noticing, he might have the opening he'd been searching for; but the type of light involved would be an important consideration in figuring out what to block the sensors with. Infrared or ultraviolet could be handled with mud or leaves. For X rays nothing short of lead foil would do him much good.

An examination of the disk might give him some clues; but that examination would have to wait. This shower had already lasted as long as usual, and he didn't want to arouse suspicions by breaking routine. Carefully, using steady pressure, he worked the disk into the slab of soap built into the shower wall. It wasn't a perfect hiding place, but it had the advantage of that extra shower wall's worth of thickness with which to block his captors' sensors. With luck maybe this time he'd get away with it.

He got the disk all the way in, smoothed over the spot as best he could, and shut off the water. Brushing the excess water off his arms and torso, he stepped out.

It was like a not-quite instant repeat of a week earlier. The four Zhirrzh standing outside his cell with gray sticks or flashlights at the ready; the two unarmed Zhirrzh inside the opened door; Thrr-gilag standing off to one side, his tongue flicking in and out, watching the whole operation. "What's going on?" Pheylan asked, a sick feeling in the pit of his stomach.

"You walk away," Thrr-gilag said.

So they'd done it again. With a quiet sigh Pheylan moved away from the shower. One of the unarmed Zhirrzh left the door, passing him and stepping into the stall. Producing a small tool, he proceeded to dig into the soap where Pheylan had hidden the disk.

"Not proper," Thrr-gilag said. "You claim not know?"

Pheylan turned to look at him. "It came loose somehow," he said. "I thought I'd take a look at it. As I told you before, we humans are curious."

For a long moment the only sounds were the quiet hum of the air system and the soft scraping noise of the Zhirrzh tool. "The Zhirrzh wrong," Thrr-gilag said at last. "You not unthinking predators. You think and plan. Too much. Tomorrow not go outside."

"That's not fair," Pheylan protested, the bitter taste of stomach acids boiling up into his throat.

"Speak fair?" the Zhirrzh in the shower retorted, emerging from the stall with the soap-covered disk held in his hand. "No fair to animal."

Deep inside Pheylan something snapped; and for that single heartbeat he didn't care anymore if he lived or died. "You want animals?" he snarled. "I'll show you animals." He took a step toward the Zhirrzh, his hands curling into fists, dimly aware that Thrr-gilag was shouting something, and that the Zhirrzh directly behind Pheylan's intended target had raised his flashlight weapon—

And without warning the whole world exploded into a flash of brilliant white light in front of him.

Pheylan staggered back, stifling a curse as he threw his hands up to his face. Across the room he heard the Zhirrzh scuttle across the floor, the door slamming hastily shut behind him.

"You not unthinking," Thrr-gilag said from behind Pheylan. "But you still predators. You create war."

Carefully, Pheylan blinked his eyes open again. Aside from some residual stinging and a massive purple blob blocking the middle of his vision he seemed all right. Around the edges of the blob, he could see the group of Zhirrzh headed for the outer door. "We don't always create the wars," he told Thrr-gilag. "But whether we do or not, we always win them. Tell your Elders that."

There was a short pause. "I will tell them," Thrr-gilag agreed.

He turned and crossed the room, and a minute later Pheylan was alone. Except, as always, for the handful of Zhirrzh techs manning the outer room's monitors.

Slowly, blinking at the ache in his eyes, feeling drained, Pheylan picked up his jumpsuit and started getting dressed. So Act One was over. That little show of submissive naïveté he'd pulled early on had gotten him this far, but now they were onto him. But that was okay. The gambit had gotten him a lot further than he'd expected it to, and he'd gathered some useful information along the way.

Among other things, that the time for subtlety was over. Whatever form his escape attempt took, it was going to have to depend heavily on simple, raw brute force.

Lying down on his bed, allowing himself to look demoralized, he closed his eyes to aid in their healing and got to work on his daily isometrics.

20

It seemed as if he had just closed his eyes when Lord Cavanagh awoke, once again, to a gentle shaking of his shoulder. "Lord Cavanagh?" a voice murmured. "It's Hill, sir. Keep your voice down."

"All right," Cavanagh murmured back, forcing sandpapery eyes open. "What is it?"

"Time to leave, sir. You need to get dressed."

Cavanagh squinted toward the window. The leaf-filtered sunlight that had been there when he'd gone to bed had been replaced by the brighter haze of artificial lighting. Apparently, the Yycromae were running their armory around the clock. "All right."

"We'll be in the cleansing room when you're ready," Hill said, stepping back and disappearing out the door.

The cleansing room was an odd melding of human and Yycroman designs: a water-efficient staggered system of slickglass sink and toilet facilities, juxtaposed with a typically open Yycroman cloudburst-shower compartment. The walls and floor were done in layers of thin gray stone crisscrossed with living moisture vine, with a cloudy sky design imprinted on the ceiling. The whole thing left Cavanagh with the strange impression of a human bathroom stuck out in the woods somewhere, which was probably not exactly what the designer had had in mind.

But, then, the designer probably hadn't intended to have a large hole picked in his slate wall between the slickglass system and the cloudburst shower, either.

"Lord Cavanagh," Kolchin nodded in greeting as Cavanagh came in. He was covered in grime and dust, with a sheen of sweat mixed in on his forehead. "Sorry to wake you, sir."

"That's all right," Cavanagh said, frowning at the damage to the wall. "How on Earth did you manage all this?"

"A Peacekeeper commando is never entirely without resources," Kolchin said, looking rather grimly satisfied with himself. "What do you think?"

Cavanagh stepped to the hole and looked in. At one edge was a rectangular duct that ran vertically inside the wall, with a parallel set of pipes running along the other edge. The space between them was filthy and discouragingly narrow. "I think it looks rather cramped," he said. "Is this supposed to be our exit?"

"Yes, sir," Kolchin said. "We can climb down the pipes to the subbasement, and from there out to the work field."

Cavanagh looked at Kolchin's grimy outfit, noting for the first time that the other seemed to be breathing a little heavily. "I take it you've already checked this out?"

"Yes, sir. Don't worry—it's easier going down than coming back up."

Cavanagh eyed the hole again. "What about Fibbit?" he asked. "I don't think she's going to fit in there."

Kolchin and Hill exchanged glances. "No, she won't," Hill said. "That's why she and I are staying here."

Cavanagh shook his head. "Out of the question. We all go or none of us does."

"We don't have any other choice, sir," Kolchin said, his tone respectful but insistent. "Fibbit can't get through the wall; and by herself she can't keep up the illusion that all of us are still here. Hill and Fibbit together can. The local government center, Vind Kaye, shouldn't be more than three thousand kilometers away from here. If we can make it down there and get in touch with the NorCoord consulate, we should be able to get a skitter message out under diplomatic seal. But we need time to do that."

Cavanagh looked at Hill. "Hill?"

"I agree with Kolchin, sir. And we really don't have time to argue about it."

Cavanagh sighed. They were right, of course. But that didn't mean he had to like it. "The Yycromae are going to have a fit when they see this wall," he said, shaking his head. "All right, Kolchin. Let's go."

The climb wasn't nearly as difficult as Cavanagh had feared it would be. Kolchin had rigged a sling sort of arrangement out of his tunic, which allowed Cavanagh to descend with less muscular exertion than would otherwise have been needed. And with Kolchin directly beneath him in case of a slip, there was little actual danger involved.

That didn't stop the climb from being thoroughly unpleasant. The dankness and musty odor kept his nose on the edge of a sneezing fit the whole way, the dust and filth made his skin crawl, and every few seconds some form of insect or other multilegged creature skittered away into the deeper recesses of the opening or into the cover of the moisture-vine roots that continually brushed against his hands and face. The trip seemed to last forever, and by the time Kolchin's hands reached up to help him down the last meter, he was half-convinced they'd missed the subbasement entirely and were tunneling their way into the planetary crust.

"This way," Kolchin whispered as Cavanagh freed himself from the tunic sling and handed it back. "Service entrance, with two aircars parked a quarter of the way around the building. There's a low decorative wall that runs most of the way—a little crawling, and we should make it."

After the musty grit of the climb, the clean dirt of the steppe ground was almost a vacation. Within minutes they had reached the end of the decorative wall; beyond it Cavanagh could see a half-dozen ground vehicles parked in a neat row near the hotel's main entrance. "Where are the aircars?" he asked.

"They're gone," Kolchin said grimly. "Must have just been couriers. Damn."

Cavanagh glanced over the wall. All around them, to the horizon and beyond, the Yycroman military preparations were buzzing along under the blazing lights. "We're not going to get very far on foot," he said.

"I know." Kolchin hissed gently between his teeth. "Change of plans: back inside."

He eased past Cavanagh and led the way back into the building and down to the subbasement. "All right," Kolchin said, slipping out of his tunic again. "I did a little looking around before Hill woke you up, and it looked like the main Yycroman business offices were one floor above us. I'm going to sneak up there and see if I can get some information on their courier schedule. If we can hop one while the pilot's inside delivering his package, we'll have our exit route."

Cavanagh looked up into the maze of pipes and ductwork. "You think you can get in there without being caught?"

"Well, if I can't, I'm sure the Yycromae will send

someone to let you know," Kolchin said dryly as he got a grip on one of the pipes. "Sit tight; I'll be right back."

There wasn't really anywhere to sit comfortably among the maze of pipes and ducts, but Cavanagh found a place a couple of meters away where he could rest some of his weight against a support stanchion. He'd changed position five times and was getting ready to do so again, when there was a muffled thud and Kolchin was back. "Here," the other said, definitely breathing heavily this time as he pressed a plate into Cavanagh's hand. "Hope it's in here—had to grab what I could and get out."

Cavanagh opened the plate and turned it on. Glowing swirls of lacy Yycroman script appeared on the screen, laid out in what seemed to be a standard index pattern. He scanned down the swirls, searching for something having to do with messages or couriers.

And as he did so, something else caught his eye. He keyed for it, fumbling a little with the unfamiliar Yycroman board layout. . . .

"Looked like they had two separate file listings," Kolchin commented, his face hazily visible in the glow from his own plate. "I grabbed a copy of both . . . here it is: courier-service schedule. Lot of flights here— I guess they're not trusting any of this to radio or laser transmission. Let's see. . . ."

The file Cavanagh had called came up; and there it was. Maps, listings, timetables—the whole works. "Kolchin."

"Looks like the next scheduled flight will be here in about twenty minutes," Kolchin said, peering at the plate. "That wall should give us enough cover if we leave in, say—"

"Kolchin," Cavanagh said again.

"What?"

"I've found their battle plan."

In the faint glow of the plate he could see Kolchin's face tighten. "Let me see."

Wordlessly, Cavanagh handed him the plate. Kolchin took it, exchanging it for his, and for a few minutes he flipped through the pages in silence. Cavanagh waited . . . and finally Kolchin looked up at him again. "How much of this did you read?"

"Just some of the part dealing with Mra-ap," Cavanagh told him. "It didn't make any sense to me."

"That's because it doesn't make any sense, period," Kolchin said. "They're hitting all the Mrach spaceport and shipbuilding facilities, but completely ignoring the rest of their transportation and industrial networks. Communications, too—they're taking out skitter launch sites but not the ground relay stations or even the satellites."

Cavanagh shivered. "Maybe they're not expecting any Mrachanis to be left to use them."

For a long moment both men were silent. "Yeah," Kolchin said at last. "CIRCE. I didn't want to believe it."

"Maybe I'm wrong," Cavanagh said. "I hope to God I am. But either they've got something unbelievably clever in the works, or else they've forgotten everything they ever knew about warfare."

Kolchin closed the plate, shutting off the glow. "We'd better get moving," he said. "We need to be ready when that courier gets here."

"Right," Cavanagh said, closing his plate as well. Somehow the darkness in the subbasement seemed more stifling now than it had earlier. "Lead the way."

"Stay close and quiet," Kolchin said, brushing past him in the darkness. Cavanagh turned to follow, and as he did so, there was an insect-light touch at the back of his neck. He reached up to brush it away—

[You will not move,] a Yycroman voice ordered softly.

Cavanagh froze, his fingertips touching cold metal pressed to the back of his neck. "Kolchin?"

There was no answer. [You will not move,] a second Yycroma said. [You have no possibility of esca—]

The word was cut off by a flash of light, lightning-bolt brilliant in the darkness. Cavanagh flinched back, squeezing his eyes shut against the afterimage of two figures struggling together. Strong hands gripped his arms—another flash burned through his closed eyelids —more Yycroman voices—the dull thud of a body hitting the floor—

And then, silence.

Cavanagh braced himself. "Kolchin?"

To his great relief the other's answer was immediate. "Here, sir. Sorry."

"That's all right," Cavanagh said, his muscles starting to shake with reaction. Their escape attempt had failed, but at least Kolchin hadn't been killed in the process.

There was a click, and a dim light filtered into the subbasement from some distant source. Three meters in front of Cavanagh, Kolchin stood motionless in the center of a group of armored Yycromae, the muzzles of two Yycroman rayslicers pressed into his stomach and up under his jaw. All around them another dozen Yycromae stood with weapons ready. Males, all of them.

Cavanagh sighed. So that was it. They'd taken their best shot, and they'd failed. "Well," he said. "Back to our room, I take it?"

[The warrior Kolchin will be returned to a new place of confinement,] a Yycroma standing off to one side said. [You will be taken to the Klyveress ci Yyatoor.]

Cavanagh frowned. "Alone?"

[Yes.]

Cavanagh threw a glance at Kolchin. There was a look in the other's eyes; a tightening of the muscles in his jaw—"It's all right, Kolchin," he said quickly. "I'll be fine. You go on back upstairs."

Kolchin's eyes flicked to his guards. "Sir—"

"Go with them," Cavanagh said, making it an order. "Fibbit's likely going crazy up there. Hill's going to need help calming her down."

Some of the tightness went out of Kolchin's shoulders. The moment had passed, and he knew it. "Yes, sir."

Cavanagh looked at the Yycroma who'd spoken. "I'm ready," he said. "Lead the way."

Considering the late hour, Cavanagh had expected to find the ci Yyatoor wearing the Yycroman equivalent of a dressing gown and looking at least slightly disheveled. To his mild surprise she was instead dressed in full diplomatic regalia, complete with ceremonial helmet and tooled cloak. [Lord Cavanagh,] she greeted him gravely as he was ushered into her suite and taken to a chair facing her. [I would speak with you.]

"I'm here," Cavanagh said, sitting down and trying to ignore the armed Yycroman males towering over him.

Klyveress opened her mouth slightly, the crocodile teeth glittering. [Guards: wait outside,] she ordered.

Silently, the males turned and left, sealing the door behind them. Cavanagh kept his attention on Klyveress, painfully aware of just how classic this setup was. She would know by now that he and Kolchin had seen their battle plan . . . and a healthy Yycroman female hardly needed male assistance to kill an unarmed middle-aged human. Quick, clean, and without the potential embarrassment of witnesses.

Also dreadfully melodramatic. Somehow he doubted that aspect would bother her any.

[I am told that in the service area you discussed the

Yycroman battle plan with the NorCoord warrior Kolchin,] Klyveress said.

For a single, frantic second Cavanagh thought about denying it. But with the plates Kolchin had borrowed already in their hands, that would be as stupid as it would be futile. "We discussed it briefly," he admitted.

[I am also told you spoke of the weapon called CIRCE.]

Cavanagh felt his chest tighten, a premonition of his death flashing before his eyes. Of course—that was what this was all about. The Yycromae knew he and Kolchin suspected them of planning to steal CIRCE . . . and the last thing they could afford would be for even a whisper of such a possibility to get back to the Commonwealth. "Did we?" he said between dry lips. "I don't recall."

For a long moment Klyveress just sat there, staring unblinkingly at him. Cavanagh gazed back, listening to his heart pounding in his ears, wishing he knew how to read Yycroman faces. Or maybe it was better that he didn't. However it happened—a sudden leap with tearing teeth, a deathly silent walk to an execution chamber, or something else—perhaps it would be easier not to see it coming.

Abruptly, Klyveress rose to her feet. Cavanagh shrank back in his seat, tensing himself for the leap. [I will tell you this, Lord Cavanagh,] the ci Yyatoor said. [We will not stand idly by and allow you to slaughter our children as you did the Pawolian warriors. If CIRCE is used, we will fight you to the last Yycroman warrior. You will take that message back to the hierarchy of NorCoord.]

She sat back down, turning her face ninety degrees away from him. [Your people approach,] she said, picking up a plate from the table beside her. [You are free to leave with them.]

Cavanagh frowned at her profile, his heart still pounding, a drop of sweat trickling down his temple. Something here was not playing according to script. Unless they planned to jump him as he walked out of the room . . . but that didn't seem like something Yycromae would do. "Excuse me," he said carefully. "I think I missed something."

Klyveress looked at him again. [The words were clear enough,] she said. [If the hierarchy of NorCoord uses CIRCE against the Yycromae, they will do so at high cost to themselves. You must make certain they understand that.]

Cavanagh shook his head. "I'm sorry, but I still don't understand. NorCoord isn't going to use CIRCE against the Yycromae. If we use it on anyone, it'll be the Conquerors."

Klyveress stared at him, her eyes darkly suspicious. [Yet you talked of CIRCE with the warrior Kolchin.]

"Yes, we did," Cavanagh acknowledged, watching her closely. This could still be a trick, he knew; a roundabout method of getting him to tell what he knew or suspected about their intentions concerning the weapon. But his instincts were belatedly kicking in . . . and what he could see in her face and manner seemed to be not so much aggression and triumph, but fear. "But we weren't discussing any NorCoord use of it. We were considering the possibility that the Yycromae might have . . . created . . . a CIRCE of their own."

Klyveress's pupils widened, an unmistakable Yycroman reaction of shock. [The Yycromae would never seek such a weapon,] she insisted. [What torn logic would bring you to think otherwise?]

"We watched your war preparations out on the steppes," Cavanagh said, nodding behind him. "And we saw your battle plan. It didn't look to us as if you had nearly enough firepower to destroy the Mrachanis. Not without a weapon like CIRCE."

She gazed at him, her pupils again dilating. [And is that what you think of the Yycromae?] she asked softly. [You, personally, Lord Stewart Cavanagh? That we would seek such total annihilation of another people?]

"Well, they're your enemies," Cavanagh pointed out, suddenly feeling very uncomfortable. The expression in her eyes . . . and the worst part was that she was right. He'd done nothing less than accuse her and her people of planning genocide. An appalling insult to anyone, made all the worse by the fact that he'd done so without even a shred of evidence. Evidence, or even rational thought. "In my experience enemies generally seek each other's destruction," he added, a bit lamely.

[Such pride,] Klyveress said, her voice still soft. [Such very human pride. Do you truly believe that all the universe can be understood through the filter-glass of human experience and knowledge? That what you choose to believe must then carry the strength of truth for all time and all peoples?]

"I'm afraid that some humans do indeed act as if that's the case," Cavanagh conceded. "I don't consider myself among them. Tell me what filter-glass I am mistakenly using."

[You assume as do all humans,] Klyveress said, laying down her plate. [You see machines of war among the Yycromae and no such machines among the Mrach. From this you conclude that the Yycromae seek war and destruction.]

"And you do not?"

[We do not. Nor did we when humans first came to Kammis. Then, as now, we seek only to protect ourselves from destruction at the hands of the Mrach.]

At the hands of the *Mrachanis*? "I don't understand."

[The Mrach seek our subjugation,] Klyveress said. [As they seek the enslavement of all peoples. They use the manipulation of words and the twisting of emotions instead of machines of metal, and so you do not recognize their attacks. But they are no less real. Nor less potent.]

Cavanagh rubbed at the stubble on his cheek. Absurd, on the face of it . . . and yet, hadn't he only hours ago been wondering what on Earth had possessed him to fly all the way out here to Phormbi just because some Mrachani had suggested he do so? "Tell me more."

[What do you wish to know? The Mrach had been attacking Yycroman culture for eight years before we awoke to the threat and tried to counter it. But such were not our abilities. After four years more we were forced to the conclusion that we could stop their attacks only by destroying their ability to come to our worlds. We were preparing that strike when the humans found Kammis and intervened.]

"Why didn't you say anything about this then?" Cavanagh asked. "Or during the Pacification?"

[At first we believed you to be subjects of the Mrach. Even after we learned our mistake, we feared you were already too heavily under Mrach influence to listen to our words against them.] Klyveress's mouth opened slightly. [You yourself, Lord Cavanagh—did you not automatically assume the Yycromae sought to inflict mass destruction? What else could that be but years of Mrach twisting of your attitudes toward us?]

Cavanagh grimaced. "I see your point."

[Besides which, your misdirected solution was precisely in accordance with our own wishes,] Klyveress continued. [Your interdiction zone was intended to protect the Mrach and hierarchy of NorCoord from Yycroman aggression, but it also served to deny Mrach access to our worlds. In protecting them from us, you also protected us from them.]

"I see," Cavanagh nodded. A spin on the interdiction zone that he doubted anyone in the Peacekeepers had ever thought of. "That probably irritated the Mrachanis no end. I'm surprised they didn't try to get the interdiction lifted."

[And risk raising doubts about how dangerously threatened they were?] Klyveress hissed between her teeth. [Even Mrach powers of persuasion have their limits. They can make blue seem green; they cannot make white seem black. At any rate, they now had an abundance of interesting challenges stretched before them. Through the Commonwealth they had been introduced to other races and peoples, all of whom they could now seek to twist to their purposes.]

Cavanagh thought back to his years in Parliament, to the numerous times the Mrachanis had brought requests before the NorCoord government. A number of the petitions had been granted; others—many of the most important—had not. "I don't think they've succeeded in twisting humanity," Cavanagh said. "At least not completely."

[The Yycroman hierarchy would agree with you,] Klyveress said. [But do not think this due to cleverness or superior resistance. You have been saved only because of the multitude of human cultures that exist among you, each markedly different from all the others. To the Mrach such cultural anarchy is bitterly confusing. But they are patient warriors. If you permit them the necessary time, they will succeed.]

"They're obviously making progress elsewhere," Cavanagh said grimly. "I suppose this explains how they persuaded those Bhurtala to work for them back in Mig-Ka City."

[They have worked hard to learn control of the

Bhurtala,] Klyveress agreed. [As haters of humans, the Bhurtala are strong potential allies to them. They have also breathed strongly on the flames of old Pawolian resentments, and sought to plant antihuman feelings in the Meert-ha and Djadar.]

"They've certainly got enough material to work with," Cavanagh agreed soberly. "Humanity hasn't always been the most enlightened or benign of neighbors."

[You have too often been tyrants,] Klyveress said bluntly. [The NorCoord hierarchy has too often served your own interests at the cost of the weaker among you, human and nonhuman both. Without the threat of Peacekeeper might, your pride and arrogance would long ago have driven others to violence against you.]

"Yes," Cavanagh murmured, wincing. *To see ourselves as others see us . . .* and it was not a pretty sight. He'd known there was a certain amount of resentment against NorCoord's leadership role, but he hadn't realized it was this deep or widespread.

He looked sharply at Klyveress, a sudden and discomfiting thought striking him. Fibbit, whose presence on the Mra-mig street had gotten them out here to Phormbi in the first place. "What about the Sanduuli?" he asked. "Are they under Mrach influence?"

[The Sanduuli?] Klyveress echoed. [For what reason would the Mrach bother with them?]

"Perhaps to use as lures," Cavanagh said. "It occurs to me that we wouldn't have been so easy for the Mrach to maneuver to Phormbi if we hadn't involved ourselves with Fibbit first."

[She is not a tool of the Mrach,] Klyveress assured him. [Or, rather, not in the way you imagine. I have looked into her case, and I do not believe she is more than she appears. The Mrach have lured several threaders such as she into similar entrapment on their worlds. Duulian threaders have an impressive natural ability to

express and influence emotion in their work, an ability
the Mrach hope can be learned from observation of
threading techniques and added to their arsenal of
weapons.]

"I see," Cavanagh said slowly. But if that was the case
—if Fibbit wasn't simply a Mrach plant—then it followed that the human in her threading was still the key
to something important. "Ci Yyatoor, how extensive is
your Commonwealth database?"

[Very extensive. Why do you ask?]

"Fibbit was going to do another threading of the man
we came here to find. If it's finished, I'd like you to scan
it into your system and see if we can find out who he
is."

[Those soon to arrive will surely have a more complete database,] Klyveress said. [Would it not serve you
better to wait for them?]

Cavanagh frowned. "What do you mean?"

[The human ship that will soon reach orbit,] Klyveress said. [Their representatives will be here within the
hour. Surely you were expecting their arrival.]

"No, I most certainly was not," Cavanagh said, feeling
a stir of annoyance. The *Cavatina* was supposed to
have gone directly to Dorcas, not come out here looking for him.

The annoyance evaporated. It couldn't be the *Cava-
tina.* Captain Teva hadn't known he was coming to
Phormbi. "What kind of ship is it?" he asked carefully.
"Civilian? Diplomatic?"

[It is a Peacekeeper warship,] Klyveress said. [Under
the authority of a human named Taurin Lee.]

Taurin Lee. Of Bronski and Lee and early-morning
hotel intrusions. Except that Bronski had been the one
in charge on Mra-mig.

Or at least the one nominally in charge. "Did Mr. Lee
give himself a title or rank?"

[He said only that he traveled under the authority of the NorCoord Parlimin Jacy VanDiver.]

Cavanagh's stomach tightened. VanDiver. He should have guessed. "Did he say why he was here?"

[To take you and your associates from Yycroman space,] Klyveress said, watching Cavanagh closely. [I do not understand, Lord Cavanagh. Is this not an ally of yours?]

"Not in the least," Cavanagh said, trying to think this through. "He works for one of those humans who seek to destroy their enemies. Or those he perceives to be enemies."

[Among whom are the Yycromae?]

Cavanagh thought about it. Yes, down deep VanDiver probably didn't think much of the Yycromae. He probably didn't think much of any nonhuman, for that matter. "Is Lee coming here to the steppes?"

[Yes. He insisted that you not be allowed to move or communicate from this spot until he arrives.]

"Then you're going to have to disperse those armed merchant ships before he gets here," Cavanagh said.

[Impossible,] Klyveress said. [The warship is already too close. It would easily detect so many movements.] She cocked her head. [I do not understand, Lord Cavanagh. Do you seek to help us against the Mrach?]

"At the moment I'm not interested in helping either of you," Cavanagh said bluntly. "You've presented me with a new perspective on what's been happening out here for the past twenty-five years, and I appreciate that. But I'm going to need time to think it through. What I want right now—what we all want right now—is to keep the Commonwealth from getting distracted with internal bickering while we've got the Conquerors breathing down our necks. That means no Yycroman attack on the Mrachanis, and no Peacekeeper sanctions against you."

[But we cannot risk the divisiveness of Mrach poison,] Klyveress protested.

"We're going to have to," Cavanagh said. "Right now the Conquerors require every bit of our attention."

He took a deep breath. It was unfair, really. He'd left politics six years ago; had left the military thirty years before that. None of this was supposed to be his job. But here he was, and he would just have to do the best he could. "We need to talk with Kolchin and Hill right away," he told Klyveress. "Pool what we know and come up with some ideas. And I want to find out once and for all who that man is in Fibbit's threading."

[I will give the orders.] Klyveress paused, her eyes boring into his face. [What will you say to Taurin Lee when he sees the armed merchant vessels outside?]

"I don't know," Cavanagh admitted. "But we've got an hour. We'll think of something."

21

"**C**lipper here, Maestro," Clipper's voice said in Aric's ear. "We're all set."

"Acknowledged," Quinn said. "Okay, Max, start your scan."

"Yes, Commander," the computer said. "Beginning sectoring pattern."

Aric took a deep breath, exhaled slowly against his faceplate, his eyes tracing the curved edge of the planet outside the Counterpunch's canopy as it cut a boundary between the dull metal of the fueler's hull above and the scattering of stars below. The first system they'd hit had been the worst: the nerve-racking wait in the close confines of the fighter cockpit, wondering when Quinn would kick the release and send them spinning out into combat with an enemy whose existence Aric wouldn't even know about until that instant. The second system hadn't been much better, but he'd permitted himself to hope that he was adapting.

He wasn't. Now, the third time around, he was just as nervous as he had been at the beginning. Sitting here in a Copperhead fighter, staring at the back of Quinn's helmet, he felt as out of place as he had as a child in his father's office, waiting for that last phone conversation or meeting of the day to be over. Beside him the Mindlink jack was a gaping reminder of just how out of place he was; the meager row of status lights beside it an even more pointed reminder that if and when that combat situation arose, he would be nothing but deadweight.

And topping it all was the fact that this was their midway point: the third system of the five the other Copperheads had agreed to help search. Three more blanks, and they would be returning to the Commonwealth, to face whatever charges Peacekeeper Command decided to throw at them.

And to abandon Pheylan to the Conquerors.

"Report, Commander," Max's voice cut into Aric's gloom. "I've located a substantial region of refined metal. Feeding location and specifications."

Aric felt his stomach tighten. Could this be it? "Where is it?" he asked.

"About a quarter of the way to the eastern horizon," Quinn said. "Looks too spread out to be a ship. Maybe a base or sections of a small city. Continue scan, Max— keep a sharp watch for vehicles. What do you think, Clipper?"

"Sounds worth taking a look at," Clipper said.

"Agreed. I'll take center; form up around me."

"Acknowledged. Let's go, gentlemen. Paladin, take point; Shrike, take portside flank. Harlequin, you're on high cover."

There was a jerk of released clamps, and the fueler bounced up and away as the Counterpunch dropped free. "What do you want me to do?" Aric asked, trying to keep the quavering out of his voice.

"Just sit back and enjoy the ride," Quinn said, his voice suddenly vague and distant as a small green light appeared on Aric's board. Quinn had engaged the

Counterpunch's Mindlink. Together he and the fighter were now a single, living entity.

With Aric as little more than excess baggage. Grimacing, he hunched his shoulders inside his flight suit and settled down to sweat it out.

The minutes dragged by. The five ships reached atmosphere without provoking any response and started down, the fighters' wing and tail-line positions continually reconfiguring as they drove through increasingly thicker air. "Got visual," Paladin's voice came. "Looks like a city, all right. Or what's left of one."

"Battle damage?" Harlequin asked.

"Or just natural deterioration," Dazzler, Paladin's tail, put in. "Can't tell which from up here. It's definitely more ruins than city, though."

"Let's take a closer look," Quinn said. "Keep the formation loose."

More minutes dragged by. The Counterpunch passed through a layer of cirrus clouds, heading down toward rolling wooded hills below. In the distance to the left Aric could see the sparkle of sunlight on water—a river or the edge of a lake; he couldn't tell which—with a suggestion of taller hills on the horizon in the other direction. Ahead, the hills they were traveling over seemed to be giving way to a flatter terrain, the trees similarly giving way to a wide grassland. Far ahead he could see the sparkle of another body of water.

"Maestro, we're over the city," Dazzler reported. "Lots of broken stone and metal, but it's all scattered around through big patches of vegetation. Looks pretty old."

"What about the ground itself?" Quinn asked.

"No obvious pits or burn marks," Dazzler said. "If there was a battle here, it must have happened a long time ago. Wait a minute."

For a moment there was silence. "Interesting," Dazzler said at last. "What do you think, Maestro?"

"Interesting, indeed," Quinn said. "Worth a closer look. Bookmaker, how's the high ground look?"

"Still showing clear," Bookmaker said. "If there's anyone here, they don't seem to have noticed us."

"Max?"

"I concur, Commander," the computer replied. "Continuing scan, but so far I've found nothing but the city."

"Must have been some war," Aric murmured uneasily.

"Not necessarily," Quinn said. "The city could have been nothing more than a base. A first-stage colonization effort someone put in and then gave up on. Clipper, form up a screen; El Dorado and I are going in."

"What are we going in to see?" Aric asked as the Counterpunch rolled partway over and dropped toward the ground.

"It's some sort of odd pyramid thing," Quinn told him. "About three meters high, white with lots of black speckles across the surface." His helmet bobbed as he nodded. "It'll be coming up on our left. Take a look."

The side of the Counterpunch dipped again, and Aric looked out. There it was: a triangular shape of glistening white, looking garishly out of place among the darker oxidized metal and broken masonry and pale-green plants. The spots Quinn had mentioned were closely but irregularly spaced, starting about a third of the way up from the bottom. Aric looked at it, lifted his gaze farther out—"Is that a fence over there?" he asked.

"Where?"

"Out there—that thick dark line a couple hundred meters away." He peered forward over Quinn's helmet. "There—straight ahead now—there's a section of it."

"It's a fence, all right," Quinn acknowledged, pulling a

sharp turn that threatened to leave Aric's stomach behind. "Close mesh, but it's not metal. Can't get a clear reading on what it is at this distance."

"Definitely looks like they're not encouraging visitors, anyway," Aric said, feeling a queasiness in his stomach that wasn't entirely due to Quinn's flying. "You suppose there might be other defenses?"

"Fair chance of that," Quinn conceded. "I'm not reading anything, but the sensors I've got aren't really designed for this sort of thing. It's your call—you want to just skip it?"

Aric grimaced. "No," he said. "It's the first lead we've had. We can't afford to pass it up. Let's go down."

"Okay," Quinn said. "Clipper, we're going in. Keep a sharp eye."

The Counterpunch swung back around toward the pyramid, its nose swinging up and then dropping again as Quinn switched to vertical landing mode and set them down. "I won't be long," he told Aric as the canopy slid back. "Stay put and keep watch."

"No," Aric said, punching his restraint release. "You stay here. I'll go."

Quinn twisted back around, a startled look on the part of his face Aric could see. "Mr. Cavanagh—"

"It's El Dorado here," Aric told him firmly, pulling himself up out of his seat and hoping sheer momentum would get him out of the fighter before he could change his mind. "And this isn't open to argument."

"It could be dangerous—"

"It sure could," Aric grunted. "And if there's trouble, whoever's out there is going to need backup. You can fly this thing. I can't. So I'm elected."

He dropped over the side of the fighter to the ground before Quinn could protest further, staggering a bit after the zero-gee of the past two days. Carefully, trying to watch every direction at once, he started toward the pyramid.

The ground was soft and uneven, with a large assortment of obstacles created by the half-hidden pieces of twisted metal and broken masonry. But no spears or snares or explosives kicked in. A nerve-racking but uneventful minute later, he had reached the pyramid.

It was, as Quinn had estimated, about three meters high, its surface a brilliantly reflective and unstained white. And as for the spots they'd seen—

"They're not spots," he said, peering closely at one of them. "They're holes. Squashed oval shape, about four centimeters across and two high and two or three deep."

"Odd sort of erosion pattern," Harlequin commented.

"More likely a shaped gunfire charge," Clipper suggested.

"It's neither," Aric told them. "For one thing, the holes are too smooth and too neatly shaped. For another, each one's got a little cover door built over it."

"A door?" Delphi echoed. "What kind of door?"

"A mesh of some kind," Aric said. "Extremely fine fibers, with a very tight weave. The material's shimmery, but I don't think it's metal. Could be spun glass, I suppose."

"You're right, it's not reading as metal," Quinn confirmed. "Neither is the pyramid itself."

"The final report on the *Jutland* attack indicated the Conquerors use little or no metal in their construction," Shrike pointed out.

"True," Clipper said. "Though that's hardly proof that this is a Conqueror construct. El Dorado, can you see through the mesh at all?"

"Quite well, actually," Aric said, moving around the pyramid and looking through the various doors. "Most of the holes seem to be empty. Wait a minute; here's one—" He frowned. Looked again. "With a thin slice of dried meat inside it."

"A *what*?" Paladin demanded.

"Well, that's what it looks like," Aric said. "A very thin slice off a small dried sausage, just lying there on the floor. Dark brown in color; about the diameter of my little finger." He glanced through several of the other doors. "There are a couple more like that, too. Most look pretty much the same, though the color varies a little. Wait; here's one slice that's a lot thicker than the others. Maybe three or four times as thick."

There was a long pause. Aric leaned close to the mesh covering that last hole, trying for a better look at the thing inside. Just like a slice of cured sausage, all right: dark brown with a hint of red, slightly wrinkled, looking old and dry. The breeze rustling through the trees grew louder for a moment, and he saw the sausage slice rock gently as an eddy current slipped through the mesh door. The breeze faded away. . . .

And Aric stiffened. Without the wind whistling past his helmet, he could hear something now. Quiet and vague, almost at the edge of his imagination. But definitely there.

A long, wailing scream.

"How are the doors sealed?" Delphi asked.

Aric jumped, the other's voice somehow startling coming in on top of that distant scream. "Sorry. What?"

"I asked how the doors are sealed."

"Uh . . ." Aric prodded the edge of one with a gloved finger. The pyramid material itself was exceptionally slippery, he noted. "They seem pretty solid," he said. "They're hinged at the top, with some kind of locking catch at the bottom. You want me to try to open it?"

"I don't think that would be a good idea," Quinn warned. "Anyone who would put protective doors on something like that might have put in other defenses against tampering. Besides, we've still got a lot of ground to cover. Max? Anything new from up there?"

"Nothing out of the ordinary," the computer answered. "I should point out, however, that the fueler's sensors haven't been designed for long-range detection of the sort of materials the Conquerors seem to favor."

"We're not much better down here," Quinn said. "You just keep watching the infrared and motion sensors. Come on back, El Dorado, and we'll get out of here."

"All right," Aric said, starting back toward the Counterpunch. "One other thing that might or might not be important. A minute ago, when everything else was very quiet, I thought I heard a faint scream."

"What sort of scream?" Clipper asked.

"I don't really know," Aric said. "Just your basic generic scream, really. If I had to guess, though, I'd say it sounded more like pain than anger."

He was at the top of the Counterpunch's flowmetal ladder before anyone spoke again. "You sure you didn't imagine it?" Quinn asked.

"I'm not sure, no," Aric admitted as he dropped into his seat. "But it sure sounded real at the time."

"None of the rest of us heard it," Clipper said. "But that doesn't mean anything, not with the cut-rate helmet mikes they've stuck us with these days."

"We can have Max scrub through the cockpit recordings when we get back to the fueler," Crackajack said. "Maybe he can dig something out."

"Maybe," Aric murmured, strapping in again. A scream of agony. Or maybe a chorus of screams—several of the niches had had sausage slices stashed away in them.

Stashed away . . . or locked away. Could the pyramid thing be a prison of some sort?

He snorted under his breath. A prison for sausage

slices. Right. Clearly, there had to be a better explanation.

Only problem was, he couldn't think of one.

The Counterpunch lurched back into the air. "Evaluation?" Quinn asked as he swung the nose away from the pyramid.

"I was afraid you'd ask me that," Aric said. "I don't have one. Nothing that makes any sense, anyway."

"Well, if it helps, you've got plenty of company," Quinn said. "I can't begin to think why anyone would put something out in the middle of nowhere like that."

"Unless it's some kind of warning," Aric said as an unpleasant thought suddenly occurred to him. "You know—that old barbarian technique of impaling your victims' heads on poles to warn off other enemies."

"You know anyone who makes war on sausages?" Bookmaker put in dryly.

"Besides, why go to the trouble of protecting something like that with mesh doors and a perimeter fence?" Crackajack added. "You *want* people to get close enough to see it."

"Point," Aric conceded with a sigh. "Where are we going to look next?"

"There's a large river about a hundred klicks to the east," Quinn said. "We'll start there."

"Commander, this is Max," the computer voice cut in. "I'm picking up a group of incoming tachyon wake-trails. Preliminary analysis indicates it to be two Conqueror ships."

Aric felt his heart skip a beat. "You sure?"

"The wake-trails match the baselines from the *Jutland* attack."

"Interesting timing," Clipper said. "Warrior's luck, Maestro. Max, what's their ETA?"

"Approximately two hours until mesh," Max said.

"Have you got a clear vector?"

"Assuming my baseline data is accurate, the vector is quite clear," Max assured him. "Sending to you now."

There was a moment of silence. Aric swallowed, looking up at the high clouds overhead. It was all right. They had two hours to get out of here before the Conquerors arrived.

Or two hours to find Pheylan. If this was, in fact, where he was being kept.

"Max, are you sure about this vector?" Delphi asked.

"Quite certain," the computer said. "Again, presuming the accuracy of my baseline information."

"What's wrong?" Aric asked.

"The vector makes no sense, that's what's wrong," Delphi said tartly. "There's not a system on that line for nearly a hundred fifty light-years."

Aric frowned. "That seems a little high."

"And nothing within ninety light-years inside a three-degree uncertainty cone," Crackajack added.

"Maybe they're coming from a station," Aric suggested hesitantly. "Something in deep space, between two solar systems."

"That doesn't make a lot of sense, either," Harlequin said.

"Maybe not to us," Dazzler reminded him. "These guys are aliens, remember?"

"Let's cut the chatter," Clipper cut them off. "Maestro, what's the plan?"

"We've got two hours," Quinn said. "We'll use the first one to continue our search. Wide spread, no overlap, and cover as much territory as you can. Harlequin, you join the pattern; I'll take over high cover for you."

"Delphi will feed you your vectors," Clipper said. "Let's get to it, gentlemen."

•   •   •

The final red light on the auxiliary board winked to green. "That's the last of the refuelings," Aric reported tightly. "How are you doing there?"

"All set," Quinn said from his seat at the fueler's main control board. "Ready to go as soon as Max gets all the numbers he can."

"Good," Aric said. He turned back to the fighter-status board, a hollow feeling in the pit of his stomach. They'd reached the fueler with a good twenty minutes to spare, and he'd naturally assumed they'd be heading out as soon as the fighters were berthed. Plenty of time to avoid the potential nastiness of an encounter with the Conquerors.

Quinn had had other ideas. The incoming ships' heat-emission numbers, he'd pointed out, were likely to be the only clue they would get as to how far the ships had come. The fueler had the proper instruments to get those numbers, and Max had the proper programming to sift through and interpret them.

And so here they waited. Sitting ducks, waiting for the Conquerors to arrive. Hoping that the newcomers would mesh in close enough for them to get a good reading, but far enough away that they wouldn't spot, track, and summarily vaporize the fueler.

"I wonder if we should change our orbit again," Aric said, drifting over to hover at Quinn's shoulder. "Moving higher up in the gravity well would let us mesh out a little faster."

"We're fine right where we are," Quinn soothed him. "That last shift should get us to apogee just about the time they mesh in." He glanced up at Aric. "Look, relax, all right? Odds are they won't even know we're here until we're long gone. Max, any change in their vector?"

"No, Commander. Still as originally computed."

"Watch out for a shift right at the end," Quinn

warned. "They might have a specific approach they like to come in on."

"Acknowledged," Max said. "They'll be meshing in in approximately one minute."

Aric looked at the display, and the hazy horizon of the planet beneath them. "What do we do if they come out on the far side of the planet?"

"We'll have to see what their orbit insertion looks like," Quinn said. He was holding the end of his Mindlink cable in his hand; with only a slight hesitation he plugged it into the jack beside the main display. "If it looks like they might come into Max's range within a couple of minutes, we'll probably hang around and try to get a reading. Get ready; here they come."

Aric held his breath, unconsciously bracing himself as he watched the displays. The timer counted down. . . .

"Vector shift!" Quinn snapped. "Coming around toward us—"

And then, suddenly, there they were: two ships, milky-white, the same linked-hexagon configuration that the *Jutland* watchships' records had burned into Aric's memory. A little below them, falling into an orbit roughly parallel to theirs.

Barely two kilometers away.

"Quinn!" Aric barked. Practically right on top of them—!

Quinn didn't answer. Aric looked down at him, a hand reflexively coming up to point at the display.

He froze, finger still pointed at the board. Quinn was sitting motionlessly in his seat, his forehead creased with concentration, his eyes staring with a chilling blankness at the display and the Conqueror ships visible there.

And on the board beside the computer-link jack, two pale-green lights had come on.

Aric looked back at the display, a tingle of eerie unreality clouding over the surge of panic. The Conqueror ships were starting to rotate their edges toward the fueler, the Corvines in sight now as they darted toward the alien ships like angry hawks defending their nest. Deadly silent, deadly serious, deadly precise. Four fighters, one fueler, working now as a single unit.

Copperheads.

Out of the corner of his eye Aric saw a light flick on beneath the display—

And with a suddenness that made him jump, the display shimmered and the Conquerors and planet vanished. "Quinn! What—? Did we mesh out?"

For a half-dozen heartbeats there was no answer. Then, slowly, Quinn's eyes came back to focus. "Yes," he said, his voice sounding strange. "We got the readings we needed and left. No damage."

"Ah," Aric said, feeling oddly out of breath. "What about the Corvines?"

"Should be right with us," Quinn said. The two lights beneath the jack had gone out; reaching over, he pulled out the Mindlink cable. "We're doing a two-minute parallel jump."

"I see," Aric said. He'd seen people try parallel jumps on occasion, never with optimum results. The twin problems of timing and drift . . . but then, those pilots hadn't had Copperhead synchronization. "Did anyone get a static bomb off?"

"No," Quinn said, his voice a little grim. "There wasn't enough time. That's why we're just doing two minutes."

Aric looked at the display, now functioning as the fueler's main status board. "What happens if they track us?"

Quinn shrugged, pulling the other end of the cable

out of the jack hidden under the hair beneath his right ear. "We fight, I guess. Don't worry, though—there's a good chance they won't be able to find us. Two minutes is considered optimum timing for the enemy to get a track on your wake-trail and mesh out after you. Since we'll be meshing in about that same time, they should wind up shooting right past us."

"That assumes they can't track a wake-trail while in stardrive," Aric pointed out. "Or that they won't wait that extra minute and notice that we've meshed in again."

Quinn shook his head. "Doubt it. So far their stardrive seems to work the same way as ours. It's unlikely their tracking system would work any differently."

"As unlikely as their meshing in only two kilometers away from us?"

For a moment Quinn was silent. "You're right," he conceded. He sat there another moment, then picked up the connector cable and reinserted it into the jack behind his ear. "Max, I want an immediate tactical scan as soon as we mesh in," he ordered, plugging in the other end of the cable.

"Yes, Commander."

One of the two green lights beside the jack came on. "Stand ready, El Dorado," Quinn said. "Here we go."

Once again the seconds counted down; and with another shimmer the stars were back. Holding his breath, Aric stared at the display. "I don't see them," he murmured. "The Corvines. Where are they?"

Silence. "Quinn?" Aric demanded. "Where are they?"

"There," Quinn said, relief evident in his voice. "There, and over there. Just had a little drift problem, that's all. They're on their way. Damage . . . not reading any."

"Great," Aric said, rubbing his hand across his forehead. It was like coming off one of those terrifying amusement-park gravity rides that he'd always hated. The kind Pheylan and Melinda had always tried to drag him onto when they were kids.

Unfortunately, this ride wasn't over yet. "What do we do if the Conquerors show up? Run for it?"

"Immediately," Quinn nodded. "Don't worry, the others all have the contingency rendezvous point. Max, how's the analysis on those ships coming?"

"It's finished, Commander," the computer said. "I'm afraid it's not going to be as useful as you hoped."

"They never are," Quinn said. "Let's hear it."

One of the side displays lit up with a false-color diagram of the two Conqueror ships. "Here are the raw data," Max said. "You'll see that aside from the beginnings of edge-effect dissipation, the infrared pattern is remarkably uniform. This implies either an extremely cool drive mechanism or else a highly efficient heat-redistribution system."

"Hull-based superconductors?" Aric suggested.

"That's one possibility," Max agreed. "Unfortunately, that uncertainty coupled with our lack of data on the hull material itself leaves us with a considerable margin of error for any distance calculation. It will be better than the *Jutland* was able to obtain, though, given the immediacy of these readings."

"Bottom line, Max," Quinn said. "Let's have it."

The false-color images were replaced by a star chart, with a vector marked in red. "I estimate the ships had traveled between twenty-five and seventy light-years," Max said.

Quinn snorted. "Twenty-five to seventy?" he echoed. "Why don't you make it an even zero to one billion while you're at it?"

"I'm sorry, Commander," Max said, sounding genuinely regretful. "Without better data that's the best I can do."

"I know," Quinn sighed. "Forget it."

Aric looked at the chart. Delphi's estimate had been right: there wasn't a single system on or near that line for nearly a hundred light-years. "It has to be a space station," he said. "That's the only way it can make any sense."

"I know," Quinn said. "I know. The problem . . ." He broke off, waving a hand helplessly at the chart.

Aric nodded, a hard knot of gloom settling into the pit of his stomach. To find a single deep-space station along a line forty-five light-years long . . . "It can't be done, can it?" he asked quietly.

"No," Quinn said. "There's not a chance in hell. Not if we had every ship in the Commonwealth to help us."

Aric looked at the red line. "So what do we do?"

Quinn looked up at him. "We go home, sir," he said. "There's nothing else we can do."

The control room was suddenly as silent as a tomb. Pheylan's tomb. "Not yet," Aric said. "We can't go yet. We can do two more systems—the others promised they'd help us search that many."

Quinn waved again at the chart. "Fine. Which two do you want?"

Aric shook his head. All those stars. Where even to think about beginning?

"It's over, Mr. Cavanagh," Quinn said into the silence. "We did everything we could. It wasn't enough. It's time to go home."

"You that eager to face trial?" Aric bit out.

"No," Quinn said. "I'm not eager to prepare for war, either. But we'll probably have to do both."

Aric grimaced. "I'm sorry," he apologized. "I didn't mean it that way."

For a minute Quinn was silent. "We need to release the others to go back," he said at last. "That was our agreement. But if you want to continue . . . I guess I'm willing to keep going. We could probably go another month on our own before we had to turn back."

"And where would we look?" Aric countered.

Quinn shrugged slightly. "Wherever you wanted."

Aric turned away from the chart, his mind churning with anger and frustration. But Quinn was right. They literally had no place to start looking. "No," he said. "You're right. There's nothing more we can do." He took a deep breath. "When do we leave?"

"The Corvines will be back here in about four hours if they stick with their current minimal-fuel course," Quinn said. "We'll get the fighters berthed and refueled and then head home. Either to Dorcas or straight on to Edo."

Aric nodded. The plan made sense, of course—they had no reason to hang around here once they'd made the decision to leave. But still . . . "Maybe we should all get some rest first," he said over his shoulder. "Could be the Conquerors just weren't able to track a tachyon wake-trail this short. They might be waiting for us to mesh out and start after us then."

"Not if we drop a static bomb first," Quinn pointed out.

"We could all still use some rest," Aric insisted. "All of us need it."

He could feel Quinn's gaze on the back of his head. "All right," the other said. "How much time do you want?"

Or in other words, how much time did he need to reconcile himself to abandoning Pheylan to the Conquerors. "Let's make it ten hours from now," Aric said. "That'll give everyone about six hours of sleep."

"Agreed," Quinn said.

Aric took a deep breath. So that was it. He had ten hours in which to pull a miracle out of a hat.

Or to find the courage to do what had to be done. And to say a final good-bye to his brother.

22 **"A**ll right," Melinda said, easing off the clamps that had been holding the Conqueror's torso open and dropping them back onto the tray. "That part's done. How are you holding up, Hobson?"

"I'm okay, ma'am," her assistant said from across the makeshift autopsy table. Words aside, he was looking a little green above his breather mask. "We almost done?"

"With this session, yes," Melinda assured him. "I'm going to have to scrounge up some specialized instruments before I can do anything with the cranium. We'll look at the tongue and then take a break."

"Yeah, I heard about that tongue," Hobson said darkly. "That's how that one iced Bremmer and Ranjithan."

"Yes," Melinda nodded, moving to the other end of the table and picking up a probe and clamp. "Open his mouth, will you? Carefully."

Hobson complied. Easing the probe under the tongue, Melinda lifted the tip out into the open and clamped it in place. "Interesting," she murmured, touching the edge.

"What are those things?" Hobson asked, leaning in for a closer look. "Look like little shark teeth."

"They're pieces of bone, I think," Melinda said, wiggling one of the dark-white triangles with her probe. "Fastened directly to the tongue muscle. Definitely sharp."

"How come they don't cut themselves?"

"They probably don't normally protrude quite this far out," Melinda said, picking up a scalpel and making a small incision between two of the bone teeth. "The muscle tissues have likely contracted somewhat over the past forty hours. Ah."

"What?" Hobson asked.

"Blood vessels," Melinda said, easing the incision open. "A fairly major set, right here at the edge."

Peripherally, she saw Hobson glance away. "Major Takara's coming," he said.

Melinda straightened and looked behind her. Takara was coming toward them through the deepening dusk, picking his way carefully around the boxes of equipment and supplies that had been piled beneath the wide rock overhang. "Major," she nodded as he stepped up to the plastic bubble of their makeshift autopsy room. "Anything from the biochem people?"

"Yes," Takara said, "and you can both relax. Turns out the Conquerors' genetic pattern isn't even remotely similar to ours. That apparently means that any viruses or bacteria associated with your subject there aren't going to have the slightest idea what to do with human body chemistry. Shouldn't be able to bother any of the native Dorcas ecosystem, either."

"And vice versa, I suppose?" Melinda asked.

"Right," Takara said, unsealing the bubble's flap door and stepping inside. "So much for any *War of the Worlds* scenarios we might have hoped for. How are you doing, Hobson?"

"I'm holding up, sir," Hobson said. "This isn't exactly my usual specialty, though."

"Consider it part of the exotic life your Peacekeeper recruiter promised you." Takara nodded at the Conqueror corpse on the table. "Looking at the tongue?"

"Yes," Melinda said. "And I think I know how he killed those two men." She touched one of the sharp bone fragments with her probe. "These bone teeth are attached to what seems to be a ridge of erectile tissue just beneath the tongue's surface. Normally, the tissue is soft and pliable, which lets the teeth float loosely. Keeps them from scratching or cutting anything in the inside of the mouth. When the tissue engorges, though, the teeth stiffen into place, turning into a sort of serrated knife along each edge. They might physically interlock, too, which would give the arrangement more structural strength. I'll have to poke around a little more to see if that's the case."

"Well, be careful while you do it," Takara warned. "The autopsy on Bremmer indicated there might have been some kind of poison in that wound. You at a break point here?"

"We could be," Melinda said, glancing past Takara's shoulder at the fading light past the overhang. Evening was coming, and they would have to quit soon anyway. "Do you need me somewhere else?"

"Colonel wants to see you in his office. Could take a while."

"All right," Melinda said, stripping off her gloves and breather mask and dropping them into the prep tray. "Hobson, can you get the body back into storage by yourself?"

"No problem, ma'am."

"And then get cleaned up and report to Lieutenant Gasperi in Command Three," Takara added. "Whenever you're ready, Doctor."

Holloway's "office"—a chair and computer desk in a corner of the tactical-equipment section of the over-

hang—was buzzing with activity when Melinda and
Takara arrived. Holloway himself was standing in front
of a map that had been fastened to the rough rock of
the wall, holding a discussion with several of his men.
Other Peacekeepers were moving back and forth between the desk and the other workstations, dropping
off reports and picking up new orders. And off to one
side, standing or sitting on the uneven floor, were a
half-dozen tired-looking men in camouflage outfits.

The group by the map broke up. "Dr. Cavanagh,"
Holloway greeted her, stepping back to his desk and
sitting down. "Sorry I can't offer you a chair, but we're a
little short of furniture here. How's the dissection coming?"

"We've made a start," Melinda told him, stepping up
to the desk and giving Holloway a quick once-over. He
looked as tired as the men by the other wall. Maybe
more so. "I've done a preliminary examination of the
exterior and a closer study of the torso area. I need to
do the head and the limbs, and then we'll move on to
microscopic tissue studies."

"I see." Holloway picked up a small plastic sample
box from the scattered electronic equipment and
stacks of paper cluttering the desk and handed it to
her. "Take a look. Tell me what you think."

Melinda took the box and looked through the lid. Inside, nestled in the palm of a camouflaged glove, was a
thin, dark-brown disk, slightly curled at the edges. "It
looks like a slice of sausage," she said. "Where did it
come from?"

Holloway gestured to the camouflaged men. "Sergeant Janovetz?"

"We found it just north of the settlement," a raw-
boned man near the middle of the group said. "In a
little cubbyhole built into a sort of white pyramid thing
the Conquerors have got set up on Overview Ridge."

Melinda frowned at Holloway. It had been barely two days since the Conquerors had invaded. "They're moving equipment in already?"

"They moved these in, anyway," Holloway said. "There appear to be four of them: one each north, south, east, and west of the settlement."

"Pretty good-sized, too," Janovetz said. "The one we saw was about three meters tall and a couple wide at the base, with probably a couple hundred of these cubbyholes cut into it."

"Some kind of defense station?" Melinda suggested. "Or a sensor array?"

"The positioning's right for either one," Holloway agreed. "Only problem is that the pyramids seem to be completely inert. No active or passive electronics, no power sources, no metal. Nothing." He nodded at the box. "Except those things."

Melinda looked into the box again. "How many were there?"

"There were four others in the cubbyholes we could see," Janovetz said. "Could have been more—we couldn't see into the top ones. Most of the holes were empty, though."

"Plenty of room for expansion, then," Melinda said.

"My thought exactly," Holloway nodded. "Means we'd better find out what the hell those things are. Preferably before the Conquerors get a whole shipment of them in."

"I understand," Melinda said. "I'll do what I can."

It was after midnight when she finally unsealed the flap door of the biochemical bubble and stepped wearily out into the dim nighttime lighting of the main medical ward. To her complete lack of surprise, Holloway was waiting there for her.

"Doctor," he murmured, getting up from where he'd been sitting against the rock wall and shutting off his plate. "Any progress?"

"Some," Melinda said, glancing at the rows of sleeping injured. Burn patients, most of them, victims of the Conquerors' laser weapons. "Can we talk somewhere else?" she whispered. "I don't want to wake them."

"Sure," Holloway whispered back. "This way."

He led her past the cots and the medic's duty station to the huge curtains that had been rigged at the edge of the rock overhang to keep light from leaking out. Holloway found an edge and a minute later they were outside in the cool mountain air. "What did you find out?" he asked.

"Not very much, I'm afraid," Melinda said. "It definitely follows the same genetic plan as the Conqueror tissue. But all that means is that it probably originated on the Conquerors' homeworld. The cellular structure is extremely tight-packed, which in humans might suggest either part of a sensory cluster or the central nervous system."

"Sensory cluster," Holloway murmured thoughtfully. "Maybe we were right about the pyramids being sensor stations."

"Maybe," Melinda nodded. "Again, that's what it might suggest in humans. We don't know what the Conquerors' patterns are like yet. One other thing: the cellular structure appears to be extremely uniform, with only the edge being made of a different material. Again, in terms of Earth biology that would suggest it's not an egg."

"Could it be a cutting or budding of some kind? I seem to remember that some plants and animals reproduce that way."

"Some do, yes," Melinda agreed. "Most of the ones we know about are fairly primitive, but that doesn't necessarily mean it can't occur in more advanced animals. I don't think the pyramids are Conqueror nurseries, though, if that's what you're getting at."

"Why not?"

"For one thing, I think I've got a good candidate for sexual organs in our Conqueror specimen," Melinda said. "If I'm right, it means they shouldn't reproduce via unisexual buds or slices or whatever. For another, why would anyone put a nursery out in the open like that? Especially in the middle of a war zone?"

"I was thinking more along the lines of an incubation site for one of the Conquerors' homeworld animals," Holloway said. "Something vicious that would help distract us from our fight against the Conquerors themselves. These things were pretty well protected—I don't think you heard, but each of the holes was covered by a little mesh door. Janovetz had to break a catch to get it open."

"No," Melinda said, suppressing a shiver. "I hadn't heard that."

Suppressed or not, Holloway noticed. "You cold?" he asked. "We could go somewhere else to talk."

"I'm all right," Melinda said, looking up at the stars and the thin clouds drifting across them. "I was just wondering whether it's safe to be out in the open like this."

"We're all right," Holloway assured her. "I don't think the Conquerors have anything that can still fly at the moment. Whatever their expertise at full line-ship combat, they don't seem nearly as adroit at this close-in planetary work. I'll have to thank your brother someday for his thoughtfulness in providing us with those Copperheads."

Melinda winced. "I'm sorry, Colonel. The idea was never to cause this much trouble for anyone."

"It's all right," he said. "I just hope they're able to find your brother Pheylan."

Melinda twisted around to stare at his silhouette. "How did—? Did the Copperheads tell you?"

"Actually, they were even more closemouthed about it than you were," Holloway said. "But it's been simmering in the back of my mind for a couple of days now. A private rescue mission into Conqueror space was the only halfway reasonable thing I could come up with. I assume from your reaction that I was right."

"Yes." Melinda looked up at the stars again. Wondering what their chances really were of finding Pheylan. Or whether he and Aric would both disappear into the darkness.

"You can't fight their part of the war for them," Holloway said quietly into the silence. "All you can do is try to handle your part, and let them be free to do theirs."

"That's easy for you to say," Melinda said.

"You think so?" he countered, his voice suddenly hard. "I have friends and family, too, you know. They're sitting in ships and ground stations all over Lyra and Pegasus Sectors, waiting for the Conquerors to attack. I can't do their worrying for them. Neither can you."

Melinda took a deep breath. "You're right. I'm sorry."

"Nothing to be sorry about," Holloway said, his voice calm again. "I've been in the Peacekeepers for twenty years now. It took me the first ten to learn how to let go. Anything else you can tell me about the sausage slice?"

"Not really," she said, forcing her mind away from Aric and Pheylan and back to the task at hand. "What I need to do now is run biochem tests on both the slice and the Conqueror body and do some comparisons. Do you suppose there's any chance of getting another slice, perhaps from one of the other pyramids? Or are the Conquerors protecting them too well?"

"Interesting you should bring that up," Holloway said. "Janovetz's team came under assault about three klicks out from the pyramid. It was his opinion that trying to get that close in again would be suicide unless we were willing to risk sending in some serious air cover, which I'm not. But I was looking over the recorder report just now, and I noticed that it was only on their way in toward the pyramid that the team encountered any real resistance. Once they were right there beside it, the attacks stopped."

"Sounds like the Conquerors didn't want to risk damage to the pyramid," Melinda suggested.

"I agree," Holloway nodded. "What's more curious is that the team was then also allowed to leave the pyramid without coming under any further fire."

Melinda frowned. "Are you sure about that?"

"It's right there in the recorder," Holloway said. "There were still bursts of laser fire chasing them away, but nothing that even came close."

"Seems odd," Melinda said, staring into the darkness. "Why would the Conquerors want to just let them go?"

"I come up with three possibilities," Holloway said. "One, the Conquerors didn't want anyone coming close to the settlement; two, they didn't care where we went as long as we didn't damage their pyramid; or three, they cared about both of the above but didn't want to risk damaging the sausage slice the team had appropriated. If Janovetz had tried going forward instead of turning back, we might have a better idea which it was. Too late now, of course."

"Yes." Melinda hesitated. "Colonel—no offense—but why are you telling me all this?"

"Mainly because you're not military," he said. "You've got an entirely different background and point of view, and that might let you see things the rest of us miss." He paused. "Besides, given that you're the one who brought it up, I thought you deserved to be kept up to date on the situation regarding the tectonic-monitoring station."

For a moment Melinda didn't understand what he was talking about. Then, suddenly, it all came back. "Is that what Janovetz was trying to get to?"

"It was one of their objectives," Holloway said. "They didn't get anywhere near it, though. And until that defense force Command promised us gets here, we're not going to get another shot at it. If the force gets here at all, of course."

So that was that. If the tectonic station was harboring one of the CIRCE components, it was likely going to stay buried awhile longer. Locked away from both NorCoord and the Conquerors. If they were lucky. "What happens if the Conquerors find it?"

Holloway shrugged. "In theory a single component's of no use to anyone. If there is one there and they get it, we wind up in stalemate mode."

For a minute they stood there in silence. "What do you think our chances are?" Melinda asked at last.

"Against the Conquerors?" Holloway shrugged again. "Probably going to depend on how well we can dig in for the long haul. Like I said, they don't seem all that good at ground fighting; and if they were going to nuke or fry us from orbit, you'd think they would have tried it by now."

Melinda thought back to that short battle after the Conquerors had shot down their aircar. "Maybe the Copperheads took them by surprise," she suggested.

"That could be part of it," Holloway agreed. "But if you add up what we've seen of their basic armament and tactics, you don't see anything very impressive. Especially for what one would expect to be their elite shock troops."

"Maybe we don't rate anything that elite," Melinda

said, a shiver running up her back. "Maybe their shock troops are busy somewhere else. On one of the more important Commonwealth worlds."

"That's possible," Holloway said soberly. "If so, we could be a long time getting any help here."

Melinda blinked away sudden tears. Her father and brothers, all separated from each other . . . "But that's their part of the war," she said. "Right?"

"That's right," Holloway said. "Save your mental energy for our corner of it." He hesitated. "If it helps any, try remembering how well we did against them after they shot us down. If they were that badly prepared to deal with us, they ought to be completely out of their depth on Edo or Avon."

He twisted his wrist up, and Melinda caught the flicker of pale glow as he checked his watch. "Anyway, I've kept you out here too long already. What with the rest of the dissection and probably another round of surgery, your day's going to be as busy as mine."

Surgery . . . "Yes, it will," Melinda said mechanically as an odd thought suddenly occurred to her. Something half-remembered from her preliminary examination of the Conqueror corpse. "I'll try to have reports ready on both the slice and the Conqueror body by tomorrow evening."

"All right," Holloway said, finding the break in the curtain and guiding her through out of the darkness into the dim light of the medical ward. "You know where you're supposed to sleep?"

"Yes, I'm fine," she assured him. "I want to check something first, though."

"All right. Good night, Doctor."

"Good night."

The Peacekeeper engineers had rigged a storage box for the Conqueror corpse out of an empty transfer pod and the refrigeration unit from a spare Icefire engine. It had been set up in an out-of-the-way spot a few meters from the autopsy area. A *dark* out-of-the-way spot, unfortunately, a factor Melinda hadn't properly appreciated when she'd headed off on this little side trip. But it couldn't be helped. This section of the overhang area wasn't yet screened from view from the outside world, and Holloway had expressly forbidden lights here until it was. She would have to make do with the diffuse starlight filtering through the trees or forget the whole thing until morning.

But she reached the storage box without anything worse than minor damage to her toes and shins. Hobson had pushed the spare equipment cart right beside it, and with a little cautious feeling around she located a breather mask and fresh pair of gloves. Putting them on, she popped open the cover.

The Conqueror body was lying faceup on the metal slab the engineers had spot-welded into the pod. Easing the head over to face away from her, she ran a hand up the neck beneath the backward curve of the cranium. If she was remembering correctly . . .

And there it was: the telltale smoothness of scar tissue. A vertical incision, slightly off center, extending most of the way between the skull and the top of the bony ridge that topped the alien's spine. Smooth, very professionally done, about five centimeters long.

And just about the right size for the removal of something the diameter of that sausage slice.

Slowly, carefully, she returned the head to vertical and closed the cover of the storage box. It was ridiculous, she knew. Completely ridiculous. And yet . . .

Behind her mask she snorted. No; it *was* ridiculous. The Conquerors had sexual organs—surely they didn't reproduce by budding. And they certainly didn't reproduce in any way that required surgery to function.

Turning away, she lifted her gloved hand to the seal on the breather mask—

And froze. There, no more than ten meters away, something was floating slowly through the air across the storage area. Something pale white in color, insubstantial in form, moving between the piles of boxes and equipment.

A ghost.

Against her cheek Melinda felt her hands begin to tremble, every ghost story Aric and Pheylan had inflicted on her as a child surging back in a bubbling flood of panic. She took an involuntary step backward, coming up short as the small of her back rammed into the cold storage box. The ghostly figure paused, seemed to turn its head toward her—

And with a flash of horror she saw that the face turned toward her was that of a Conqueror.

It vanished at that moment, disappearing instantly into nothingness. But it didn't matter. Melinda's scream was already on its way.

"I'm all right," she said, taking one last sip of hot liquid and handing the cup back to the medic. Her hand, she noticed, was still trembling slightly. "Thank you."

"You sure?" Holloway asked.

"Yes. I'm sorry, Colonel."

"It was a perfectly reasonable reaction," Holloway assured her. "I'd probably have emptied a full clip into it, myself. Is there anything else you can tell us about it?"

Melinda shook her head. "Not really. It was definitely there, definitely three-dimensional, and definitely a Conqueror. And definitely looked like something straight out of a ghost story."

Beside Holloway, Major Takara shook his head. "This

doesn't make sense, Cass. Even begging the question of how they did it, why bother running a hologram into the base in the first place?"

"Maybe to shake us up," Holloway said. "Create a ruckus so they could get an idea of personnel and weapons placement by seeing how and where we react. *If* all it was was a hologram."

"What else could it have been?" Takara asked.

"I don't know," Holloway said. "But we're dealing with aliens and unknown technology. And a slice of something that Dr. Cavanagh suggested might be part of a sensory cluster."

Takara frowned at him. "You're not suggesting that sausage slice is part of a high-tech retrieval system, are you? With a hologram as the far end of it?"

"Yes, it's a ridiculous idea," Holloway nodded. "I agree. But Dr. Cavanagh said it was floating around the equipment dumps; and at this point I don't care about looking ridiculous. Have we got anything out here with half a chance of blocking whatever sensor system the Conquerors might be using?"

Takara already had his plate out. "Well, we could rig another pod like the one holding the body back there. But that wouldn't—wait a minute. Here we go: the darkroom."

"What's that?" Melinda asked.

"Electronics reconfiguration chamber," Holloway told her. "Multilayered steel, lead, soft iron, and a couple others. Designed to block out anything that might damage unshielded crystallines, up to and including a fair percentage of cosmic rays. That's perfect, Fuji. Get the slice moved over there right away."

"Got it," Takara said. "What about the body? You want that moved in there, too?"

"Yes," Holloway said. "Dr. Cavanagh can continue her

dissection work in there tomorrow." He looked at her. "If you feel up to it by then."

"I'll be fine," she promised.

For a moment his eyes searched her face. "All right," he nodded. "But don't push it."

He glanced toward the overhang. "Chances are we're going to have plenty of time out here to get things done."

23 **"S**o nice to see you again, Lord Cavanagh," Taurin Lee said, positively radiating self-satisfaction as he and his entourage passed between the silent male Yycroman guards and crossed to where Cavanagh and Klyveress sat waiting for them. "You know, I would have sworn you told Bronski you were going to be staying in Mig-Ka City."

"I changed my mind," Cavanagh said, glancing at each of the other six men now spreading out behind Lee. One of Bronski's men was among them—Garcia, if Cavanagh remembered his name correctly. Bronski himself was nowhere to be seen. "Shifting circumstances and all that. Speaking of Mr. Bronski, where is he?"

"I'll ask the questions, if you don't mind," Lee said. "You made quite a mess getting out of that hotel. The Mrachanis were absolutely furious."

"Given that they intended all along to maneuver me here, I hardly think they have any right to complain." Cavanagh caught Garcia's eye. "Garcia, where's Mr. Bronski?"

"I told you, Cavanagh—"

"He's out inspecting that little impromptu shipyard outside," Garcia said.

"Shut up, Garcia," Lee snapped, throwing the other a knife-edged look as he pulled a card from his tunic. "This is a NorCoord Parliament carte blanche, Lord Cavanagh," he identified it. "I'm in charge here. As I was on Mra-mig, if that matters to you."

"I see," Cavanagh nodded. He'd already figured that part out, but it was useful to know what authority Lee was operating under. "So what great leadership act are you here to perform?"

"For starters, I'm going to put you under arrest," Lee said. "You and your journalist friend both."

"You mean Ezer Sholom?"

Lee lifted his eyebrows in mock surprise. "I thought you didn't know who he was."

"I didn't," Cavanagh said. "I identified him the same way you did: by scanning one of Fibbit's threadings of him into a computer. Did you take the time to read his complete record?"

"He was once a journalist," Lee said, looking at one of his men and nodding sharply toward Cavanagh. "That's all I need to know," he continued as the man stepped forward.

[What do you intend to do?] Klyveress asked.

"I intend to put him under arrest, Klyveress ci Yyatoor," Lee said as the man moved to Cavanagh's side. "Either he's already broken the Official Secrets Regulations or is intending to break them. Either way, that's adequate cause for a presumptive arrest."

[He is on Yycroman soil,] Klyveress pointed out. [Is he not bound therefore by Yycroman rather than NorCoord law?]

"If I were you, ci Yyatoor, I'd stay out of this," Lee said, his voice deadly quiet. "That shipyard out there is a serious and blatant violation of the Pacification treaty.

Trying to defend Lord Cavanagh will simply buy you more trouble than you and the Yycroman Hierarchy are already in.

[Commonwealth interdiction forces have been withdrawn from Yycroman space,] Klyveress reminded him. [We thus lie undefended beneath the Conqueror threat. Would you have us sit idly by and allow our worlds to be destroyed?]

Lee snorted. "Do you really expect me to believe that's what all those ships are for?"

[Do you call me a liar?] Klyveress countered.

A couple of the other men seemed to wince. Lee either didn't notice or didn't care. "I call you a twister of the truth," he said bluntly. "I don't believe for a minute the Hierarch would be foolish enough to send barely armed merchant ships against an enemy like the Conquerors."

"What else do they have?" Cavanagh put in, watching Garcia. "The Commonwealth took all their real warships away from them."

Garcia's lip twitched. Not much, but enough to show he knew about the Yycroman warship out there.

A fact that apparently had been kept from his temporary boss. "Maybe the Hierarch will hire you to defend them before the NorCoord Parliament," Lee said sarcastically, no hint of Garcia's reaction registering on his face. "Otherwise, I suggest you start cooperating. Before I slap a charge of treason on top of the Official Secrets violations. Now, where's Sholom?"

"He's not here," Cavanagh said, feeling a ring of sweat beginning to collect beneath his collar. *Treason.* Did Lee know about the fueler he'd sent to Melinda? Or about the Peacekeeper fighters Aric and Quinn had borrowed?

Or could that even have fallen through right at the beginning? Were Melinda and Aric even now in custody, with Lee simply playing a spider's game with him? "I think he's still on Mra-mig, unless the Mrachanis have moved him. And there's a good chance he's in trouble."

"He sure is," Lee said grimly. "All right, let's go."

"No," Cavanagh shook his head. "I mean *real* trouble. If I could talk to Bronski—"

"I already told you I'm in charge," Lee cut him off. "Daschka, take him to the shuttle. We'll finish up here and—"

"There," Cavanagh said, pointing to the doorway as Bronski and two other men walked into the room. "Mr. Bronski, I need to speak to you. Immediately."

"You can talk to him aboard ship," Lee said. "What are you waiting for, Daschka? Get him moving."

"This can't wait," Cavanagh insisted as Daschka took his arm and levered him to his feet. "It's absolutely vital to Commonwealth security."

"Save it for your hearing," Lee said. Across the room, behind Lee's back, Garcia had stepped over to Bronski's side and was whispering in his ear. "Get him out of here, Daschka. And put him under communications quarantine—he's not to talk to anyone aboard ship without my permission. Now, as for you and the Hierarch, ci Yyatoor—"

"Just a minute," Bronski said.

Slowly, deliberately, Lee turned to look at him. "What did you say?" he demanded, his voice deadly.

"I said just a minute," Bronski told him. "I'd like to hear what Lord Cavanagh thinks is this vital to Commonwealth security."

"In private, Mr. Bronski," Cavanagh added. "For the moment I think this should be for your ears only."

"Cavanagh—"

"It's all right, Mr. Lee," Bronski cut him off. "There's nothing he can tell me I'm not cleared to hear. Where to?"

[There,] Klyveress said, gesturing toward one of the other doors leading from the main room of the suite. [It is private, and there is no other exit.]

The room was a small sleeping chamber, with a Yycroman bed pushed all the way to one wall and two human-sized chairs facing each other in the center. "Interesting," Bronski commented as Cavanagh sealed the door behind them. "Human chairs and everything. You and the ci Yyatoor had this already set up, didn't you?"

"As I said, this is something that needs to be discussed privately," Cavanagh said, taking one of the seats and gesturing Bronski to the other.

"What, with an assistant liaison from a small Commonwealth diplomatic outpost?" Bronski asked, pulling the chair a few centimeters back.

"No," Cavanagh said. "With a senior member of NorCoord Military Intelligence."

For a second Bronski seemed to freeze halfway down into the seat. "That's an interesting accusation," he commented, continuing the rest of the way down. "Totally ridiculous, of course."

"Of course," Cavanagh agreed. "All Commonwealth diplomatic personnel routinely carry concealed flechette pistols. Just in case they should happen to find themselves in an unexpected face-off with Bhurtala on a Mrach world. It was also just coincidence that your assistant Garcia happened to twitch a few minutes ago when I suggested all Yycroman warships had been taken away from them after the Pacification, which you and he know is not strictly accurate." He cocked an eyebrow. "And, of course, all Commonwealth diplomatic liaisons are issued with forged Mrach red cards. I'd guess that would make you—what? A colonel? Senior colonel?"

For a long moment Bronski just looked at him. "Brigadier," he said at last. "Let's hear about this threat to Commonwealth security."

"Ezer Sholom," Cavanagh said. "The man Fibbit made a threading of in Mig-Ka City. What do you know about him?"

Bronski shrugged. "Ezer Ronel Sholom. Born May twenty-second, 2234, in Crane City, Arcadia. Joined the StarNet News Service in 2257 and became one of the most popular journalists of his day. Covered the Pawolian war and guerrilla insurrections on Tal from the front lines and did daily analysis during the Yycroman Pacification. Wrote about a dozen books, did the lecture circuit, hobnobbed with the rich and famous. Retired about fifteen years ago to a small estate on Palisades."

"Is he still there?"

"It's still his official residence. Whether or not he's there at the moment I don't know. What's this about?"

"It's about a book he set out to write but which was never published," Cavanagh said. "I don't know if it's even in his file, but right after the Pawolian war he was appointed by the head of NorCoord Command to write the history of the CIRCE project. The *official* history, including everything that wasn't classified."

A muscle in Bronski's jaw seemed to tighten. "No, that wasn't in his file," he said. "I've never heard anything about it."

"As I said, it was never published," Cavanagh said. "It may not even have been completed. I seem to remember speculation at the time that the only reason he'd been given the assignment was that the whole Commonwealth was clamoring for information about CIRCE, and NorCoord wanted to shut them up. Once the noise had died down, someone high up in the government apparently decided to reclassify everything about CIRCE and stillbirthed the book. But Sholom had definitely made progress before that happened. He talked to my cleanup unit, and to the officers and crews of every ship that took part in that battle. I'm pretty sure he talked to the heads of NorCoord Command, too."

"So what are you suggesting?"

"I'm suggesting that in the course of his research, he might have learned something vitally important about CIRCE," Cavanagh said. "I think the Mrachanis know it and are trying to find out what that something is."

Bronski rubbed at his lower lip. "You really think a journalist could have figured out something that significant?"

"Sholom was sharp as a cross-saw," Cavanagh said. "He'd also spent a lot of time already with the military. He knew how they operated and how to read between the lines of what they said. And it wasn't until Fibbit started talking about him to me that the Mrachanis began to get nervous."

"Maybe," Bronski conceded. "If they are, I think they're shooting in the wrong barrel. Still, we can't have nonhumans kidnapping or leaning on Commonwealth citizens. All right, let's go find him. You're going to want to come along, I suppose?"

"Definitely," Cavanagh said.

"Fine," Bronski said, getting to his feet. "We can consider you under house arrest till we sort out whatever this Official Secrets stuff is Lee keeps ranting about."

Cavanagh stood up. "One other thing. What are you planning to do about that Yycroman shipyard out there?"

"I'm going to report it, of course," Bronski said. "They've broken the Pacification treaty. They have to be slapped down, and they have to be slapped down hard."

"What about the Conquerors?"

"What about them?" Bronski retorted. "You can't blink at treaty violations just because someone nastier is waiting over the next hill. Especially not from people like the Yycromae. Bad enough they were able to hide a couple of warships from us for twenty years—something like this proves they're out for blood again."

"We need all the fighting ships we can get right now," Cavanagh said. "And you can't seriously suggest the Yycromae should allow their worlds to stay undefended."

"You really believe self-defense is all they've got in mind?" Bronski countered.

"The ci Yyatoor has given me guarantees," Cavanagh said. "I can show them to you aboard ship."

Bronski's eyes narrowed. "Since when have you had authority to negotiate treaties and accept guarantees?"

"Since it became necessary for someone to do it," Cavanagh said. "And since I was the man on the spot."

Bronski snorted. "I'm sure that'll play real well with Lee and his boss. I'm starting to see why VanDiver wants your head on a plate."

"There are a lot of reasons," Cavanagh said. "Whether he gets it this time depends on whether you're willing to help me smooth the whole thing over."

"And why would I do that?"

Cavanagh shrugged. "Loyalty to the Peacekeepers, perhaps. The realization that opening a second front against the Yycromae would be a dangerous waste of resources."

Bronski snorted again. "Forget it," he said, stepping toward the door. "Come on, let's go find your journalist friend."

"Or," Cavanagh added, "perhaps the fact that, unlike the NorCoord Parliament, Military Intelligence has known about the Conquerors for the past six months."

Bronski froze, his hand still reaching for the door release. "What are you talking about?"

"I'm talking about that contact between the Mrachanis and a Conqueror ship six months ago off their Mra-kahie mining world," Cavanagh told him. "The one where both sides took a quick look at the other and hightailed it for home. The Yycromae may not have much military left, but they still have an excellent intelligence service. Klyveress told me all about it."

"Well, salutes all around to Yycroman Intelligence," Bronski said. "Doesn't have anything to do with us."

Cavanagh shook his head. "Sorry, Brigadier, but that won't wash. By your own admission you, a senior officer, came charging personally all the way over from Mra-ect when word reached you that I was on Mra-mig asking about contacts with the Conquerors. As it happens, I was only looking for details of that two-hundred-year-old legend, but you didn't know that. And even if you had, you couldn't risk someone there spilling the rest of the soup to me."

"So why didn't I haul you in right then and there?" Bronski demanded.

"Because somewhere between the spaceport and my hotel suite Taurin Lee intercepted you," Cavanagh said. "He was nosing around on his own and must have decided that attaching himself to your party would be a good way to find out what I was up to. Does he know who you really are, by the way?"

Bronski's lip twisted. "No."

"I didn't think so," Cavanagh said. "And as a minor Commonwealth liaison, of course, you could hardly refuse to honor his carte blanche. Unfortunately, that meant you were going to have to confront me with a high-ranking parliamentary aide in the room. Your superiors hadn't bothered to inform the NorCoord Parliament about the Conquerors, so you couldn't tell him the real reason you were there; and you knew he wasn't likely to swallow the flimsy excuse you'd concocted about Fibbit and deportation orders. About all you could do was look around some, throw around a lot of weak bluster, and then leave, planning to come back later after you'd gotten rid of him to finish the job properly."

Bronski shook his head. "This is nonsense," he said. "Complete soap-bubble nonsense."

"Fine," Cavanagh said. "Let's go back to the main room, then, and ask Lee why Commonwealth Commerce suddenly decided to restrict the transfer of human technology six months ago. Or why during that same period Peacekeeper Command has been spending money like sand. A Parlimin like VanDiver would be most interested in learning how far they'd been left out of this."

"Be careful, Cavanagh," Bronski warned softly. "You're treading on very dangerous ground here."

Cavanagh sighed. "I have no interest in precipitating a governmental crisis, Brigadier," he said. "If I did, I'd have said all of this in Lee's presence in the first place. All I want is to sweep this Yycroman thing under the rug until we've dealt with the Conquerors."

Bronski chewed at his lip. "And just how do you suggest we do that? Walk away and pretend the shipyard doesn't exist?"

"Of course we can't do that," Cavanagh said. "What we'll have to do is invent a legitimate explanation for it. Create a secret agreement between the Peacekeepers and the Yycroman government, postdate some order—something along those lines."

"Put our professional necks on the block, in other words."

"Under the circumstances," Cavanagh reminded him

quietly, "I think parliamentary investigations are likely to be the least of a Peacekeeper's worries."

Bronski grimaced. "I'll think about it," he said. "In the meantime we've got your journalist friend to find. Get your people together and let's get moving."

There was a breath of air from behind him, and Aric turned to see Quinn hovering in the control-room doorway. "Maestro," he said. "Good timing—I was just about to come and get you."

"I came by to remind you we'll be leaving in an hour," Quinn said, pulling on the doorjamb to propel himself across the room. "You found anything?"

"I think so, yes," Aric said. "A possibility, anyway. Max, put up that last display, with the red line and mark."

The star field he'd just been working on appeared on the display. "All right," he said as Quinn braked to a halt behind his chair. "The red mark is the system the Conquerors chased us out of a few hours ago. The red line is the vector they came in on."

"With nothing at the other end of it," Quinn said.

"Right," Aric said, holding up a finger. "Nothing at the other end; *if* you assume the Conquerors came in a straight line. Max: the green line and points."

Another line appeared, this one intersecting the red line at a not quite ninety-degree angle. "Let's assume instead that the Conquerors were originally on this green vector, and that they changed to the red line approximately seven light-years out from the system. Assume further that they were originally traveling between two systems, and that Max's estimate of twenty-five to seventy light-years is accurate. If you pivot all possible course segments around that point, it turns out there's only one pair of systems that meets those criteria. That's them, marked in green."

"Interesting," Quinn said. "Any particular reason why you picked seven light-years for the intersect point?"

Aric braced himself. "That's the distance a stardrive would take them," he said, "if someone on the planet called for help the same time we hit atmosphere."

He could feel Quinn's gaze. "You realize what you're saying," the other said at last. "You're suggesting that the Conquerors have a method of true interstellar communication."

"I'm aware of that," Aric said soberly. "I'm also aware that that's considered scientifically impossible. But it's the only way this makes any sense."

"They could have come from a deep space station."

"And meshed in practically on top of us?" Aric countered. "That wasn't just coincidence, Quinn—I ran the whole thing through Max earlier. If you hadn't made that last course adjustment to the fueler, they would have meshed in flanking us. They had to be getting concurrent data from the surface. Observational data, at the very least."

"So where was this observational data coming from?" Quinn asked. "These Conquerors who supposedly were screaming for help—where were they?"

"Maybe they were hiding somewhere," Aric said. "Possibly on the part of the planet we didn't get to." That scream he'd heard when he was standing beside the pyramid . . . "Or maybe they were right there in front of us."

"What, those sausage-slice things?" Quinn snorted. "That's ridiculous."

"Maybe," Aric agreed. "Being ridiculous doesn't mean it's not true."

"It's a wild-snipe chase," Quinn insisted. "Ninety-nine percent chance of that."

"I know," Aric said quietly. "But it's all we've got."

Quinn sighed. "Max, what do we have on those two systems?"

"The one closest to Commonwealth space is currently being claimed by the Mrachanis," Max said, "even though it lies more than fifteen light-years outside their generally recognized territorial sphere. They have a pilot mining operation on the second planet, which they've named Mra-kahie."

"What about the other one?"

"I have nothing but observatory data listed," Max said. "Spectral data indicates G2 class; planetary probabilities unknown but considered moderate. The system is seventy-one light-years from Dorcas and sixty-six light-years from the *Jutland* battle."

"How far away are we from it?"

"Twenty-eight light-years," Max said. "Fuel reserves are more than adequate for a trip there and back."

"How about if we have to fight a battle at the other end?" Quinn asked bluntly.

There was a slight pause. "They would still be adequate," Max said, "provided the battle lasted less than four hours."

"Yeah," Quinn muttered under his breath. "Well, with the Conquerors that's not likely to be a problem. All right, Max, go ahead and compute us a course. Something evasive, with four or five vector changes along the way to confuse their trackers. And don't use more than two of our static bombs."

"Yes, Commander." The red and green lines vanished from the display, to be replaced by a zigzag of yellow lines from their position to the target system. "The static bombs would be dropped at the blue marks," the computer added.

"Looks good," Quinn said, peering closely at it. "Go ahead and get us started."

"Yes, Commander."

Quinn shook his head. "I hope you're wrong about this," he said to Aric. "I really do. If the Conquerors have genuine tachyonic communication, then it's all over except for the shouting. The Commonwealth won't have a prayer."

Aric looked at the jagged yellow line, striking at the green mark like a frozen bolt of lightning. "Makes it that much more important that we find out now. One way or the other."

"I suppose," Quinn said. "Well . . . you'd better go get some rest. We've got another eleven hours to go, and you won't want to hit that system half-asleep. I'll let the others know about the change in plans."

"All right." Aric hesitated. "Quinn, maybe this is none of my business. But under the circumstances . . . why did you quit the Copperheads?"

There was a brief silence from behind him. "It's hard to explain," Quinn said at last. "Have you ever done any kind of computer linking?"

"I did gamer links a few times when I was in college," Aric said, turning to look at him. "That was an inductive type, of course, not an implant."

"It's not the implant itself," Quinn said. "At least, not directly. It's . . ." He paused. "You have to understand that the Copperhead Mindlink is absolutely unique. It feeds data to us at least a thousand times faster than any business computer-link ever created—probably ten thousand times faster than the best inductive gamer type. You're not getting just a game scenario or sheets of numbers and flow vectors when you link up this way. The data literally floods over you, running in over every sensory input your brain's got. You don't just see the combat—you feel and smell and taste it, too. Every image razor clear and razor sharp; every thought you have turned instantly into vectors and curves on a tactical overlay. You feel your team like an extension of your own mind and body, with their thoughts flowing in and complementing your own. It's like nothing else that mankind has ever created. Like nothing you could ever imagine."

"Sounds a little frightening."

"No." Quinn shook his head. "That's just the point, a point most of the Parlimins who questioned me never really understood. The problem wasn't that the programmers did their job poorly; the problem was that they did it too well. The Mindlink is a tremendous experience—exhilarating, challenging, and not the least bit frightening. There have been many computer links over the years that have claimed to be complete realities. This one genuinely is.

"And it was a reality that too many of my teammates didn't want to leave."

Aric looked at him, a shiver running through him. "You mean like an addiction?"

"I mean like a total withdrawal from reality," Quinn said bluntly. "They walked around offlink like ghosts. Just going through the motions of living, doing whatever they had to do so they could get out of this pale imitation of reality and back to the real thing. Some of them went so far as to steal wireless jack connectors so that they wouldn't have to face the real world at all."

His lip twitched. "Some of those never came back. Not even when the Mindlinks were forcibly taken away from them. They never came back."

Aric gazed at his face. At the lines of tension in his jaw . . . "You feel it too, don't you?" he said.

Quinn turned away. "All Copperheads do," he said. "And I'm convinced that it does damage to us every time we link up. But the Peacekeepers didn't want to give up the program. Neither did NorCoord." He shrugged fractionally. "They're screening the applicants better these days—we got that much out of Parliament at the hearings. Maybe it was enough. I don't know. I'm not sure I want to."

Aric grimaced. "I'm sorry. Sorry, too, for dragging you into this in the first place."

Quinn turned to face him again. "Don't be," he said. "I told you all this so you could try to understand, not so you'd waste time with sympathy. When lives are at stake, you do what you have to, whether it's personally comfortable for you or not." He cocked an eyebrow. "I doubt this was something you really wanted to do, either, if you want to get right down to it."

Aric shrugged. "It's not exactly the same situation."

"It all comes together in the end." Quinn looked up at the display. "Anyway. Now you know. Better go get some sleep. We could have a really busy day ahead of us."

24 **W**ith a start Pheylan woke up, a twisted and tortured dream evaporating in the dim nighttime lighting of his prison cell. For a moment he lay on his cot without moving, blinking the sleep from his eyes and trying to figure out what had happened to shock him awake that way. In the room outside four Zhirrzh techs were puttering about as usual, the consoles with their gray-tone displays looking as normal as they ever got. The clock on one of them indicated it was just after dawn outside, at least if Pheylan was reading it correctly, an hour or two earlier than he was accustomed to waking up. There was no indication that any of the aliens had just come in, slamming a door behind him; nothing on the floor that would suggest someone had dropped something with a crash. From outside he could hear a distant, barely audible roar, growing fractionally louder as the vehicle circled around coming toward them.

Pheylan frowned. It was an odd sort of sound, now that he was concentrating on it. An aircar? No, more likely a spacecraft. One whose engines made an unusual sort of twittering drone. . . .

And suddenly every muscle in Pheylan's body went

rigid, his throat tightening as he strained to hear. Half-afraid he was imagining it . . . but there was no mistake. The sound was unique and unmistakable.

A Mrach ship.

With an effort Pheylan forced his muscles to relax, the hammering of his pulse abruptly loud in his ears. This was it. His best chance—maybe his only chance—of getting out of here. His training at the academy had included a unit on Mrach ships, instrumentation and flight technique both. If he could get to it, he would be out of here.

If he could get to it.

He lay there another minute, running through all the nebulous gambits and wild schemes he'd thought up in the past three weeks. None of them were all that terrific, but there was no time now to come up with anything better. Outside, the drone of the Mrach engines had fallen silent, and there was no way of knowing how long it would be before the ship took off again. It was now or most likely never.

Taking a deep breath, he propped himself up on one elbow. "Hey," he called plaintively, pointing to one of the techs as they all turned to look at him. "You. Go get Thrr-gilag. I don't feel well. I think I'm going to be sick."

The tech turned back to his console and began speaking quietly into the intercom. Pheylan stayed where he was, rubbing his stomach and making all the faces he'd learned to use on his mother when he wanted to stay home from school and his symptoms were only marginal. The Zhirrzh had learned a lot about humans from him, but there were one or two things that might still surprise them. And if it surprised them enough . . .

Half-hidden behind its console, the prep-room door swung open and Thrr-gilag stepped through. "Good day, Cavv-ana," he said. "You not well?"

"Not at all," Pheylan said, screwing up his face in agony. He had no idea whether or not Thrr-gilag could even read human body language, but this was no time to go half throttle. "Fact is, I'm bloody sick. You've got to let me get out into the sunlight right away."

"It only three days," Thrr-gilag reminded him, moving up to the glass wall and peering at him. "You without sun seven days before."

"I wasn't coming down sick with something then," Pheylan said.

"Why sunlight help?"

"Because it will," Pheylan said, suppressing a grimace. Clearly, Thrr-gilag wasn't going to give in for the performance alone. He was going to have to go all the way with this. "I know this sickness. It's common among humans—" He broke off, letting his face go stricken as he kicked off his blanket and swung his legs over the side of the bed. "Oh, God—here it comes."

He stood up, throwing a hand up the glass wall to steady himself. His other hand went to his mouth; and under cover of the motion he stuck his finger into his throat.

And vomited at the wall directly in front of Thrr-gilag.

The Zhirrzh jumped nearly a meter backward in a single leap, barking something startled sounding. The four techs scrambled into motion, two of them heading toward Pheylan's cell door, the others running toward the prep room. "They bring suit," Thrr-gilag told Pheylan, his voice noticeably higher pitched than usual. "What that happen, Cavv-ana?"

"Like I said, I'm sick," Pheylan said, weaving his way to the shower on trembling legs and starting to have some belated second thoughts about this. He'd expected the cramps that were twisting through his stomach muscles, but he hadn't counted on this sudden weakness that had hit his legs. If he wasn't ready to act when the time came, this wasn't going to work at all.

Still, he had a few minutes before it came to that. Turning on the shower full blast, he stepped halfway into the stall, shoving his face into the stream and spitting mouthful after mouthful of water onto the shower floor. "What this for?" he could hear Thrr-gilag shouting over the noise. "Cavv-ana? What this for?"

"I'm rinsing my mouth," Pheylan said, shutting off the water and stepping wearily out to lean against the side of the stall. Good; his legs were starting to settle down again. "These stomach juices are full of acid. Very bad for my skin and mouth. The vapors aren't good for my lungs, either. You've got to let me out of here."

From the prep room the two Zhirrzh techs reappeared and hurried toward the cell door, one with the obedience suit flapping in the breeze behind him, the other fumbling with the black trigger gadget Nzz-oonaz normally handled. One of the two techs at the cell door reached over to unlock it, stopping at a sharp word from Thrr-gilag. More instructions, and the Zhirrzh with the obedience suit stooped to stuff it through the dog flap. "You can put on?" Thrr-gilag asked Pheylan.

"I'll try," Pheylan said, straightening up and making his way across the cell. So much for doing this the easy way. He'd rather hoped that this startling new behavior from their pet human would have rattled Thrr-gilag enough to forget either the obedience suit or the standard procedure concerning it. Clearly, the other had more presence of mind than that.

Which just meant Pheylan would have to do this the hard way.

He got the obedience suit on as quickly as he dared, trying to balance the feigned weakness of his illness with the need to make his move before more Zhirrzh could be called in on the crisis. "All right," he said, leaning briefly against the doorjamb as they got the door open. "I'm—wait a minute," he interrupted himself, reaching again to his stomach. Turning around again, he stumbled back to the toilet and dropped on his knees in front of it.

There was even less available to come out this time around, and about all Pheylan got for his efforts was dry retching and another bout of cramped stomach muscles. But that was all right. All he really wanted was an excuse to get back into the shower . . . and by the time he staggered out again, the obedience suit with its wonderful water-wicking action was well and thoroughly soaked. "All right," he said, mopping his face uselessly with an already saturated sleeve as he returned to the waiting knot of nervous Zhirrzh. "Let's go. Before it happens again."

The sun was still mostly hidden behind the swaying tops of the gray-green trees as they emerged from the prison building. The air was cool, turning Pheylan's breath into little puffs of smoke and slicing through his wet jumpsuit like a set of sharpened icicles.

But he hardly noticed. There on the landing area, no more than a hundred meters away, was his ticket home. And arguably the most beautiful sight he'd ever seen.

A Mrach *Premra*-class courier ship.

Or at least, what was left of one. The thing had gone through the wars, all right, or at least a typical Zhirrzh battle. The distinctive Mrach flowing-metal design was blackened and pitted, crisscrossed with bubbled-edge slashes that looked as if they'd cut completely through the outer hull before the interior sealant had caught up with the damage. Nearly all of the port-bow hull was missing completely, the gaping hole having been filled in by a rough white material that didn't look like anything the Mrach used. But the aft section looked relatively untouched, and it had clearly made it in through the atmosphere under its own power. On the near side a group of Zhirrzh had gathered together near the exit ramp, a scene reminiscent of his own arrival three weeks ago.

That could be trouble. If any of them were armed . . .

"It good?" Thrr-gilag asked from beside him.

Pheylan turned his face a few degrees away from the ship to face into the rising sun. "Yes, it should help," he said, shivering as a breeze intensified the chill soaking through his skin. "It'll take a few more minutes before I'll feel any effect."

Thrr-gilag was silent a moment. "It not work," he said.

Pheylan's heart seemed to seize up. "What do you mean?" he asked, a cold chill running through him that had nothing to do with the air temperature.

"I say it not work," Thrr-gilag repeated, his tongue sliding out to point at Pheylan's soaked jumpsuit. "You try damage with water. But it not damage."

Pheylan breathed a quiet sigh of relief. Thrr-gilag was smart, all right. But for once he was being smart in the wrong direction. "I'm not trying to damage the suit," he said, looking casually around. Three of the four techs who'd come out with them were standing around him about an arm's length away; the fourth, the one holding the obedience-suit trigger, was facing him from about twice that distance. Beyond them a pair of Zhirrzh had left the group by the Mrach ship and were heading toward him, those compact flashbulb guns of theirs hanging loosely in their hands.

It was now or never. Turning his back to the Zhirrzh with the trigger, Pheylan took a step away—

And suddenly his knees buckled beneath him, pitching him face first into the dirt with a thud. A thud, and a spray of water from the saturated jumpsuit.

A spray of water that turned the dirt where he'd landed into instant mud. Coating the entire front of his obedience suit . . . including the sensor disks embedded there.

Thrr-gilag made a strangled sound in his throat; but whether he thought his prisoner had hurt himself or whether he'd suddenly realized what had just happened Pheylan never knew. Before anyone could react further, Pheylan rolled onto his back, leaped to his feet, and charged at the Zhirrzh tech holding the obedience-suit trigger.

The other was backing desperately away, firing the trigger uselessly at him, as Pheylan caught up with him. With one hand he grabbed the Zhirrzh's arm, wrenching the trigger out of his grasp with the other and stuffing it down the front of the obedience suit. Yanking the alien toward him, he swung him bodily around, bent him over at the waist, and jammed his head and neck into a football-style grip between the magnet rings under his left armpit.

An instant later the other four Zhirrzh were on him, clutching at his arms and head as they tried to free their trapped comrade. But their thin arms and double-thumbed hands were no match for human musculature. Pheylan swung his shoulders and his prisoner at them, shaking and throwing them away from him.

All but one of them. Grabbing Thrr-gilag's arm, Pheylan swung the Zhirrzh into shield position in front of him. "Call them off," he snapped, releasing the arm and shifting quickly to a grip across Thrr-gilag's neck. "Those two Zhirrzh. Call them off or I'll break your neck."

"Not allow escape," Thrr-gilag said, his voice gone suddenly high-pitched. "Zhirrzh not allow escape."

"That's entirely up to you," Pheylan bit out. The two Zhirrzh were still coming, their flashbulb guns raised into firing position now. "But they either let me go or they kill me," he told Thrr-gilag. "Those are the only options they've got left." He gave the other's neck a sharp squeeze for emphasis. "And if they kill me, you two will go too. Your decision. Make it fast."

Clutching his two captives tightly against him, Pheylan started walking toward the Mrach ship. He had the full attention of that whole group now, and two gray sticks had joined the flashbulb guns that were pointed in his direction. Pheylan kept walking, feeling utterly naked behind Thrr-gilag and wishing now that the slightly taller Svv-selic hadn't been demoted from spokesman position. Holding the Zhirrzh tech upright instead of under his arm would give him a better shield; but the minute he did that, he'd be open to the spare obedience-suit trigger they undoubtedly had stashed away somewhere. This way they would have to sacrifice the tech if they wanted to stop him. He could only hope the tech had lots of friends here.

The two closest Zhirrzh guards had stopped, their flashbulb guns still targeting him. "Tell them to put their weapons down," Pheylan hissed to Thrr-gilag, looking slightly away from the weapons and keeping his right eye tightly closed. "Now."

Thrr-gilag took a deep breath. *"Kasar!"* he called.

And in reply both flashbulb guns went off together.

Pheylan stopped in his tracks, keeping a firm grip on his prisoners as he blinked hard against the double purple blob blocking the view from his left eye. It didn't seem as bad this time as it had been in his cell, possibly because he'd been looking away. Ahead, he could hear and dimly see the two Zhirrzh running toward him. He waited, shifting his balance onto his left leg; and as they reached him, he opened his right eye and kicked the lead Zhirrzh hard in the torso.

The alien hit the dirt like a dropped sack of cement,

throwing a cloud of red dust into the air. The other Zhirrzh gasped something, swinging his flashbulb gun up again as he tried to brake to an emergency stop.

Neither effort proved successful. Pheylan's second kick caught him the same place as his partner, dropping him neatly to the ground beside him.

"That wasn't very smart," Pheylan said, giving Thrr-gilag's neck another squeeze. "I could have killed you right then, you know."

"I know."

"Good. Now let's try it again, shall we? And get it right this time. Otherwise I may have to kill you, this tech here, and all the rest of that group over there."

"The Zhirrzh right," Thrr-gilag said. "You predators."

"You're damn right we are," Pheylan agreed. "It's up to you what happens here. What's it going to be?"

He could feel Thrr-gilag take a deep breath. *"Shalirr i crr'arrea mazzasprr akrr'trr i parrsavva crri,"* he called. *"Parr've krrti."*

Ahead, the gray sticks seemed to waver. *"Krrti svarr?"* one of the Zhirrzh called.

"Parr've krrti," Thrr-gilag repeated.

They kept at it for another half-dozen exchanges. Pheylan resumed walking toward the ship, his right eye closed again in case they decided to try that stunt a second time. The three Zhirrzh who guarded the white pyramid had come out of their domes now, he saw, but they didn't seem to be making any move to come join in the festivities.

And then, to Pheylan's mild surprise, the weapons pointed at him lowered to the ground. "So what's the decision?" he demanded.

"You allowed to leave," Thrr-gilag said. "They agree."

Pheylan smiled grimly. Sure they did. He'd seen far too much of the Zhirrzh to believe that one for a minute. They had something up their sleeves, all right, something that would probably involve a brief fire fight in the upper atmosphere. But that was all right. Short odds or not, once in the air he would at least have a fighting chance.

The group by the Mrach ship had moved a respectful distance back by the time Pheylan and his two unwilling shields reached the landing ramp. "You leave us here?" Thrr-gilag asked as Pheylan awkwardly backed the three of them up the ramp and into the ship.

"That depends on whether I can find something to tie you up with," Pheylan said, glancing quickly both ways down the corridor. There was no one in sight. Sidling over to the hatchway control, he jabbed it with an elbow. The panel slid down; and as it did, he let go of the Zhirrzh tech and gave him a hard shove toward it. The other stumbled, off balance, and hit the ramp. Pheylan got a glimpse of him beginning to roll down it as the hatchway sealed.

"Lie down," Pheylan ordered Thrr-gilag, pushing him toward the floor. "On your face. Stay there or I'll break your neck."

Silently, Thrr-gilag obeyed. Keeping an eye on him, Pheylan stripped off the obedience suit and used the sleeves to tie Thrr-gilag's arms behind him. "All right," he said, hauling the Zhirrzh back to his feet. "Let's go."

The cockpit was at the end of the corridor. "Sit here," Pheylan ordered, pushing Thrr-gilag down into one of the seats and using the legs of the obedience suit to tie his legs together. The rising sun was shining brightly nearly straight ahead through the canopy, its light glittering off the edges of the strangely curved Mrach control panel.

A canopy, like his glass-walled cell, that the Zhirrzh lasers would be able to shoot through. But there was nothing Pheylan could do about that except try to get out of here before they got their sharpshooters into position. Mentally crossing his fingers, keeping his head down, he climbed into the control seat and keyed the engines.

They came on with a muffled roar. Pheylan studied the instruments, trying to dredge up that unit on Mrach ships from his memory. The injection feed control . . . there? Tentatively, he eased it forward, and as he did so the roar beneath him changed pitch and tone into the familiar twittering drone.

So far so good. Shift to preflight: check. Activate stardrive and run internal-operations monitor: check. Confirm Icefire ducts in lift position. . . .

There was a faint sound behind him. Pheylan looked up, started to turn around—

And jerked back against the contoured cushions. Floating over the control-board displays, less than a meter in front of his face, was a full-size image of a Zhirrzh.

Pheylan gasped, the shock of it freezing his muscles as effectively as a jolt of electric current. Pale white, insubstantial yet sculpted in exquisite detail, the image hovered half in and half out of the cockpit like something from one of the ghost stories Aric had loved to tell as a child. The mouth moved, and as if from a great distance he could hear what sounded like Zhirrzh speech—

And then, abruptly, something jabbed like a hot needle into his right shoulder.

He spun around, the paralysis broken. Thrr-gilag stood at his side, his tongue just retracting again into his mouth, the part of the obedience suit that had restrained his legs hanging in tatters around his waist.

And on Pheylan's shoulder a drop of blood had appeared. "Damn!" he snarled, spinning out of the seat and grabbing for Thrr-gilag with both hands.

Or rather, trying to grab him. To his bewilderment his

right arm had suddenly become inexplicably heavy. He tried again to force it upward; but even as it dropped limply to his side, he stumbled and dropped to his knees on the hard deck.

He barely felt the impact. His whole body was going numb . . . and in front of him Thrr-gilag's image was beginning to waver. "Damn," he murmured.

The image faded away . . . and with his last thought Pheylan wondered what death would be like.

And whether the men and women of the *Kinshasa* whom he'd failed would be there. And would be able to forgive him.

"There's no doubt at all, Commander," Max's voice said in Aric's ear. "I've run three different samples of neutrino and gamma emissions. There's definitely a Mrach ship down there. One moment: I'm now getting tachyon emissions. Most likely a stardrive self-monitor."

"A Mrach ship," Quinn murmured. "Interesting. Does he have lift yet?"

"No," Max said. "Engine emissions are still at pre-flight levels."

"Let me know the minute he goes up," Quinn said. "Clipper? What do you think?"

"Oh, we're going in, all right," Clipper said. "The only question is whether we go cold or risk letting Max fire up the active sensors first."

"They must know we're coming," Dazzler put in. "That last static bomb is still burning out there."

"Knowing we might be coming is a far cry from our setting off a flare in their faces," Clipper countered. "Max, have you spotted anything down there besides that cleared area?"

"Not so far," Max said. "I'm still searching. I do have a good scrub of the cleared area now."

"Pipe it down," Quinn said.

"How does it look?" Aric asked, staring at the half-darkened planetscape stretched out above them.

"There's not much there," Quinn told him. "Two linked-hexagon buildings that look a lot like the way the Conquerors build their ships. Three or four smaller structures in between them . . . make that a definite four structures. Looks like one of them might be another of your screaming pyramids. A good-sized landing strip, with one small ship on it. Mrach design, all right. The whole area's surrounded about a kilometer away by a fence. Could be some people around the ship, too—the compound's near the terminator line, and it looks like we've got some narrow shadows, but the fueler's telescope isn't good enough to resolve anything that small."

Aric clenched a hand into a fist. "So are we going down?"

"Commander, the Mrach ship has shut down its engines," Max said before Quinn could answer.

"Malfunction?" Clipper asked.

"Nothing I could detect from the emissions," Max said.

"Someone must have changed his mind," Bookmaker suggested.

"Or else they've spotted us," Clipper said.

"Our cue, either way," Quinn decided. "Combat code red; let's do it."

The clamps released with a jolt, and the fueler fell away above him; and suddenly Aric was jammed hard into his seat as Quinn threw full power to the drive. "How soon?" he called over the roar from behind him.

"Five minutes," Quinn called back. "Maybe less. Hold tough—it's going to get a little hot back there."

"I can handle it," Aric gritted. Already he could feel the air heating up around him as the Counterpunch sliced through the upper atmosphere at near-meteor speed. The drive was a violent roar in his ears, drowning out the pounding pulse he could feel but not hear. Directly ahead, past Quinn's helmet, the dark of space met the dark section of the planet, giving him nothing to look at but blackness; only later did it occur to him that Quinn would have deliberately chosen that vector so as to hit the Conqueror compound with the rising sun at their backs.

"Maestro, we've got visual," Dazzler's voice came suddenly. "A definite on aliens down there. A whole group of—"

"We're drawing fire," Paladin cut him off. "Medium-intensity lasers—probably light arms."

"Target and destroy," Quinn ordered. "All fighters, go to—"

"There he is!" Dazzler cut him off. "Maestro, we've got him!"

"Go to laser link, damn it," Quinn snapped. "All ships."

The voices went silent. "Quinn?" Aric murmured.

"It's him," Quinn confirmed tightly. "It's Commander Cavanagh. He's being carried out of the Mrach ship." He hesitated. "Looks like he's unconscious."

Aric's heart seemed to freeze. "Unconscious? Or dead?"

"We'll find out in thirty seconds," Quinn told him grimly. "Hang on; we're going in."

The Counterpunch dipped suddenly, throwing Aric into a half second's worth of free fall, then pulled into a tight turn with gee forces that left him gasping for breath. Above the roar of the engine he could hear the sputtering bursts of precision antipersonnel guns. Another surge of gee force as the Counterpunch's nose swung up—something slammed into the underside of the fighter as the engine roar suddenly cut back—

And above him the canopy slid back. "He's there to the right," Quinn shouted. "Get going."

Aric ripped off his helmet and scrambled up and over the cockpit side, throwing a quick look around as his feet found the top of the flowmetal ladder. Twenty meters away was the Mrach ship; ahead and to the right was one of the two complexes Quinn had mentioned. Overhead, three of the Corvines were screaming tight circles over the area, spitting death at anything that moved.

And lying sprawled on the ground five meters away was a naked human form.

Pheylan.

Later Aric would never fully remember the leap to the ground and the mad dash across the eye of the war zone, or the task of hoisting Pheylan up over his shoulder, or the even more formidable task getting the two of them up the ladder and into the cockpit. Only one solid memory would remain from those few seconds: the terrifying coldness of his brother's skin.

And then the canopy closed over them, and the Counterpunch was again clawing its way through the air. "How is he?" Quinn called.

"Not good," Aric gritted back, struggling to reach around Pheylan's legs to get to the small medical pouch behind Quinn's seat.

"Get the diagnostic band out of the medic pouch," Quinn said.

"I'm trying," Aric snapped back, finally getting the pouch open. His left arm was pinned beneath Pheylan's back, but the band was designed for one-handed operation, and a few seconds later he had it secured just above Pheylan's knee. "Okay," he said, plugging the lead into the jack beside the pouch. "Max?"

"Heartbeat is slow but regular," the computer reported. "Blood pressure and nerve function are similarly low."

"What's wrong with him?" Aric asked.

"Unknown as yet," Max said. "There are several unidentified factors in his blood, but some are undoubtedly from alien foodstuffs. One moment. Indication of a mild poison in his bloodstream."

Aric looked down at Pheylan's right shoulder, and the slow oozing of blood from a small puncture wound there. "I can see the injection point," he said. "Should I try the snakebite technique?"

There was a short pause. With his free hand Aric dug through the medic pouch, searching for a knife or field scalpel or something else sharp and wishing desperately that Melinda were here instead of him. If it came to deliberately cutting into his brother's skin, even to save his life—

"That won't be necessary," Max said, relief evident in his voice. "His vital signs have bottomed out and are beginning to come back. Is there a general stimulant injector in the kit?"

"It's the bright-orange one," Quinn said. "You know how to use it?"

"Yes," Aric breathed, pulling out the orange injector and popping off its cover.

"Start with one dosage," Max said. "We'll see how it goes from there."

"Right." Pressing the flat edge of the injector against Pheylan's skin, Aric touched the trigger. "Any change?"

"One moment," Max said. "Yes, it's definitely helping. I believe he's out of danger, at least for the moment."

"We can do a more complete check when we get back to the fueler," Quinn added. "Might as well get some use out of that miniature pharmacy your sister stuffed aboard."

Wrapping his arms around his brother, Aric hugged him as he hadn't since childhood. They'd done it. They'd really done it. "Thank you, Quinn," he said quietly, his eyes filling with tears. "And all of you."

"Our pleasure," Quinn said. "Let's go home."

"We've decided to head directly for Edo," Aric said, hovering in the doorway. "Dorcas and the Mrach worlds are closer, but Quinn thinks that Colonel Holloway might still be too mad at us to listen before he threw us all into the stockade."

"Probably wouldn't be able to do anything even if he wanted to," Pheylan said, taking a sip of coffee—real, genuine Earth coffee—from his squeeze bottle. "Not unless Command's reassigned some warships to the region."

"True," Aric agreed. "They hadn't as of four days ago, anyway. And under the circumstances, none of us liked the idea of taking any of this into Mrach space."

"Can't say I blame you," Pheylan said. "Though I have to point out that the whole idea is probably a waste of time. Even if Command authorizes an expeditionary force to go back there, we're talking a good eighty hours of transit time, plus whatever it takes to throw the force together. Plenty of time for the Zhirrzh to pack up shop and clear out."

"Quinn knows that," Aric said. "There might still be some rubble left worth sifting through."

"Maybe. Might be a pleasant diversion from court-martial paperwork for them, anyway."

"Thanks for the reminder," Aric said, making a face at him. "I trust you'll be able to find time during your busy debriefing schedule to come by as character witness for the defense."

"Don't worry," Pheylan promised. "Trust me—I'll lay 'em dead in the aisles."

Aric's smile faded. "You were lucky," he said quietly. "You know that, don't you? They should have killed you the second they knew we were coming. All I can figure is that they thought they'd already finished you off."

Pheylan sipped again at his coffee, freshly aware of the dull throbbing in his shoulder where Thrr-gilag had stabbed him. There was sense in that, of course. He'd learned a lot about the Zhirrzh during his captivity; surely they wouldn't have wanted him rescued to take all that information back.

And yet . . . "No," he said slowly. "I don't think Thrr-gilag was trying to kill me. You haven't seen those tongues of theirs, Aric—damn things work like gutting knives. He could have ripped me clear to the bone and dumped in enough of that poison to kill me where I sat. Or skipped the poison routine entirely and just sliced my throat."

Aric shivered. "Maybe."

"No maybes about it," Pheylan told him. "He had to have been just trying to knock me out so they could haul me back to my cell. With that hologram sent in to distract me while he sliced up the obedience suit and took his shot."

"Must have been one impressive hologram," Aric said. "That still doesn't explain why he didn't change his mind when Paladin came roaring in over the trees at them."

Or why he or the Zhirrzh tech hadn't attacked long before they reached the Mrach ship, come to think of it. Had they been afraid Pheylan would be quick enough to break their necks before he succumbed to the poison? "Maybe he didn't have time," Pheylan said. "Maybe he panicked. Or maybe . . ."

"What?"

"It's a long shot," Pheylan said. "A real long shot. But maybe those little seeds of uncertainty I tried to plant in Thrr-gilag were finally starting to take root. Maybe he'd started to wonder if his leaders had lied about what happened at the *Jutland* battle."

"I suppose that's possible," Aric said doubtfully. "But I wouldn't count very hard on it if I were you. You're asking him to take the word of an alien over his own people."

"He was thinking about it," Pheylan insisted. "He really was. He'll check into it."

"Maybe." Aric rubbed his cheek. "Speaking of aliens, you have any thoughts about that Mrach courier ship?"

"Not really," Pheylan shook his head. "The most likely possibility is that they ran into it at that mining world you mentioned, shot it out of the sky, and took it home as a souvenir."

"Figuring out how to fly it en route?"

"It would have been a little tricky," Pheylan conceded. "But on the other hand, I was outside pretty soon after it landed and never saw any actual Mrachanis." He shrugged. "Though on the other hand, the Zhirrzh could have just gotten them inside quickly."

"That's what I like about you, Pheylan: you always keep things clear-cut," Aric said dryly. "Well, at least that one's not our problem."

"Just as well," Pheylan said, setting his squeeze bottle on its patch and adjusting the straps on his sleep pad. "We're going to have enough on our hands just getting you, Dad, Quinn, and Melinda out from under all this."

"Not a problem," Aric assured him, dismissing it with a wave of his hand. "Quinn and I are heroes now, you know, and you can't jail your heroes. And with Dad's connections, he and Melinda are probably already back home wondering what's taking us so long."

"I hope you're right," Pheylan said.

"Of course I'm right," Aric soothed him. "Besides, medical types with Melinda's credentials are far too valuable to lock away somewhere." Reaching into the room, he switched off the light. "Anyway. Max says you should get some rest. War may be looming on the horizon, but that's no reason we shouldn't catch up on our sleep."

Pheylan reached up to rub his sore shoulder. "If the war hasn't already started," he said quietly. "It wasn't more than three days ago that Thrr-gilag was asking some rather insistent questions about the Copperheads."

Aric grimaced. "Well . . . if it's started, it's started. We'll know one way or another soon enough. You just get your rest. For the moment, anyway, the Cavanaghs are out of it."

25

They found Ezer Sholom buried away in a surprisingly elegant apartment in an otherwise nondescript part of Mig-Ka City, barely five blocks from the run-down apartment house where Fibbit had been living.

Buried away, looking frail and old. And barely breathing.

"What's happened to him?" Cavanagh asked as one of Bronski's men wrapped the diagnostic band of a Peacekeeper medic box around his wrist.

"I don't know," Bronski said, sniffing the air suspiciously as he looked around the room. "Stress, maybe. Old age." He glanced around, gestured to one of his men. "Daschka, I want you to start checking out the area. All the bordering apartments, likely outside spots for bouncer setups—you know the routine. Leave Cho Ming on the door; you can take everyone else. You find any Mrachanis hanging around, you put 'em under detention—my authority and to hell with any diplomatic niceties."

"Right," Daschka nodded. "You heard him, gentlemen. Let's go."

He left, taking the rest of Bronski's squad with him.

"What are they looking for?" Cavanagh asked, taking a couple of experimental sniffs of his own. He couldn't smell anything.

"There's a smell in here that could be the residue from a hypnotic inducer," Kolchin told him. "If the Mrachanis were in a hurry to get information out of Sholom, they might have used something like that."

"Or abused something like that," Bronski growled. "Hypnotics are tricky to handle, and I doubt the Mrachanis have had much practice using them on humans."

"You might be surprised," Cavanagh said. He looked over at Lee, glowering out one of the windows. "Certainly seems to have been worth the effort to come find him."

Lee didn't reply. He hadn't said much at all since Bronski had pulled rank on him and taken them off Phormbi sixteen hours ago. "Well, they were certainly treating him like peerage otherwise," Bronski commented, glancing around the apartment. "We're definitely going to want to backtrack this. Find out when and how they got him to move in here."

"Sir, I've got a positive on a foreign substance in his bloodstream," the man crouched over Sholom said. "You were right on the nose: it reads out as a hypnotic. The box is mixing up a counteractive—he should be all right in a few minutes."

"Good job, Eisen," Bronski said. "Stay with him."

"Yes, sir."

There was a movement across the apartment, and Cavanagh turned to see Bronski's man Garcia come in. One look at his face—

"What is it?" Bronski asked.

"You asked me to go pull the Peacekeeper file from the last skitter into Mra-mig," Garcia said, his voice as grim as his face. "I didn't think this was something I should put across the phone system. Seems the Conquerors have hit Dorcas, Kalevala, and Massif."

Bronski's lip twitched. "Confirmed?"

"We've got two confirmations on the Dorcas attack: one from a man named McPhee from Parlimin VanDiver's staff, the other from the captain of Lord Cavanagh's private yacht. No information yet as to damage or situation. The Massif and Kalevala hits have yet to be confirmed. Command is sending task forces to check things out."

"Yeah," Bronski growled. "Well, it's started."

"Yes, sir." Garcia looked at Cavanagh. "One other interesting bit of information in that packet: Lord Cavanagh's son and daughter have been charged with grand theft of Peacekeeper property."

"I knew it," Lee snapped, turning away from the window. "I told you he was dirty, Bronski—I told you a hundred times. But you wouldn't listen."

"Shut up, Lee," Bronski said. "The report say whether the son and daughter are in custody?"

"The son isn't," Garcia said. "He's off somewhere with some stolen Peacekeeper fighters—there weren't any other details. The daughter is in detention on Dorcas."

Cavanagh's chest tightened. "On Dorcas?" he demanded. "You just said Dorcas was under attack."

Garcia shrugged. "Apparently, this VanDiver aide was supposed to take her out, but at the last minute the local commander decided to keep her there. That's all we know."

"Probably all we're going to know for a while, too," Bronski said. "All right. Daschka's out looking for whatever surveillance post the Mrachanis had set up here. Go give him a hand."

"Yes, sir." Turning, Garcia left the apartment.

"We have to get out there right away," Cavanagh said

quietly to Kolchin as Garcia left the apartment. "Call Hill—tell him to charter us a ship. We'll need to get to Avon, connect back up with the *Cavatina*, and get out to Dorcas."

He'd been talking quietly. Apparently, not quietly enough. "Don't even think it, Cavanagh," Bronski said, looking over at him. "You're not going anywhere until we get all this straightened out."

"Brigadier, my daughter's in a war zone."

"And you're *especially* not going into a war zone," Bronski added. His lip twisted, a glimmer of sympathy edging through the professional cast-metal set of his face. "Look, I know how you feel. But the last thing we need is a civilian spinning around getting in the way. Let the professionals deal with it, all right? They'll get an attack fleet there; NorCoord will put CIRCE back together—"

"CIRCE," a weak voice murmured.

They all looked down at the old man lying on the floor. "Mr. Sholom?" Bronski said, dropping to one knee beside him. "I'm Brigadier Petr Bronski of NorCoord Military Intelligence. How are you feeling?"

"Absolutely wonderful," Sholom said, a dreamy smile creasing his face. "I'm floating where no one has ever seen."

"Yeah," Bronski said. "Well, it'll wear off soon enough. Anyway, you're safe now."

Sholom's smile turned bittersweet. "Safe, you say? Safe? No. It's all false, sir—all of it. No one is safe. The Conquerors are coming."

Bronski frowned at Eisen. "What is all this?"

"Residual effects of the hypnotic," Eisen told him. "I've seen this before. There'll be a few minutes of it while he comes back up out of the overdose."

"Okay. It's all right, Mr. Sholom. You'll be all right in a minute."

"Will I?" Sholom countered. "Will I really?" He shook his head. "None of us are going to be safe, Brigadier Bronski. Not from the Conquerors; not from anyone. I know, you see," he said, his voice dropping conspiratorially. "I figured it out. No one knew that I had; but I did. And I never told anyone. It was a fluke of nature, you see. A million-to-one coincidence. Maybe even a billion to one. But NorCoord was clever. Or maybe just desperate. Or maybe just too proud to pass up the chance. They took what happened and ran with it. Came up with a soap-bubble explanation and name and a way to use it. And it worked. It ended the war."

Bronski looked at Eisen again, got a puzzled shrug in return. "I don't understand," he said to Sholom. "What are you talking about?"

"Celadon, of course," Sholom said quietly. Suddenly the dreaminess was gone from his face; and in its place was the same guilt-tinged fear that Cavanagh had seen in Fibbit's threading of him. "It was the surge from a massive solar flare. That's all it was. Coming up just as the Pawolian ships sprung their trap. It came up behind them, you see, just as they left the protective cover of the planetary umbra. They couldn't see it coming, of course—they were in the umbra. A million-to-one coincidence. Maybe a billion to one."

"Sir?" Eisen put in urgently, jerking his head toward Cavanagh. "I don't think civilians should be hearing this."

"It's all right," Bronski said, his voice grim. "Anyway, it's already too late. Go on, Mr. Sholom. What happened then?"

Sholom's lip twisted. "What do you mean, what happened then? It killed them, of course, that's what happened then. All that radiation surged right up through the drive nozzles where there weren't any dipole protection fields. And then it just bounced around inside the ships. Focused and concentrated by all that superdense metal and liquid reflectors that were there to keep radiation out." He gazed out at nothing. "Bounced around until it killed them."

Bronski's face was that of a man walking through a graveyard at midnight. "Are you saying," he asked quietly, "that CIRCE doesn't exist?"

Sholom shook his head. "It doesn't. It never did. I figured it out, you see. I wondered why no one had even heard of something like that being in development until it was announced after Celadon. It was because there was never anything. I figured it out. But I didn't say anything."

"Why not?" Cavanagh asked.

Sholom shook his head again, his eyes filling with tears. "It was keeping the peace; don't you see? It was the threat of CIRCE that kept the Pawoles from fighting. It kept the Yycromae from fighting. It kept everyone from fighting."

"It's not going to keep the Conquerors from fighting," Kolchin said.

Sholom closed his eyes. "I know," he murmured. "I know. Perhaps NorCoord should have admitted it a long time ago. Such pride, to think they could use a myth to ensure peace. Such foolish, foolish pride . . ."

He trailed off, and for a long minute the room was silent. Cavanagh stared at the old man, the pounding of his heart like the sound of the universe crashing down around him. CIRCE had given him his life once, ending a war that might otherwise have killed him. Later it had given him hours of fear as he waited for it to begin the series of wars that would rip the Commonwealth apart and burn civilization down to ash. And then, three weeks ago, it had once again given him hope. Hope, this time, that the unstoppable Conquerors could in fact be stopped.

And none of it had been real. None of it.

Bronski took a deep breath. "Is he stable yet? Eisen?"

Eisen's eyes seemed to come back from a long way away. "Yes, sir, he'll be fine," he said, the words coming out with difficulty.

"All right," Bronski said. "Everyone in this room is hereby remanded to full quarantine confinement. Get that strap off him—"

"Wait a minute," Lee cut him off as Eisen set to work on the medic box. "You can't lock us up like junior officers, Brigadier. As a member of Parlimin VanDiver's staff—"

"Shut it down, Lee," Bronski advised him. "At the moment I don't care a Meert's moltings who or what you are. You're going into quarantine until I can find out whether any of this is true. And what the hell we do if it is."

"There'll be records," Cavanagh murmured. "Radiation records from the NorCoord ships at the battle. Brigadier, what about my daughter? I can't just sit back and do nothing when she's in danger like this."

"I'm sorry, Lord Cavanagh, but I've got no choice," Bronski gritted. "And to be perfectly honest, after that little private talk of ours on Phormbi, you were for the lockbox anyway. Eisen, go out and get Cho Ming off the door."

"Yes, sir," Eisen said, getting up and heading for the door.

"You're making a serious mistake, Brigadier," Lee said, biting out each word. "You can't make a parliamentary aide simply disappear."

"I can and I—*damn!*" Abruptly, Bronski grabbed for the inside of his jacket—

And froze there, his face stiff and unreadable, his eyes focused on something over Cavanagh's shoulder. Chest tightening again, Cavanagh turned to look.

Kolchin was standing there quietly, Eisen's limp form on the floor at his feet, Eisen's flechette gun in his hand. Pointed at Bronski. "Nice and slow, Brigadier," he advised. "Pull your hand out. Empty."

"Are you insane?" Bronski hissed, easing his hand away from his jacket again. "You can't get away with this."

"Lord Cavanagh needs to see to his daughter, sir," Kolchin said mildly. "He can't do that locked up in a quarantine cell."

"He's going to be there for life if you don't put that gun down," Bronski snarled. "Cavanagh—tell him."

Cavanagh looked at Kolchin. Bronski was right, of course. It was insane to think he could do anything for Melinda.

But to be locked up, unable to do anything at all, while the Conquerors began a war around her . . . "The *Jutland* fleet tried to stop the Conquerors," he reminded Bronski, stepping up beside him and carefully relieving him of his concealed flechette pistol. "They couldn't do it. If CIRCE is really nothing more than a well-crafted myth, we're going to need some brand-new approach to fighting them."

"And you're the one who's going to come up with this genius weapon?" Bronski bit out. "*And* while on the run from every cop and Peacekeeper in the Commonwealth? Get back on the ground, Cavanagh."

"The Commonwealth's going to have more pressing problems than chasing down a single fugitive," Cavanagh said. "Especially since there are a lot of people who are going to wonder why you're bothering with me. Don't worry; neither Kolchin nor I will say anything about what we've heard here today."

Lee took a step toward him. "Let me come with you," he said.

Cavanagh shook his head. "Sorry, Mr. Lee. Whatever

the truth about CIRCE, massive panic is the last thing the Commonwealth needs right now. I can trust Kolchin to keep this to himself; I'm afraid I can't say the same about you and Jacy VanDiver. I'd put a double guard on him, Brigadier, if I were you."

"You're making a mistake, Cavanagh," Bronski said quietly. "A big, big mistake."

"It wouldn't be the first time. Kolchin, should I try to find something to tie them up with?"

Five minutes later they were ready to go. Two minutes after that, Kolchin having arranged for the guard at the door to join the group inside, they were driving down the street in Bronski's car.

"What about Hill?" Cavanagh asked as Kolchin maneuvered through the Mrach traffic. "Should I risk giving him a call?"

"Better not," Kolchin said. "Even if Bronski's people have left him his phone, odds are they'll be tapping into any messages that come into it. Besides, he'd never be able to sneak out without Fibbit noticing and kicking up a fuss."

Cavanagh nodded heavily. "So we're back to the Phormbi escape plan. Just a couple of days late."

"And with a lot more people on our tail." Kolchin threw him a hard look. "Sir, I want to make sure you understand what we're getting into here. We've become fugitives now; and I can promise you it won't be fun. If you want to go back, we can do it. I acted without orders; you'll still be pretty clean."

"They'll still lock me away," Cavanagh reminded him. "Bronski's already said he was going to do that. Anyway, I'm already in serious trouble over what Aric and Quinn did. What's a few more years added on to my sentence?"

Kolchin shrugged. "I suppose that's one way of looking at it."

Cavanagh looked up into the blue sky. "Whatever's happened on Dorcas, Melinda's right in the middle of it. I can't just sit this one out. Any more than I could for Pheylan."

Kolchin didn't answer. But it wasn't hard for Cavanagh to figure out what he was thinking. Pheylan could easily be already dead; and it was Cavanagh's refusal to accept that possibility that had now put Melinda in danger.

Or had already cost her her life.

"Where are we going?" he asked Kolchin.

"Back to that fighter/courier dump in the hills," Kolchin told him. "Even if the Mrachanis told Bronski where we picked up that courier, odds are he won't expect us to try the same place again. It's our best shot, anyway."

"The Mrachanis might be guarding it this time."

Kolchin smiled tightly. "Let them try."

ABOUT THE AUTHOR

TIMOTHY ZAHN is one of science fiction's most popular voices, known for his ability to tell very human stories against a well-researched background of future science and technology. He won the Hugo Award for his novella *Cascade Point* and is the author of over a dozen science fiction novels, including the bestselling *Star Wars* trilogy: *Heir to the Empire, Dark Force Rising,* and *The Last Command;* the novels *Conquerors' Pride, Conquerors' Heritage,* and *Conquerors' Legacy;* and three collections of short fiction. Timothy Zahn lives in Oregon.

Turn the page for a special preview of CONQUERORS' HERITAGE by Timothy Zahn

Timothy Zahn's epic Conquerors saga turns next to the perspective of the Zhirrzh—and a series of stunning revelations that will change your perception of the struggle between this alien race and humanity. Packed with the wondrous speculation and gripping adventure that have catapulted Timothy Zahn to the top rank of science fiction authors, *Conquerors' Heritage* is an essential reading experience. Here, in an early scene from the novel, Thrrgilag is called to a meeting at the highest level of Zhirrzh authority: the Overclan Prime.

The testimony was finished, and the Speakers were filtering out for the midarc meal, when the summons Thrr-gilag had been dreading finally came.

"You are called to the private office of the Overclan Prime," the Elder told him, his voice and manner short. "Follow me."

Thrr-gilag sighed silently. "I obey," he said.

It was a long, lonely railcar ride—nearly half a thoustride long, in fact—down the deserted underground tunnel that led from the rear of the Overclan Seating chamber back to the two main office buildings of the complex. Eventually they reached the end and returned to ground level. Leaving the railcar, Thrr-gilag followed the Elder to an elaborately carved door with large wooden rings in place of the usual doorknobs, and the look and smell of great age. "Enter," the Elder said, gesturing to the door. Taking a deep breath, Thrr-gilag gripped the ancient wooden ring and pulled the door open.

The room turned out to be a small, intimate conversation room, furnished with no tables and only a handful of couches. Three Zhirrzh were waiting for him: Cvv-panav, the Speaker for Dhaa'rr; Hgg-spontib, the Speaker for Kee'rr; and the Overclan

Prime himself. None of their expressions were especially encouraging. "Come in, Searcher," the Prime said gravely, gesturing to a row of *kavra* fruit on a ledge beside the door. "I presume you know the Speakers for Dhaa'rr and Kee'rr."

"Yes, Overclan Prime," Thrr-gilag said, nodding politely to each of them in turn. Picking up one of the *kavra* fruit, he sliced through it twice with the cutting edges of his tongue and dropped it into the disposal container beneath it. "How may I serve you?" he asked, wiping his hands on the cleaning cloth hanging beneath the ledge.

"The alien prisoners have been brought to the complex," the Prime told him. "They're being prepared for interrogation in the medical center."

"I see," Thrr-gilag said. Strictly speaking, he should have been informed of any transfer of the aliens. Under the circumstances, he wasn't really surprised that he hadn't. "How well did they withstand the journey across from the landing field?"

"I'm told they're quite weak, but that their metabolic readings are stable," the Prime said. "I expect to be able to speak with them in a few hunbeats." He eyed Thrr-gilag. "Before we do, though, Speaker Cvv-panav has some questions concerning your testimony of this premidarc."

"More specifically, concerning your glaring breach of security," Cvv-panav bit out. "I want to hear what you know about the Prr't-zevisti incident on Dorcas. And how you learned of it."

"I spoke with my brother, Commander Thrr-mezaz, just before we were evacuated from Base World Twelve," Thrr-gilag said. "He told me that Prr't-zevisti's *fsss* cutting had been captured and that Prr't-zevisti himself had not been seen since then. That's all I know."

"And did Commander Thrr-mezaz happen to mention that this incident was to be kept a secret?"

Thrr-gilag felt his tail speed up. "No, Speaker, he didn't."

"Do you generally consider discussions with warrior commanders to be the stuff of casual conversation?" Cvv-panav persisted.

"Not at all, Speaker," Thrr-gilag said. "I've always treated such information as private and privileged."

"And yet you simply blurt out this private and privileged information without any thought whatsoever?"

Thrr-gilag looked him straight in the eye. "I would not have thought, Speaker, that testimony before the Overclan Seating would be considered casual conversation."

"I would agree." Speaker Hgg-spontib spoke up from his couch on the Prime's other side. "In fact, I'd venture to say there are many other Speakers wondering why it required a slip of a young searcher's tongue for us to learn of this incident. One might think the Dhaa'rr were attempting to keep vital information to themselves, for their own private purposes."

"The death of a Dhaa'rr Elder is a private matter for the Dhaa'rr clan," Cvv-panav growled back. "Not a gossip item for idle conversation."

Hgg-spontib's midlight pupils visibly contracted. "Are you suggesting that members of the Overclan Seating have nothing better to do than indulge in idle gossip?"

"What the Seating does or does not do hardly matters at this point," Cvv-panav snapped. "There were probably two thousand Elders observing the meeting, not counting those of the Overclan itself. Thanks to this loose-tongued young fool, the news is probably all over the Elder community by now."

"You overstate your case somewhat, Speaker Cvv-panav," the Prime observed mildly. "Any such leaks probably occurred four fullarcs ago, when Searcher Thrr-gilag first learned of Prr't-zevisti's disappearance. The pathway for that conversation involved seven Elders, including three without warrior security classification."

It was Cvv-panav's turn to narrow his midlight pupils. "And how would you know that, Overclan Prime?"

The Prime met his glare without flinching. "Because one of the communicators in the pathway was of the Overclan."

"Was he indeed," Cvv-panav said, his eyes dark with suspicion. "An interesting coincidence."

"Hardly a coincidence," the Prime said. "All nonwarrior pathways between Zhirrzh outposts and expeditionary forces have been going through the Overclan ever since that first contact with the Human warships."

Cvv-panav threw Hgg-spontib a look. "I don't recall the Seating being consulted on this matter, Overclan Prime."

"No reason why you should," the Prime said. "I considered it a matter of Zhirrzh security, and therefore acted without consulting the Seating. As was both my right and my duty."

"I'm not sure all the Speakers would accept such an interpretation of the Agreements," Cvv-panav said. "One might think the Overclan was attempting to keep vital information to itself, to paraphrase my colleague Hgg-spontib. For its own private purposes."

"Walk carefully, Speaker," the Prime warned him quietly. "Inflammatory accusations can be as damaging as any security breach."

"So can the appearance of impropriety, Overclan Prime," Cvv-panav countered coolly.

"Indeed," the Prime said. "But before you slaver too much indignation, allow me to point out that the reason Searcher Thrr-gilag was using a non-secure pathway was that the Dhaa'rr clan had not yet provided another properly secure Elder to fill the pathway gap left by Prr't-zevisti's disappearance. Two entire fullarcs after that disappearance, I might add."

Cvv-panav looked at Thrr-gilag, as if suddenly remembering that there was a low-level witness sitting in on this high-level argument. "With your permission, Overclan Prime, we'll continue this discussion at a more convenient time," he said stiffly. "In the meantime, perhaps we should see if our prisoners are ready to answer some questions."

"Yes," the Prime said. "Communicator?"

An Elder appeared. "Yes, Overclan Prime?"

"Go speak with the healers in the medical center. See if all is prepared."

"I obey."

Thrr-gilag cleared his throat. "I would remind the Overclan Prime that the prisoners are still very weak," he said. "If pushed too hard, they may die."

"All the more reason to question them while we can," the Prime said. "In any event, that decision is now in the hands of Searcher Nzz-oonaz."

Thrr-gilag felt his tail twirling faster. "May I assume, then, that I've been removed as speaker of the mission?" he asked, just to make it official.

"Be thankful you haven't been removed from the mission entirely," Cvv-panav put in acidly, his tone making it clear that he'd argued for precisely that outcome. "By all rights the escape of your Human prisoner should have earned you far more than simply a demotion. A public censure at the least, perhaps even criminal charges."

The Elder reappeared. "All is prepared, Overclan Prime," he said. "The healers and alien specialist group are waiting."

"Very good," the Prime said, rising from his couch. "Speakers, Searcher: come."

The medical center turned out to be a somewhat more compact version of the room on Base World 12 that the technics had hurriedly converted into a prison for Pheylan Cavanagh. In the middle of the room, lying on rolling beds and covered by a portable glass security dome, were the two prisoners. Nearly forty Zhirrzh were present, busy at the various monitoring consoles along the walls or gathered four-deep around the dome gazing at the aliens. Thrr-gilag spotted Svv-selic and Nzz-oonaz standing beside the glass, along with a number of the technics and healers who'd been with them on Base World 12. Only a handful of the observers appeared to be Speakers from the Overclan Seating.

And nestled in among them Thrr-gilag spotted someone else, someone he hadn't seen for several cyclics. Gll-borgiv, an alien specialist from the Dhaa'rr clan.

"Searcher Nzz-oonaz will perform the interrogation," the Prime said as a technic by the door handed each of the newcomers a translator-link earphone. They crossed to the dome, a respectful path opening up for them through the crowd as they did so. For a few beats the Prime gazed at the aliens, then nodded to Nzz-oonaz. "You may begin."

"I obey, Overclan Prime," Nzz-oonaz said, sounding more than a little nervous. "During their brief conscious period back on Base World Twelve we established that they spoke at least some of the language of our Human prisoner. I'll try that first."

He pressed a little more closely against the dome and cleared his throat self-consciously. "Aliens of the Mrachanis," he said in the Human language. "I am Nzz-oonaz; Flii'rr. Can you hear me?"

For a dozen beats nothing happened. Then, slowly, one of the aliens opened his eyes. "I hear," he said, his voice almost too soft to hear. A beat later the words were echoed by the translator-link in Thrr-gilag's ear slits. "I am Lahettila. Ambassador to your people from the Mrachanis."

"Did he say *ambassador*?" Hgg-spontib muttered from beside Thrr-gilag, pressing his translator-link tighter against the side of his head.

"Yes," Thrr-gilag confirmed, frowning at the aliens. Yet according to the warriors who'd captured it, the alien ship had opened fire on them with the same Elderdeath weapons the Humans had used.

Nzz-oonaz was obviously thinking along the same lines. "Do Mrachani ambassadors usually attack an unknown spacecraft on sight?" he demanded.

For another few beats the Mrachani's gaze seemed to drift around the crowd gathered around him. Almost, Thrr-gilag thought oddly, like a dramatist measuring an audience before beginning his performance. "We came to bring warning," the alien sighed at last, closing his eyes tiredly. "And to offer the assistance of the Mrachanis in your struggle against the *Mirnacheem-hyeea*."

Nzz-oonaz threw Thrr-gilag a questioning look. Thrr-gilag flicked his tongue in a negative: the word didn't mean anything to him. "What is this *Mirnacheem-hyeea* you speak of?" Nzz-oonaz asked.

"The *Mirnacheem-hyeea* are those who attempt to dominate all within their reach," the Mrachani said. "In their language the name means Conquerors Without Reason." He opened his eyes, closed them again. "The Humans."

Conquerors Without Reason. Thrr-gilag let the words roll around in his mind, tasting the implications. Ominous implications indeed.

"We appreciate your warning," Nzz-oonaz said. "What assistance do the Mrachanis offer?"

"The Mrachanis need your help," the alien murmured, his voice fading even further. "We need your—" He took a deep, shuddering breath. "Help."

"What assistance do the Mrachanis offer?" Nzz-oonaz repeated.

There was no answer. "Healer?" Nzz-oonaz asked, looking over his shoulder at one of the consoles.

"He's gone back to sleep," the healer reported. "And their metabolic efficiency appears to be dropping again. Shall I attempt to awaken them?"

Nzz-oonaz looked at the Prime. "Overclan Prime?"

The Prime was gazing at the aliens, his face hard. "How much risk would there be to their lives, Healer?"

"I don't know," the healer admitted. "We still know very little about their biochemistry."

"We won't risk it, then," the Prime said. "Let them sleep, and we'll continue the interrogation later. I want a full watch to be kept, healers and Elders both."

"I obey," the healer said. Gesturing to a technic, he began issuing orders.

Cvv-panav took a step closer to the Prime. "I should like to continue our discussion of last full-arc, Overclan Prime," he said quietly, but with a note of insistence in his voice.

"No need," the Prime said, turning to Hgg-spontib. "I'm sure Speaker Hgg-spontib will not argue that this contact has grown far beyond the proprietary rights of the clans who first contacted the Humans." He looked over at the sleeping aliens. "Or perhaps we should call them the Human-Conquerors," he amended grimly. "At any rate, I'm assigning Gll-borgiv; Dhaa'rr, to this study group."

"I protest, of course," Hgg-spontib said. "The Dhaa'rr have yet to suffer any damage at the hands of either of these alien species. If any new searchers are added, they should be from the Cakk'rr, who at least have the claim of having captured these Mrachanis."

"I've already discussed the matter with the Speaker for Cakk'rr," Cvv-panav put in. "There is no searcher of the Cakk'rr of adequate expertise. She has therefore agreed to defer to the Dhaa'rr in this matter."

Thrr-gilag pressed the top of his tongue against the roof of his mouth, keeping his mouth firmly shut. The Zhirrzh alien specialist community was a reasonably small group, and he could name at least three Cakk'rr experts right off the end of his tongue who would be capable of working with the Mrachanis. Clearly, putting a Dhaa'rr on the group was a political decision, not a scientific one.

"The Kee'rr still protest," Hgg-spontib said in the tone of one who knows a lost battle when he's lost it. "And what of Searcher Thrr-gilag?"

"The Dhaa'rr insist on a full investigation," Cvv-panav put in before the Prime could answer. "The escape of the Human—the Human Conqueror—must be properly examined."

"Your insistence is premature," the Prime told him. "An inquiry board is examining all the records from Base World Twelve. Until they come to a decision, Searcher Thrr-gilag will be permitted to observe all proceedings involving the Mrachani aliens."

"But not to speak to them," Cvv-panav insisted.

"Proper protocol will of course be followed," the Prime said. "He may offer questions through Searcher Nzz-oonaz." He looked at Thrr-gilag. "Do you accept these limitations?"

As if he had a real choice. "I do," Thrr-gilag said, a flush of shame twitching through his tail. Svv-selic had let Too'rr domination of this mission slip from his grasp by letting the Human prisoner get too close to the Elders' pyramid. Now Thrr-gilag's mistake had similarly lost the speakership for the Kee'rr clan.

How long would it be, he wondered, before Nzz-oonaz made his mistake and Cvv-panav demanded that Gll-borgiv and the Dhaa'rr take charge? He doubted it would be very long.

"You look as if you have something else to say, Searcher," Cvv-panav said, an edge of challege to his voice.

"No," Thrr-gilag said, resolutely turning away. Arguing any of this would just give them an excuse to throw him off the mission completely. "With the Overclan Prime's permission, I'd like to leave the complex for a time."

"What of the aliens?" the Prime asked. "If they should awaken, you'd be needed."

So at least the Prime thought of him as a useful part of the group, even if Cvv-panav didn't. That was something, anyway. "If our shipboard experiences are a guide, they should sleep at least four or five tentharcs," Thrr-gilag said.

"Very well," the Prime said. "You may leave, but I don't want you more than a few hunbeats away from this room. And be certain to update your location with the servers at the Overclan shrine."

"I obey," Thrr-gilag said. He turned away, easing through the crowd toward the door—

"One other thing," the Prime's voice said quietly from beside him.

Thrr-gilag looked over, a bit startled. He hadn't realized the Prime had followed him. "Yes, Overclan Prime?"

"There are certain things you and your group are aware of that have not been released to the general Zhirrzh public," the Prime said.

Thrr-gilag winced. Yes; Prr't-zevisti. "I understand fully," he assured the Prime. "I'll be careful not to say anything outside the complex."

"I'm sure you understand the sort of thing I'm talking about," the Prime went on, as if he hadn't spoken. "Stories which would spread rumors and fear. Panic, even, particularly among those who are unaware of the full scope of the countermeasures Warrior Command is taking." He gazed hard at Thrr-gilag. "And I don't refer only to those outside the Overclan complex."

Thrr-gilag frowned at him. What in the eighteen worlds was the Prime getting at?

And then, abruptly, he got it. CIRCE. The Humans' ultimate weapon.

The Prime was still studying his face. "You understand," he said.

"Yes," Thrr-gilag said, shivering. He understood, all right. If even a hint leaked out at this point that their enemies had a weapon against which there might not be any defense at all . . .

He looked sharply at the Prime, the other's almost offhanded comment suddenly registering. *Not only those outside the Overclan complex . . .*

"May I inquire," he asked carefully, "who among the Zhirrzh are aware of this aspect?"

"I am," the Prime said. "So are a handful of the supreme commanders at Warrior Command, the former Overclan Primes, and perhaps thirty other high-security Elders. Plus your alien study group, of course."

Thrr-gilag pressed his tongue hard against the inside of his mouth. "And the Overclan Seating?"

The Prime didn't flinch. "It would not be advisable for them to know as yet."

"I see," Thrr-gilag murmured. Suddenly it all made sense, this mad rush to throw beachheads and encirclement forces at the Human worlds. Warrior Command wasn't looking for territory to conquer; it was trying desperately to capture or entrap one or more of CIRCE's components before the Humans could gather them together and reassemble the weapon.

And in the meantime the Overclan Prime was trying equally hard to prevent Zhirrzh society from exploding into hysterical terror at the thought of the potential genocide facing them. And if that meant hiding the truth from even the Overclan Seating, then that was what they were going to do.

"You understand the situation," the Prime said. "I could lock you and the others away somewhere, but that would attract unwelcome attention and questions. So for the time being you're free to move about; but be assured that if you tell anyone about this thing, you and your whole family will suffer greatly. Do you understand?"

"I do," Thrr-gilag managed. "And if I may say so, Overclan Prime, there's no need to make threats. I understand as well as you the need to avoid a panic."

"Just so long as we understand each other," the

Prime said. "Where exactly will you be going right now?"

"Just to get something to eat," Thrr-gilag said. "There's a place nearby called the Lapper's Paradise I thought I'd try."

"Very well," the Prime said. "But I meant what I said about staying close to the complex. These Mrachani aliens may hold the key to our survival against the Human-Conquerors."

Survival. Previous Overclan Primes throughout history, facing other aggressive alien races, had spoken not of survival but of victory. Or so the histories said.

But then, none of their other alien enemies had ever had a weapon like CIRCE. "I understand," Thrr-gilag said quietly. "I'll be close."

SF 3 2/97